Advance praise for Aimie K. Runyan and *Promised to the Crown*

"This gr ... ageous women fro ... rance. Aimie Run ... ewards of life on th ... *n* is an absorbing a

—Jenni ... *ar*

"A capti ... abeth, and Nicole ... author Aimie Run ... her as seamlessly ... *own* is an unforget ... ill stay with you lo

—Anne ... *Doll.*

"In her ... *rown,* Aimie Run ... enture from Franc ... ry and start a new ... riend-ship, love, ... nce to educate, en

—Pam ... *ch*

"An engaging, engrossing debut. Runyan's gift transports you to the distant, frozen landscape of seventeenth-century Canada, but Rose, Elisabeth, and Nicole feel as real as if they live next door. A romantic, compelling adve..."

—Greer Macallister, U...
The Magician's Lie

[illegible]ance praise for Aimie K. Runyan's *Promised to the Crown*

"[illegible] gripping debut brings to life the saga of three courage[illegible] [illegible] disparate backgrounds starting over in New France. [illegible] deftly guides us through the hardships and [illegible] of life on the early Canadian frontier. *Promised to the Crown* [illegible] adventure with heart."

—[illegible] Laam, author of *The Secret Daughter of the T[illegible]*

"[illegible] captivating tale of three courageous women: Rose, Eliz[illegible] and Nicole, bonded by adversity, friendship, and love. In [illegible] Runyan's skillful hands, their stories are woven togeth[illegible] as were their fascinating lives. *Promised to the Crown* [illegible] unforgettable saga of strength and sisterhood, one that w[illegible] [illegible] long after the final page."

—[illegible]irard, author of *Madame Picasso* and *Platinum Do[illegible]*

"In [illegible] original and well-written debut, *Promised to the C[illegible]* [illegible] evokes the story of three young women who [illegible] [illegible] to Canada in the seventeenth century to marry [illegible] start a new life. It is a heart-wrenching and timeless tale of [illegible] and hope that skillfully blends history and romance [illegible] entertain and inspire."

—[illegible]noff, author of *The Last Summer at Chelsea Bea[illegible]*

PROMISED TO THE CROWN

AIMIE K. RUNYAN

KENSINGTON BOOKS
www.kensingtonbooks.com

KENSINGTON BOOKS are published by

Kensington Publishing Corp.
119 West 40th Street
New York, NY 10018

All Kensington titles, imprints, and distributed lines are available at special quantity discounts for bulk purchases for sales promotion, premiums, fund-raising, educational, or institutional use.

Special book excerpts or customized printings can also be created to fit specific needs. For details, write or phone the office of the Kensington Sales Manager: Kensington Publishing Corp., 119 West 40th Street, New York, NY 10018. Attn. Sales Department. Phone: 1-800-221-2647.

eISBN-13: 978-1-4967-0113-8
eISBN-10: 1-4967-0113-5
First Kensington Electronic Edition: May 2016

ISBN-13: 978-1-4967-0112-1
ISBN-10: 1-4967-0112-7
First Kensington Trade Paperback Printing: May 2016

10 9 8 7 6 5 4 3 2 1

Printed in the United States of America

To Allan, for being my port in the storm,
my partner in crime,
best friend, and the love of my life.

And to Ciarán and Aria, for teaching me the
kind of motherly love that made this book possible.

ACKNOWLEDGMENTS

As with any first book, the list of people to thank is so long that I am sure to forget someone crucial to the creation of this book: My profound apologies in advance.

Many thanks to:

My rock star agent, Melissa Jeglinski, my wonderful editor, John Scognamiglio, and the entire crew at Kensington for believing in this project and spending countless hours to make it shine. I am immeasurably grateful to you.

Susan Spann, for being my first friend at Rocky Mountain Fiction Writers and for taking me under her wing. She embodies all that is great in the writing community. And RMFW? You're the best tribe there is.

The wonderful women of the BWW: Jamie Raintree, Katie Moretti, Gwen Florio, Andrea Catalano, Theresa Alan, and Orly Konig-Lopez for the unwavering support from first query to release day. You're all amazing, and I couldn't do this without you. I love you all.

Jill Furman and Melony Black for reading this when it was rougher than tree bark and not hating me for it, and to Abby Polzin for all the great cleanup edits. Thanks to all who read this work in its infancy and adolescence. It is better because of you.

The wonderful women of the Tall Poppies, thank you for welcoming me into the fold. You're some of the most talented writers in the biz, and I'm proud you let me sit at the cool table with you.

My wonderful family, especially Wayne and Kathy Trumbly and Bob and Donna Runyan for their love and support.

Most of all, to Allan, Ciarán, and Aria. The three of you made me a wife, a mother, and a much busier, much happier woman. You are the best things in my life.

Adversity draws men together and produces beauty and harmony in life's relationships, just as the cold of winter produces ice-flowers on the window-panes, which vanish with the warmth.

—Søren Kierkegaard

PART 1

1667

Louis XIV's colony in Canada needs women.

Surrounded by the British, the King needs to tie his settlers to the land with farms, wives, and children to defend in the event their enemies should invade.

The King's ministers devised a plan by which young, strong women of good character would be sent at the King's expense to wed the soldiers, farmers, artisans, and fur trappers who populated the colony.

History would remember them as the King's Daughters and the Daughters of New France.

CHAPTER 1

Rose

June 1667, The Salpêtrière Charity Hospital, Paris

One, two, three strokes up . . . Rinse. One, two, three strokes down. Rinse. Move three inches to the right. . . .

Rose Barré scoured the floor on her hands and knees, her once fine hands now raw, cracked, and bleeding, as she tried to rid the small room of the stench. The battle was futile. One painfully clean dormitory cell would not mask the stink of filth and disease that permeated the dozens of other cells surrounding it. The fetid smell of mold, piss, and unwashed flesh hit Rose in the face each morning as she opened her eyes and kept her from her sleep at night, despite all the promises that she would grow used to it. This was one of Rose's bad days, where, no matter what she did, she could not stop scrubbing, even though her *officière* had forbidden the endless scouring. No matter how Rose tried to reason with herself, she could never get the room clean enough to sate the urge. She wiped her black, matted curls from her forehead with the back of her hand and moved the brush three inches to the right.

The church bells rang not far from Rose's room, causing her to look up from the soapy scrub marks. She tossed her brush in the bucket of murky water with more vigor than necessary. *I'm going to be late.* Missing a lesson would not be worth the resultant reprimand, no matter how much Rose longed to continue her attack on the perpetually grimy floor. She looked down at the water stains on the knees of her dingy canvas apron. *Oh well, I haven't another. I'll bear the disapproving eyes of the Sisters as I always do.*

Before she reached the door to the classroom, Rose heard voices raised in argument coming from Sister Vérité's rooms. She scuttled past the open door on her way to the catechism room with every attempt at silence. She laid her hand on the classroom's door handle when Sister Vérité called her name. She froze. *Curse my luck!* Rose groaned quietly. Rose turned back and entered the well-ordered apartment that served as Sister Vérité's office and living quarters, leaving the musty hallway behind. The familiar rooms smelled of candle wax and book dust, not unpleasant for a room in the Salpêtrière. As she entered, Rose saw Sister Charité, the Supérieure herself, seated behind the large walnut desk.

"Hello, Sister," Rose stammered.

She realized that raised voice had been Vérité's; the younger *officière* had dared to argue with the Supérieure. Rose felt a cold stone growing in the hollow of her stomach as she took the proffered chair.

"Sister Vérité and I were just discussing you, my child," Sister Charité said.

Rose felt the rock in her stomach grow larger still.

"Me, Sister?" Rose asked. Given the immense scope of the Supérieure's duties, Rose figured her goings-on were as significant to the head of the massive establishment as the scurrying of ants.

"Yes, my dear," the Supérieure said, looking Rose over. "You know that your skills and talents, your education, have not gone unnoticed by Sister Vérité. Therefore, you have not gone unnoticed by me. The question, child, is where your talents are best spent."

Sister Vérité's preference for Rose was no surprise. From her arrival at the charity hospital three years prior, the Sister earmarked her as a "*bijou,*" a gem. Rose learned this meant that she was being groomed to be an *officière* herself one day. Sister Vérité's kindness in those early days, Rose was certain, was the only thing that kept her heart from breaking. She had shadowed the young woman ever since. More recently, she'd taken on the unofficial role of assistant. *They're here to make me a* sous-officière, Rose concluded, but was relieved only momentarily. *My appointment wouldn't make Vérité displeased. Surely, one as young and inexperienced as I wouldn't be asked to serve in La Force to work with the lunatics and thieves.* The stone turned to bile that threatened to escape its confines as she pondered the possibility. Life in the dormitories felt like purgatory, but from what Rose understood from the stories, the hospital prison was hell itself.

Sister Charité shifted position in her seat, seemingly adjusting her thoughts as well. "You are, without question, of great use to us here. Sister Vérité vehemently supports taking you on as an *officière.* I have no doubt you would serve us admirably in that capacity. The King, however, needs young women to go to New France as brides for his settlers there. In his wisdom, His Majesty has ordered us to send some of our best, that they might marry and end their reliance on the Royal treasury and solve His Majesty's colonial woes in one gesture. I think you would be an ideal choice. You are young, you are strong and healthy—a good worker, too."

The room filled with a heavy silence as the Sisters waited for some response from Rose, who stared downward at her splotched apron.

"I leave the choice to you," Sister Charité said. "I suggest you consider your options carefully. I will expect your answer in the morning."

Sister Charité gave her *officière* a pointed glare and left the room with her usual efficiency. *New France?* Rose's hands shook at the very prospect. All she knew was that it was a cold, lonely place, far to the west. Only the bravest of men attempted the voyage, and fewer chose to make a life there. Could the good Sister, who preached to the inmates about the virtues of femininity and the place of women in the home, be serious about sending her—and others—to the colony?

Vérité looked at her charge with pleading eyes. "Sister Charité would not wish me to sway your decision, Rose, but I must speak. You cannot think to leave. Not for some desolate patch of wilderness that the King has taken a fancy to."

"Truly, Sister, I do not know what to think." Rose, who had never in the course of her life been given leave to make her own decisions, now had less than twenty-four hours to decide her own fate.

"You are needed here, Rose," Sister Vérité said. "The children admire and love you. You have purpose here, helping the poor of Paris. Stay and be an example to them. What awaits you in New France? Bitter cold? A man, gone half-savage, who expects you to keep his shack? Child after child until bearing children kills you? Is that what you want?"

Rose looked at her mentor. Vérité's eyes shone with terror. Rose thought of a husband. One to treat her each night as her uncle had. Callous. Uncaring. Cruel. Rose had no desire to relive the torture she had endured at his hands.

Vérité smiled at Rose, taking the girl's hand in her own. "The Salpêtrière isn't paradise, but it *is* safe. Now, hurry along to class."

Rose's prayers and responses to the questions on her catechism that afternoon were distracted at best. If Sister Jeanne, normally a stickler for attentiveness, noticed Rose's comportment, she said nothing. The lenience made more sense when Rose remembered that Sister Charité had mentioned others would go to New France as well. The *officières* would certainly know who the candidates were. *There are no secrets in a place like this. Not ones anyone can keep for long.*

After catechism came supper, an ample bowl of hearty beef soup and crusty bread, a substantial degree better than the usual fare. It still tasted as pleasant as soot in Rose's mouth that night. Excused from her evening duties, Rose returned to her room after supper and paced the floors, still dingy for all her toils. A fatigue, much deeper than she had ever felt, washed over her. She felt crippled by the enormity of the decision. She thumbed through her prayer book, but knew it would give her no solace that night. She looked at her ratty mattress, but knew sleep would not come. She opted for the hard wire bristles of her scrub brush instead.

Even three long years weren't enough for Rose to adjust to the cesspool that was her prison. Her heart still broke with each injustice. All it took was a letter from a well-connected member of society to the right people, and a woman was imprisoned in this "charity hospital" for the rest of her days. A girl who refused to marry a man a quarter century her senior, another who took a profession as a secretary without her father's blessing, women branded as mad by husbands who wished to be rid of them. Most common were the countless orphans, like Rose, whose families simply couldn't be bothered with their care. These were Rose's companions now, so very unlike the ones her beloved father had envisioned for her.

As she scrubbed, Rose remembered her father's face, lined with kindness. A successful merchant, he'd lost his life over a hand of *vingt-et-un* with a disgruntled client when Rose was barely twelve years old. Her mother died giving birth to her, and Rose was sent to live with her aunt and uncle on their estate outside of Paris. A palace of crystal chandeliers, gilded furniture, and gardens manicured to the point they no longer resembled anything from nature. For two and a half happy years Rose's aunt doted upon her niece and Rose reveled in spoiling her young cousins. Then her uncle took notice of Rose's developing breasts and soft red lips.

Too frequently, Rose remembered that first evening when she gently shut the door to the nursery and released a grateful sigh that the day was coming to a close. She had just finished tucking in little Luce after three stories and a promise of more tomorrow, and Rose was ready to find her own bed.

"Tired, my dear?" asked Uncle Grégoire, approaching his niece from a spot in the shadows farther down the hall.

Rose gasped, not having heard her uncle approach, and not used to his presence in this wing of the house. His children, while necessary for the protection of the estate, were of little interest to him in many respects. "You gave me a start, Uncle!" cried Rose. "Yes, yes, I am tired. The children were particularly energetic today."

Grégoire clucked his tongue in disapproval. "You work too hard, my dear. You were not brought here to be a servant, you know."

"Of course, Uncle. But I enjoy the children immensely."

"Let their mother and the servants attend to them, my dear." Grégoire was now standing only inches from Rose, and his proximity was beginning to make her nervous. She would have taken a step back, but she was all but pinned to the nursery door. Rose looked at her uncle, not knowing what to say by way of a response.

"You're not a chatty girl," remarked Grégoire, running a finger down his niece's flushed cheek. "I like that. You please me a great deal, you know." His fingertip reached its objective . . . the swell of her lower lip.

"I do?" muttered Rose, covertly looking for a way to escape. She saw none.

"Oh yes," said Grégoire. "I don't want you wasting your energies on the children. I will keep you as my pet. Do you understand? Your aunt must never know."

Before she could answer that she, in fact, did not understand what her uncle wanted from her, his mouth was upon hers. Trapped, Rose had no choice but to press herself against the door. His right hand moved from her hair to the front of her dress, grabbing the soft swell of her breast, causing Rose to whine in displeasure.

"To your room, now," he commanded, pulling away from her and grabbing her arm, forcing her to follow.

Once in the small bedchamber, he divested himself of most of his clothes and began to yank her dress from her shivering frame. He shoved her to the bed and tears rolled down her cheeks as he took her roughly, without consideration for her innocence.

"Good girl," he said, throwing his clothes back on before Aunt Martine noticed his absence. "You will wait up for me each night unless I give you leave otherwise. Do you understand?"

"Yes, Uncle," she said, wiping the tears from her face.

"You will come to enjoy it, little pet." He cast a glance at the bloodstains on her bed. "Now see to your sheets before your aunt notices the mess."

And so it continued for six months. Uncle Grégoire did not miss an evening, and despite his assertion to the contrary, she never came to enjoy his unwanted attentions. Each month, Rose feared she would miss her course and she would be utterly ruined. Worse, Rose began to worry her uncle would never tire of her and continue his nightly visits forever. She longed to tell her aunt, but didn't want to break her heart when she learned what a monster her husband was. She knew she was ruined for marriage, but she hoped that if the whole disgusting affair stayed secret she might remain a sort of spinster aunt who cared for the children and eventually their own children.

That was until one night when, without preamble, Rose's bedroom door was flung open just as her uncle was dressing to leave.

"You little whore." Aunt Martine looked with hate, not at her half-naked husband, but at Rose, who lay trembling, trying to forget his embraces.

The next morning Rose was taken from her bed with nothing but her oldest dress and most basic belongings in tow. With one word from her aunt, she was now a ward of the state and a prisoner of the Salpêtrière. Stripped of all she ever knew and loved, she was terrified of this new hell in which she found herself.

Rose was abandoned, screaming, at the gates of the Salpêtrière. The fear gripped her like the cold fingers of death. She was certain she wouldn't live out the night, so she wasn't afraid that her screams would earn her a beating. Seeing the dawn light through her cell window proved a disappointment that morning and many afterward.

Rose thought of her father often. Sometimes she indulged in the fantasy that he was miraculously returned to life. She imagined his face as he saw her on her knees scrubbing the floor in a tattered dress. When he learned where she was, what his brother had done to her, there would be another duel, this time with a far more satisfactory outcome. In her childhood, she was given every whim of her heart, coddled and loved by him and a long string of overindulgent governesses. He loved to tell Rose how much she looked like his beloved, lamented wife. So far as Rose knew, he never loved another woman. She treasured the thought like a precious jewel. Like the emerald brooch of her mother's that now her aunt surely kept for herself.

Before her confinement, Rose had been only vaguely aware of the charity hospital's existence. The vast, imposing compound of moldy brick and human stink had terrified her, as it did most children. As the sheltered daughter of the bourgeoisie, Rose had only rarely visited the sector of Paris where the specter of the Salpêtrière loomed over the surrounding streets. She didn't realize, then, how fortunate that made her.

She had assumed that, like many institutions of its kind, the Church had the running of the Salpêtrière, but Rose learned with surprise that the staff was a secular one. Adopting the title "Sister" and abandoning given names for religious monikers was only ceremonial. Despite the lack of official ties to the Church, the members of the staff were all deeply religious. They espoused the virtues of routine and constant occupation. Prayer, study, chores, meals. No idleness to tempt the "weak souls" in their charge. She overheard the *officières* use the term more than once. *Are we really weak? Or merely inconvenient?*

Can I truly stay in such a place? Her grip on the brush was painful, but she gave it no heed.

Vérité was right; in the hospital, Rose's life had purpose. The children, the staff—they needed her, appreciated her, treated her well. But what awaited her in the Salpêtrière? A larger room? A salary? One day a month to escape into Paris under the watchful eye of a chaperone?

Were those small liberties enough?

Rose imagined that Vérité was also right about what awaited her in New France: harsh conditions, certainly . . . but perhaps a family of her own as well.

Papa had been wonderful, but he alone did not constitute a family. In the years before she lived with her uncle, Rose had always pictured herself with a large brood of children, to make up for her own lack of brothers and sisters. That would never happen without a husband, though the thought sickened her. It would never happen in the Salpêtrière.

In her logical mind she knew that not all men were such demons, but she could not separate the marriage act from the memory of her uncle's careless, often painful, fumbling. Though her governesses and nannies had never discussed the topic with her, she'd had a vague idea of what happened between a husband and wife. She imagined it was a gentle, loving act of submission where the woman entrusted her body, soul, and heart to the man of her choice. Her uncle had shown her it was a brutish, animal act that she had no interest in ever repeating. The rough hands, putrid breath, his complete disregard for her pleas to stop . . . She could live happily never letting another man come so close to her ever again.

* * *

All too soon, dawn's weak sunlight peeked into the minuscule window of Rose's cell, stripes of light painting her scrubbed floor. Rose would have to meet with Sister Charité soon, yet still she had no answer. She made up her mind, and changed it, a dozen times over the course of the sleepless night.

As she walked the long corridor to Sister Charité's office, Rose prayed the answer would come to her.

Do I go? Risk the bitter cold? The savages? Starve in a strange land?

Do I stay here and wither in this rancid building? Scour the floors and say my prayers?

What exactly would I pray for?

No answers came. When she reached her destination, she knocked on the open door to announce her presence.

"Come in, Rose." Sister Charité did not look up from her document, but motioned to an empty seat opposite her massive desk. Rose, never having visited the room before, took in the sparse furnishings, noticing that every object had some purpose. The Sister did not appreciate decoration or unnecessary trappings. Despite the Spartan nature of the room, the gently crackling fire created a welcoming ambiance, its warmth driving back the unseasonably cool weather.

"What is your decision, my child?" The Sister sat back in her chair, giving Rose her full attention.

Rose looked at her hands, willing herself to speak. A stack of books on the Sister's desk, the top volume askew by a matter of a fraction of an inch, drew her attention. She itched to straighten it, but didn't dare. After a moment she sputtered, "I don't think I can go, Sister."

"Then you are a fool." Rose felt Sister Charité's brown eyes searching her soul and casting judgment. Disappointment mingled with the lines of experience on the old woman's face.

"Excuse me, Sister?" Rose looked up from her hands, eyes wide, glancing away from the book.

"You heard me, child," Sister Charité said. "You're a fool. What's worse, you're a fool with a good brain and an education—that's the worst kind of fool to suffer."

"Sister. It's just so far . . ." Rose began.

"Yes, it is," Sister Charité said. "And it's cold. And the men are not as civilized as in Paris, if indeed any man can truly be called 'civilized.' A rough life, to be sure. Vérité most likely convinced you of this, despite my orders.

"However, it *is* a life, Rose. I have seen you are miserable here. Some women thrive on confinement and discipline. Some women stay here of their own free will because they need our guidance. Yet our regulations only serve to stifle a girl like you."

"I'm not unhappy here, Sister. Truly. I love the children—helping them with their lessons. I like being useful to Sister Vérité." *Do not touch the book.* Rose gripped her hands, as though in prayer, against the compulsion.

"Of course," Sister Charité said. "Who does not wish to live a useful life? But there are uses for you in the New World as well, my dear. More than you can take on alone, I am certain. But then, you would have your own children to guide and teach."

"I don't wish to marry, Sister." Rose forced herself to look directly at Sister Charité as she spoke the words aloud at last. Looking at Sister Charité, focusing on the woman's honest face, kept the image of her uncle, the stink of stale whiskey, and the nights of endless torture from resurfacing. Her interwoven fingers went white.

For weeks she tried to plead with him to stop. He merely covered her mouth with an unwashed hand that reeked of tobacco and his own filth and took her anyway. He was at least a measure gentler on the nights she didn't protest. After a few weeks, she couldn't even summon tears. She would lie back, close her eyes, and pray that he wouldn't make her pregnant. Pray he would tire of her and that somehow she might be able to go on with life as she had before. But it could never be. She was forever changed. Broken.

After he left each night, she imagined barring the door against him. She imagined confessing the whole affair to Aunt Martine. She imagined begging the priest for help. In her mind, each attempt to win her freedom from her uncle's cruelty always resulted in a beating or her public disgrace. Worse, the insufferable pity of a priest in her uncle's employ who would tell her that suffering was a woman's lot in life and that she could learn the valuable lesson of forbearance and self-effacement from her ordeal. In the end, her tenure in the Salpêtrière had confirmed her worst suspicions.

"It is the idea of marriage that bothers you, not the reality of it, my girl," Sister Charité said.

"I don't think that's true, Sister," Rose replied.

Sister Charité's eyes flashed in surprise at the severity of Rose's tone. Rose was almost equally shocked, not having felt much conviction in her own opinions these past three years.

"Go to the colony, girl," Sister Charité said. "You may not find happiness in marriage, but I can promise you, without equivocation, that you will not find it here."

Rose took in a deep breath and looked the older woman in the eye as an equal. *She means what she says. She thinks this stinking prison will kill me—sooner rather than later. And I can't find anything in my heart that tells me she's mistaken.*

"If I must," Rose said, and with the deft movement of one hand, straightened the off-kilter book.

"Finally some sense," Sister Charité said, glancing away from the book and back to Rose. "You will leave Paris for Rouen in two weeks. There, you will meet the rest of the girls who will travel with you to New France. From Rouen, you will go to the port in Dieppe to meet your ship. Several of our girls are going. I want you to keep a special eye on Geneviève and Vivienne for me. They are very young and will be grateful for your attentions."

"With pleasure, Sister." Rose knew the girls from their catechism classes. Geneviève and Vivienne were orphans as well, only a few months into their sojourn at the Salpêtrière. Both seemed sweet natured and eager to learn, though neither were gifted scholars. They never looked particularly happy, and Rose was glad Sister Charité had selected them. They were the pale, slight type of girl that, all too often, slipped from life in the middle of a chilly night in the dank prison.

"Very good. I trust you will make sure these last two weeks are profitable ones," said Sister Charité by way of dismissal.

Rose walked slowly back to her dormitory. She hoped that Sister

Charité was right, and that a useful life awaited her in New France. Rose enjoyed her duties at the Salpêtrière, but the *officières* could replace her. The putrid edifice would continue to rot beneath the feet of its inmates whether Rose taught catechism or not. In fact, there was only one person Rose would truly miss. Without realizing where her steps had led her, Rose found herself in front of Vérité's apartment.

Rose opened the door when bid to the sight of Vérité at her desk, bathed in the light of early morning, poring over her record book. Taking notes on the behavior and progress of her charges, as Rose had helped her to do countless times.

How can I disappoint her? Maybe even break her heart? Rose's breath caught in her throat. *The decision is made and I must not waver. I am not a coward.*

"I am going," she announced, instead of giving a proper greeting. She kept her gaze on Vérité, not wanting to show hesitation.

"Stupid girl," Sister Vérité said. "You will die a martyr to this New France. You will wish you had never left. I can promise you that."

"I'm sorry you feel so, Sister." Rose felt a pain in her chest to see the flash of anger in Vérité's eyes.

"I am not your sister anymore, am I? Call me Pauline if you must speak to me at all." Vérité attempted to keep her tone stoic, but Rose could hear an unmistakable quiver in the undertones.

"Pauline." The name felt strange on Rose's tongue. "You will always be a sister to me." She reached for Vérité's hand, but the Sister rebuked her.

"Then how can you leave me?" Something in Vérité's countenance escaped Rose's understanding, but she grasped the accusation of betrayal in Vérité's voice all too well.

"Your friendship has meant more to me than anything," Sister Vérité said. "Your arrival here brightened my life, yet you cast my friendship aside. You cast me aside. You cast aside your very life."

"I will find death sooner or later, Pauline," Rose said. "Who can say whether it will come any sooner in New France than in the Salpêtrière? Either way, I cannot stay."

"Do what you will." Vérité stood and opened the door of the

pleasant apartment to the gloomy hallway beyond. "The choice was yours, and you made it."

"I do not leave for two weeks, Sister Vérité," said Rose, reprising the title for the sake of a few young girls within earshot. "We needn't say good-bye—not yet."

"You're already gone," was Vérité's farewell.

Indeed, for the next two weeks, Rose lived like a shadow in Vérité's presence—there, but never noticed or acknowledged.

Please speak to me! Rose wanted to shout as she assisted the silent Vérité in her duties. She knew it would accomplish nothing, so she held her tongue. Worse, she feared any attempt to break the silence might cause Vérité further grief.

On the day the three girls left for Rouen, Sister Charité stood beside the carriage in the weak spring sunlight and presented each one with a rosary and a benediction.

"Go and do your duty, my daughters," Sister Charité said as she opened the door to the carriage. "Know that my prayers and good wishes go with you."

Rose forced a weak smile for the formidable woman. She waited for Vivienne and Geneviève to take their seats before claiming her own. Rose hesitated as she climbed onto the step of the carriage and onto the worn leather seats. The last carriage she'd traveled in, more than three years before, had been far grander, but brought her to the place of her nightmares. *Please God that this rattletrap take me to a brighter future.*

"Wait!" Vérité called from behind them.

Rose turned to see her friend rushing from the doors, gasping from the exertion of her run.

When Vérité reached Rose she removed her necklace, a small silver medallion depicting St. Agnes, and clasped it around her neck. Then she took Rose's face in her hands and kissed her cheeks.

"I am so sorry . . . these past weeks . . . I just couldn't . . ." Vérité struggled.

Rose silenced her friend with a hearty embrace.

"Please don't forget me, Rose." Vérité did not bother to restrain her tears.

"Never," was all Rose could manage.

Rose forced herself to board the carriage and watched as Vérité . . . Pauline . . . grew smaller and smaller in the distance. She watched until she could no longer see the face of the one person who had truly loved her these past three years.

Once out of sight, as much as it pained her, Rose forced herself to turn around and look forward.

CHAPTER 2

Elisabeth

August 1667, On the Atlantic Ocean

Hell isn't fire; it's a frozen abyss. The streets of Paris would be stifling this time of year, Elisabeth Martin thought with a pang of regret. *I'll never be properly warm again, will I?* She looked out over the vast gray ocean, her wheat-blond hair blowing loose in the wind, and longed to feel the sun on her shoulders as she wandered the narrow avenues of the Saint-Sulpice district arm in arm with her father, Pierre. The crew said it was colder than usual for summer, but at least the bone-chilling rain had given way to fog. She could only imagine what winter would be like on the open sea.

To summon warmth on the fog-blanketed ship deck, she tried recalling one of the many fine afternoons in that same Parisian sun that she spent with her father, when they closed his bakery for an hour or two to scout their competition. They judged a baker first by his inventory. Was his supply overflowing at noon? Gone by ten in the morning?

"A good baker makes what the people want," Pierre repeated to his daughter almost daily, "and enough of it, too. But not so much that it goes to waste. No matter what they preach in the churches, there's no greater sin in my book, girl."

Next, they assessed the creativity of his offerings. Did he sell only baguettes and buns, or did he venture into pastries and cakes? At last, they would taste.

Truth be told, the tasting was their main objective.

From the age of fourteen, Elisabeth worked in the bakery as her father's equal partner. She inherited his work ethic, and he freely admitted her technique and creativity surpassed his own. Were Elisabeth a boy, she might have become a preeminent Parisian pastry chef. As a girl, she could work in her father's shop, but no more. He raged at the injustice on her behalf, but she loved the days at her father's side too much to fret over the missed chance at renown.

Now, after a month at sea, Elisabeth had become so inured to the cold that she could barely summon the memory of the Parisian summer sun. The salty spray that seeped into her bones reminded her of the chilly late-winter day when Elisabeth stood next to her mother in the cemetery, her own large frame towering over the diminutive woman, and watched the grave diggers lower her father into the cold dirt.

Though the stale air of the hold held no enticements for Elisabeth, the chill of the ocean breeze soon chased her below decks. There, girls huddled in various states of illness from the constant rocking of the ship. Those well enough to fight through the nausea nursed those who were not.

A lone girl, Nicole, lay on the edge of her bunk, head over the side and buried in a bucket as she heaved. Nothing remained for her queasy stomach to expel, which Elisabeth knew made the experience even worse. No one attended her, so Elisabeth climbed into the bunk to sit behind Nicole and hold her chestnut mane away from her face.

"Thank you," the girl muttered between gagging spells.

"Don't you worry. Just try to relax and breathe." Elisabeth spoke in soft tones and rubbed the girl's back. It was the only relief she could offer.

Eventually, Nicole lay back on her bed. The heaves no longer racked her body, but the girl still shivered violently. Elisabeth covered Nicole's shaking frame with the blanket from her own bed.

Nicole nodded gratefully but did not attempt to speak.

Not knowing what else to do, Elisabeth went to the ship's

kitchens. The crew didn't appear to appreciate passengers milling about during a squall and did not seem happy about the intrusion. Elisabeth could not walk into a kitchen without making an assessment, and the ship's galley seemed reasonably well organized. Pierre Martin himself would have found no real fault. The quantity of wine seemed a bit excessive, but sailing was a monotonous career, after all.

"Excuse me, Monsieur Aubin," Elisabeth said. "May I have some bread and ale for one of the women? She is very ill."

"They always is, mademoiselle," said the rough-hewn sailor who ran the galley. His gray beard was patchy and his teeth were black with decay. He did not look up at Elisabeth from the salted meat he chopped for that night's stew. "It ain't suppertime yet, so she'll have to wait."

"Sir, this young lady has had neither breakfast nor dinner, I can assure you," Elisabeth said. "You can certainly spare her a portion of bread and a cup of ale to soothe her stomach."

The man glanced up from his carving board with watery blue eyes, the parts that should have been white gone yellow from too many months at sea along with too much ale and rum.

"Fine, then." He pointed to a pile of bread he'd baked three days before. "Take what you want, but don't complain when we starve two weeks off the coast."

"Thank you," Elisabeth replied, in a tone laced with syrup.

She saw as soon as she boarded the ship a month before that it was best to pretend the sailors were gallant gentlemen, even though most were as far removed from it as a man could be. The chaperone sent to protect the young women from the sailors had proven a necessary measure, though the chaperone in question spent most of her time moaning on her bunk, even sicker than her wards.

Elisabeth returned to the bunk room and forced Nicole to eat the bread and sip the ale. Elisabeth shook her head as she parceled out the bread. Her father would have closed his doors rather than sell the crumbling mess. It looked as though the sailor used sawdust rather than proper flour—too much like the biscuits Elisabeth hid in her handbag when forced to visit the awful Madame Thibault with her mother. The memory of the spiteful old woman and her fondness for unctuous lectures—long ones—evoked an involuntary yawn Elisabeth didn't bother to stifle.

When Nicole finished the bread and ale, she remained far from well, but her color had improved.

"Some air," suggested Elisabeth.

Nicole nodded, though her stance wobbled when she rose from the stale mattress. Supporting Nicole by the arm, Elisabeth led the weakened girl to the main deck of the ship. Though the waves still churned, the girls found a sheltered place to sit away from the spray and biting wind.

"I don't think I can survive another two months of this," Nicole said, staring off into the angry black water.

"You can and you will." Though Elisabeth spoke with conviction, she knew that passengers died regularly during voyages of this length. She wrapped her arm around the shivering girl, tucking a strand of wayward hair behind Nicole's ear. "It won't be easy, but we will make it to the New World."

"I was mad to think this was a good idea." Nicole rested her head on Elisabeth's shoulder, weak after hours of torment. "I should have stayed home with Maman and Papa and carried on somehow."

"Tell me about your home, and your family," Elisabeth encouraged.

"We had a farm outside Rouen." Nicole raised her head and looked at the horizon as if seeing the silhouette of her farmhouse against the sunset. "Papa grew wheat. It was a beautiful place. Rolling green hills, fat cows. But the crops stopped growing and Papa had to use my dowry to buy more land."

A cloud passed over the girl's face and Elisabeth squeezed Nicole close. "The dowry had been spoken for, hadn't it?"

Nicole nodded. "His name was Jean. Jean Galet. He was a farmer like Papa. A good man. We would have been happy."

"I'm very sorry. And I'm sure he is, too." Elisabeth rubbed Nicole's back, knowing her heart has to be broken at the boy's callous behavior.

Nicole straightened her spine and stared forward. "He'll manage as we all must. But there you are. Once our engagement was broken, our priest told me of the King's need for young ladies—"

"So you decided to try your chances in New France," Elisabeth summarized.

Nicole nodded.

A common tale among the ship-bound women: a father deceased, land gone bad, a dowry misspent, and a girl with few options. Outside of marriage, a woman had few ways to survive in the world, as Elisabeth was learning.

Elisabeth volunteered information about her father's death. Each time she mentioned it, the words tasted like ash in her mouth.

"So your mother encouraged you to go?" Nicole asked. The cold air forced color back into her cheeks, and her eyes seemed far less glossy than before.

"Hardly." Elisabeth laughed. "My mother arranged a marriage for me. My dear friend helped me find a way out."

"You weren't pleased with your mother's choice?" Nicole's tanned face and large brown eyes looked up at Elisabeth.

"Not at all. He was the most shiftless man in all of Paris." Elisabeth felt like spitting to punctuate her words. She remembered the scene, only hours after her father's funeral, when her mother announced Elisabeth's betrothal to Denis Moraud over a cup of coffee, as though relating some piece of idle gossip. The resultant argument was unpleasant, but had doubtless entertained the neighbors. During the exchange, Elisabeth learned that her mother planned to marry Denis's father, Jacques. Elisabeth had inherited her father's even temper, but when she learned that her mother plotted a second marriage before her husband was even dead, Elisabeth raged. Connections, ambition, scheming: This was Anne Martin's world.

As her thoughts returned to Nicole and the ship, Elisabeth felt glad that she had severed ties with her mother, and that world, for the rest of her days.

"But your mother eventually agreed to let you go?" Nicole asked.

"No," Elisabeth said. "I'm twenty-five years old. I didn't need her consent. I obtained an affidavit of good comportment from my priest, and needed no more."

"I'm just nineteen," Nicole said. "Papa wasn't going to let me go. He kept changing his mind. Maman and I had to reason with him for weeks. I think he finally realized I'm better off going away. He didn't want to see me as a maid in some great house with no life of my own."

For a solid hour, the women recounted all the details of life in a Parisian bakery and on a Norman farm. As a city girl who rarely had the opportunity to venture outside of Paris, Elisabeth thought Nicole's youth was idyllic and peaceful. Nicole seemed equally enraptured with her new friend's tales of life in the capital.

At the center of the ship, a bell rang, indicating supper. The ladies were allowed the modesty of dining alone, in the ship's main dining room. The crew ate when the guests had finished. Of the nineteen young ladies and two chaperones, only five felt well enough to leave the bunk room and brave the burnt stew and stale bread.

I will be grateful for this meal, Elisabeth willed. *For though this food may not be to my liking, there are many who have none.* The words had come from her father, who repeated them to Elisabeth, time and time again, when they visited the shop of a less-skilled baker, or when, heaven forbid, Elisabeth's mother attempted to cook a meal. That had not happened since Elisabeth turned twelve and took over the family kitchen, to the benefit of all.

"How is Vivienne?" Nicole asked a black-haired girl of about eighteen years.

Elisabeth knew the girl's name was Rose, but they had not spoken much. Rose kept close to her young companions and nursed them faithfully through their seasickness.

"Not well," Rose said. "I see you are better, though."

Nicole nodded. "Thanks to Elisabeth. She's looked after me all afternoon."

"My thanks," Rose said, nodding to Elisabeth. "Vivienne is quite ill. I couldn't attend to them both. I would not be here now if Geneviève didn't finally feel well enough to look after Vivienne for a while."

"My pleasure." Elisabeth smiled at Rose. Though young, Rose seemed quite capable of assuming authority. She nursed the sick with patience and recruited those who were well enough to help in various tasks that made her makeshift hospital a little less hellish. Sick buckets had to be emptied and rats chased from the mattresses. Pleasant or not, it had to be done.

As they talked, Elisabeth and Rose discovered they both came from Paris, and they luxuriated in reminiscing about their favorite spots in the city. Though they had not lived in the same neighborhoods, they knew a few of the same restaurants and theaters.

Night closed in over the Atlantic Ocean, and a merciful calm swept over the sea. The restless pitch of the waves slowed to a gentle rocking. Sleep became possible, even for the sickest among them. Elisabeth woke several times to check on Nicole, but every time the girl breathed evenly, deep in restful sleep despite the stench of the livestock and the unseasonable cold that kept Elisabeth from her rest.

A determined girl, Elisabeth mused. *She may be shy and scared, but she's made of stronger stuff than she realizes.*

Several bunks over, Rose held a vigil over small Vivienne. The child claimed to be fifteen but looked no older than twelve. Elisabeth remembered Vivienne's frightened face when Madame LeMaire, one of the chaperones, lectured them about the proper comportment of the King's wards. The old woman, whose crisp white hair and lined face gave her the look of a head of garlic, waxed on about the virtuous women needed to found this great new territory, beloved of His Majesty. The women cared more about the realities of the voyage—three months of stale and moldy food, days trapped in a bunk room that smelled increasingly of vomit and shit as the sea flung the ship about like a toy—than founding a country. They worried more about avoiding frostbite and being scalped by the rumored savages during their first winter in Canada than preserving the honor of the Crown and the Church. Elisabeth knew poor Vivienne had felt the same, perhaps felt it even more keenly than the rest. The small girl shook in her sleep, and Rose wrapped an arm around her.

"Is she any better?" Elisabeth asked, joining Rose at Vivienne's bedside.

"Hard to say," Rose said. "She moans. She hasn't eaten all day."

"Let me see if I can coax her," Elisabeth offered. "She must eat something."

Elisabeth wrapped her shawl tightly around her shoulders and found the stairwell by the light of one dim candle. Though most of the crew slept, the ship maintained a skeleton watch even in the dead of night. What they kept watch over, Elisabeth knew not, and preferred not to think of it.

The galley was empty, and Elisabeth offered silent thanks that she need not banter with the crotchety cook to secure rations for Vivienne. She tore a portion of bread from the nearest loaf and tucked it away. She could not open the ale barrel, so she grabbed a mug from the pile of clean dishes and made to return belowdecks where she would seek out a few precious ounces from her personal barrel of fresh drinking water.

"Where are you going, you little thief?" a voice behind Elisabeth asked.

"Excuse me, Monsieur Aubin." Elisabeth put on her sweetest tone as she turned to face the revolting cook. "Another of the girls is quite ill. The bread will settle her stomach."

"Settle yours, more like." The cook growled, his foul breath spoiling the air between them. "Fat cow that you are, you're taking it for yourself."

At some cost, Elisabeth restrained her tongue. She was tall, built like her father, and did not take her mother's pains to keep her frame slender. She was used to a full day's work and to eating rations that gave the energy she needed. Despite the years of reprimands and her mother bemoaning her daughter's masculine frame, jibes still hurt Elisabeth more than she cared to admit.

"I assure you, sir, I find your bread no more palatable than wood shavings. It does, however, settle the stomach reasonably well. If you doubt me, come below and see the girl yourself. I suggest you bring a bucket and mop, and help with the vomit while you're there."

The cook grabbed Elisabeth's arm and pinned her against the galley door frame.

"Don't talk to me like that, you little tramp," he hissed. "I know what all you 'ladies' are. You're good ol' Louis's way of emptying France of whores. Why not save that lip and offer to earn that bread like a good little slut?"

He pushed his reeking body close to hers. Elisabeth felt the bite of acid in her throat. Rather than stepping away, and letting him pin her more firmly to the door, she pushed him, slamming his back against the opposite side of the door frame.

I don't regret my "mannish size" and "unladylike figure" at the moment, Maman. Not for all your lamentations.

"Don't you ever touch me again, you piece of filth. If I need to feed an ill woman, I'll do it without your say-so. If you so much as speak in my presence again, I'll fling you overboard to feed the fishes. Do I make myself plain?"

The old man released Elisabeth's arm, or, rather, dropped it in abhorrence and left the galley. Perhaps he wasn't used to being refused. Elisabeth wondered how many sea voyages with scarce rations had made young women desperate enough to allow his advances.

Back belowdecks, Rose sat at Vivienne's side, worry etched on her delicate features. Elisabeth handed the bread and water to Rose and took a seat on the nearest bunk.

"Please eat, darling." Rose broke off a corner of bread and tried to tempt Vivienne. The girl made no response, just stared at the bunkroom ceiling.

"Water, then." Elisabeth helped to sit Vivienne up on her pillows to take the cool liquid. Rose lifted the cup to Vivienne's mouth and tilted it, but the water came back as soon as it reached the lips.

"She's burning with fever," Elisabeth said, her tone no louder than she would dare to use during Mass.

Rose and Elisabeth exchanged a worried look. Real illness could spread through a ship in days and cause unspeakable devastation. Rose took a scrap of fabric and wetted it with the precious clean water. She pressed it to Vivienne's forehead.

"We need a doctor," Rose snapped to no one in particular.

"We haven't got one." Elisabeth took the cloth from Rose's hand. "You need rest. I haven't seen you as much as nap in two days. If she's contagious, you need your rest and your strength. Sleep. Now."

If Rose thought to countermand Elisabeth's orders, she did not say so. Her shoulders sagged in defeat and she climbed under the thin covers on the sour-smelling mattress.

"Wake me if she needs me, please," Rose mumbled, almost incomprehensible.

"Of course," Elisabeth promised.

For the next six hours, Elisabeth doused the rag with water and applied the compress to the girl's forehead and face, repeating the process whenever the rag grew warm. Vivienne's small body shook against the fever, the shivering broken only by periods of unintelligible babbling. Vivienne's breathing grew shallow, and Elisabeth recognized the signs she had seen as she nursed her father through the hours before his death. The glassy eyes, the sallow skin . . . it was all the same. She had coaxed her father with broth and bread, but he would not eat. Elisabeth had sat, alone, by Pierre's side as he left this world. As the hours passed, she grew certain that Vivienne would soon join him.

"Rose." Elisabeth shook Rose from her slumber. "You need to come. Vivienne . . . Vivienne needs you."

Rose looked up at Elisabeth and wiped the sleep from her eyes. It took just a moment longer for comprehension to cross her face. Rose leaped from her bed to Vivienne's bunk and took her right hand, Elisabeth the other. Rose brushed the hair from Vivienne's forehead and whispered sweet words that Elisabeth could barely make out when she strained. *They aren't meant for my ears, anyway.*

Elisabeth watched Vivienne's chest rise and fall, until the moment came that it rose no more. Elisabeth wiped the tears from her cheeks, but Rose remained impassive, kissing Vivienne's forehead and closing the dead girl's eyes for the last time.

"I'm so sorry I failed you." Rose buried her head in her hands for a moment, then stood, smoothing the front of her dress.

Elisabeth, over a head taller, wrapped her arms around petite Rose.

"I'm so sorry, Rose. You didn't fail her. You were so brave."

"I was brave for her sake," Rose said, pulling away from the embrace, but squeezing Elisabeth's shoulder as she released her. "I couldn't break down in front of her. She didn't need to spend her last moments comforting *me*."

That afternoon, Elisabeth organized a small memorial as Vivienne's body was buried at sea. There was no priest to bless the body, but Elisabeth could not see the frail child laid to rest without a proper farewell. *Were it me, I would want at least a few words, though there is no one left on earth who would care if I slipped away.* Elisabeth banished the morbid thoughts with no small measure of self-castigation. This was an occasion to mourn for poor Vivienne, not to indulge in pity over her lonely state.

Geneviève wept for her dear friend, tucked in Rose's arms, as the sailors lowered the small, shrouded corpse into the cold abyss. Nicole, taught to read by her convent-educated mother, read from her tattered Bible while the handful of mourners listened with quiet respect. The crew, none of them strangers to loss at sea, kept the bustle to a minimum as the women held the short memorial for the girl they had known for such a short while.

Good-bye, sweet girl, I wish I could have known you better so I could grieve for you as well as you deserve. Elisabeth looked out onto the vast midnight-blue ocean that Vivienne would soon become a part of. She drew in a deep breath and willed herself to be strong. Nicole needed her to be strong. Rose needed her to be strong. But as the sunburned sailor slid Vivienne's shrouded body into the frigid waters, her strength failed her. The burning acid rose in her throat and she wanted nothing more than to give in to her grief. *One diseased rat could kill this entire ship. One minor miscalculation with the food, and we could starve. Any one of us could follow in poor Vivienne's wake.*

A vision of her father's disapproving face flashed in her memory. *You're better than this, Elisabeth. You'll survive this crossing, flourish in this New France, and die an old woman, warm in your bed. Just to spite your mother.*

When the service concluded, Elisabeth and Nicole convinced Rose to partake in supper that evening, though Geneviève was beyond persuasion.

"Another two months," Rose said, looking down at her uneaten soup.

"We'll manage," Elisabeth said, eyeing the murky concoction. Though unpalatable, the soup was warm and rich, but each day the mixture would grow more and more watery as rations grew sparser. "Others have before us, and others will long after we've safely arrived on shore."

"I spoke with one of the crew. He says we've passed the worst," Nicole volunteered. "So long as we don't hit any more storms, he thinks we may arrive early."

"Lot of good that did Vivienne," Rose mumbled to her dinner plate. "I should have stayed up with her."

"Don't blame yourself, Rose," Elisabeth said. "You did what

you could, as did I. A doctor might have helped, but maybe not. She was so ill, there was nothing left to do. She passed on knowing that we cared. Try to take solace in that."

"I promised to care for her," Rose said. "I promised Sister Charité."

"Rose, I nursed my father for weeks before he died," Elisabeth said. "I know what you feel. I felt it, too. I still feel that gut-wrenching pain—the guilt—two months later. The only way I managed to forgive myself is by realizing that Papa would not want me to take the blame. Vivienne would feel the same."

"I didn't realize you'd lost your father so recently," said Rose. "I'm very sorry."

"As am I," Elisabeth said. "But I can hear his voice in my head: 'It was just my time, 'Lisie. Have a good cry for me—I deserve that much—and move on.' So that's what I'm trying to do. As you must, also."

The others giggled at Elisabeth's impersonation of her father's jovial tone. Even Elisabeth smiled. It became less and less difficult to think of Papa without pain. However, thoughts of her mother still forced her anger to rise to the surface like a festering blister. The scoldings for her disinterest in running a house. The jibes at her size. The spiteful way she disregarded Elisabeth's talent in the kitchen. Elisabeth hoped someday she would learn to reflect on her childhood with a sense of peace.

"Your father sounds like he was a wonderful man," said Nicole.

"The best of men," Elisabeth agreed. "I miss him terribly. It's silly, but I brought his favorite rolling pin with me. I knew he'd want me to keep it, so I tucked it in with my petticoats." There was also a ridiculous handkerchief in her trunk that she tried not to dwell on.

"My *maman* sent me with a pearl brooch that belonged to her mother," Nicole said. "And Papa made me a wooden bird to remember him by. When we were small he used to carve little toys for us out of scraps of wood in the evenings as he sat by the fire."

Rose cleared her throat. "I have a doll from the Orient my papa bought when I was a girl. Maman died when I was born, but I have her looking glass—Papa saved it for me. My aunt didn't notice I'd taken it."

"It's wonderful that we all have little remembrances," Elisabeth said. "We have to remember where we came from, especially as we leave it all behind. We also have to bear in mind that where we're going is just as important."

For the rest of the evening, the women exchanged stories of home and family. The warmth of their memories cast out a bit of the cold. Elisabeth noticed that Rose ate a portion of her meal as she shared the details of her childhood in Paris. Nicole spoke of the green hills of Normandy, and Elisabeth shared about every nook of her father's shop to the point where all three could smell the browning butter laced with sugar and longed for one of his pastries.

Chapter 3

Nicole

September 1667, Approaching the Docks in Quebec City

These will be my friends and neighbors. Nicole surveyed the docks as she gripped the rail of the gangplank on her way down from the loathsome ship. She scanned the faces of the dozens of settlers eager to catch a glimpse of the prospective brides, anxious to find a glimmer of kindness among them. *How long will it be before I'm so starved for new society and a taste of home that I clamor to the docks to see the next arrival of passengers with the rest of them?*

Distracted, her boot caught a ridge on the gangplank and she gathered herself just before she toppled into Elisabeth. *Steady your nerves, you dolt,* Nicole chastised herself. *There's no need to make a fool of yourself before they even know your name.* The solid ground felt foreign beneath her feet as she stepped onto the dock. After three months, she wasn't sure she trusted it to remain firm. Nicole squeezed Rose's hand as she saw that Rose dried her tears on a grimy handkerchief. Only ten of the women would stay in Quebec City, the others bound for Ville-Marie or Trois-Rivières. Though the old crone of a chaperone had been too ill to spend any amount of time with them, she had decided on the town assignments without consulting the ladies themselves, nor would she brook any arguments to the list. Because of this, Rose bid Geneviève a tearful farewell as the latter was destined for Ville-Marie. Though incensed that the chaperone separated Rose from Geneviève, Nicole was elated that she was to remain with Rose and Elisabeth in Quebec, at least until they were married.

At the dock, near the throng of settlers, the governor, the bishop, and a handful of other officials waited on a platform to greet each of the ladies who would stay in Quebec City. Nicole mustered a stiff curtsy and a vague smile for the men dressed in finery as impressive as she'd ever seen in the grandest parts of Rouen. Satins, silks, brocades, and even starched lace. She looked down at her tattered woolen skirt and patched jacket and wished for a moment that she had allowed her mother to make her some new things for the journey. She had refused, wanting them to save every *denier* for new fields, but she couldn't help but feel shabby next to these important men.

You came here to ease the burden on Papa and Maman, to give the little ones a chance, not for yourself. Nicole cast her eyes down, knowing that wasn't the complete truth. The afternoon in April when Father Augustine found her in the churchyard, sobbing, she was not thinking of her family. When he offered her a place on the ship, she didn't accept out of selflessness. She was thinking of her own broken heart as she stood, moments before, in the back of the church as she watched Jean Galet, her Jean, pledge himself to another woman not three weeks after he was supposed to marry Nicole. *Her* broken heart, *her* embarrassment. Not her family's improved lot with one fewer stomach to fill. Not the dying fields that lay beyond her father's front door.

She knew it was stupid to give one's heart to a man before marriage. *Too many hours distracted by his roguish brown curls and wicked dimples. Too many hours congratulating myself on my good fortune to find such a match meant too many hours of anguish when it all came to nothing.*

Chin up and eyes forward, Nicole told herself, summoning the words her father, Thomas, had said almost four months prior as she entered the Rouen Cathedral to meet her shipmates. It was his motto, and Nicole decided it was high time she adopted it as her own.

The governor cleared his throat, preparing to offer a formal welcome to the brides, but a tall nun—a contradiction of a woman, with a lined face and a youthful step—silenced him.

"My good sir, I should like to see the ladies out of the cold air and settled in the convent as soon as may be. They are exhausted from their voyage and not used to the climes here. We would be honored to welcome you at any time if you wish to greet the girls properly."

The bishop opened his mouth, looking as if he wished to object, but glanced to the governor already bidding the ladies a cheerful farewell, and stayed his tongue.

Nicole blessed the woman as she claimed her spot in the open wagon. The Ursulines lived not far from the docks, so it was less than a half hour before Nicole and the others found themselves in the convent common room, warming themselves before a well-fed fire as the dozen or so nuns of the order introduced themselves. Nicole had thought the Sisters would find the arrival of ten energetic young women a disruption to their staid and solemn lifestyle, but they seemed all too happy to welcome their guests, even if it meant their solitude was shattered like a china cup on a stone floor.

Upstairs, the girls were allowed to choose from the rooms appointed to their use, and Rose and Elisabeth claimed a cozy room with Nicole. The wooden floors looked sturdy and not given to drafts. The beds were draped with sensible green canvas curtains and warm, clean bedding. More comfortable than her own tiny bedroom in her father's farmhouse, to be sure. Their trunks appeared before long, but the emptying of their finery into the armoire was the task of minutes.

Following the others' example, Nicole shrugged off her shoes and slid under the warm covers of her new bed. She relaxed every muscle in her body, sinking into the soft mattress. Her eyes welled up with tears of gratitude. *Never again will I cross that damned ocean. Come what may, this place is my home and I will make the best of it.*

Nicole smiled throughout the meal and answered questions with a polite expression, but the weight of fatigue still hung heavy on her, despite the short nap. Her eyes felt rough, as though her lids were lined with sand. Every muscle felt sore and overused—reeling from the lack of rock and sway on the solid stone floor. The beef stew and warm bread was the most appetizing thing she'd seen since embarking the ship, perhaps months before then, if she was honest with herself, but after the first few mouthfuls, she couldn't force any more down, sure her papa and *maman* would not be eating so well that night.

"I understand from your parish priest that you have an impressive education," Sister Anne, a plump nun with a sweet face, said to Nicole. As all their priests sent along letters to the Ursulines, the bit of information did not surprise Nicole, even if being the subject of correspondence between her confessor and a stranger was more than a bit off-putting.

"My mother was brought up in a convent, Sister," Nicole explained. "She taught us all to read, write, and do some simple figuring."

"A solid foundation, my dear," the nun replied. "We must be sure to find you a young man with some wit about him."

Nicole nodded, not giving much thought to the prospect. The thought of "husband" and "Jean Galet" was still too synonymous for her to think of anyone else.

All around, the Sisters questioned the young ladies about their lives in France, just as Sister Anne questioned her. Not just a method of getting to know their new housemates, but a tool for matchmaking, Nicole realized. The apple tart before her lost all appeal and she pushed it to the side where it was soon claimed by one of the other girls. Despite the lectures that laid the expectations plainly before the King's wards, Nicole had managed before now to shove the reality from her mind. They were to marry, and to do so as soon as they were able.

"My dear ladies, if I might claim your attention for a few moments before you seek out your beds?" The eldest of the nuns, the one who had interceded at the dock, stood at the head of Nicole's table. "I am Sister Mathilde and will be responsible for your welfare while you are with us. We are so pleased to welcome you to our little convent and hope your time here will be enjoyable and profitable."

Not an eye in the room wavered from the old woman's face. Her voice was as sure as her step, and confidence emanated from her in equal measure with kindness of spirit.

"While you are here, we hope you will voice any deficiencies you might have in your domestic education. If you have little skill in the kitchen, you will find yourself before a stove more often than you might like. If you cannot sew, we expect to see you with needle in hand for at least an hour each day. Likewise, we expect you to share your talents for the benefit of your shipmates and the order while you are here."

Nicole looked to Elisabeth, who harbored a small smile on her lips. Elisabeth's talents were obvious. *At least Maman sent me with her favorite knitting needles,* Nicole thought. *Blankets and scarves won't come amiss with winter so near.*

"We want you all to take advantage of your time afield, for many of you will settle quite far from here. You may well find yourself at quite some distance from any neighbor who is able to instruct you, nor will it be likely that she—or you—will have the time to spare. And, ladies, I cannot caution you enough, make your choice of husband carefully. You will have your pick, I assure you, but not all the men are equally deserving. Above all, you must ask any prospective suitor if he has built upon his land. We don't want to see you with less-than-adequate lodging in the midst of one of our winters. You are here to keep houses, but not clear the land for them."

Sister Mathilde continued her speech for a few more moments, but Nicole felt it impossible to focus on her words. Within days, the single men of the settlement would descend on the convent, each vying for the attentions of the ladies, hoping to secure a bride. Nicole had a vision of a cattle auction where the group of farmers schemed to purchase prized stock for their herd. Looking for wide hips and straight teeth in his future bride as he would look for a rounded rump and strong legs in a dairy cow? Dinner churned in her stomach, and Nicole suspected it had very little to do with the richness of the food.

They retreated upstairs to their room after the speech, Nicole happy to leave the chatter of the group behind. She changed into her nightdress and all but launched herself into bed. Nicole's affection for her decadent mattress grew with each moment she wallowed in it.

"Isn't it exciting?" Elisabeth asked, straightening her bedcovers. "To think our arrival is such an important event? That the settlers are so anxious to meet us all?"

"Nerve-racking, more like," Nicole said, pulling up her blanket. "What if we choose poorly?"

"We must take our time and be prudent, that's all," Elisabeth answered, stretching before climbing into her own bed.

"Spoken with such confidence," Rose said with a chortle as she placed her skirt in her trunk. "I suppose you did a fine job selecting from all your suitors in Paris."

"Ha ha." Elisabeth lobbed a pillow at Rose's head. "I was too busy working to bother with suitors. Though I can assure you, I rejected my one offer with great enthusiasm. I can tell you, you'll know the bottom of the barrel when you see it. If you need any help, I'll be sure to point them out for you."

Rose laughed, but Nicole couldn't summon it.

"Cheer up," Elisabeth said, peering over at Nicole from her bed. "What's bothering you?"

"I've never in my life made such a decision without my parents," Nicole said. "Papa arranged the match between myself and Jean. I'm sure we'd have been terribly happy . . . if there'd been money at least."

She didn't tell them how much she'd cared for him. How much she was *certain* he cared for her. Even though the match was arranged, she'd rejoiced in her father's choice.

"The Sisters will guide us, I'm sure," Rose said. "They don't want to see us settled in misery. You heard Sister Mathilde. We're the 'mothers of New France' and a valuable resource."

The image of the cattle auction resurfaced in Nicole's mind and did not settle her troubled thoughts. Not for the first time since she'd left France, Jean Galet's face came to mind. The sweetness of his dimples, the mischief in his greenish-blue eyes. *Will any of those young men clamoring for brides be as kind as you, Jean? Will any of them make me as happy as you would have done?*

Nicole choked back her tears, but had far less success with her doubts.

A week after their arrival, the benches and podiums of the town hall gave way to a bower of autumn leaves and a refreshment table to welcome the new ladies and their prospective suitors. A group of younger men played melodies on their well-worn instruments off to the side. Though they did not play well, the tunes were lively, which inspired the conversation to be likewise. None danced, however, for the clergy did not approve. The Sisters watched the proceedings with the attentiveness of hawks on the hunt, ensuring any lapse in decorum was rooted out on the spot.

Nicole lurked toward the edge of the gathering, sipping from a cup of cider, taking stock of the assembly. Rose, having grown up in society, was undaunted by the reception and chatted with a rather tall man with a weak chin. She seemed attentive, but Nicole could not tell if it was due to politeness or genuine interest. *An impressive skill, but not something one learns on a farm milking cows.* Elisabeth, too, bore a sweet smile as she conversed with two eager men. Nicole imagined at Elisabeth's father's side in the bakery was as good a place to learn conversation as any ballroom.

Be brave, Nicole told herself. *The men seem no different from those at home. Smile. Seem friendly. They will come to you.* She took a deep breath and placed the cup on the table. She stepped out of the shadows and affixed a smile that she hoped appeared sincere. Within moments, a gangly man in his twenties bowed before her.

"Alphonse Quentin," the man said by way of introduction.

"Nicole Deschamps," she replied, pleased that no warble of her voice betrayed her nerves.

"Your hair is the color of warm chestnuts," he said, staring at his feet.

"I—I thank you?" Nicole stammered. *Was that meant to be a compliment?*

"I grow some of the finest oats to be seen in the settlement," the man said, appearing to summon some confidence.

"That's . . . wonderful for you," Nicole said.

"My dear Mademoiselle Deschamps." Sister Mathilde swooped

in, taking Nicole by the arm. "I have need of you. I'm sure Monsieur Quentin will forgive me."

Quentin nodded, but his face betrayed his disappointment. Though he might not forgive Sister Mathilde's intrusion, he would never dare to voice it.

A few yards away, the old woman leaned into Nicole. "Alphonse Quentin is a good man, but a simple one. A girl with any schooling at all would be wasted on him. I've a much better plan for you."

Nicole found herself standing before a man who looked about as happy to attend a social event as he would his own hanging. He stood a good six inches taller than Nicole and cut a striking figure. His features looked chiseled from marble, but the fringe of jet-black curls that framed his face did marvels to soften his statuesque visage. Nicole could tell his stormy gray eyes were assessing her, but his conclusions remained a mystery.

"Monsieur Alexandre Lefebvre, may I present Mademoiselle Nicole Deschamps of Rouen," Sister Mathilde said, pushing Nicole forward. "I thought you two should get better acquainted."

Monsieur Lefebvre nodded. Sister Mathilde whisked away to another part of the hall, leaving Nicole alone with the man. She looked to her friends, but saw no polite means of escape.

"Good evening," Nicole said, after an awkward moment.

"Good evening," Lefebvre echoed, arching his brow.

Was I too bold in speaking first? Nicole looked at her shoes, praying the floor would swallow her whole.

"So you are from Rouen," Lefebvre said. "I assume your father has passed. That seems the usual tale."

"Very near Rouen, monsieur," Nicole said. "But my father lives. He has a farm outside of the city."

Lefebvre paused with his mug of cider half raised to his lips. "Indeed. Then how did he allow you to come here?"

"Our land was depleted. I had no dowry." Nicole willed that words of her family would not trigger the tears that seemed forever pressing behind her eyes. "I preferred to leave than to be a burden."

"He would have done better to keep you in France." Lefebvre's voice, for reasons unknown to Nicole, seemed laced with acid.

"You do not like New France, then?" Nicole wondered what on earth could inspire such venom.

"It is no place for women," Lefebvre said. "A desolate place. The King is a fool for risking your lives to build his colonies."

"If I may be so bold," Nicole asked, "why are you here, monsieur, if you find this place distasteful?" She grew weary of this man's scornful tone. Hard enough to accept her new life, without a stranger telling her that she'd made a dreadful mistake.

"The lot of a second son, mademoiselle," Lefebvre replied. He offered a barely perceivable nod and left without another word.

Though she had no particular reason to heed this stranger, Nicole felt somehow wounded by his slight. She admitted an appreciation for Lefebvre's poise and comportment. He seemed more refined than the men in the Norman countryside, and made Nicole feel somehow backward and crude.

Quite the introduction to society, Nicole thought. *A simpleton and a man too presumptuous and arrogant by half. Why can't I find a man with Jean's sweetness and quick wit?* Jean's boyish face and brown curls flashed in her memory, and she knew she could not depend upon herself to keep the tears at bay.

She sought out her cloak and left the reception, hoping no one noticed her departure. The bitter wind blew, as always, but the snowfall was light and Nicole could see the convent from the town hall even through the falling snow.

"What on earth are you doing out here?" a male voice yelled.

Nicole turned to see Lefebvre, who must have left the gathering just before she did, untying his massive sorrel horse. Lefebvre's eyes blazed with intensity as though she had done him a great offense.

"Going home, monsieur." Nicole pulled her cloak tighter but did not slow her pace.

"You should know better than to go out in a storm alone," Lefebvre said. "This is not France; the winter here is not to be taken lightly."

"Thank you for your concern, monsieur, but I think I can find my way fifty yards in light snow," Nicole replied.

"Don't trifle with the weather, girl," Lefebvre said. "A light snow can turn into a blizzard in moments."

Nicole bit back a reply and set out toward the convent. Though tempted to engage the infuriating man in a shouting match, she held her tongue and left him behind. She reached the convent without incident, but sought the warmth of the fire as soon as she crossed the threshold. She wondered if she would ever adjust to the perpetual cold.

She took the least austere of the chairs and pulled it close to the crackling flames, enjoying the warmth as she watched the figures in the blaze. It was a game she had played with her mother as a girl. Some people looked for sheep or rabbits in the wispy clouds, but she sought out the kittens frolicking in the dancing fire.

But her plans of a solitary end to her evening ended when Sister Mathilde entered the room to see which woman had returned so early.

"You are back already, child?" Sister Mathilde claimed the seat by the roaring fire next to Nicole's, a cup of warm cider in hand for each of them.

"I have enjoyed my share of company, Sister." Nicole sat back down on the spindly chair in front of the fireplace. "I see you came back early as well."

"The younger women of my order can supervise once things are underway," Sister Mathilde said, savoring a sip from her cup. "I weary too easily now, to spend the late hours away from my convent. I noticed Alexandre Lefebvre showed you his usual charm."

"You saw?" Nicole was embarrassed that the conversation had not been more private.

The Sister nodded. "I hoped you might soften him a bit. Poor man."

Sister Mathilde looked into her cup. She seemed tempted to say more, but kept her thoughts to herself.

"Do not be discouraged, my dear," Sister Mathilde said. "Some women find their matches almost at once, others take time. You seem one of the latter variety. Nothing wrong with that. You'll be tempted before long."

"I hope you're right, Sister." Nicole looked back at the fire and sipped the warm cider. *Something that tastes of home, at least.*

"Tell me, child, are you unhappy here?" Sister Mathilde asked.

"No, Sister, not exactly." It was the truth. Nicole didn't dislike anything about the colony in particular—except, perhaps, the cold. "I miss my family a great deal, though."

"As a good girl should," Sister Mathilde said. "Just remember, your place is here and you must make the best of it. You will find contentment here, my dear, and perhaps even happiness, but you must allow yourself to find it."

In other words, Nicole thought, *chin up and eyes forward.*

CHAPTER 4

Elisabeth

October 1667

Flour . . . sugar . . . yeast . . . salt . . .

Elisabeth gathered the ingredients for bread, along with eight bowls and plenty of clean cloths. Dawn had just broken, and her lesson wasn't for hours, but her impatience kept her from idling in the warmth of her bed. Today was her first day as a teacher and she was determined to get things right. Sister Mathilde stressed that the most coveted quality of a wife was her usefulness, and Elisabeth knew that baking bread would soon become a part of the life of all her shipmates. Good bread meant good health, and Elisabeth could not bear the idea of not imparting some of her knowledge to the women who had become her dearest friends. Six of her shipmates and even two of the Sisters agreed—eagerly—to take lessons when Elisabeth volunteered.

People do care what I do, Maman. People care about what I have to say.

The recipe she taught today would be a simple one, so preparing ingredients was the work of minutes. Kindling the oven to the proper temperature was another matter. Sister Éléonore had started the task for their breakfast, but the fire wasn't ready to bake bread. A few more sticks of firewood and a good blast from the bellows set things on the right course. The convent's bread oven was in the interior of the house, much to Elisabeth's delight. It posed a fire risk, to be sure, but it saved the inconvenience of going outside to bake bread in the snow. Her shipmates who married homesteaders would certainly know that pleasure soon enough.

Unable to resist the temptation of being alone in a proper kitchen for the first time in months, she set to work. *Millefeuilles,* Elisabeth decided, noticing the quantity of excellent cream. *No man with a mouth can resist them*. Thursday afternoon was the designated time for the gentlemen of the colony, and she had no doubt the pastries would sate grateful appetites. Almost without thought, she mixed the ingredients and set the dough in the coldest part of the cellar where it would rest before she rolled it out and baked it in sheets.

Elisabeth luxuriated in swirling the cream mixture together. This was the heart of the *millefeuille*. In the bakery she had time for neither careless haste nor leisure, so it was only on the rare occasions when she had the time to develop a recipe in the family kitchen that she had the chance to enjoy her craft.

Without warning, her mother's face entered her thoughts. She had to slow her hand and steady her breath, or risk turning the cream into butter as she stirred. Over the years she had to learn to calm her temper where her mother was concerned. Pastry dough, in particular, required gentle handling, so it served as a useful tool for cooling her anger. *Nothing that ever escaped Anne Martin's mouth is worth ruining one batch of pastry or one loaf of bread.*

It was three years before that Elisabeth taught herself this recipe . . . sneaking in some baking time before her mother awoke just before mid-morning. It was one of the horrid days when her mother insisted she stay home to practice some loathsome domestic skill. Sewing and a social call that day.

Anne was convinced that one of the silver-haired, dour-faced women would convince Elisabeth to give up her hours at the bakery, though her own nagging could not do it. Once every month or so it was the same: *A woman has no place running a business if she has the means to do otherwise.*

"Her sister is a countess, Elisabeth! Imagine that. You cannot think she'd give you poor advice," Anne would say. Elisabeth held her tongue, knowing no amount of time would help her mother to understand that she was not as impressed by rank as she. No sister of a countess, aunt of a duke, or cousin to a foreign prince made any progress.

The tedious lecture then led to a stern reprimand about the sheaves of wheat Elisabeth had embroidered on her brown linen jacket. If there was one thing Anne couldn't stand, it was anything that attached her to the working classes. *Including me. Including Papa.*

When her father came home, the day was forgotten. He praised the embroidery as being fit for a baker and all but drooled on the table in praise of her pastries. So it always was on those days. As soon as her papa crossed the threshold, all the bitterness and frustration of the day evaporated, and she was herself again.

Elisabeth summoned Pierre's face from her memory to replace Anne's and she felt the tension ease from her shoulders. She looked down at the same brown jacket, now threadbare, and smiled at the little sheaves of wheat as she fetched the pastry dough from the cellar. With movements as deft as a dancer's she rolled the pastry into thin sheets and placed them in the scorching oven. Within moments, the scent of butter laced with sugar filled the air. Elisabeth sat, stealing a few minutes' rest before the girls arrived for their course, and breathed in the aroma. *Thank God that some things never change.*

Not long after, her pupils assembled around the scarred oaken worktable and looked to Elisabeth expectantly. *They're waiting for me,* she realized. *Say something!* Elisabeth felt the words stick in her throat like dry bread. Rose and Nicole awaited instruction eagerly, some of the others less interested—one gazing out the kitchen window with a martyred expression as though she'd been waiting a month for Elisabeth to open her mouth.

"Be-begin by putting all the flour in the bottom of the bowl," Elisabeth said. As though by magic, eight women did as she commanded. Elisabeth tucked her shaking hands in her apron pockets. Her father's voice entered her head as she continued the lesson. *If there is one thing you know, girl, it's how to bake a loaf of bread. You have no reason at all to doubt yourself in private, so don't sell yourself short and do so in public.*

Step-by-step, the ladies followed Elisabeth's instruction for making a loaf of plain bread with white flour. The mixtures came together with more than passable results as she inspected the dough that rested under warm damp cloths near, but not too near, the fire. She would have them come back in an hour or so to shape the loaves. Nothing so elaborate as her favorite baguettes from home, but a nice oblong cob shape would be serviceable for their families. She disliked making her loaves round if they were of any real size—too difficult to cut and tear into smaller chunks for dunking in soups and stews. *Given some flour and yeast, these women and their families will not starve. And I've helped them.*

"Ladies, tonight we will dine like queens of France," Elisabeth said with pride. "We'll set the loaves baking in a few hours. Now hurry and spruce yourselves up. Your beaux will soon be here, and they will want to hear of your culinary prowess, no doubt."

At four that afternoon, just before the sun set into another long autumn night, a dozen suitors swarmed to the boardinghouse to visit the King's wards. Elisabeth smiled at the fine waistcoats and *justaucorps* the men wore in hopes of impressing potential brides. She scanned the eager faces in search of a certain broad-featured gentleman with large brown eyes. She placed her pastries, cut with precision and drizzled with caramel, on the large table that dominated the room.

Soon, Gilbert Beaumont's tall frame appeared toward the back of the crowd. Elisabeth ignored the flutter in her stomach at the sight of the sturdy man with his serious brown eyes. They had met at the reception, and Elisabeth found herself looking forward to his visits with more enthusiasm than she dared to show. *Smile,* Anne's voice commanded. *Young men like cheerful young ladies.* Though it pained Elisabeth, the conjured advice was sound.

"Mademoiselle Martin, how wonderful to see you." Gilbert bowed to Elisabeth in greeting as they met toward the edge of the room.

The nine other young women sat in their preferred spots, with one or more suitors vying for each lady's attention. Another small group of men waited, with a remarkable guise of patience, for a chair to open up near the lady of his choice. The waiting men filled the time conversing about crops and hunting.

As they crossed to some vacant chairs, Elisabeth saw Jacques Piaget, an established farmer, hoping to attract her attention. His expression betrayed no lost affection for Gilbert Beaumont.

If only Maman could see me, Elisabeth thought as she offered Gilbert one of her pastries and a mug of spruce beer. *All those years she lamented of me ever finding a husband, and here I have my pick. Parisian men may prefer petite beauties, but New World men want solid wives who aren't afraid of work.*

"Delectable, Mademoiselle Martin," Gilbert said after swallowing a bite of the flaky pastry. "You have great talent."

"My father taught me well." Elisabeth sampled her efforts thoughtfully. "I had to make do with a caramel sauce, as it seems chocolate hasn't made its way to New France."

"And more's the pity. I care for it myself," Gilbert said. "I studied as an apprentice baker in Bayeux, as I'm sure I have told you."

"Indeed, Monsieur Beaumont." Elisabeth smiled behind her mug. "Perhaps as often as three times now."

The smart suitors mentioned their skills at every opportunity. Those with talent managed to do so without appearing boastful. Elisabeth had to admit that Gilbert knew her weakness and used it to his advantage.

"What I haven't said before is that my fondest wish is to start my own bakery," Gilbert said. "I have repaid the three years of service for my crossing and have no love for farming, so I've saved enough to open a small bakery here in town."

"How wonderful," Elisabeth said. At once her mind started formulating the needed inventory and organizing the stockroom. *Slow down,* she told herself. *He may see the business as his own. He may wish to see you at the counter, charming the customers, not in front of his ovens. He may not be as forward thinking as Papa.*

"I understand there are only four bakers here; I'm sure they will appreciate another to ease the demand." Elisabeth chose her comment with care, hoping it would show her interest in the business without seeming too eager.

"You're right, Mademoiselle Martin, as always," Gilbert said. "More to the point, though I'm a solid baker, I have nothing like your gift. I hoped you would join me in my efforts. I have no doubt we could forge a successful . . . business . . . together."

Elisabeth hid her smile behind her mug. There was a dash of her papa's humility in Gilbert that she loved.

"Perhaps you are right, Monsieur Beaumont." Elisabeth's heart thudded against her rib cage. *He's going to ask. I've known him three weeks, and he's going to ask.*

"Would you consider—would you consent to join me, to be my wife?" Gilbert raised his eyes to hers, the crease between his eyes grown deep as he waited for her response.

Elisabeth appraised the man before her. He seemed humble, hardworking, and honest. His qualities reminded her of her father, all the more so because he had no qualifications of which her mother would approve.

Elisabeth cast a quick glance at Jacques Piaget, who stood with some of the other men and kept an eye on Elisabeth. Jacques had already cleared his land; his farm was an enviable success. He had money and servants. He was the respectable choice.

Gilbert had not settled, and his future was far less certain. But Gilbert did not seek to find a bride who would rub his feet after a long day of toil; he wanted to share his life with her. He showed her respect. Piaget could assure a full stomach and physical comforts, but Gilbert offered the chance to create something more. She knew which man her mother would have picked for her, and which her father would have persuaded her to take. The decision was not a complicated one.

"Monsieur Beaumont, nothing could make me happier."

Gilbert's eyes shone. For a few seconds, he seemed unable to find his voice. Then, in a bold gesture, he took her hand and laced his fingers through hers.

"I hoped you would agree to be married in two weeks' time," Gilbert said. "I want you as my wife before the year ends. I hope that is not too soon for you, my Elisabeth." His voice trembled with restrained emotion, but she also detected a note of pride as he tested the familiarity of her given name on his tongue.

"The sooner the better, Gilbert," Elisabeth replied with a smile. "I don't need months to know my heart. Name the day, and you will find me at the church."

She longed to smooth the wayward lock of hair from his forehead, but did not dare.

Gilbert kissed her hand, pleasure radiating from his gentle features. "Monday the seventh."

"You have a bargain, monsieur."

"The first of us to marry," Nicole exclaimed that evening as they climbed into bed, her voice laced with dreaminess. "Are you excited, Elisabeth?"

"I'm the oldest of the lot. It's only fair that I wed first," Elisabeth said, tossing a pillow at Nicole's head. "And yes, I *am* excited."

"I'm surprised you picked so quickly," Rose said. "Monsieur Piaget was hurt."

"I know." Elisabeth's countenance fell for a few seconds as she remembered the unpleasant scene that followed when she announced her proposal to him. "But he wasn't what I was looking for. Nor was I well suited for him, though he doesn't see it yet."

"Perhaps not," Nicole said. "But he was handsome and well off."

"And utterly boring." Elisabeth pulled the covers up to her chin and giggled. "Not for me. Gilbert may look somewhat plainer than Monsieur Piaget, and has less money, but he is a good man. With the bakery, I'll prove a far bigger service to him than I would to Monsieur Piaget. I don't know the first thing about life on a farm."

"I think it's lucky you found one another," Nicole said. "You seem well matched."

"I agree," Elisabeth said. "I hadn't even the audacity to hope that I might find a baker in need of a wife. Especially one who wants me to help run the shop the way he does. Not many men would welcome a wife as a business partner."

"He's tasted your cakes and pastries," Rose said, grabbing the spare pillow from Nicole and lobbing it back at Elisabeth. "He's not missing taste buds, nor is he a fool. You credit him with too much selflessness."

The girls erupted in giggles loud enough to elicit a knock on the door from one of the Sisters.

"Apologies! We're going to bed now!" Elisabeth called back in a loud whisper.

For several minutes the girls tried to quiet their giggles, but each time one sequestered her laughter, another would start, causing the third to erupt again.

"But seriously, Elisabeth," Nicole asked when she controlled herself in earnest. "You've known him only a few weeks. How do you know he's the right choice?"

"I don't," Elisabeth said, now solemn. "But I don't think there is such a thing as a right or a wrong choice in matters like these. Just better or worse. I could marry Jacques Piaget tomorrow, be well looked after, have a measure of comfort, and find a reasonable happiness. He could have been a *good* choice, but I think a future with Gilbert offers more, which makes him a *better* choice."

"You don't believe each man is destined for one woman? In true love?" Nicole asked, with the mock dreaminess returning to her voice.

"That's the question of a girl whose *maman* told her too many fairy stories as a child." Elisabeth's laugh was biting.

A snort of derision came from Rose as well.

"And I suppose your *maman* never told you any?" Nicole retorted.

"My mother had no time for stories or games," Elisabeth said. "Perhaps that's why I chose Gilbert. One of the reasons, anyway."

"What do you mean?" Rose asked, turning to her side.

"Gilbert seems the type who will play with our children. He's quick to laughter. He has a soft heart. That's what I want, for myself and for my family. Children deserve kindness. They have time enough to learn the world's rough nature when they're older."

"True, but the truth may come as a ruder shock when learned too late. Don't shelter them," Rose advised.

Elisabeth nodded. Rose's years in the Salpêtrière doubtless provided a harsh education.

"No. You're right," Elisabeth said. "Kindness is one thing, but I'm not the sort for fairy stories either. I suppose I have *that* in common with my mother."

"Than I wager you have a better chance of happiness than most," Rose said, ending the conversation.

Today I become Madame Beaumont. A luckier woman there never was. As a sign of appreciation for her teaching, the nuns gave Elisabeth a length of fine brown wool and white linen. The others helped her fashion a lovely jacket, skirt, and fichu for her to wear for her wedding, but Elisabeth insisted on embroidering the collar herself. Sheaves of wheat, once more, to honor her father and her new husband.

How I wish you could see me, Papa, Elisabeth thought as Rose braided her hair. *And you too, Maman, if you would hold your tongue.* Elisabeth pushed Anne from her mind. She would not allow the thought of her mother to poison her wedding day.

"I'm so glad you won't be going far," Nicole said. "Though it will be lonely here without you."

"I'll visit as often as I can," Elisabeth promised. She knew the visits would not be frequent, but the prospect of busy days ahead pleased her to no end. She despised being idle—yet another inheritance from her father.

"Sister Anne said she'd stay behind and make sure all the last-minute details for the supper are seen to," Rose said. The girls had insisted that they host a small dinner for Elisabeth and Gilbert. When she heard of the plan, Elisabeth took over planning out the menu herself. She allowed the others to do much of the cooking, but prepared the cake and breads herself. She could not offer Gilbert a proper gift, but she could at least make this gesture.

At last Elisabeth stood at the door of the church with Rose and Nicole. She took a deep breath as she entered, feeling keenly the absence of her father's arm at her right side. At the altar, Gilbert took her hand, and a peace settled over her. *He is why I came here. I have found my place.*

"Dearly beloved . . ." the priest began, and continued on with the words that priests had spoken before such couples since time immemorial. Elisabeth looked into her soon-to-be husband's eyes with no reservations. *I hope I will make you as happy as you've made me.* The thought of children running around the bakery on their sturdy little legs brought a smile to her face that she was sure the small congregation found ridiculous for a bride.

With the union blessed and notarized, the couple returned to the convent for the meal.

"You must have worked for a week!" Gilbert said when he saw

the feast before him. He was careful to sample every dish, paying special attention to those prepared by Elisabeth herself.

"The almond cake is amazing, sweetheart," Gilbert praised his bride. "I imagine these would do very well in the shop near Easter time."

"My thought as well," Elisabeth said. "And the butter pastries at Christmas."

Gilbert nodded agreement. Elisabeth cast him an appreciative smile. He would take her advice to heart, at least in the matters of the bakery.

"Discussing business on your wedding day," Rose said, clucking her tongue. "If it isn't a sin, it ought to be." She softened the rebuke with a wink, which caused Elisabeth to giggle as she hadn't done in years.

"I do believe the happy couple would like to find their way home," Nicole said.

Elisabeth noticed the cue came from the painfully obvious way Gilbert eyed the door.

Sister Mathilde presented them with a hamper of food and a soft baby blanket. "To a happy and productive union, my dears," she said, and her smile, not a frequent feature of her face, let Elisabeth know she approved of the match. It meant more than Elisabeth realized it would.

Gilbert's shop lay only minutes away by carriage, in the heart of the small settlement. Elisabeth had never seen her future home, nor ever been alone in Gilbert's company.

"Here we are, my darling," Gilbert announced as he pulled the horses to a stop. He had arranged for a neighbor to see to the horses, and Elisabeth's things had been sent over earlier, so the couple entered their marital home together.

The building was simple, and made of wood, not stone. The ground floor housed the bakery, the living quarters above stairs. The smell of baking bread never quite left the air. *Just like Papa's shop.*

Elisabeth surveyed the shop and saw the signs of success: few remaining loaves of day-old bread, a floor showing signs of gentle wear from a steady flow of customers, and a clean, well-ordered working area at the back.

"I know it isn't much. . . ." Gilbert interpreted her silence as disapproval.

"It's perfect," Elisabeth breathed. And it was. Small, and simple, but theirs.

Gilbert took Elisabeth in his arms, and took her mouth with his. She did not know how to react to the strange sensations at first, but at last allowed herself to relax in her husband's embrace.

I am home at last.

CHAPTER 5

Rose

November 1667

Rose stood before the looking glass in despair. Thursday had come, and again she was forced to go downstairs with the rest of her companions to visit with gentlemen callers. Every week her dress grew shabbier. Every week, she had to feign interest in the prattle of young men who sought her hand. As she descended the stairs, she thought of Sister Charité, her duty to the Crown—to marry and bear children—but none of it served to raise her spirits.

You knew what they expected of you and it does no good to let your feelings get in the way of doing your duty. You've not been all that successful in making good on your promises as it is. Rose may have failed in her duty to Vivienne, but at least she'd had a letter to let her know Geneviève was engaged and would marry soon. Rose allowed herself to take a small measure of solace in that, at least.

Now go and be charming, Rose told herself. *Or at the very least, don't embarrass yourself.*

"My dear Mademoiselle Barré," Rémy Peltier greeted Rose as she entered the common room. "How wonderful to see you again."

He hadn't missed a visit in three weeks, and she hadn't expected him to miss this one. "Welcome, Monsieur Peltier." Rose's attempt at a convivial smile went only as deep as her lips. "I trust you are well."

"Indeed," Peltier said. "Never better."

Rose winced at his contrived buoyancy.

"I'm glad to hear it," Rose said, picking at a loose thread on her sleeve. She could think of nothing else to say. *He is going to think me a simpleton. But perhaps that's what he's after anyway.*

For a few moments, the silence sat heavy on the pair. *Say something, you dolt.* But it was Peltier who broke the silence.

"I'm pleased to tell you, my homestead is nearly ready to live on," Peltier said. "My home will be built in four or five months, as soon as the ground has thawed."

"You must be glad for more comfortable accommodations, monsieur," Rose said, continuing her assault on the wayward thread. *What a stupid thing to say.*

"Yes," Peltier agreed, "but I hope I will not have to live there alone for long. I had hoped . . . Mademoiselle Barré, I was hoping you would be so kind as to marry me."

A hole now appeared at her sleeve and she clasped her hands to avoid making further damage. *You knew this was coming.* Peltier had singled her out, and the time had come for him to declare himself. Rose had seen more than one suitor disappointed by waiting too long to make his intentions clear. *Why can't I have Elisabeth's conviction? Or at least her decisiveness.*

"Monsieur, I . . ." Rose paused. She could think of no rational reasons for accepting or refusing this man. He looked at her, expectant and hopeful.

His manners may be a bit stiff, but he is a good man. Can I do better? Could I share my life with him? Try though she might, she found no ready answers to her questions.

"I know these things happen quickly here," Peltier said, with a gentle smile. "If you need more time, I can wait. It would have to be several months before we marry, in any case."

"*Remember your first and only duties in New France are to take a husband and mother as many children as God sees fit to populate these new lands.*" Sister Charité spoke the words before she left the Salpêtrière *and* she'd heard a dozen variants since her arrival. *It does not matter how you feel; you must do your duty. He's as good a man as you can hope to expect here.*

"I appreciate your consideration, but it won't be necessary," Rose said. "I accept, monsieur."

Even as she said them, Rose wondered how the words found their way to her lips. *At least you made a decision.*

He smiled. "I am so pleased. We can have the contract drawn in the new year and marry just before Lent. I am sorry my home prevents us marrying earlier."

"Do not worry, monsieur," Rose said. "In the grand scheme of things, four months is very little time."

By the time the first of December's storms shook the convent, four girls remained in residence with the Sisters. The rest of the residents had been plucked by eager suitors, who wished to be married before Advent. The parlor was the only comfortable room in the house that night; it was too much trouble to keep all the house fires lit. The parlor air was thick with the smell of burning logs.

Rose sat, enjoying the warmth of the fire as she embroidered a dress collar, when a banging at the door shattered the pleasant quiet.

Sister Mathilde opened the door, revealing a half-frozen man.

"*My wife,*" he panted. "She's gone into labor. The baby is coming too early and I don't know what to do."

"Why have you not gone for the doctor, Monsieur Laurier?" Sister Mathilde asked, her tone scathing.

"You were closer, and I was afraid the roads might not be passable." Joseph Laurier stood in the doorway, shaking from cold and fear. He seemed willing to accept the nun's abuse if doing so might win assistance for his wife.

"Gather sheets, blankets, and firewood," Sister Mathilde barked. "Rose, you'll come with me."

Why me? What use can I be? Rose wanted to open her mouth, to shout to Sister Mathilde that she had no useful training, but no words emerged from her mouth. One of the Sisters loaded Rose's arms with a pile of clean sheets. Another came with an assortment of infant clothes. Taking a breath, she fetched her market basket for the linens. *I guess it doesn't matter if I can help or not; I suppose I'm going to.*

She made her way to Joseph Laurier's horse and cart, where a line of freezing girls and nuns loaded a giant heap of firewood into the open cart bed. Sister Mathilde was already seated in the cart, with a case on her lap. Rose assumed the case contained medical supplies.

The moment the last stick of wood was thrown into the cart, Joseph Laurier jumped in the driver's seat and whipped his horse into movement. Rose held on with a death grip as the rickety carriage rattled at a breakneck pace over treacherous, wintry roads. Relief radiated from her as Joseph halted the horse before a precarious-looking wooden house on a lonely bit of farmland far outside the settlement.

The Laurier home offered little protection from the biting winter wind. Pretty, young Gislène Laurier huddled in the bed, alternately shivering with cold and sweating from the efforts of her labor. Rose began to shake. *God, she's in agony. I couldn't bear it.*

"Rose, listen to me," Sister Mathilde scolded. Rose had not heard the Sister's first command, so she forced herself back into the present. "Rose, boil water on the fire and rip a sheet into strips. When the water boils, use it to clean my shears and then dry them in the cleanest cloth you can find. And you, put wood on that fire and keep it roaring hot. No baby would survive that chill," Sister Mathilde snapped at Joseph as she scrubbed her hands and arms as far as the elbows.

Sister Mathilde took Gislène's fragile hand and stroked her brow. The nun's orders to the expectant mother sounded gentler than those she issued to Rose, and far kinder still than the ones she snapped at the nervous father.

After kindling the fire, Joseph found himself without an occupation, and took to pacing in clumpy boots from one end of the minuscule one-room house to the other.

"For the love of all the saints and my poor nerves, Joseph Laurier." Sister Mathilde kept her volume down, but laced her words with the venom of irritation. "Calm yourself or leave this house so the child can be born in peace."

Joseph sat in a rough-hewn chair at the dining table, too nervous to take offense at the woman's orders. He barely managed to keep his hands from fidgeting as the sounds of his wife's struggles filled the room.

"Breathe deeply," Sister Mathilde said. "Just keep breathing through your nose. There you are, dear—you're doing wonderfully."

Rose was unsure of how to aid Sister Mathilde but endeavored to fill the role of makeshift midwife as well as she could. She fetched objects and followed orders with an almost comical speed. Even so, she wished she could anticipate the needs of both patient and midwife. *Oh Lord, my governesses taught me all the wrong things. I might be able to conjugate verbs in Latin and know how low to curtsy to a Prince of Sweden, but now all of that is as useful as a satin parasol in a blizzard.*

"Rose, the strips!" Sister Mathilde cried an hour later. "And the shears! Quickly!"

A fearful amount of blood gushed from Gislène, along with a baby girl. Sister Mathilde tied the baby's cord with a strip of sheet and cut it with the efficiency of a Paris surgeon.

She thrust the howling newborn at Rose, with orders to clean the baby, turning her attention back to Gislène at once.

Rose had never touched an infant so young and fragile, but had no time for fear to overtake her. With gentle movements, Rose cleaned the baby and swaddled her tight in the blanket Nicole had made for the expected infant weeks before. *She is a sweet little thing,* Rose admitted to herself. *Even if she doesn't look like much yet.*

Joseph had drifted off to sleep in the rigid chair, but woke with a start when the baby's cry echoed through the cabin.

"A healthy girl, monsieur," Rose said, passing the baby off to her father with a quick kiss to the infant's forehead, and returned to Sister Mathilde's side.

"Your stomach is still hard, Gislène," Sister Mathilde said after massaging her patient's abdomen. "There may be another child. That would explain the early arrival."

How can she endure it again? So soon? Rose continued to fetch and follow orders in between silent prayers that the exhausted woman would survive the ordeal. *I am sure I would not. Could not. Cannot.*

A half hour later Gislène's cries again echoed throughout the cabin. Though Sister Mathilde kept a serene countenance, Rose saw a trembling in the hands that were usually as steady as anchors. Once more, the nun passed over a child covered in muck—a boy this time. Rose wiped and cleaned the child, but he remained limp.

"Sister, something isn't—" Rose began.

"Do what you can, girl," Sister Mathilde said. The nun looked up from her patient to Rose for only the briefest of moments, but her expression spoke volumes. *This child won't survive.*

Rose cleaned and swaddled the boy, who never opened his eyes. After a few moments he let out a weak rasp and was gone from the world. Not knowing what to do, she held him close to her breast and swayed with him as she would with a living child. She prayed it would somehow give his soul some comfort, even if it was too late for his body.

Sister Mathilde, still tending to Gislène, exhaled, her shoulders dropping in relief. Rose noticed the worrisome amount of blood, but saw that the pool wasn't growing larger. *We almost lost her, too. It's a wonder any of us pull through.*

"The boy?" Sister Mathilde asked, standing, stiff from her stint on the hard stool and walking over to Rose, who still cradled the baby in her arms.

"I am so very sorry—" Rose whispered.

"There was nothing to be done," the Sister assured her, taking the child and examining his face. "He was never strong enough. Sometimes there are miracles, but today was not that day, I'm afraid. I'll tell the mother. You tidy things as best as you can."

Gislène's shoulders shook with violent sobs as Sister Mathilde relayed the news. Joseph stared at the floor in disbelief.

"My son is dead," Joseph said in a hollow voice.

"But your daughter is alive," Sister Mathilde declared, "and she will need all the love and care you can give. She may be strong, but she is small, and winter is hard upon us. Do not dwell on your sorrows to the neglect of your blessings."

"She is a pretty thing," Joseph said, handing the swaddled baby to her mother.

"She's beautiful," Gislène agreed, wiping tears from her puffy cheeks.

"Let's call her Nathalie, for your *maman,*" Joseph suggested as he rubbed a finger against the baby's downy cheek.

"She would have liked that," Gislène said.

Sister Mathilde gave the new parents instructions on caring for the fragile child and her recovering mother. Dawn crested over the eastern mountains as Joseph carted the women home to the convent.

The warmth of the sitting room fire felt as welcoming as anything Rose had ever known. Once properly warm, she started to feel the effects of the evening's efforts. Rose stumbled up the stairs to seek the refuge of her bed, still shivering from more than the vicious winter chill.

"How is the baby?" Nicole asked as Rose changed into her nightgown.

"Mother and daughter are well," Rose answered, without mentioning the son that was lost.

The tenor of her voice betrayed her weariness and desire to cut their usual chatter short.

Rose remembered the pale Laurier son as he took his first and last breaths in her arms. She thought of Vivienne, who had died in her arms only months before.

Vérité was right. Rose toyed with her mentor's silver medallion that hung from her neck as her thoughts pounded in her brain. *This place brings nothing but death. I will die here, surely as Vivienne and that poor baby did.*

Try as she might, Rose could not banish Gislène Laurier's anguish from her mind.

"Rose, I brought you some breakfast." Nicole knocked on the bedroom door at mid-morning and entered without waiting for an answer. She carried a tray laden with the most inviting foods from the convent kitchen.

Rose stirred, but had not yet summoned the fortitude to rise.

"Thank you." Rose sat up and wiped the sleep from her eyes. "How thoughtful."

"You earned a lazy morning, after last night," Nicole said. "I'm happy to do it."

Rose ate the toast and moved the rest of the food on her plate, nibbling out of politeness.

"Are you unwell?" Nicole asked. "Did you catch a chill last night?"

"No, no. I'm fine," Rose said, without making eye contact. "Just tired."

"No doubt," Nicole said. "You had a long night."

"Indeed," Rose said.

"What did Madame Laurier name the baby?"

"She named the little girl Nathalie." Rose took a small bite of toast and gazed out the window, then back to the sweet brown-eyed girl who knew that Rose was concealing something. "I'm not sure what they will call the little boy. He didn't survive."

"Oh, how awful," Nicole said. "Those poor people."

Rose nodded. "He died in my arms."

Nicole embraced her friend but offered no words of comfort. Rose abandoned any pretext of calm, and let the tears flow on Nicole's shoulder. *That poor baby, born into the world just to die moments later. What was the point of all that poor woman's suffering?*

Rose wasn't sure how long she wept in Nicole's arms, but at length, the tears subsided and she pulled back from the embrace.

"Thank you," Rose said. "You're a dear friend."

"Don't mention it," Nicole said. "You'd do the same for me."

"I just don't know if I can go through with it all," Rose said, smoothing out her quilt. "She had such pain . . . and then the baby died. . . ."

"That's why the task falls to women," Nicole said. "We're strong enough to handle it."

"I hope you're right," Rose said. "I have my doubts."

"Things go wrong, but there's no reason to dwell on them," Nicole said. "I'm sure you'll have a legion of healthy babies before long."

Rose wanted to smile at her friend's assurances, but could not force her lips to comply. *I am not made for this life, yet I must carve one for myself from this frozen rock even so.*

CHAPTER 6

Nicole

March 1668

It may not be spring yet, but I can certainly pretend it today. Nicole leaped at the chance to escape the confines of the convent to fetch some supplies for Sister Mathilde in town. Basket in tow and her chin pointed upward to absorb the fledgling sun, Nicole walked, enjoying the warmth on her face like the kisses of a long-absent lover.

She was shaken from her reverie when the toe of her boot caught the edge of a rock, pitching her forward into a pool of mud. Before she finished gathering her wits and the contents of her basket, she felt a steady hand at her elbow, helping her rise from the quagmire.

"Oh, thank you!" Nicole looked up to see to whom the helpful hand belonged. She found herself looking into the face of a tall man in uniform—a man of rank, but young. His features were soft and boyish, and his curly brown hair gave him an air of youth. *Jean, how is it you came to be here?* She silenced the question a heartbeat before it escaped her mouth. Jean Galet was married and back in France. This man could not be him. A moment's study revealed that this man stood taller than Jean, had a leaner frame, and the features of a man rather than a boy.

"Of course, mademoiselle," the young officer said. "I hope you are unhurt."

"Only my pride is injured. Thank you again, monsieur. . . ." Nicole willed, in vain, for the blush to leave her cheeks.

"Pardon me," the officer said with a bow. "It's Jarvais, Luc Jarvais."

"I am pleased to meet you," Nicole said, trying not to wince as cold mud slid down the inside of her boot. "I am Nicole Deschamps."

"At your service, mademoiselle," Luc said, kindness emanating from his voice. "May I accompany you somewhere?"

"Unfortunately, I must return home." Nicole looked down at her mud-coated dress. "I am not fit to be seen in company, though it is a shame to waste a fine day."

"Indeed it is," Luc remarked. "Will you at least allow me to escort you home?"

"Thank you, yes." Given the circumstances, Nicole doubted the Sisters would object to her walking with him unaccompanied.

"Are you newly arrived to the colony?" Luc asked.

"Relatively. I arrived last fall, though at times it seems like I've been here for years."

Indeed, the streets of the settlement town had become more familiar to Nicole than the bustling streets of Rouen.

"I know what you mean. I've been here for almost three years and haven't seen my family since."

Nicole noted a slight trace of sadness in his voice.

"You are homesick, too," she observed.

"At times," Luc said. "I remember, at first, I thought myself truly alone in the world. I can promise you it does get easier, though. I still pine for home, and especially for my youngest sister, Babette, but it's not as unbearable as it was."

"Is she much younger than you?" Nicole asked.

"Four years my junior, though she will always be a tiny girl to me."

"I suppose time does not stand still for the people we love any more than it does for us." Nicole considered her siblings and how changed they might seem if she ever saw them again.

The thought of her sisters Claudine and Emmanuelle married, or her baby brother Georges a landowner, sent a pang to her heart.

"It is a shame," he said. "How comforting it would be if it could all stay the same. Not very interesting, however."

"Indeed," Nicole agreed, with a smile.

"But my service is nearly complete. I'll have leave to return home soon, if I choose."

Nicole felt a twinge of regret in her chest. *You've only just met this man. Why should you care that he's going home, aside from the fact you wish you could be going yourself?*

Just then, they arrived at the door to the convent. Luc left Nicole with a deep bow and a polite brush of his lips on the back of her hand.

As Nicole shut the door behind her, she heard Rose set aside her mending to see who had escorted Nicole home.

"Well done!" Rose teased.

"I hope my dress isn't ruined." Nicole looked down at the garment in dismay.

"Not that, you goose!" Rose said. "The handsome young officer! Here I thought you were just out for some fresh air and flour for Sister Mathilde."

"And so I was," Nicole said, exasperated. She did her best to remove her boots without getting any more mud on the floor than necessary.

"You're going to leave me here all alone, aren't you?" The merry glint had not left Rose's eyes. "For some handsome soldier who comes, banner flying, to rescue you from the muck."

"I must admit, it was a romantic morning," Nicole mocked. "A mud-bog rescue is definitely a choice first encounter with a prospective suitor."

"So you say." The false nonchalance in Rose's voice grated in Nicole's nerves.

"Honestly, he pulled me from a mud puddle and walked me home. He showed no affinity, at least none that I noticed. Now be a lamb and come help me out of this mess."

"No doubt he'll come calling Thursday," Rose said, feigning disdain as they climbed the stairs.

"He did ask if he could," Nicole admitted, shucking off her muddy skirt.

"And the Thursday after, and the one after that, until you say yes," Rose predicted, gathering the soiled clothes for the washtub.

"Unlikely. He's nearly released from service. He can go home if he chooses." Nicole rubbed her cold legs with a dry cloth.

"I bet you could persuade him to stay. Do you think he's handsome?" Rose asked.

"I have eyes, Rose," Nicole said. "Anyone who did would believe he is."

"Would you say yes?" Rose asked, loosening Nicole's corset.

Nicole laughed. She agreed that Luc was a very suitable match, in many ways. As an officer, he would have both education and understanding. In France, his rank would almost certainly have ruined any chance for a match between them. But here, in New France... Nicole cast the thoughts aside as quickly as they came. He was going home, and a clumsy stumble and muck-covered skirts were no way to entice a gentleman into courtship.

The next day, a warm and welcoming Wednesday, Nicole decided to help Rose with the massive pile of mending rather than risk falling into another mudhole.

Mending was tedious work, but it occupied the hands, though not the mind. When a knock at the door interrupted the chore, Nicole rose to answer.

"Monsieur Lefebvre." Nicole was astonished to see him, of all men, at the door. He had never come to visit Nicole, or anyone else, during visiting hours, and she hadn't expected him to. She had no affection for the man, but she did still remember his tirade on the rare occasions when she ventured into the snow alone. His chiseled chin and nose had etched their way into her memory; though she would have much rather Luc's boyish face and sweet dimples take their place.

"Yes," Lefebvre said. "And you're Mademoiselle Deschamps, if my memory serves."

He stood at least six inches taller than she and exuded wealth, education, and class far beyond her own. Nicole nodded, fearing her voice would falter. *Stupid git, speak! Don't let him know he intimidates you.*

"Monsieur Lefebvre, we ask gentlemen to call on Thursday evenings," Sister Mathilde said as she approached the entryway. "However, we can make an exception just this once. Please come join us in the common room, where you can visit with Mademoiselle Deschamps in more comfort."

"Sister, I have not come courting." Lefebvre's tone bordered on the uncivil. "I am doing a favor, delivering a case of cider from the Ferrier farm. I had business nearby and Monsieur Ferrier asked me to save him the trip into town."

"Of course," Sister Mathilde said. "Your man can take it to the kitchens. Please stay and have some cider along with a piece of Mademoiselle Deschamps's excellent cake." *Stop forcing this, Sister. I beg you!* Nicole bit her tongue to keep the words from escaping.

"I have been out on errands all day; it might be nice to sit with a bit of refreshment," he admitted.

"Of course," Nicole said, plastering on a smile. "Please make yourself at home while I fetch you some."

She hurried off to the kitchen to cut a slice of the butter cake that Elisabeth had coached her in making that morning at the bakery. Sister Éléonore passed her a mug of the good cider with a wink. *Don't get your hopes up, sweet lady. He has no more an eye for me than King Louis would have for a pockmarked tavern wench.*

She placed the food and drink before him at the long table in the common room, careful not to spill the drink or cause a clattering sound as the plate touched the table's surface.

"This looks lovely, thank you." He sampled a small morsel of the cake, chewing slowly and thoughtfully. "Clearly, you've learned from your friend, Madame Beaumont."

"She's a very patient teacher." Nicole looked down at her hands. Anywhere but at his too-intense gray eyes.

"And you, an able pupil." He took a sip of the cider, looking her over as he drank. Assessing, as he had done at their last meeting.

Why must you look at me as though you were looking for a second head? What have I done to make you act this way?

"How are you finding our settlement, now that you've endured one of our winters?"

The weather? Really, Monsieur Lefebvre? I bore you so completely? "I'm not sure if one can come to love the bitter cold, but the settlement is lovely." *Not the dismal picture you painted before.*

"I'm glad you're adjusting well," Alexandre said, playing with a bit of thread on his trousers.

"Truly?" Nicole's tone was wry. He had seemed content to send every last one of the King's wards back on the next ship.

"Of course. I wouldn't have you miserable." *How gracious of you.*

They sat in uncomfortable silence for a few minutes as Alexandre finished his cake. *At least he approves of me in some measure.* She thought of her easy conversation with Luc Jarvais and longed to be on a stroll along the riverbank with him rather than cooped up in the convent's common room with stodgy Alexandre Lefebvre.

"I'm afraid I must attend to some other business. Thank you very much for your trouble." Alexandre stood, brushing a few tiny crumbs from his front.

"It was a pleasure, monsieur." Her tone conveyed a great many sentiments, pleasure being the least of them.

"Now that you've learned what a talented cook we have in Mademoiselle Deschamps, I hope you'll come visit us with the other gentlemen on Thursdays, Monsieur Lefebvre," Sister Mathilde chimed in. It was rare she involved herself—at least directly—in the courtships that transpired under her roof. Nicole shot her a glance and wished she'd continue her pattern.

Alexandre looked at Nicole, his expression unreadable. Annoyance? Boredom? Even fear, perhaps?

"I'm afraid I'm very busy, Sister. I'm not sure I can spare the time."

"What a shame, monsieur. Very well though, thank you for your troubles." Sister Mathilde offered him a hopeful smile. "We hope to see you soon."

He nodded farewell to the nun and made no gesture toward Nicole.

"I wish you wouldn't, Sister," Nicole said when she was certain Alexandre was out of earshot.

"My dear, Alexandre Lefebvre is a good man. He just needs some persuading." She resumed her place in her favorite chair and motioned for Nicole to join her.

"Sister, he doesn't care for me. You have to see that." Nicole sat back and folded her fingers. Her mending wasn't within reach and her hands were foreign to the lack of occupation.

"Don't cast him aside yet, my girl. He's a prize worth catching." The Sister opened her book as a signal that the conversation was closed for now. Nicole fetched her mending from across the room and worked as the pious woman studied by the afternoon sunlight that peered in through the window.

You're a wise woman, Sister, but you need to recognize a hopeless cause when you see one. Alexandre Lefebvre would sooner court you *than pay me any mind.*

Alexandre Lefebvre was not among the visitors that Thursday, but Luc Jarvais was in attendance, as Rose had predicted.

"These are for you, mademoiselle." Luc handed Nicole a bouquet of young wildflowers that had only just begun to bloom.

"Thank you, Monsieur Jarvais," Nicole said. "These must be the first of the season."

"Indeed, the first to appear on my fields this year."

Nicole looked down at the bouquet, little more than a bundle of stems, tied with a fine yellow ribbon.

"Please, Monsieur Jarvais," Nicole said, remembering her manners. "Would you care to have a seat in the front room?"

"Thank you, mademoiselle." Luc followed Nicole into the adjacent room, looking around the cozy surroundings as he took the chair Nicole offered him.

"These are lovely, Monsieur Jarvais." Nicole accepted a vase from Rose and arranged the bouquet on the mantelpiece. "Thank you again."

"Say nothing of it, Mademoiselle Deschamps," Luc said. "They seem particularly fine this year."

"I would imagine," Nicole said. The subject of wildflowers exhausted, she racked her brain to find another topic of conversation. Luc seemed fascinated with the scarred wooden floors, or something on the tip of his boot. Nicole opened her mouth to make a comment, but a loud crash and a muffled curse from the kitchen cut her off.

Rose emerged from the kitchen a moment later, carrying a small tray loaded with cider and butter cake. She set the tray on the table nearest Nicole and left the room more stealthily than she had arrived.

Luc accepted the cider and a slice of the tender cake, but paid little attention to the refreshments.

"I'm glad you're well," he said at length. "I was worried you might catch cold after your spill."

"Thank you, monsieur," Nicole said, fiddling with a crease in her apron. "I am quite well. I was able to change and warm myself before chill set in."

"I am glad to hear it," Luc said, with a smile that did not conceal his nerves. He took a sip of cider. To his credit, he controlled the shaking of his hands with a degree of success.

"Have you been in service long, monsieur?" Nicole asked to break the silence.

"Five years," Luc said. "Three here, two back home in Tours."

The silence weighed on the room, but Luc found the courage to speak again.

"Mademoiselle Deschamps, I must confess that I did come to inquire after more than your health." He spoke the words with such haste that it took Nicole a moment to decipher his meaning.

"As you know, young women are not in abundance in this part of the world," he began with determination.

"With the exception of this house, you are quite right," agreed Nicole.

"I have wanted to start a family for some time now," Luc continued, rising to pace the room but never making eye contact with Nicole. "Until now, I thought I might have to return home to find a suitable wife. The truth is that I care for the settlement a good deal . . . that is . . . Mademoiselle Deschamps . . . if you would be willing . . . would you consider . . . becoming my wife?"

"Monsieur Jarvais, I . . ." Nicole could not find the words to articulate her thoughts.

Rose gave up any pretense of subtle eavesdropping and poked her head through the door that connected to the kitchen. With pleading eyes, she urged Nicole to answer the poor man, one way or the other.

"I know this is quite sudden," Luc said.

"Indeed it is," Nicole agreed, finding her voice, and scowling at Rose behind the suitor's back. Rose retreated to the kitchen.

"We have only spent a few moments in one another's company," Nicole said.

"I know I must seem rash, imprudent even," Luc said, having found his confidence. "I hope I haven't offended you, but I wanted to declare my intentions now, before another claims your affections. Your position as a ward of the King marks you as a respectable young lady. My position assures you that I can provide for you and our family. I know this is a hurried business, but I hope you will find it in your heart to say yes."

Nicole took a moment to consider the man before her. He was a kind and serious man, but little better than a stranger. Few brides in the colony could say otherwise about their grooms, though most had the advantage of knowing their husbands for at least a few months before they married.

Despite this, Nicole could not find it within herself to refuse.

"Yes," she answered after she found her voice. "I will be your wife."

Luc gave an audible sigh of relief and knelt before his bride, taking her hands in his.

"Mademoiselle Deschamps . . . my dear Nicole, if I may. I promise I will do everything in my power to make you happy."

He placed a gentle kiss on her knuckles.

Nicole gazed into his eyes and saw no malice, just goodness of heart and kindness of spirit. She knew his promise was sincere and hoped she would manage to do the same for him. He would endeavor to take care of her. Perhaps even come to love her, someday. No one in her acquaintance could boast of any more.

CHAPTER 7

Elisabeth

April 1668

The smell of yeast, flour, water, and salt transforming into the staff of life never left the timbers of the Beaumont Bakery. Elisabeth rested her swollen ankles while the last loaves of bread rose in the oven. Five months pregnant, she was already bulging and uncomfortable. Little Pierre or Adèle was expected in late summer, much to the expectant parents' delight.

Though she tired easily, Elisabeth refused to give up her duties in the bakery. She trained Gilbert that arguing was futile, and she guessed that he went along in order to obtain a stronger position for the later months of her pregnancy, when he would have to insist that she rest.

"Thank you," Gilbert said when he saw his wife using the chair he had placed near the oven for her.

"My pleasure." Elisabeth offered a fatigued smile as she kneaded dough from her seat. "I think this baby of ours may turn out to be a giant."

"Just big and strong, sweetheart," Gilbert said as he stroked Elisabeth's fair hair.

She returned the caress, and, since there was no one visible through the window, offered him a less-than-chaste kiss.

"I hope so, too. I love you, Gilbert."

"Affectionate today," he said, taking another kiss while there was peace. "Not that I'm complaining."

"Careful now," she said, seeing the shadow of movement outside. "No need to expose ourselves to public ridicule."

"Nothing more ridiculous than loving one's wife." He smeared flour on her nose with a boyish grin as he turned to the opening door.

"Good afternoon, Monsieur Levoisier. What can we get for you today?"

Elisabeth smirked at her husband's buoyant greeting from behind her hand as she wiped her nose.

"Good afternoon, Monsieur and Madame Beaumont," Levoisier said. "Nothing today, but I have a letter for Madame Beaumont that came in on the ship last Tuesday. From France."

Levoisier produced the letter with a self-satisfied smile. Had they not known his kindly nature, they might have thought him a tad too pompous. In truth, he was proud to spread happiness by bringing news to people separated from their families.

Gilbert thanked him with a few coins and a bun.

Elisabeth longed to be able to read the letter herself, but handed it to her husband.

> *To Elisabeth Martin, New France:*
>
> *I am ashamed that any child of mine, raised with care and devotion, would so easily disregard my wishes. M. Delacroix told me of your departure a week after you set to sea, far too late for me to intervene. I was a fool to ever permit your association with that family. I was wrought with worry until he told me of your whereabouts, and then I find that you heartlessly abandoned me. You destroyed any chance for an alliance with the Moraud family. I am now forced to live as an impoverished dowager aunt with my brother Roland and his family. The embarrassment is too much to bear.*
>
> *You are an ungrateful child, and solely responsible for my current state. I cannot believe that you are so*

quick to forget all I have done for you. I will never speak your name again. It is just as well a vast ocean separates us, as I no longer have a daughter.

Anne Martin, as dictated to Roland Clément

"Pay it no mind, sweetheart," Gilbert said, handing Elisabeth the letter.

Knowing her husband as she did, Elisabeth could read the look in his eyes: *I wish the post had come when she was out or asleep and I could have burned the letter before she knew it existed.*

"How very much like my mother." Elisabeth punched the ball of dough and tossed the letter into the oven, hoping its acerbic words wouldn't sour the bread.

Gilbert took his wife in his arms and rested his chin atop her head, stroking her hair the way she liked. "She doesn't matter."

"No, though I'm not surprised that she feels the way she does," Elisabeth said. "What surprises me is that she went to the trouble of dictating a letter to tell me so—and paying the post. Mother prided herself on never lowering herself to such gestures. It seems unusually petty."

"*Petty* is a good word...." Gilbert held Elisabeth close, then released her, lest the neighbors see and laugh at the folly of a couple in love. "Your mother would not approve of our marriage, would she?"

"No," Elisabeth answered without hesitation. "She would not. Our marriage gains her no advantage in society. Though you are the best of husbands, she would not have permitted this union. But Papa would have loved you, Gilbert."

"I wish I could have known him," Gilbert said, rubbing a finger across her cheekbone. "So much I could have learned from him."

"Maman has always been such a bitter woman." She breathed a sigh of annoyance as she returned to her labors.

"She's an ocean away," Gilbert said, caressing her from behind.

Her muscles, sore from the expansion and the foreign movement inside her, as well as her day of toil, melted like pastry dough left to soften by the oven.

Gilbert smiled. "Just you worry about growing us a healthy baby and banish all her bitterness from your heart, my love."

"I'll do my best." Elisabeth closed her eyes. *He truly is the best man I have ever known,* she thought. *Papa, how I wish your marriage had been as happy.*

In the following week, Elisabeth tried to take her husband's advice, but it was not an easy task.

Questions plagued her at every moment.

Why did Mother bother writing? Why is she so embarrassed to stay with Uncle Roland, a man of such good standing in society that Mother would not take her baker husband and plain daughter to visit him? Why did Jacques Moraud break off an engagement that was advantageous to him, despite my refusing Denis?

These questions, and others, flitted through Elisabeth's brain as she kneaded balls of dough, despite her efforts to keep her mind on her work.

"Bailiff Duval, good afternoon," Gilbert said, causing Elisabeth to look up from the tray of dinner buns she was shaping for the ovens. The tall man with his impressive gut was charged with carrying messages from the courts, along with other clerical duties, and was very pleased with himself for the important job.

"Afternoon, Beaumont," Duval said, not charmed as others by Gilbert's convivial nature. "I've come to speak with Madame Beaumont."

"What business could you possibly have with my wife?" Gilbert stepped around to the front of the counter.

"Just a few questions, Beaumont." Duval stood tall, as though trying to impress Gilbert with his stature, both physical and social.

"It's all right, Gilbert," Elisabeth said, placing a calming hand on her husband's bicep. "I'm happy to answer the bailiff's questions, as long as he doesn't mind me taking a seat."

For a moment, Bailiff Duval considered her words as though she was serious in her request to take a seat in her own shop. "Fine, fine," he said.

"Ask your questions then," Gilbert said, his patience gone.

"There has been some question as to whether your documents were in order when you arrived, Madame Beaumont," the bailiff said. "The judge sent me to look at them, if you please."

"I'll get them," Gilbert said before Elisabeth could stand.

He bounded upstairs and produced her affidavit of good comportment and the copy of her baptismal records.

"Very good." Duval examined the sheaves of parchment. "And how old are you, Madame Beaumont?"

"As you can see on my baptismal record, I just turned twenty-six, monsieur," Elisabeth answered.

"And you were how old when you left France, madame?" asked Duval.

"I had just turned twenty-five, monsieur," she replied.

"Good, good." Duval leaned against the counter, examining the documents. "Judge Arnaud will want to see these. I hope you don't mind if I take them. The utmost care will be taken."

"Of course," Elisabeth said, puzzled by the request. "For as long as you have need of them."

"Very well," the bailiff said. "The judge will send me for you in a few days, I would expect. Good day, madame, monsieur."

Gilbert nodded Duval wordlessly out of his shop.

"Self-righteous ass. What in the world is all this about?" Gilbert muttered, not realizing he had spoken aloud.

Elisabeth expelled a breath with a sigh. "The only thing that makes sense is that Mother has complained to someone who matters."

"Does a widow in her situation have that much influence?" asked Gilbert. For a moment, Elisabeth envied her husband's rural upbringing. He knew nothing of politics and position. He could not, as he had told Elisabeth so many times, imagine a mother that would put her own interests before her daughter's. When the farmers arranged for their daughters, feelings might not be the first concern, but they weren't the last. The picture both he and Nicole painted of the Norman countryside made Elisabeth wonder if her beloved Paris actually was the haven she imagined it was.

"She was a Clément, and that still means something. Mother alone might not have much pull anymore, but Uncle Roland certainly does if she can persuade him to act."

"Let us hope he has the sense to see her as the meddling shrew that she is and that he won't aid her in this whole mess," Gilbert said, kissing her brow.

"Not likely," Elisabeth said, her expression grim. "He has no particular attachment to me, and will do anything to silence Mother. She can be—tenacious."

"Let's not borrow trouble just yet, sweetheart," Gilbert said.

"Don't you see?" Elisabeth said. "It's already here. We must prepare ourselves. If Mother can cause trouble, she will. If the authorities here adhere to their laws as I've heard they do, they may very well send me back to France."

"Not while I live and breathe," Gilbert said, his eyes flashing. He grabbed the back of a nearby chair, his knuckles whitened by his angry clutch. "You're mine and you aren't going anywhere."

"Let's hope so, my sweet," Elisabeth said. "For there's nowhere else I'd rather be on this earth."

Elisabeth let herself go limp in her husband's embrace, taking deep breaths to slow her heart. She was happier with Gilbert than she had been in her life. She knew she had found her place and her purpose, but her mother would see her plucked from it in a moment, just for spite. She looked down at her swollen belly. Unquestionable proof that she was no longer a maid. Would Denis Moraud be persuaded to take her, despite the baby, if her marriage to Gilbert were nullified? Probably, dim-witted thing that he was, he could be persuaded by his father to do anything.

The baby. If she were expelled back to France, Anne would see the child cast aside like a bastard. She placed a hand on her abdomen as if to shield the growing child. But as Gilbert cradled her in his arms she knew the baby might well be the best defense she had to stay where she was. She was sent to the New World to make children and had shown herself equal to the task. She would have to leave Rose and Nicole behind as well. They were the dearest friends she'd ever had and she knew that finding their like in France would be miraculously lucky. *I've sworn to protect you, my darling baby. I'll do whatever it takes, but we need you to do your part and grow strong. We need you as much as you need us right now.*

For a moment longer, Elisabeth allowed herself the indulgence of her husband's embrace. For all his ferocity and optimism, she could not convince herself that the outcome was in any way certain. She did not mark his shirt with her tears, however, not wanting to mar with her grief what could be one of their last embraces.

* * *

"Madame Beaumont, have your prices for the twelve-pound loaves gone up?" Madame Huillier, possibly the sweetest old woman in the settlement, looked down at the coins with a furrowed brow.

"No, madame, still eighteen *sous,*" Elisabeth said. "As they have been for months."

"Then I'm afraid I'm five *sous* short, madame." The woman looked as though the error were somehow of her own making and turned red as a turnip. Despite the embarrassment, the elderly woman could not afford to let the mistake pass. There were few who could.

"Oh, my apologies!" Elisabeth handed the woman the missing coin without preamble. If anyone were less likely to cheat the Beaumonts, Elisabeth didn't know who it was. "Please take two of these nice cakes to enjoy after supper."

"Madame, it was a simple mistake," Madame Huillier said. "It's not necessary."

"I insist," Elisabeth said, wrapping up two of the buttery confections and pressing them into the woman's hands, gnarled by long days of hard work.

"Bless you, my dear," Madame Huillier whispered, eyes downcast as she left the shop. Only at Easter and Christmastide could the Huilliers afford the luxury of Elisabeth's good cakes.

Flustered by her blunder, Elisabeth waited on Madame Dupré, a woman considerably less charitable than Elisabeth's previous customer. The dark-haired, wiry woman looked over her change overlong before nodding her way from the shop.

"A rather extravagant gesture. Giving away two cakes worth six *sous* apiece for an error of a five-*sous* coin," Gilbert said as the shop cleared.

"I know," Elisabeth said. "I just felt so awful. I couldn't bear the thought of that lovely woman thinking that I'd dream of cheating her of a single *denier.*"

"I'm sure she doesn't," Gilbert said, wrapping his arm around his wife, rubbing her back, made sore from the added girth of the baby mingled with the hours she spent on her feet. "Go to the convent and see the girls for a few hours. Take some cakes with you."

"But the supper rush—" Elisabeth protested.

"Can be managed by me. Now run along." Gilbert pointed to the door, a comical arch to his eyebrow.

Elisabeth felt she ought to protest further. The bigger the baby grew, the more duties fell onto Gilbert's lap. She wanted to keep up her old pace, but the pregnancy sapped more of her strength than she had ever imagined it would. For weeks, however, she had found herself longing for the carefree days after their arrival. The late-night chats with Nicole and Rose, basking in the warmth of their bedroom fire. But Elisabeth's marriage had ended that chapter in their lives. She longed for the days before her mother's meddling.

Elisabeth accepted Gilbert's offer, packing her basket with a sampling of her finest pastries, and walked slowly toward the narrow street that housed the convent. Both Rose and Nicole used the time before supper for mending, needlework, knitting—whatever had to be done. Winter made for longer than usual engagements and a lack of new courtships altogether. Elisabeth was lucky to settle her marriage before Advent, and snow made weddings a challenge. It was as good a time for a chat as Elisabeth would find. She lost no time distributing her pastries and the contents of her mother's letter.

"We both fear the judge will want to pursue the matter further," Elisabeth said, sipping from a mug of her favorite cider. It tasted bitter in her mouth and it was all she could do not to spit it back in her cup. When the others had their eyes occupied elsewhere, she sniffed the contents of the mug. *It smells just fine. Why must everything I love taste so foul to me these days?*

"Can your mother do such a thing?" Nicole asked, casting aside her knitting as Elisabeth recounted the substance of her mother's letter. "Can she really cause such a fuss?"

"Easier than you can dream," Rose answered. Elisabeth nodded to her friend. Better than anyone, Rose knew the power of a letter written to the right people. Rose's late-night confessions to her roommates at the convent had made an indelible mark on Elisabeth's heart. She'd always endeavored to believe the best about people, but Rose's tale of her uncle's barbarism was enough to break the illusion that people were, despite their flaws, generally good. Elisabeth had clung to a young girl's love for her mother, but she knew now it was not, and probably never had been, reciprocated.

"Gilbert thinks it wouldn't be worth the trouble and expense to send me back," Elisabeth said, abandoning her cup and leaning back in her chair, resting her hands on her swollen bulge. "He's being optimistic for my sake, but you know how the authorities here are when it comes to matters of propriety. They'd sooner deport a woman than have her sully the King's colony."

Nicole nodded. "They 'want the colony to be the best that France has to offer,'" she quoted in an unctuous voice. "We've heard the Sisters lecture us on it enough times."

"Well the others on our ship were such a rowdy lot. So unlike us, am I right?" Elisabeth smiled despite herself.

Rose snorted, ignoring a glare from Sister Anne.

"I want to tell you they can't do anything," Rose said. "I wish that were true. Whatever the law states, in the end, they will do as they please.

"Were I you, I would emphasize how quickly you married, the child you carry, and the business you're establishing—that is, the business *Gilbert* is establishing and in which you *help* tirelessly. That is what they want to hear: hardworking women who know their place and have plenty of babies for the colony."

"Well, I'm doing my duty by God and King as I promised to do," Elisabeth said, patting her belly. "And this little settler can't come soon enough."

"I worry that you're so uncomfortable so early on," Rose said, arching her brow with concern.

"I'm sure it's fine. You'll be rocking that sweet little one before you know it, and Rose and I will be mad with jealousy," Nicole said, sampling an apple tart and going back for a second mouthful with vigor.

"So long as his father and I are together to welcome him into this world, I'll be as patient as I can," Elisabeth said, willing the ache in her spine to subside, even for a few blessed minutes.

CHAPTER 8

Rose

April 1668

Rose tucked away her winter cloak in her wardrobe, perhaps the only woman in the colony to do so with regret. All welcomed the capricious weather of March giving way to April. It meant lighter fabrics and looser clothes for those who had them. At least a measure less of misery for those who did not. A hard lot in life, Sister Mathilde often said, is always easier to bear under blue skies than gray.

What I wouldn't give for another month of winter, though the entire colony would see me hanged for thinking it. Rose slammed the lid of her trunk, smirking at the satisfying *crack* of wood on metal.

Rose worshipped the warmth and the sun like an idle cat, but the price of this summer was a good deal too heavy. Her marriage to Rémy Peltier loomed closer. Every day of fine weather brought his home one day closer to completion. Once his homestead was ready for her, the reasons for delaying the marriage would grow feeble. Until now, the engagement offered Rose a sort of protection. It provided her with an excuse to ignore the attentions of other men.

For months, Rose accepted Peltier's visits with a façade of

sweetness and devotion. He was kind to her, bringing her trinkets every week when he came to visit, and paid her pretty compliments with an air of sincerity. She didn't dread Thursday afternoons as a rule—they added some variety to the monotony of the week—but she didn't look forward to Peltier's visits as she felt she ought to.

Like a fiancée should. Like a wife should.

Rose looked to Nicole, who, every Thursday after lunch, dashed upstairs to freshen her dress, wash her face, and even take a brief nap if time allowed, so that she was at her very best when Luc came to call. Nicole took extra pains in the kitchens on Thursday mornings to ensure the gentlemen callers had plenty of refreshment. To entice him, she learned a few of the pastry recipes Elisabeth was willing to share. The finest examples of Nicole's handiwork—where the glazing shone, the shape was perfect, and the filling just plump enough so that it didn't spoil the look of the pastry—were always reserved for Luc.

Rose did not descend the staircase fifteen minutes early with the false pretense of knitting in order to snare the best seats in the common room. She took no special pains with her dress or her hair. In fact, it was now past time when the gentlemen should start to arrive. Peltier, no longer the overeager suitor longing to secure her hand, would not be among the first to arrive. He would not be long in following, however, and might well be waiting for her below.

Go to him and do your duty, Rose chastened herself. *It's what you came here to do. If you wanted to live like a nun, you could have stayed at the Salpêtrière. At least Vérité would have been happy.* She touched the silver medallion at her throat as she thought of the girl, long since lost to her. Rose had written when she arrived in the colony seven months before, but there had been no reply. She had given up hope of one.

Rose placed one foot in front of the other, more out of habit than duty or willingness of spirit. She passed by the Sisters' study before entering the common room. She stole a glance at the black-clad women, some poring over texts, others lost in prayer. Rose felt a pang of jealousy in her core. No husband to mistreat them. No childbirth to cut short their lives. Few things of this world concerned them—only the prospect of paradise in the next.

Rose looked at them and envied their tranquility and wished beyond measure that she could share in it.

"Some spruce beer, Monsieur Peltier?" Rose offered. Despite their engagement, Rose clung to the formality of a title. It seemed natural for her, and he made no complaint on the subject.

"Thank you, yes." Peltier smiled, pleased with her solicitousness. "I am glad to see you are well, my dear. You will be pleased to hear that building continues. We may even complete the house a week or two ahead of schedule."

"I am sure you are anxious for its completion." Rose picked at a nonexistent crumb on the tablecloth.

"Indeed." Peltier's smile was laced with arrogance. "I am sure my homestead will be far more to your liking than the convent. Far more amusing, I would think."

"Oh, life here is never dull," Rose said. "With a house full of young people and plenty of work to be done. It's a happy life here."

Peltier looked askance at Rose, as though finding pleasure in the convent were anathema to him. "Really. How very . . . resourceful . . . of you to find a measure of contentment here. Though I am certain it won't compare to your own home, of course. Our home."

"I'm not sure how true that is, Monsieur Peltier." Rose's mind traveled to the small chapel where the Sisters sat deep in prayer. So tranquil. The envy she felt at her very core, like a ball of ice, had yet to melt. She felt the words spring from her mouth before she could even bring herself to draw them back in.

"Monsieur, I cannot marry you." Rose made herself look Peltier in the eyes. She gripped her mug tightly, refusing to betray her shaking hands to him.

"You cannot be serious," he said.

"I am very sorry, monsieur." Rose longed to look away, but maintained her composure.

"You're overtired, my dear Mademoiselle Barré," Peltier said, clucking his tongue as a mother would do to downplay the tantrum of an overweary toddler.

"I'm very well rested, Monsieur Peltier." Rose set down the cup. *How could I have ever thought to marry such a man?*

"Who is it?" Peltier demanded. "Who has tempted that faithless heart of yours?"

The look in his eyes was at once reminiscent of Aunt Martine in their final moments together. When her aunt had opened the door to find Uncle Grégoire just having defiled her, the kind aunt who had taken the place of her long-deceased mother turned as cold and unfeeling as a serpent. The long months helping tend her young cousins and being Aunt Martine's closest confidante were erased in moments. It was the worst outcome from her nightmares, and now the man before her treated her with the same cold contempt. Rose felt the pangs of remorse vanish. She sat straighter and breathed deeper than she had since Peltier's arrival.

"Indeed, no one, monsieur." Rose kept her temper at bay, but only just. She gripped the edge of the scarred wooden table to give her hands an occupation. "I no longer intend to marry at all. I plan to ask the Reverend Mother about taking orders."

"You cannot be serious," Rémy repeated, as stunned as if she had announced an intention to transform into a fish.

"I am very serious, monsieur," Rose said. "New France was a mistake for me. I hope, since I cannot fulfill my promise to marry, that I may serve my new country through her Church."

In Rose's mind, the newborn plan felt sound. She would have less freedom than as an *officière* of the Salpêtrière, but at least the fetid environs would not kill her.

"I cannot believe you would consider a religious life," Peltier scoffed, sitting back in his chair, legs askew, fingers pressed to his forehead, ignoring the presence of others. "A vibrant young woman has no place in a convent."

"I hope to make my own place, wherever I choose, monsieur," Rose said, her eyes flashing defiance.

"As you wish." Peltier gathered his cloak and hat and made his way to the door without another glance at Rose.

"So, you wish to join our little order, do you?" Rose started at Sister Mathilde's question.

Of course, her conversation would not have gone unheard, but the Sisters' remarkable ability to hear everything while remaining unnoticed was, at times, unsettling.

"Yes, Sister," Rose replied.

"When did you come to this conclusion, my dear?" Sister Mathilde asked.

"It's been a while, Sister. It's been coming along gradually, I suppose."

"And these feelings began perhaps five or six months ago? Sometime in the neighborhood of the birth of the Laurier baby, or soon thereafter, perhaps?" the nun asked.

"Yes, Sister," Rose admitted. "It was."

"I am not surprised that you were frightened, Rose," Sister Mathilde said. "That is why I took you with me. I see much fear in you, and wanted you to see what you will come up against as a wife and a mother here. However, I did not take you there to frighten you behind a veil."

"But, Sister, when the baby died . . ." Rose said.

"I know," Sister Mathilde said. "It happens all too often, for reasons only the Lord can understand. What you must see is that Gislène Laurier lived. She has a healthy daughter and a devoted husband, despite his flaws. She suffered a great loss that day, but has far more to be thankful for.

"If you are still serious about taking orders six months from now, I will speak to the Reverend Mother myself. In the meantime, you will come to this room every Thursday when the young men come to call. Is that clear?"

"Yes, Sister," Rose replied.

Faithful to her word, Rose descended to the common room on Thursdays to greet the gentlemen of the colony. She sat, each week, mending in hand, displaying a look of utter indifference to the young men who came to call. They seemed to understand her meaning, for no one had bothered to disrupt her sewing in weeks. Although she was engaged, Nicole had taken to doing her knitting with Rose to keep her company. Of course, Rose suspected that Nicole hoped for an unannounced visit from Luc, but she gave *most* of the credit to her friend's kindness and not her self-interest. With just a month until her wedding, Nicole had plenty of sewing to keep her occupied. *And, mercifully, she doesn't prattle on about Luc. At least, not too often.*

Then, when six weeks after her refusal, Peltier entered the common room, Rose drew on every ounce of her restraint to greet him with civility.

"Monsieur Peltier," Rose said. "I had not thought to see you. . . ."

"Mademoiselle Deschamps." Peltier ignored Rose's greeting and approached Nicole instead. "I am very glad to find you at home today."

Nicole looked at Rose, puzzled. Never once had Peltier paid attention to her before. He seemed to prefer Rose's innate refinement and dark good looks to Nicole's plainer manners and more subtle beauties.

"How may I help you, monsieur?" Nicole could not keep the astonishment from her voice.

"I was wondering, mademoiselle, would you consider allowing me to pay you court?" If Peltier felt any hesitation at making an offer to Nicole in front of his former fiancée, his voice did not betray it.

"Excuse me?" Nicole asked. "I'm afraid I don't. . . ."

"I have seen you, often, during my visits," Peltier said. "You seem a gentle young lady who would make a good wife."

"Thank you for your compliments, but I am promised to another," Nicole answered. "And I am happy with the arrangement I've made."

"Commendable. You keep your promises better than your friend," Peltier said, no small amount of venom behind the words.

"Monsieur Peltier, I am not ignorant of your situation," Nicole said. "You also seem to forget that the woman in question is standing no more than three feet away as we speak."

"Mademoiselle Barré ended our engagement for reasons that had nothing to do with me. There is no reason I should not pay court to another," Peltier said, no sympathy in his voice.

"She deserved . . . deserves . . . more courtesy," Nicole said. "You let pride and injured feelings get in the way of finding out why she chose to end the engagement."

"You display admirable loyalty to your friend." Peltier shifted his gaze from Nicole to Rose and back again. "My apologies. I should have asked you in private."

"Indeed you should have," Nicole said, attempting to control her rage. "Nonetheless, my answer remains the same. I have no desire to know you better. Good day, monsieur."

Nicole turned her back on Peltier and returned her attention to the soft wool blanket that took shape in her hands—hands that shook with satisfaction after serving the dreadful man a bit of his own bitter medicine.

The echo of Peltier's angry footsteps resonated through the convent.

"Thank you," Rose said, at last.

"It was, most assuredly, my pleasure," Nicole said.

"Can you tell me what you two are playing at?" Sister Mathilde approached the mantel, making no attempt to lower her voice, drawing stares from the other young ladies who had just bid farewell to their suitors.

"What do you mean, Sister?" Rose set the garland aside.

"The pair of you came here to marry—and came at the King's expense, I will remind you. Yet you treat this sacred duty without reverence. I know your intentions, Rose, but I won't have you turning others from the King's instructions. I expect more from you as well, Mademoiselle Deschamps. Promised or not, you had no right to treat an honorable proposal with contempt. The pair of you set the example for the prospective brides in this convent, for good or evil."

"Yes, Sister," Nicole said. "It's just that Monsieur Peltier . . ."

"Is a conceited popinjay, I know. He's not my first choice for any of you. But all you need do was rebuke him kindly and hint that someone else has captured your interest. That would have caused him no insult. Casting him off on your friend's account makes you appear spiteful."

"Yes, Sister," Nicole said, eyes downcast. "I understand."

"Good. This is not the society of Paris you are used to, Mademoiselle Barré. The loan of a few sticks of firewood can mean the difference between life and death on a homestead in the winter. You cannot afford to lose friends—or make enemies—here."

Oh, I am sure I've already made my share of enemies, Sister. When the town learned that I was depriving the town of another wife—another prospective mother, most of them made up their minds about me. The veil will protect me from their scorn—and a good deal more.

CHAPTER 9

Nicole

May 1668

The evening before her wedding, Nicole lay alone in her room, listening to the sounds of a quiet house. The scratching of mice. The purring of the striped black-and-gray house cat, Chaton, too old and too spoiled by Sister Éléonore to hunt them. The soft snores and murmured prayers of the Sisters that traveled through the walls. Silence could be deafening. Nicole reasoned with herself, pulling the blanket to her chin. She ought to sleep, to be the picture of health and happiness at the church the next day. Nicole had excused herself from the common room, unable to focus on her knitting, but now she wondered if she would have done better to stay up until she was well and truly exhausted. Rose padded into the room a half hour after Nicole had begged her leave.

"Have I made a mistake?" Nicole asked from under her covers.

"For heaven's sake!" Rose cried. "I thought you were asleep! I just jumped a mile inside my skin!"

"I'm sorry, Rose," Nicole said, sitting up. "I just can't sleep."

"Excited?" Rose asked.

"Nervous," Nicole said. "Scared."

"Of course you are," Rose said. "You're getting married."

"To a man I've known for less than two months," Nicole added. "Am I a fool to be rushing into this so fast?"

"I have to admit, I thought the courtship might last a month or two longer than it did," Rose said. "But we've seen faster courtships here. It's not like France where couples can be engaged for months and months. You have the rest of your lives to get acquainted. He's a good man, Nicole. The Sisters vouch for him."

"I know he is," Nicole said.

"And that's all that matters," Rose concluded. "Sonnets and ballads don't put food on the table. So get some sleep. You'll think more clearly in the morning."

Mercifully, sleep did come, but she was up with the sun the next morning and preparing for her departure from the convent. Nicole realized she had seen Luc only six—perhaps seven—times since his proposal. Many men in the settlement didn't wish to see their intended overmuch and expose their flaws and risk a broken engagement. There were too many competitors for the brides for a man to assume that any engagement was safe until the ring was placed on the lady's finger. Nicole sighed, thinking that perhaps Luc was hiding something. Something serious. She had to keep her mind from racing to terrible scenarios.

Things are so different in France. Nicole focused on keeping her breathing deep and even as she finished packing her trunk. Jean Galet had come to visit at every chance. He hid nothing from Nicole, so far as she knew, and she felt no need to conceal anything from him. The earnestness in his eyes inspired Nicole's confidence. Perhaps too much. *Stop this! Luc's a good man and you are going to the church in less than an hour to pledge yourself to him.* Casting the doubt from her mind, she dressed in a soft yellow gown that had been Nicole's mother's best dress until her daughter left France. Nicole longed for her mother and her words of wisdom on her wedding day. She imagined her mother at her side, folding the odd petticoat and placing it in the trunk, helping her daughter as she had done on the morning she left for the ship in Dieppe.

That day, a year before, long before dawn on the morning Nicole had left to gather with the other King's wards at the cathedral,

Nicole had packed her clothes, just as she did now. Bernadette had padded into her daughter's bedroom without a knock.

"I'm sorry, Maman, did I wake you?" Nicole had asked as she placed a tattered petticoat in her valise.

"No, *chèrie.* I couldn't sleep," Bernadette answered, taking a kerchief from the bed and folding it into a crisp square.

"Neither could I." Nicole hadn't mentioned the nightmares to her mother, though her sleep had been troubled for weeks.

"The voyage will make you sleep again," Bernadette had said. "The house is emptying so fast, Nicole. Your papa and I filled it, but one by one you have to leave us."

Nicole placed a hand on her mother's back to comfort her. To Nicole's great relief, her mother did not break down in tears, but managed to calm her ragged breaths. Bernadette reached her cracked, calloused hands into the pocket of her stained apron and pulled out her pearl brooch. A simple circle of yellowed pearls set in gold.

A few months prior, Bernadette had entrusted Nicole to take them to a jeweler to sell them. The spiteful troll of a man declared the pearls to be false and the brooch worth just three gold *livres.* He insisted the price was generous. Such a small sum hardly seemed enough to merit parting with her mother's favorite possession. Though Bernadette's dresses were ragged and a pearl brooch would only look ridiculous at the tattered collars, Nicole could not accept the man's offer.

"It isn't worth anything," Bernadette said, pressing the jewel into her daughter's hand, "but I want you to have it. It will still be pretty to wear when you're married. A little keepsake to help you remember your old *maman.*"

"I could never forget you, Maman," Nicole said with tears in her eyes.

"I wish I could be there for your wedding, my darling girl." Bernadette had cupped her daughter's face in her hands. Though she had tried not to show her favoritism, Nicole knew she had always been her mother's sweetheart. For twelve years, she was the baby of the family, doted on by her parents and two older brothers, Christophe and Baptiste. Claudine's arrival was a shock to the entire village, that had long assumed Bernadette was not to be blessed with a large family. Emmanuelle and George's births were just as stunning.

She took her mother in her arms and held her close, as Bernadette had done to her as a child. The two women cried, but regained their composure without much delay. Tears would make nothing easier.

Now, on the morning of her wedding, Nicole pinned the pearl brooch to her collar and banished the painful thoughts of her family. She would be a cheerful bride.

Nicole left the room and made her way down the stairs to where her friends awaited the bride's descent. Sister Mathilde smiled and nodded approval. In moments, the entourage whisked Nicole away to the church where Luc and the rest of the congregation were waiting.

At the altar, Luc looked nervous but dignified in his best uniform. Nicole reminded herself to breathe and focused her attention on placing one foot in front of the other, necessary since she did not have her father's sturdy arm to steady her.

Luc beamed at the sight of her. She was not the most elegant bride in the colony, but in that moment, those gathered would have thought Nicole Deschamps the most beautiful bride in creation if they took the groom's expression as their measure.

In only moments, they were husband and wife.

The newlyweds and their small band of well-wishers celebrated the union with a hearty meal, thanks to Rose's efforts. The majority of the guests left gifts to help Nicole set up housekeeping in Luc's modest farmhouse. Embroidered pillowcases and table linens would give the cabin a feminine touch, while cast-iron pots and good knives would help in her daily chores. A kind neighbor had even given them several fine chickens to use for eggs and meat in the coming years.

Rose offered Nicole a warm scarf and several blankets she had knit from soft wool, while Elisabeth gifted the couple a gorgeous blue-and-yellow star-patterned quilt along with a massive hamper of baked goods. Sister Mathilde pressed a prayer book into Nicole's hands along with another hamper filled with good food, and offered her customary blessing for a happy and productive marriage.

As they left, Luc's wagon strained under the weight of the generous gifts from friends and neighbors. Nicole watched as the convent shrank and then disappeared from view. She knew that she was a welcome guest there at any time, but never again would she call it home.

Nicole watched the abundant trees and rocky hills whirr past as their faithful plow horse trudged them along the ill-kept road—or path, more accurately—that led to the farm. It was beautiful land, even if it did appear so much more savage than the manicured hills of Normandy. Luc's homestead lay an hour from the settlement when the weather was fine and the roads clear. Luc held a one-hundred-acre farm, with the expectation that he would live on the land and make a living from its produce. Many men who were granted a tenancy ended up forfeiting the land because the growing season proved so short and other pursuits, like trapping furs, were more profitable. However, Luc did not have that option.

As an officer of the King's army, he was expected to set an example. Farming was the surest way for the King to keep hold of his settlements. Luc had been a part of the Chambly company in the Carignan-Salières regiment. From what little he'd shared with Nicole, they'd spent three years building forts, liaising with the natives, and protecting the settlers from invasion when talks weren't successful. Now that his term was up, he had been presented with two choices: return to France, or marry and help settle their fledgling nation. He told Nicole repeatedly that she had made the decision a very easy one for him.

"Here we are," Luc announced as they crossed onto his land. "This is all ours."

Nicole surveyed the land, but made no reaction. There were large patches bereft of trees and bramble that looked ready to cultivate. The thick-rooted vegetation of the north still claimed much more of the land than he'd been able to clear.

Nicole took Luc's hand as he helped her down from the wagon. She dared not look at his face, else the tears welling up in her eyes would spill over and betray her anger.

She stood just past the threshold, and listened as the wind whistled through gaps in the timbers. Rusted pots, strategically placed around the room, collected water from the roof that succeeded in keeping out rain only when the weather was fine. The draft in May made the hairs on her arms prickle in the chill. In November it would be unbearable. The skeleton house would provide no relief from the summer sun, nor would it keep the rodents from her pantry . . . when there was one.

Nicole circled the cabin once as Luc emptied the wagon of the wedding gifts. The cabin was the size of the convent's common room, with no walls to divide the living areas from one another. There was a rickety bed in one corner with a patched, thin quilt. The kitchen was an open fireplace next to a roughhewn table that would have to hold office as Nicole's work area as well as dining table. Two dining chairs, and two in the middle of the room. Three small windows with cloudy glass, and a floor that creaked like an arthritic old woman with every step trod upon it.

Nicole removed the worn bedding and replaced it with Elisabeth's fine quilt and the Sisters' embroidered linens. The extravagance made the cabin seem all the dingier for the effort. *I left Maman and Papa for this? Will this be any better than life as a maid in a fine house?* The fear and regret rose from the pit of her stomach to her throat with a lurch as though she were in a carriage driven by an ill-mannered horse.

"It needs some work," Luc said, looking down at his feet as he placed Nicole's trunk at the foot of his—their—bed.

Nicole had no reply, but summoned every ounce of her energy to restrain her tears as she smoothed the bedcovers.

"You're displeased," Luc said. It was not a question.

"You said you had a house," Nicole said, wrapping her shawl tighter around her shoulders rather than discarding it as she crossed to the kitchen table.

"And so I do. I've been spending my time clearing land so we'll have a harvest this fall. It's more important than the house." Luc stared at his feet, his hands on the back of one of the two chairs in the room.

"You told me the land was cleared and that you had a comfortable home." Nicole's voice remained calm, measured, as she organized the contents of Sister Mathilde's hamper, hoping the mice would stay away. She made a mental note to ask what few neighbors there were if there were any spare barn cats to be had.

"Nicole . . . I knew that I couldn't wait to have this place ready if I wanted to marry you." Luc took a seat in his chair and rubbed the bridge of his nose. "In a year, you'd be married to someone else. Expecting his child. I couldn't bear the thought of it."

"You never thought to tell me the truth?" Nicole kept her voice low. She was beyond shouting. "You never thought that I might be willing to wait for you?"

"I couldn't chance it." Luc did not look up at his wife, but seemed to study the calluses on his hands.

"But you can risk me." Nicole closed the lid of the hamper and tucked it in a corner. "Do you think this place will hold in winter?"

"I plan to shore it up before then."

"Between planting your first crop and clearing more of the land?" Nicole sat next to her husband, clutching the armrests until her knuckles went white.

"Something like that." Luc glanced up at Nicole, but did not make eye contact. *I hope this means you know how wrong you were.*

As she looked at her new husband, Nicole noticed the fine lines under his eyes. The grayish tone to his skin that could only come from night after night of too little rest. She cast her eyes around the cabin a second time. She had seen that it was poorly built. She saw that it was terribly small. She had not, at first glance, noticed that every surface was scrubbed clean. She had not seen the vase of wildflowers on the solid wooden table. She had not noticed that the chair on which she sat was new, purchased for her to match his own. He'd had less than two months to make the homestead livable and his attempt was admirable given those time constraints. His fellow soldiers must have helped him throw together the cabin at little more than a moment's notice. *A generous donation of their time and resources—all so he could marry me.*

Though the chair would not find welcome amid the décor of Versailles, it was well made. Possibly the most expensive item in the room. It had to have cost him more than he earned in a month, but he had saved the money to provide her with a small measure of comfort. She looked at the handsome chair, then at her husband. In that chair she would spend countless hours knitting or reading after a long day's toil. There she would comfort her babies. Were she a lucky woman, there she would seek respite from the physical torments of advanced age.

Nicole reached over and grasped Luc's hand, took a tentative breath, and pressed her mouth to his. His eyes shone at the bold gesture, and he enveloped her in his arms, strengthened from clearing the land of myriad trees and shrubs, and pulled her onto his lap.

She looked up at Luc's features, a curious blend of a chiseled nose and curved jaw. She wondered how she had ever seen anything of the boy, Jean Galet, in him. There was none of the boyish charm she had seen in Jean's face; instead, she saw the face of a man who knew work. *God knows, the company of a man will mean more than that of a boy in this place.*

"It needs work, but fortunately, you have me to help with it," Nicole said, offering another slow kiss.

"A greater blessing I've never had," Luc said. "I thought I'd be alone the rest of my days."

"In a desolate place such as this, not such a far-fetched idea," Nicole said, laying her head against his chest, closing her eyes against the unpleasant thought of such a good man spending his life alone. She pushed it from her mind and ran her hand up his chest. He perfumed the air with the scent of clean man flesh, pine trees, and good Marseilles soap. *He must have saved a bar from home.* Nicole lamented leaving the soft soaps from home behind. The rough bars forged with animal fat and potash left her with a slimy coating like a frog's. "I hope I'll make you happy."

"I have no doubts on that, my dove," he said. "Though I must confess I won't have the funds for much improvements to the house until next year. You'll manage, won't you?"

Nicole eyed the gaps in the walls and holes in the roof. It would be tolerable with summer hard on their heels, but winter would be another matter. When the vicious winds howled through the ramshackle building, no fire would drive out the cold.

"Nicole, say something," Luc implored. His eyes seemed to search hers, as though puzzling over an enigma.

"When winter comes . . ." Nicole began, biting her lip.

"We'll be bundled up under the covers," he said kissing his way down her jawline. "We won't feel the cold, I promise."

"What if we have a baby?" Nicole asked, pulling away. "We could have a baby by February. Do you really think we could keep a baby warm here in the coldest part of winter?"

Luc's brow furrowed, adding years to his appearance. He

stroked the side of her face and the worry melted. "Let's not worry about that just yet, my dove. These things often take a few months. We'll welcome our baby next summer, I'm sure of it. We'll have time to fix things up. I swear it."

You promised that the land was clear and that the house was sturdy. Neither of those things were true. How much trust can I place in your promises?

Nicole buried her face in his chest and drew in a breath, enjoying his masculine scent. *I have no choice but to trust you. My fate is tied to yours.*

She melted at his caresses, adjusting to the foreign sensations of allowing his physical affection. She wanted to lose herself in his kisses, but found it difficult to push aside the worry that she had made a serious mistake.

CHAPTER 10

Elisabeth

May 1668

"You are how old, Madame Beaumont?" Judge Arnaud asked. He rubbed the bridge of his nose, closing his eyes. Whether shutting them against a headache or in annoyance, Elisabeth knew not.

As Bailiff Duval predicted, Elisabeth was summoned to Judge Arnaud's chambers. The judge had business in Ville-Marie that had delayed the proceedings for almost two months. Though it meant a reprieve, the waiting was worse than the questioning itself. If the judge decided against her, she might be sent away at any time. The window to sail was open for the year, and he would not delay until the next. If it meant the child would be born at sea on a maggoty bed surrounded by the stink of human filth, he would not spare a second thought for a woman he considered a lawbreaker. He would not spare a thought for the innocent baby.

The dank stone courtroom was cold, even in late spring, and smelled of stagnant water. The judge explained that this was not a formal trial, just a questioning, but that did not stop Elisabeth from shaking, though she tried to for the baby's sake—and Gilbert's. Rose and Gilbert sat in the chairs designated for guests, his arms crossed over his chest, looking both angry and frightened at the whole ordeal. Rose sat with an even expression, a welcome vision of calm and patience. Elisabeth suspected her husband had expected some sort of reprieve. That the questioning was so absurd it would never take place. Elisabeth clung to no such delusions. She had to be strong for him.

"Twenty-six monsieur. As I told your bailiff," Elisabeth said. "My baptismal records say the same."

"That they do," Judge Arnaud said. "The problem is that your mother sent an affidavit saying you had your records falsified. She claims you were two months from your twenty-fifth birthday, not two months past it. Which means you were a minor and left France without her permission."

"That is patently false," Elisabeth said, using all her reserve to control her temper. "My baptism records are genuine, monsieur."

"Why, for the love of all the saints, would your mother contest your leaving France?" Arnaud asked, leaning back in his chair. "You are married, and no longer a burden on her resources. She should be grateful to the Crown for its assistance."

"Monsieur, she attempted to arrange a marriage for me in France." Elisabeth decided that honesty was prudent. "The marriage was advantageous for her, but not in my best interests, I assure you. I left rather than let her badger me into such a union."

"You took your mother's wishes so lightly?" The judge frowned. "Even if you were the age you claimed to be, did you not consider that your mother might know better than you?"

"Monsieur, she proposed the engagement on the day of my father's funeral. She'd been planning her own marriage to the young man's father before my papa even died. You will excuse me if I did not take her counsel to heart that day." Elisabeth failed to keep the acid from her tone.

"Indeed." Arnaud looked as if he saw Elisabeth's vision of Anne Martin, and did not find it endearing. Though she'd heard remarriage was a quick business in New France, Elisabeth herself had seen a woman publicly shamed for taking a new husband only three weeks after burying the first. Anne's plotting won her no friends in the settlement.

"So what say you, Arnaud?" Gilbert asked, no longer able to sit in silence. Arnaud ignored the breech of etiquette and leafed through the papers strewn on his bench.

"I need time to counsel," the judge said. "I'm calling for a recess. Be back in an hour and I'll deliver my decision if I am able."

If I am able? What can that mean? Elisabeth wanted to scream at the delay. *Send me back or let me stay, but make up your mind!*

Rose and Gilbert waited with her in the outside chambers as they listened for the bailiff's call to order. Gilbert held her right hand and Rose her left. The calm exterior left her, but she did not fall into hysterics. She felt hollow and was certain her face looked blank. When either her husband or her friend spoke, they had to repeat themselves several times in order to elicit a response.

They are going to take me from Gilbert. They are going to take the baby from him. I'm going to die at sea, and Mother will smile from malice, happy that if she could not get her way, at least I didn't get mine. No cajoling could bring her thoughts to a better place.

Arnaud returned to the chamber a half hour later than announced, his expression a mixture of annoyance and frustration. His counselors, men of the Church and the State, clearly differed in their opinion as to what should be done. Elisabeth clutched the arms of the chair, as though they might haul her away by force. She was beyond controlling her shaking, and solemn-faced Gilbert made no attempt to comfort her.

The judge cleared his throat and motioned for Elisabeth to rise. Though he was not invited, Gilbert took his place beside her and held her hand.

"If Madame Beaumont were unmarried, and the affidavit were true, I would have no choice but to send her back to France," Judge Arnaud said.

Elisabeth felt her knees buckle, but Gilbert steadied her before she could sway or tumble in front of the assembly.

"As I have no way of reliably proving the validity of her baptismal records, I'd be tempted to send her back anyway because of the time it would take to verify them on this end. Some of my counselors would see you returned to ensure that the honor of the colony isn't compromised, regardless of what we were to discover.

They feel that your disregard for your mother's wishes shows a want of character that is unsuitable for His Majesty's colony. The priest even offered that the marriage could be annulled on these grounds. And ought to be."

Just say it. Send me back and have done with it, but no more of this! Elisabeth saw the vein in Gilbert's neck throb, a rare indication of his temper. The local priest, a sour-faced man named Cloutier, sat ramrod straight in his chair.

"However," the judge continued, "Madame Beaumont married almost at once upon her arrival. She is a hardworking woman. She has shown her value to our community. She is doing her duty to the Crown and our settlement." Arnaud turned to his clerk. "As such, even if she had been twenty-four years old when she left France, she still would have been of age at the time of her marriage. The most I would be willing to do then is fine you the ten *louis* and the cost of your trousseau, to repay the Crown for the deceit.

"But, seeing as Madame Beaumont has done what her king asked of her, and both Monsieur and Madame Beaumont are model citizens, I see no reason to impose this hardship on you, regardless of her age. You are free to go."

"Your Honor, I must object—" The priest stood, clutching his Bible with purple knuckles.

"I've heard your argument, Father, and I've made my decision." Arnaud did not do the priest the honor of turning to address him. "You will abide by it without complaint."

The priest glared at the back of Arnaud's head and spun to exit the room without taking his leave of the judge, stopping only to spare a disgusted look for Elisabeth. *An enemy I'd have done well not to make.*

"Thank you very much, Judge Arnaud," Elisabeth said, finding her voice. She was just able to offer a weak smile of relief.

"My pleasure," Arnaud said. "And, Beaumont?"

"Yes, Judge?" Gilbert turned around, but his hand did not leave his wife's arm.

"You're a lucky man," Arnaud said.

"Thank you." Gilbert cast a smile at his wife. "I believe I am."

"And luckier still that your mother-in-law is an ocean away."

"That, also, I cannot disagree with," Gilbert said, with the first earnest laugh Elisabeth had heard from him in days.

Several days later, Gilbert padded up behind his wife and encircled her with his arms, kissing the soft skin at the base of her neck as she washed the supper plates.

"You're so quiet these days, sweetheart," Gilbert said. "Promise me you're not worried about your mother."

"It's just . . . I'm so angry. Why would Mother have done this to me?" Elisabeth placed the plate on the countertop. "I always imagined, once I was gone, she'd let it go. Be happy to be rid of me."

"I don't know your mother, so I cannot say what was in her head, but it truly doesn't matter." Gilbert tightened his embrace around her. "You're my wife now and the good judge has had the sense to recognize our union. She has no recourse now."

"No, she doesn't," Elisabeth said. "And you're right, she doesn't matter anymore. You and the baby are all that matter now. Still, I can't help but wonder why she would be so adamant that I be returned."

"I know, sweetheart." The smell of warm bread wafted from his skin as he leaned in to kiss her forehead. "Perhaps she loved you more than she ever could show you."

Elisabeth was unable to contain her snort of derision. "All I can think is that she hoped I remained unmarried, and that she could have me deported back home," Elisabeth said, picking up another plate. "Perhaps to force me into marrying Denis Moraud, or someone like him."

"Too late," Gilbert said, smiling into the gentle curve of her neck.

"Yes she is," Elisabeth said. "Thank God."

Gilbert took the plate from Elisabeth's hands, turned her around, and kissed her in earnest. "Come back to me," he said.

She was there in body, but none of her spirit reached her lips.

"I think I need your help with something, my love," Elisabeth said.

"Anything, sweetheart," Gilbert said.

"I want to answer her letter," Elisabeth said. Gilbert did not question her decision. He fetched a quill and paper and waited for her to speak.

Dear Madame Martin,

Thank you so much for your letter. I am glad M. Delacroix told you of my departure. I asked him to do so. You will be pleased to hear I am safe and well in New France. I have done my duty to my king and country, and have married one of the settlers here, a good man, Gilbert Beaumont. We have a bakery that is beginning to thrive, as Papa would have wanted.

Since you were good enough to speak so plainly in your letter to me, I will offer the same kindness. You regretted your marriage to Papa. You thought he was beneath you. It's you, madame, who were always unworthy of him. He was a good man who loved us both, and you repaid him with coldness and scorn. He offered you affection, comfort, and respectability, and you shunned those gifts.

I will spend the rest of my life appreciating those same gifts from Gilbert, and loving my husband as you should have loved your own. You were a poor wife and a poorer mother. I am glad that my child will be welcomed into a home where he will be loved and appreciated by both his parents. From this moment, I disown you as you have disowned me. I will not speak your name, or spare any thoughts for you. You are not deserving of any such attention.

Good-bye,

Elisabeth Beaumont

Elisabeth signed her own name, as Gilbert had taught her, adding what she hoped was a stylish flourish. She wanted her mother to understand she had signed it with her own hand.

"We will send it with the courier when the ship arrives next month," Gilbert said, kissing his wife's hand as she sealed the letter with a bit of candle wax.

"No." Elisabeth stood.

She walked to the oven and deposited the letter in the fire, banishing her mother from New France, and her life, forever. She would not trouble couriers and sailors with this missive.

Elisabeth watched as the flames lapped against the paper, turning it to embers. *You deserved better from her, Papa, and so did I.*

Chapter 11

Rose

June 1668

Rose gritted her teeth as she carried the tray of cakes into the common room to meet with the weekly contingent of suitors. *Last week, I escaped on an errand; the week before, a cold. Of course my good luck wouldn't hold for a third week.* She'd played Sister Mathilde's game and sat week after week, pretending to be open to letting the young gentlemen of the settlement pay her court, but in truth she hid behind the safety of her embroidery and mending basket, biding her time until she could take orders.

"Ah, there you are, Rose. Monsieur Henri Lefebvre, I wish you to meet our Rose Barré." Sister Mathilde presented a young man of perhaps twenty-five, with wavy dark-brown hair and hazel eyes.

The young Lefebvre had to be some relation to the Alexandre Lefebvre whose lecture to Nicole was infamous within their little circle. To Rose's relief, Henri's expression held quite a bit more humor than Alexandre's. *A good thing, too. I don't think I could endure an hour of Alexandre Lefebvre's sarcastic manner.*

"You must try one of her cakes, monsieur. She has become quite the cook," Sister Mathilde said, eyes piercing Rose as the nun retreated to the comfort of her chair. Her meaning was clear: *Be polite. Be charming. Make an effort.*

"Cold spruce beer, monsieur?" Rose asked, noticing Sister Mathilde's stealthy retreat. "Cider, perhaps?"

"Cider, please," Henri replied. "You have finer cider here than the best Norman orchards."

Rose showed Henri to a rigid wooden chair near a window that afforded a view of the narrow street outside. Beyond the panes, passersby bustled along, keen to take advantage of the fine weather.

"I'm glad to finally meet you, mademoiselle," Henri said, looking up from the froth of his cider.

"Finally?" Rose asked.

"I've been here the last three weeks, hoping to meet you," he confessed. "I noticed you at Mass when I first arrived, to visit my uncle, and hoped to make your acquaintance."

"I had no idea. I am sorry I kept you waiting, monsieur." *Polite, as you wanted, Sister.*

"Beauty's privilege," Henri said with a smile.

Oh spare me! No more Peltier-like flattery. Rose frowned, but willed herself to keep control of her countenance. She saw his eyes darken. *Try harder, Rose, or you will never be allowed to take orders.*

Her inner voice barked a hearty laugh. *I have to be one of the only prospective nuns in history to bide her time before entering the postulancy by courting men, I'll wager.*

"Tell me more about yourself," Rose said. She glanced at Sister Mathilde and saw an almost imperceptible nod of approval.

"Not much to tell, actually," Henri said, taking a sip from his mug and causing a drop to inch down the side. Rose longed to wipe it away before it reached the wooden tabletop, but forced her eyes to Henri's face. "I grew up near Amiens. My family has an estate there. I help my father run his affairs. I came to Canada to confer with my uncle Alexandre before moving on to my father's holdings in Martinique."

"You do not plan to stay?" Rose asked, tracing her finger along the ridge of her own mug to divert her hands from reaching over with her thumb to dry the bead of cider on his. "How long are you here for?"

"Another few weeks, before I sail for the islands. I needed to regain my legs before heading back to sea."

"I cannot fault you for that." Rose remembered her own crossing without affection.

"May I visit you while I am here?" Henri looked away at some unknown object instead of making eye contact with Rose. "I would very much like to see you again."

"Of course," Rose said, setting her mug aside and folding her hands on her lap. "Though I must be forthright with you, monsieur. I have plans to enter the Church, very soon. I can offer you nothing other than friendship."

"I confess I couldn't have asked for more with my departure so imminent. But I am surprised that you still accept callers."

"My arrangement with Sister Mathilde is unusual. All the same, I will welcome your visits," Rose said. Henri kissed her hand with the elegance of a courtier and bowed his leave.

Not for me, Rose thought, wiping the side of the discarded mug and the tabletop with her apron, *but at least he has more humor than his uncle to temper that affectation.*

A week later, Rose arrived mid-morning at the Beaumonts' bakery, armed with her usual commissions from Sister Anne.

"Sit and have some cider," Elisabeth offered. "Gilbert will get your order ready. We've got fresh stock in the ovens."

"It smells like heaven, but I came to work rather than rest." Rose crossed to the flour-doused work surface in the kitchen, bypassing the small table reserved for refreshment and gossip. "I'd like to take a try at your almond pastries if you've time for a lesson."

"Always, for you." Elisabeth gave Rose a quick squeeze and took her place across the table, but grabbed a stool to rest her throbbing ankles.

She ordered Rose about, making the younger woman gather ingredients and measure them out with painstaking precision. While Rose worked, Elisabeth asked about the boardinghouse. Engagements made, engagements broken, and successful weddings were the most coveted news in the settlement.

Rose answered patiently—thoroughly, too—until Elisabeth voiced the real question she wanted answered.

"Why the sudden interest in pastry making?" Elisabeth looked away as if to downplay the question's significance.

"Just something to do." Rose didn't look up from the dough taking shape beneath her fingers.

"Not a common occupation for a nun." Elisabeth's nonchalance was betrayed by a telltale squeak. "However, they say that the way to a man's heart is through his stomach."

"Excellent point." Rose's blue eyes shot Elisabeth a freezing glare. "A good skill to have when I am a Sister in a convent full of courting women, don't you agree?"

Elisabeth nodded and continued the lesson. "So Alexandre Lefebvre's nephew has nothing to do with this?"

Rose punched the innocent dough with an angry fist. "Merciful heavens, there are times when I miss city life. You can't use the privy in this settlement without everyone knowing how long it took."

Elisabeth's laugh resonated from every surface in the kitchen. "First of all, don't overwork the dough or you'll be left with a mess. Second, if you want to refute idle gossip, don't steam like a boiling kettle."

"It isn't funny," Rose said, rolling the dough back into a respectable ball, hoping to make amends.

"I suppose it isn't, but I thought you ought to know."

"You're right, I'm sorry," Rose said.

"So is it true he came to see you?"

"Yes." Rose nodded. "He saw me at church, and wanted a friend. He's leaving in just over a week now. . . . He only wanted to get to know me."

"Do you really think that's true?" Elisabeth asked. "With so little time, why would he go to the trouble?"

"Maybe because he's been traveling and he's been lonely? How would I know? I've spent an hour in his company." Rose took the rolling pin and spread the dough with skill enough that Elisabeth arched her eyebrow in appreciation.

"Really? The reports I've heard are far more romantic, but I doubted the truth in them." Whether she wanted it or not, Elisabeth heard the gossip from every corner of the settlement.

"It's a mercy you can tell the truth from an overembroidered fable. I told him I'll be taking the orders soon," Rose said. "He knows this can be nothing more than a friendship. If he wanted more than that, I doubt I'll see him this afternoon. He seems a man of good sense, not one to waste his time."

"I'm sure you're right," Elisabeth said. "But what if he did want more? Would nothing change your mind?"

"No." Rose placed the pastries in the oven. "I don't want to be a wife. I don't want to have children." She looked down at Elisabeth's rounded bump and did not feel the pang of jealousy the childless woman was meant to feel. Childbirth could be so brutal. She could hardly welcome it. Why so many women did, she knew not.

"Then I'm going to ask a hard question: Why did you come here? You knew what was expected of us."

"I thought I could do it," Rose said, accepting the almost-forgotten mug of cider and seat at Elisabeth's side. "But I know now that's not the life I was meant for."

"It's not easy being a wife," Elisabeth agreed. "And I can only imagine the challenges of being a mother. But I think there are few women who would give up their families, despite all the hardships."

"I know . . ." Rose said. *What do I know? That I've been treated so badly by my aunt and uncle that the idea of loving anyone else frightens me? That I miss Papa so much that the thought of marrying without his blessing makes me ill?* The lewd images of her uncle's advances mingled with the sensation of a walk to the altar without her father at her side, and it was all she could do to keep from curling into a ball on the flour-dusted floor. "I just can't do it."

"Rose, I can't pretend to know your heart better than you do," Elisabeth said, caressing her friend's arm. "But I know you are capable of a great many things. I hate to see you trade a chance at happiness for a life of bland contentment."

"It's all I need," Rose said, wondering if the words would become true if she spoke them often enough.

"The people in town think you're using the Church as an excuse," Elisabeth said. "They think you're being overparticular."

"I'm sure Rémy Peltier has nothing to do with that rumor." Rose's tone dripped acid. She'd feared hurting Rémy when she refused him, but his spiteful behavior since had banished whatever remorse she originally felt.

"He has," Elisabeth said, "but plenty of others have tongues of their own. My advice is to deal with Henri honorably and take your vows—if that's what you want to do."

"Of course it's what I want. Prayer, study . . . it's fulfilling. It's interesting. I've even thought of asking about doing some teaching for the native girls as I was being trained to do . . . back in Paris." Rose refused to say the word *Salpêtrière,* as though the name of the prison might somehow summon her previous misfortunes.

"I think you mean what you say," Elisabeth said. "You'd be a marvelous teacher. I also think the people in the settlement will think better of you once you've taken vows or a husband.

"But, as a friend, tell me," Elisabeth said, rescuing the pastries before they burned to a crisp. "Why did you come here for baking lessons?"

"If I'm going to be a nun it's not like I have to keep an eye on my figure, is it?" Rose asked.

The women burst into an uncontrollable fit of laughter. Even Gilbert's shaking shoulders betrayed what he thought was his expert eavesdropping from the shop.

"I suppose that's true," Elisabeth said, wrapping up the warm pastries with the order for Sister Anne. "But put these to good use."

Henri Lefebvre arrived at four, despite Rose's predictions to the contrary.

"Monsieur Lefebvre, what a pleasant surprise." Rose crossed the room and curtsied before him. *Some skills are never truly lost, are they?*

Sister Mathilde glanced up from her seat, surprised at Rose's cheerful greeting, as the young man bowed in response.

"I asked last week if I might come again." Henri's brow furrowed in confusion as he looked down at Rose.

I never realized how tall he is. I must look idiotic next to him, Rose thought.

"I just thought . . . considering . . . No matter," Rose said. "Would you like to have a seat?" She gestured to the spot by the window they had occupied the week before.

"If you don't mind, Sister Mathilde has given permission for us to take a stroll. It's such a lovely day. It seems a shame to not take advantage of the sun." Henri's hazel eyes looked hopeful. She ignored the tingling in her stomach. *Just eager for an excuse to be out-of-doors, nothing more.*

After months on a chilling ocean and several more months of travel before him, it seemed cruel to deny Henri the sun on his face and firm ground beneath his feet.

"That sounds wonderful," Rose said. "Will you permit me one moment?"

Henri nodded. Rose rushed into the kitchen, wrapped up the almond pastries, and placed them in the basket the Sisters used for light errands. A moment before leaving, she turned back and added a smaller bottle of spruce beer from the cellar and two wooden cups to her bounty.

"A refreshment," Rose said as she rejoined Henri, indicating the basket.

"Brilliant idea," he said, offering her his arm.

She accepted, and they headed out to the streets of the settlement, alive with activity on the warm day. They wandered around town and to the edge of the river. There, they sat on a patch of dewy grass and enjoyed the crisp, fresh liquid and soft pastries while they watched the water rush by.

"I can see why my uncle is so fond of the colonies," Henri said. "Father doesn't understand him, but then again, they never agreed on much."

"I don't know your uncle well, but I see he might not be the easiest man to get along with." Rose stretched her legs out before her and brushed the crumbs from her white canvas apron. Her jacket and skirt were plain gray and black linen, but they were new, thanks to the Sisters' generosity. Her rough woolen dress from the Salpêtrière had retired to rags months before. Rose considered the garment better suited for dusting than it had ever been for clothing.

"Uncle Alexandre isn't all that bad once you know him," Henri said. "A better mind for business you'll never meet."

"That I can well believe. He has an excellent reputation in the colony—for that, at least." She kept the reports about his haughty nature and his banter with Nicole to herself.

"The talk about town is that you're one of the smartest ladies the King has ever sent overseas," Henri said, voice dropping.

"I'm not sure how worthy I am of the compliment." *If indeed that's how it was meant,* Rose thought. *No one faults a woman for her lack of schooling here.*

"I hoped you might accept this as a token of my esteem," Henri said, taking a small book from the breast pocket of his *justaucorps.*

"*Verses of the Trouvères,*" Rose said, reading the title. "Medieval poetry. My father used to read to me from this before bedtime. I shouldn't accept such a precious gift."

The book she held in her hand was the first, aside from a prayer book or a Bible, she had held since leaving her uncle's home years before. Even the aroma reminded her of her father. They had laughed over the poems as he promised her a future filled with knights victorious and ladies fair. *How wrong you were, Papa.*

"I insist," he said, clasping his hands over hers. "I promise you, it will give me pleasure to know you have it."

"Then I accept it gratefully. Thank you, monsieur," Rose said. "I miss my father's library. A new book will help break the monotony."

"Life with the Sisters would be less dreary than the life of a frontier wife, I imagine," Henri mused, looking over the expanse of the Saint Lawrence River as smaller boats and a few larger ships bustled about the nearby docks.

"I think so," Rose agreed. The image of the dying Laurier baby still loomed in her mind. *At least he understands to some extent. So many men think we hold our breath anticipating how we might serve them.*

"It wouldn't have to be that way," Henri said, very gently taking Rose's hand again. "Being a wife. Come with me."

Rose felt her stomach churn. Could she accept a man she'd only met a few times before? It wouldn't be the first time in this colony. She thought of the next crop of young ladies who would arrive at the convent within a few weeks, and was sure it wouldn't be the last. Could she be happy to spend the rest of her life across the table from those kind smiles and mirthful hazel eyes?

For the first time she had to admit she might be. But there would still be children. He would still expect her to be a proper wife in every respect. . . .

Every night she would have to push aside the image of Uncle

Grégoire from her mind as Henri performed his duty as her husband. She would struggle to hide her disgust that would cause a good man needless pain. Perhaps she'd grow to accept his embraces without disdain, but at what cost to her nerves and his heart? And the inevitable arrival of the children. Risking her life and health with each lying-in. It was all too much to consider putting herself through, let alone a decent man like Henri.

Rose looked at Henri, but said nothing. *Please don't, Henri. Oh, please, don't.*

"I could provide for you, care for you in a way these good, honest farmers cannot. You wouldn't have to work yourself to death."

Rose knew he felt the calluses on her hands, and she knew he assumed they were from her hard work at the convent. He had never seen her relentless scrubbing, which had continued from her days at the Salpêtrière, and which she could never control when she was anxious or frightened.

He doesn't know how broken I am, Rose thought. *He doesn't need this. Even if he will give me all the comforts this place could afford me, there would still be children.*

She pried her hands from his and clutched the book to her chest. "I'm so sorry, Henri. I can't do it." She thought about handing back the book of poems, but didn't wish to insult him any further.

Rose felt a tear slip down her cheek and ran back toward the convent before he could see the rest.

For three days the scrubbing did not stop, and the bleeding from her fingers was unceasing. Rose managed to curb the involuntary tears most of the time, but that awful hour before supper, and the even worse hour before bed, was her time for weeping. *I made the right decision*. Rose repeated the mantra over and over to herself. *My place is here.* She hoped that if she said the words often enough, she would believe them.

"Rose, be a dear and fetch some bread from Beaumont's Bakery, will you?" asked Sister Mathilde, knocking on Rose's bedroom door. "Father Levesque is coming to supper. I'd like a good cake as well."

"Yes, Sister," Rose said and was gone without further preamble.

She didn't remember running to the bakery but was soaked with sweat when she arrived at the door.

"What in the world have you been up to, Rose?" Elisabeth asked upon seeing her friend's frazzled state. If she noticed Rose's cracked and bleeding hands, she said nothing.

"Sister needs bread and a cake for supper," Rose said, catching her breath.

"And for this you come all the way from the convent at a dead run?" Elisabeth asked, showing Rose to a chair. "What is really the matter?"

"Nothing," Rose said. "I refused Henri Lefebvre, but it was the right choice. My place is at the convent."

At least out loud, she thought the words sounded convincing.

"Then why are you so upset?" Elisabeth asked.

"I don't know," Rose said. "He was nice, I enjoyed our visits, and then he had to bring up marriage. He was supposed to leave. I wasn't prepared for him to ask. . . ."

"You're afraid you hurt him," Elisabeth said, rubbing the taut skin of her swollen abdomen.

"That must be it," Rose said. "I should apologize."

"That wouldn't do any harm," Elisabeth said. "And neither would this almond tart. I'll send the other things on to the convent with Gilbert. It will keep him from clucking over me like a nervous chicken for a good half hour."

Rose accepted the parcel and found her way to Henri's uncle's residence near the main market square, in the very heart of Quebec City. She thought of Henri's kind face, his willingness to continue their friendship despite her declarations for the Church. He'd never pressured her for more, aside from his proposal. *And one can't blame a person for asking for what they want.* She never felt anxious in his presence. There was something so inherently good in his being. *I can't be too late. I can't. He has to forgive me. . . .*

She stood before the massive wooden door and summoned the courage to knock. After a time, Alexandre answered the door, displeased with the disruption.

"Hello, monsieur, you do not know me, but I am Rose Barré, a friend of your nephew's," Rose explained, tripping over her words. "I was hoping I could speak with the younger Monsieur Lefebvre, please."

"I'm sorry, mademoiselle," Alexandre said. "He's left for the Antilles. I thought he made you aware of his plans."

"Indeed he did, monsieur," Rose said. "But I thought he wasn't to leave for several days."

"He had an opportunity to leave early," Lefebvre said. "As his business was concluded here, he had no reason to stay."

"I see," Rose said. "And do you expect him back in Quebec before long?"

"I seriously doubt he plans to return at all," Alexandre said. "I manage his father's affairs here, for the most part, so Henri doesn't have the bother of coming here."

"Please take this," Rose said, thrusting the basket into his hands. "Thank you, monsieur."

She rushed from the doorstep and was gone before the tears spilled over.

CHAPTER 12

Elisabeth

August 1668

Pain seized Elisabeth's body and refused to relinquish its grip. For ten hours, the labor contractions held her hostage, with only moments of reprieve between the surges. At first, everyone told her it was normal, just as, for weeks, they had called the swelling normal. They said not to worry that the baby came later than expected.

But nobody said things were normal now.

Elisabeth tried to find her voice, but it failed her.

How much longer? Why isn't the baby here yet? Can't you make it stop?

She longed to voice her questions. Scream them. Beg.

Her tongue would not obey. Her body seemed a foreign thing and she wanted more than anything to regain control.

Sometime later she lost that urge . . . all she wanted was to slip away from the misery. She cared not how.

Sunlight streamed in through the smudgy window. The moment Elisabeth awoke, she knew she'd been unconscious for hours. She tried to sit up, but the pulled and torn muscles in her abdomen forbade it.

Gilbert and Rose rushed to her side, adjusting her position and smoothing the hair from her face.

"The baby," she said.

"She's here," Rose said. "A girl. Your little Adèle."

"I want to see her." Elisabeth's voice was not her own. It sounded like a weak and raspy shadow of itself.

Gilbert and Rose exchanged a glance.

Elisabeth accepted the baby from Rose and looked down at the miniature features, so much like her own mother's. A warmth spread from her core. Tears spilled onto her pale cheeks.

"She's so perfect. So beautiful." Elisabeth cooed at the sleeping baby, stroking her soft skin.

"That she is," Rose agreed.

Elisabeth looked at Gilbert, wondering why he remained silent.

She held Adèle to her breast, expecting the baby to suckle, but the infant did not stir.

"Perhaps—" Rose fumbled. "Perhaps she's not hungry. Sister Mathilde told us to give her goat's milk when you were asleep."

"Don't—" Gilbert began. "We must—"

Elisabeth saw the anguish in her husband's eyes, so keen it seemed to cut her soul. "What's wrong, Gilbert? What's wrong with Adèle?"

Gilbert buried his face in his hands.

Rose sat on a corner of the bed, the tears brimming in her eyes, and took Elisabeth's hand.

"Elisabeth, the baby isn't well." Rose began trembling. "Sister Mathilde says she's very weak—she won't—"

"She won't what?" Elisabeth's voice found some substance.

"My love, the baby can't survive." Gilbert finally spoke, tears streaming down his face.

Elisabeth clutched the sleeping bundle tighter to her bosom. She felt angry that her body was torn apart, only for her beloved daughter to be taken from her, and furious with herself for sleeping away any of the few hours the child would have on this earth.

It can't be true. I won't let it be.

"I'll feed her. If she'll just eat, she'll be fine." Elisabeth sat up, her muscles screaming in protest, and gently forced her nipple into Adèle's perfect bow-shaped mouth.

The baby still refused to nurse, so Elisabeth massaged her breast, trying to release a few drops of nourishing liquid.

"She wouldn't eat before," Rose said gently. "Sister Mathilde says she's just too weak."

"*She's wrong!*" Elisabeth screamed. "Just get out. If you won't help me save her, just get out."

Rose padded from the room, her footsteps barely making a sound against the hard wooden floors. Gilbert remained, seated in a straight-backed wooden chair that usually resided at the supper table. Elisabeth's eyes, however, were only for her precious daughter.

"Eat, my little one," Elisabeth said, coaxing a few more drops of clear liquid into the baby's mouth and massaging her throat. "Please eat for Maman."

Gilbert's manful sobs from alongside the bed caused her to look up. His head was buried in his hands, shoulders shaking.

He's given up on you, my love, but your maman *won't. You're my good girl and you're going to grow to be big and strong. You must.*

Elisabeth held the baby for hours, not bothering with the swaddling clothes that many midwives insisted upon. She massaged what nourishment she could from her aching breasts until her hands cramped. With every movement, every pulled muscle and torn fiber of her body tried to reel her back into rest, but she ignored it. She ignored Rose's and Gilbert's pleas for her to entrust the baby to them and to rest. She ignored the growing seed of doubt that blossomed with every passing hour and choked her breath.

Adèle occasionally opened her blue eyes for a brief moment, filling her mother's heart with hope. But Elisabeth ignored the shallow breath becoming shallower. She ignored it until she could ignore it no longer.

"Gilbert, fetch the priest." Elisabeth's voice was whisper soft and several octaves lower than her usual tone. It felt as foreign to her as the rest of her battered body.

He said nothing but walked from the room. Elisabeth listened to his footsteps that fell morosely down the stairs to the shop below and onto the street. Rose took his place at Elisabeth's side, but did not offer to take the baby this time. She offered a hand, and nothing more.

Thank you. The words stuck in her chest, but she knew they need not be spoken.

Less than twenty minutes later, Gilbert returned without Father Cloutier.

"Where is he?" Elisabeth demanded.

"Writing his sermon. He said he would be here before nightfall if he's able to complete it."

"We . . ." Elisabeth faltered, but drew her breath. "We don't have that much time. Get the holy water. Now."

His eyes had a hollow look she'd never seen before but his face betrayed no emotion.

You're stronger than I am, Gilbert. Bless you for it.

The glass flask was soon in her hand and she unscrewed the lid while resting Adèle on her lap and left arm, careful not to disturb her. She dribbled a small amount of water on her right hand and made the sign of the cross on her daughter's forehead, sternum, and both sides of her birdlike rib cage.

"In the name of the Father, and of the Son, and of the Holy Spirit, I baptize thee . . ."

"The child cannot be buried in consecrated soil if it was not baptized." Cloutier stood at the foot of Elisabeth's bed dressed in a black cassock looking like the angel of death. Elisabeth still held Adèle's little body close to her breast, though the infant had breathed her last a few hours before.

"I blessed her with holy water myself," Elisabeth said. The priest leaned closer to hear her strained tones. "My mother kept a flask of it in the house at all times when my father was ill. The priest told her she could administer my father's last rites."

"That's not the same as a baptism," Cloutier said, shaking his head.

"The priest in my village always made sure mothers who were on the point of giving birth had holy water on hand for cases just like these," Gilbert said. His arms folded across his chest, barring any opposition from the obstinate priest.

"If you had made me aware of the direness of the situation . . ." Cloutier turned his attention to Gilbert, his voice a condescending sermon.

"I'm not sure how more evident I could have made things for you. 'The baby is dying' is as direct as a man can be."

"Parents often exaggerate these situations," Cloutier continued.

"Obviously, we were *not,*" Elisabeth said, raising her voice to its usual volume. *Do not exert yourself and drop the baby.*

"Clearly," the priest admitted, a mask of insincere sympathy plastered on his face.

Elisabeth looked at the scrawny, tall man, so very like the scarecrows out in the fields on the outskirts of Paris. Like them, he had no flesh, bone, nor beating heart beneath the tattered clothes. But she could understand his detachment, at least in principle. *You see babies die all the time. You minister to the fathers. Console the mothers. You speak of God's will and the importance of forging on. You cannot care for Adèle as we do. But I* will *see my daughter buried in consecrated ground.*

"I am very sorry, but I cannot allow the child to be buried on Church land." There was no room for debate in his expression. "I will be happy to say a blessing over the child wherever you decide to hold the funeral."

"Your blessing won't be needed." Elisabeth set her teeth and looked down at the motionless babe in her arms. There were no words he could offer that would soothe a mother's soul or mend a father's broken heart. So innocent a creature did not need such a man to commend her soul to heaven.

The priest uttered some condolences and left Elisabeth with her child, Gilbert following him to the door.

"Would you like me to hold her for a little while so you can sleep?" Rose entered the room, bringing a mug with some milk. She apparently knew better than to try to offer food.

"No." Elisabeth latched her eyes onto Adèle's face. *I can only spend so many more hours . . . minutes with you, little chick. You'll be with me the whole time.*

"Darling—"

"Don't. Don't even ask, Rose. I can't let her go. Not yet."

"I'm not asking you to, dear. Just please listen. You must rest. You must get better. You've lost a great deal of blood and you've torn badly. You must take time to heal."

"Why? What does it matter now?" For the first time the salty drops spilled over. She realized she'd been in too much pain to let her tears loose before.

"Gilbert." Rose sat on the edge of the bed, wrapping her arm around Elisabeth's shoulders. The warmth felt good around her sore muscles . . . even those in her neck had been wrenched from her attempts to push her child into the world.

Gilbert. He will need me as I need him.

"I'll rest," Elisabeth promised. "When she doesn't need me any longer. I will."

Rose nodded. "Is there anything you need?"

My daughter, but there's nothing you can do for her.

"Write to Nicole, please," Elisabeth said after a few moments. "Spare her the details. I wouldn't want to frighten her. But she should know. She'd want to know. I'd want to know if it were her." *God forbid. I wouldn't wish this on anyone, let alone a woman I cherish like a sister.*

"Of course. I'll send her your love," Rose said, her arm squeezing her friend's shoulders gently as she kissed Elisabeth's sweaty temple.

"Thank you, Rose."

"Don't you dare. But please, do try to drink some milk. It will help you feel a little better."

Doubtful, you sweet girl. But I will. For you. For Gilbert.

The next day, the three of them buried Adèle beneath Elisabeth's favorite evergreen tree, just outside of town. Far enough from the settlement that the tree was sure to stand for years to come yet, and close enough that Elisabeth could come and see her sweet daughter without too much difficulty. Unable to sit, even for the ten-minute ride outside of town, Elisabeth lay in the back of the wagon, Adèle still tucked safely in her arms.

Gilbert dug a hole deep enough so no beast would disturb Adèle's slumber. The sweat poured from his brow, but he let it drip into his eyes. Elisabeth knew his tears made him oblivious to the sting. She sat up, with Rose's help, when the hole was dug. He retrieved the impossibly small wooden coffin he'd built the previous night and removed the lid.

Elisabeth pressed her lips to the baby's cold forehead. *You must let her go. You must. Let her rest.*

Shaking, Elisabeth placed the child's limp body in the box Gilbert held out. The baby wore a simple nightdress that Elisabeth had embroidered with sheaves of wheat. *Your grandpapa would have loved it. He'll recognize you coming, my sweet girl. He'll take care of you for me.* Without looking down, Gilbert placed the lid atop the coffin. Adèle was gone.

Rose, as Elisabeth had requested, read a passage from the Bible. Something to do with the time and season for all things. Elisabeth didn't listen to the words, but was just glad someone spoke them. Elisabeth stood with Gilbert's help and sprinkled some holy water on her daughter's grave. Adèle might not have the Church's blessing, but she had her mother's, and Elisabeth was certain that it would have to count for something.

When the time came for Gilbert to fill the hole, Elisabeth could not bear to watch. She lay back down in the wagon as the shovel connected with the dirt and covered her precious child. *Clank, swoosh. Clank, swoosh.* She closed her eyes against the oppressive August sun, but she could not muffle the sound from her ears, no matter how she tried. *Clank, swoosh. Clank, swoosh.*

She felt the warmth of a body slide behind her in the bed of the wagon and wrap a slender arm around her aching, broken body. Elisabeth reached up and grabbed Rose's hand and tucked it to her broken heart in wordless appreciation.

"You will be well again. In time."

I don't see how, my dear friend. But I will trust that, somehow, you know better than I.

Chapter 13

Nicole

Late September 1668, Jarvais Homestead

Nicole approached the edge of the fledgling farm, weary but satisfied. It had taken Nicole just a few hours after her arrival to learn that French agriculture was a far more civilized affair than farming in the colony. Starting a farm on virgin soil meant waging war against vegetation that had claimed the land centuries before. Trees, vines, roots—all had to be cut down, dug up, and either burned or used for lumber to make proper fields for growing crops. Luc had begun the war against the land, but he needed Nicole to help win the last backbreaking battles. She spent much of her summer toiling in the Quebec sun that was every bit as nasty as her winter storms.

Luc's plot gave them a decent harvest, however, and by autumn the rest of the land was cleared and ready for spring. It would be easier next year.

"Supper's ready, then?" Luc rested on his hoe and wiped the sweat from his brow and patted her protruding midsection. Another miscalculation. Despite Luc's assurances that their child wouldn't make an appearance before summer, the first Jarvais child was expected in late February or early March. It was bad timing in more ways than one. It left them no time to improve the house and kept Nicole from spending many hours in the field when she was most needed.

"Yes, indeed," Nicole said, wiping a sweaty lock from his brow. She looked down at his hand on her abdomen and smiled. "We're both ready to eat."

Luc took her hand and they walked back to the farmhouse. It was still small enough that you risked rolling out of bed and into the kitchen, but Nicole had made modest improvements to make the house a bit more comfortable. The pantry she fashioned from their fallen timbers looked as though it was on the verge of collapse each time she opened the door, but it still held. Each of them famished, Luc by his labor and Nicole by the baby inside her, they dug into the supper with ardor. It was a simple meal of bread and chicken stew, but satisfying after a day of work. They ate in relative silence, as was their custom, reserving conversation for after the meal.

Afterward, Nicole sat in her wedding-gift chair near the fire, knitting a small blanket from soft wool that Sister Mathilde had sent once she'd heard the news of the impending arrival. Luc, much like Nicole's father, could not bear to sit idle, so he sat sharpening the blade of his favorite knife whose increasing dullness he'd taken to complaining about for the past week. Nicole relaxed and took in a purifying breath. This was her favorite part of the day, where they granted themselves permission to relax.

"The harvest will see us through winter," Luc said, having assessed their haul that day. "Praise be."

"That's wonderful." Nicole smiled at her husband's relief. He was not as used to the uncertainty of farming as she was.

"So now, the question is, what to do with myself during these cold months." Luc continued scraping his blade on the stone as he spoke.

"Staying in and getting fat on my cooking isn't good enough for you?" Nicole asked, winking at her husband.

"Tempting as that sounds, we need a cash reserve, Nicole," Luc said, no humor in his voice. "The harvest was fine this year, but what about next? Or the one after?"

"That's the way farming works, Luc," Nicole said. "We'll have bad years from time to time. We'll get through it."

"I don't want to 'get through it' or 'make do.' I want better for us. Better for the both of you." Luc looked up from his blade to assess his wife's reaction. "I'm going trapping with some of the fellows from the regiment next week. We plan to be out three or four weeks at most."

"You're going to leave me here alone?" Nicole asked. "There's no one for miles."

The remote location of their homestead made Nicole nervous. In France, she had lived an easy walk from Rouen.

"You'll be fine," Luc said. "You can always go into town and stay with Elisabeth if you want."

"She's busy enough," Nicole said, thinking of the heartbroken missive Rose sent after Adèle passed. Being so far removed from her friends was a hardship she had not yet conquered. It brought to mind that there was nothing at all keeping the same tragedy from befalling her. She placed her hand on her abdomen, where it was greeted with a distinct flop from the growing child, a reminder of the delicate nature of life in these early moments. "I don't like it, Luc."

"For three or four weeks, you'll be fine here, Nicole," Luc said, inspecting the edge of the blade in the weak candlelight. "And with the profits I'll make, we'll be set all year."

Nicole couldn't argue. The money could help repair the ramshackle cabin. Though she held her tongue on the subject, Luc knew the condition of the house paired with the arrival of a baby made Nicole anxious.

"Luc, I'd really prefer that you stay here." Nicole set aside her knitting and took her husband's hand. "As you said we'll be fine for the winter. Anything could happen."

"If the natives come calling you're a better shot than I am," Luc said, laughing at his joke and returning to his knife.

"Don't make light of it." Nicole gripped her knitting needles to keep from hurling them at his head.

"Calm down. It's three weeks." Luc's expression changed to annoyance, as though her fears of wildlife, storms, and hostile natives were the products of an overly vivid imagination.

"If you think you have to, go," Nicole said, throwing her knitting in its basket and retreating to the lonely bed on the other side of the room. Luc was an endearing man. Perhaps too much for Nicole's own good, but he was never so infuriating as when he would not listen to reason. There would be nothing she could say or do to sway him from his course, and she had to let him go.

Curse Luc Jarvais for leaving me here. Nicole would have screamed if she weren't too busy shivering under her blankets. The howling winds cut through the rickety cabin and the October air was as merciless as she'd feared. *How could a baby survive here in February? How would I?*

For the first two weeks after Luc's departure, it was the loneliness that plagued her. Her family's farm was active and bustling; the convent, too, was alive with life. By contrast, her little home felt eerie and foreign. Nicole was unused to solitude and refused to make friends with it. In two weeks she scrubbed every surface clean to the point of sparkling, mended every scrap of clothing, and knitted miles of baby blankets and other garments. She passed the time, but felt unable to cast off her restlessness. Then the weather turned, and it was all she could do to keep from freezing. The paltry stack of firewood Luc had left was long since depleted, and it was all she could do to chop enough on her own to keep the fire going. Luc had been sure the storms would not hit so early. Yet another miscalculation.

There was a persistent *thump-thump-thump* at the door, which Nicole assumed to be the wind, until she realized the rhythm was too regular. She sat up in the bed and set aside the blanket with a regretful glance. *It might be Luc, unable to open the door if the wind has barred it with snow.* She saw the shotgun, always loaded, that stood next to the door. *Or it might not be.* She grabbed the gun with a silent prayer that she wouldn't be forced to use it.

On the porch stood a young girl, four or five years of age. She was lithe like the white-tailed deer so abundant in the woods, with night-black hair styled in two messy braids and large black eyes filled with fear. Nicole guessed she was a child of the Huron people who had a settlement close to the farm. She was dressed from head to foot in thick leather and fur pelts, but still looked frozen to the porch.

"Hello." Nicole spoke slowly, unsure if the girl could understand French.

The child responded with a few words in her own language. Nicole shook her head to show that she did not understand.

"Are you hungry?" Nicole pointed to the cauldron that hung with the frozen remnants of her supper from two days ago.

The child shook her head and grabbed Nicole's hand, pulling her into the glacial October night. The child barely gave Nicole the chance to grab her cloak and shut the door with another prayer that none of the candles would burn the house down before they returned from wherever the child was dragging her. Still, the child's panicked expression made Nicole unable to refuse the unknown request. Perhaps the child had a sibling in trouble and Nicole was the nearest adult to help. Whatever the reason, she had to go.

"Where are we going?" Nicole asked.

The child offered a few words, none of which Nicole understood.

They continued for a quarter of an hour into the heart of the woods where Nicole had never dared to venture. If the child left her, she would never find her way back, especially since the snow kept her from seeing more than a few feet in front of her. When the child dropped her hand and darted forward, Nicole's stomach churned with fear.

"Stop!" she yelled. "Wait for me!" The snow stole the words from her mouth. The Huron child wouldn't be able to hear her cries, no matter how loud.

She cursed her slowed movements and awkward gait. The Huron girl peeked back from around a tree and motioned for Nicole to join her.

At the base of the tree lay Luc, arrows lodged in his shoulder and thigh.

"Oh God!" Nicole dropped to her knees at her husband's side. "Luc, no, please!"

She forced herself to take a few steadying breaths and gather her wits. She saw that his chest rose and fell, though the breathing was shallow and irregular.

Thank God, Nicole thought.

She examined his wounds, hesitant to touch them, but knowing he would have no chance otherwise. The arrows came out, taking hunks of flesh with them. She ripped strips from her petticoat and wrapped them on the wounds as tight as she could, though the bleeding refused to cease.

The Huron girl emerged from the forest, and Nicole scolded herself for not noticing that the girl had disappeared.

The child bore a large branch and ran back for another. She then rooted through Luc's sack and found a thick woolen blanket that had been Luc's bed since he left the farm. Taking a knife, the girl made slits in the fabric every few inches. Nicole was impressed by the girl's skill, thinking she must be older than she looked, but didn't spare the time to comment on it.

When the girl began to weave the blanket onto the branches, Nicole understood and helped the child fashion a crude stretcher to drag her husband home.

Nicole managed to lift and roll Luc's considerable frame onto the stretcher and secure him the best she could. The girl gathered the supplies and hoisted Luc's pack, almost as large as she was, onto her back and set off toward the farmhouse.

Nicole looked down at her husband, kissed his brow, and lifted one end of the stretcher, dragging the other behind her. She had to stop every few moments to catch her breath. The muscles in her back screamed against the odd contortions and exertion. The snow, for the first time, proved an asset. The makeshift stretcher slid with relative ease over the snow, though it demanded every ounce of Nicole's strength to pull it.

The trek into the woods had taken fifteen minutes. It took close to an hour, cloaked in complete darkness, to return. Nicole all but wept when she saw the farmhouse and redoubled her efforts until she reached the door.

Inside, Nicole resisted the urge to collapse on the floor. She worked on freeing Luc from the stretcher. The blanket was soaked through with blood; Nicole's hands were slick with it as she attempted to loosen the wet knots. Once she freed him from the stretcher, Nicole gathered clean cloths and made proper bandages for the wounds. Nicole fought rising nausea as she removed the old bandages that had done little to stem the flow of blood from his shoulder and thigh.

His flesh was cold. Too cold.

Sometime during her slog back to the cabin, Luc had died.

She lay down next to her husband and surrendered to the tears. Despite his faults, he had been a good man, a kind husband.

No more late-night embraces, no more sweet boyish face to greet her. The injustice had yet to occur to her. The pain was all she could comprehend at that moment.

The Huron girl sat next to them, barely stirring except to stroke Nicole's hair.

Within minutes, Nicole's hips screamed for her to rise off the hard wooden floor, and she had no choice but to listen. She covered Luc's broken body with one of the embroidered sheets she'd received as a bride and cleaned herself of his blood. The dress was frozen stiff with snow and caked with crimson. She looked down and shook her head, knowing it was destined for the rag pile.

What a thing to think of at a time like this. Nicole growled at herself as she found her warmest nightgown. *You have another. Many could not say the same.* Her pragmatic nature forgave the errant thought. Replacing her dress would be months off, especially now. If she hadn't another, God knew how she'd be able to clothe herself until she regained her pre-pregnancy figure.

The little girl looked expectantly at Nicole. *God, her parents must be sick with worry with her missing out in this storm.* Nicole looked out the one window and saw that the snow still fell steadily and the night was moonless. *There is no way I can take the child home in this. She's better off here for the night. Her parents will be glad for it despite their sleepless night.*

The Huron girl accepted one of Luc's old shirts with a questioning look, perhaps confused by the need to change clothes for sleep. Nicole changed into her nightgown and climbed into bed. Every aching muscle shouted at her; she did her best to drown them out.

Though she did not think sleep would come, she knew she needed to rest for the baby.

A slender arm the color of warm cedar wrapped around Nicole and provided her with some warmth against the frigid night.

Sleep came faster and deeper than Nicole expected, and she was surprised when sunlight woke her the following morning. As she prepared breakfast for herself and the Huron girl, she felt more grounded, if not better. The Huron girl sat in the seat Nicole preferred, closest to the fire, and waited for her meal, hands placed demurely on her lap and black-brown eyes trailing Nicole around the kitchen. There was so much to be done. She had to see Luc buried properly. She had to figure out what to do with their home. Where to go. But before she could do any of those things, she had to see the little native girl fed a decent breakfast.

"I hope you like this," Nicole said, setting a plate of good bread and salted pork before the child. To Nicole's relief, the girl ate with enthusiasm.

"Nicole," she said, patting her own chest. It embarrassed Nicole that she hadn't thought of this before. *Of course, we were busy last night,* Nicole reminded herself.

"Nicole," the girl repeated.

"Yes!" Nicole said with a smile. She pointed in the girl's direction. "You?"

The girl responded in Wendat, but Nicole could not wrap her tongue around the syllables. The young girl shook her head at Nicole's efforts. "May I call you Manon?" Nicole asked. "I've always liked that name."

"Manon," said the girl, trying the name on her tongue. "Manon." She pointed to herself and nodded.

The rest of the meal was spent with Nicole naming objects in French and Manon mimicking her pronunciation. It was a good—if fleeting—distraction from the myriad duties at hand. Nicole looked toward the entry where Luc's body still lay. The trip into town could not be put off. Luc needed a proper funeral and burial, and the Sisters would be able to find out who the child was and where to take her. The idea of seeing a familiar face was also a comforting prospect.

She had never hitched the horse to the sleigh before, but managed without too much trouble. Luc's old nag, Gillette, looked at Nicole with martyred patience but seemed happy enough to stretch her legs.

Manon was delighted with the horse and disappointed that Nicole refused to let the girl hold the horse's reins as they drove along.

They left Luc's body behind. Nicole worried that she might hurt herself further if she tried to load him into the sleigh. She felt sure his friends from the regiment would collect their fallen comrade for burial.

Though not an accomplished horsewoman, Nicole urged Gillette on as quickly as she dared, anxious to reach town. *I can't believe you left me here all alone, Luc. You were convinced nothing would happen to me or the baby. You never stopped to think about what would become of us if something happened to you. . . .* Nicole channeled her anger to urge the horse through the snow.

Less than two hours later, Manon sat on the floor of the convent's common room, deep in conversation with Rose. Nicole was deeply impressed by her friend's grasp of the language after a month of study with Sister Hortense, who led most of the catechism courses with the native girls, but was unable to focus for long on the conversation. She mostly stared into the fire and tried not to think. Luc's death had yet to fully register, and she knew the pain would come soon enough. For now, finding out where little Manon belonged was her chief concern. It kept the angry thoughts about Luc's carelessness at bay. She wanted to think well of her departed husband, but found it difficult now that she faced a future with her unborn child without the protection of a spouse.

At one point, Manon giggled, jumped up, and ran toward the convent kitchen.

"I've sent her to watch Sister Éléonore make bread," Rose said. "She's a sweet child."

"That she is," Nicole agreed. "What have you learned?"

"She lives with the Huron tribe that lives not far from your homestead, as you guessed. She saw what happened. She says it was an accident. Two of the Huron men were hunting. They mistook Luc for a deer. She thinks they left because they feared trouble with our law."

"Reasonable enough," Nicole said, knowing the laws in New France were often unkind to the native people. "She must want to get back to her family."

"She lives with an elderly grandmother. Her parents died," Rose said.

"Poor baby." Nicole glanced toward the kitchen.

"She doesn't seem happy," Rose said. "It sounds to me like the grandmother is ill. Perhaps gravely so. She says she's seen eight summers to her grandmother's eighty."

"She's really eight years old? She looks like she couldn't be any older than five or six." Nicole, not knowing what to do with her hands, folded them in her lap.

"So she claims," Rose said, looking in the direction of the giggles from the kitchen. "I don't doubt her based on the way she spoke. She's bright."

"Yes. And capable." Nicole thought of the way the girl fashioned the stretcher in the midst of the storm, but could not bring herself to speak of it to Rose.

"Is there anything we can do?" Nicole wondered.

"I'll go to the tribe and ask," Rose said. "They're pretty friendly. They've allowed several of the girls to take classes here."

"Thank you, Rose," Nicole said. "If it weren't for her, Luc would still be out there."

She shivered at the thought of her husband dying alone in the woods. Tears began to fall.

Rose took her friend in her arms and rubbed Nicole's back as she sobbed. "He was almost home," Nicole sputtered. "Twenty minutes at most and he would have been home."

"Madame," said a male voice from the door to the common room. "We've collected Luc. He's at the church. We cleaned up . . . as best we could."

After a moment, Nicole recognized the young man from Luc's regiment. Something-or-other Gérard. A nice young man, from what little she knew.

"Thank you very much," Nicole said. "I'm grateful to you all."

"Say nothing about it, madame," the soldier said. "We're terribly sorry it happened. Be happy to find the red-devil bastards who did this to him. Begging your pardon, madame."

"No need. We've learned it was an honest accident." Nicole did not feel the need to explain all Manon had done. The soldier was the type who would always think of retribution first.

"As you say, madame." Though he looked unconvinced, the young man bowed his way out of the room.

Rose cast an annoyed look after the soldier. In her talks with Nicole, she revealed that the more she learned about the native people, the more she cared for them. Accidents like these were dangerous to the delicate relations between the settlers and the Huron. Too many on both sides considered violence as the most efficient form of diplomacy.

Luc Jarvais was laid to rest the following day in the settlement cemetery. As the priest spoke, Nicole did not weep or rage at the injustice of a life cut far too short. She felt a numbness, a disbelief, that had yet to dissipate.

"Thank you," Nicole said to one of the numerous soldiers who offered a kind remembrance of Luc to his widow. So many of them descended upon her after the burial that their faces began to blur.

"You're exhausted," Elisabeth said, rubbing her friend's back. "Let's get you home."

Elisabeth scanned the small crowd for Rose, who stood at the edge of the group in deep discussion with Sister Hortense, Rose's mentor and friend.

Elisabeth caught Rose's eye and gestured her intent to take Nicole back to the convent.

"I wish I had words for you," Elisabeth said as she installed Nicole in the common room with a cup of crisp spruce beer.

Nicole had refused food, and for today Elisabeth and the others would not press.

Manon, rarely out of Nicole's sight since the night Luc died, sat on the floor playing with a simple cloth doll that Sister Anne had fashioned for her.

"I do remember from when I lost my father. Words don't help much anyway," Elisabeth said.

"Not really," Nicole agreed. "I am so glad you're here. I thought you might be burdened enough."

"I'm glad I was able," Elisabeth said.

Nicole squeezed her friend's hand, wishing she had better means to express her gratitude.

"Have you any plans?" Elisabeth asked.

"Not yet," Nicole said. For the moment, she lived hour to hour. Anything beyond that seemed too colossal.

"You'll stay here as long as you need," Sister Mathilde said, entering the room and joining the two women near the fire with mugs of spruce beer for all of them. "You don't want to be alone when the child is born."

"Yes," Nicole said, tone wooden. Another of the countless worries she had yet to consider.

"I suggest selling the rights to the homestead if you don't wish to manage it yourself," Sister Mathilde said, "and sooner rather than later. You'll fetch the best price while the land is cleared and the house is in good repair." At that statement, Nicole bit her tongue. If the good Sister saw the condition of the house that Luc described as "being in good repair" she would have cursed him for ever taking one of her girls to live there.

"A sound idea," Nicole said. The room swirled at the thought of managing a hundred acres.

"You don't need to make any decisions today, or for a few weeks yet," Sister Mathilde said, patting Nicole's shoulder. "I don't mean to be callous, dear, but there are decisions that ought to be made."

"Of course, Sister," Nicole said.

Sister Mathilde was one of the least callous people Nicole knew, but the nun was ruthlessly practical. "Thank you for letting me stay here. Your kindness means so much to me. I hope I can be of some service while I'm here."

"Our pleasure to help," Sister Mathilde said. "Just rest and protect that child of yours. That is the biggest service you can provide."

"I'll do my best." Nicole looked down at her abdomen that had begun to swell with child, and felt an overwhelming sadness for the child who would never know firsthand how much his father loved him. But as she sat, absorbing the warmth of the fire, grateful for the absence of wind blowing through timber gaps in shoddy walls, she knew she was better off here. She rubbed her swollen abdomen; *the baby certainly will be, despite Luc's grand plans and good intentions.* That night she wept herself to sleep. Not out of grief for her husband, but out of shame that she would not miss him like a wife should.

CHAPTER 14

Rose

October 1668

"The—the fat b-brown cow yumped . . ." Manon stuttered.

"Jumped," Rose corrected.

"J-jumped," Manon repeated. "Jumped." The girl's satiny brown brow furrowed, branding the word and its corresponding sound into her memory through brute force of will. She sat slouched over the scarred wooden table in the convent's common room, appearing oblivious to all the other occupants of the room as well as the crackling of the fire and the swirling snow that painted ice flowers on the windowpanes. Nicole usually gave Manon her French lessons, but a headache kept her in bed that afternoon. Rose suspected the inconvenience of selling the homestead and dealing with Luc's affairs were the root cause.

"Very good, my darling girl. You're making wonderful progress." Rose rubbed Manon's back as she arched over the book, concentrating as though the pages contained the great mysteries of the universe and not a compilation of children's rhymes.

"Not fast enough." Manon spoke as much to the book as to her tutor. *The frustration of an eight-year-old is a powerful thing.*

"Dearest, several weeks ago you didn't speak a syllable of French. You're coming along better than any of us could have dreamed.

Don't be so hard on yourself." Rose scratched the small square of skin between Manon's shoulder blades, causing the girl to purr like a kitten.

"I am stupid," Manon said, pronouncing each word with deliberation.

"No you aren't, and no one who knows you thinks that either, my dear. I worried that the people in England thought the same of me when Papa took me to London and I couldn't order my own supper. I was just about your age, maybe a year older." Rose chuckled as she remembered the fire of her indignation at the waiter's gentle scoff—a fury unmatched by anyone over the age of ten. How dare he laugh at her? The stupid man was much older than she and didn't know a word of French. She imagined that Manon must feel the same when people smiled at her lilting pronunciation that Rose found more beautiful than the most cultured Parisian accent. Rose hoped the girl wouldn't lose it entirely. But she knew that speaking as the settlers did was in Manon's best interest.

"Where is Eng-land?" Manon asked.

Rose took advantage of the distraction to give Manon a break from the text. She opened the Sisters' atlas, so old it contained no reference to the land on which they stood, and she turned to the outdated world map.

"Here is France, where I'm from. I was born in Paris, just here." Rose pointed to the large, scripted words that dominated the center of the country. "London is there."

"That isn't far," Manon said, measuring the distance with her fingers. "Only this far away."

Rose stifled her chuckle at some cost, covering her efforts with a cough. "It's actually quite a distance, dear. The real distance wouldn't fit on the page. That's why we have maps, so we have at least some idea of where countries are in relation to one another."

"That is smart," Manon said, studying the map. "My people don't have maps. This way is better." If Rose had been a less observant woman, the dark cloud that passed over Manon's face would have gone unnoticed.

"Did someone you know get lost?" Rose asked.

"My papa," Manon said, not taking her eyes from the atlas. "He was hunting. He never came home."

"I'm so sorry, my darling," Rose said, her voice hushed. Losing her father at an older age than Manon's had been an impossible lot to bear. This small girl had lost all the people who had cared most in less than a year. Manon's attachment to Nicole made all the more sense to Rose.

"This is Rouen," Rose said, indicating the large town in the northwest. "Nicole was born on a farm just outside of it."

"It must be a lovely place," Manon said.

Rose had visited Rouen three or four times in her youth, but the town had made little impression after a childhood bathed in the splendors of Paris. "Why do you say so, my dear?"

"Because she's a lovely person. She must come from a lovely place." Manon's sweet, girlish logic brought stinging tears to the corners of Rose's eyes.

"Quite right," Rose said, clearing her throat. "Let's take a break and do some needlework, shall we?"

"Very well," Manon said, sighing as she closed her book. As challenging as the book work was for Manon, it held her interest much more than domestic tasks.

Rose pulled Manon's small sampler from the basket and gave her directions on how to proceed with the design. Forming the letters stitch by stitch, Rose reasoned, would help etch them into Manon's memory.

"And how are the studies coming, my dear?" Sister Mathilde asked, taking a seat near the student and pupil.

"Brilliantly," Rose answered, smiling at Manon.

The Sister flipped through the texts and asked Manon the occasional question, observed her progress in the needlework, and looked over the samples of her attempts at handwriting. "Manon, dear. Why don't you go ask Sister Anne for something to eat? You've been working very hard. Tell her I sent you."

With no further prompting, Manon dashed in the direction of the convent kitchen.

"My dear Mademoiselle Barré, you have made tremendous progress with our young pupil. I had not thought your education plan to be as ambitious as it seems to be. In just a few weeks she has more ability than many in the colony. At least in terms of reading and writing."

"And you shall have my skills at your disposal, Sister," Rose said. "You told me I had to wait six months before you would speak to Mother Marie. It's been that and more. I'm still determined to take orders."

"And what of young Lefebvre?" Sister Mathilde asked. "I thought the two of you were becoming friendly. Whatever happened?"

"He has gone to the Antilles, Sister," Rose said. "And has no plans to return, according to his uncle."

"That is a shame, my dear." Sister Mathilde arranged Manon's papers in a neat pile, unable to let her hands rest idle. "But since you found one agreeable young man, I am sure you can find another."

"No, Sister," Rose said. "If you will not speak to the Reverend Mother for me, I will do it myself."

"Very well, child." Sister Mathilde folded her hands and looked into Rose's eyes. "I have business with her tomorrow and will speak to her then. I hope you are prepared for this life. There are many sacrifices you will be called to make."

"I know, Sister, but I have only one way to find out."

Two days later, Rose waited in the dark corridor outside Reverend Mother Marie de l'Incarnation's small office. Rose jiggled her foot to no beat or rhythm, unable to shake the feeling that she was a petulant child awaiting punishment from the headmistress. Memories of her meeting with Sister Charité swam through her brain. If anything, the cold iron in the pit of her stomach weighed even heavier this time.

Sister Mathilde opened the door and motioned for Rose to enter, then left the young woman alone with the head of the Ursuline order.

Wordlessly, Mother Marie motioned to a severe-looking chair that seemed created to keep visits brief. Mother Marie was somewhat of a legend. Rose heard the Sisters speak of her in whispered tones. She was the founder of the Ursuline order. A true pioneer. Rose could imagine what the settlement was like when Mother Marie first arrived. It must seem as bustling as Paris to her now.

Mother Marie was a slip of a woman with a face lined with the experience of a founding mother of a country. No shaded cloisters and grand cathedrals for many years. Though she was slight, Rose could see why Mother Marie inspired such reverence in her Ursulines. The serenity of her spirit, her presence, was enough to startle Rose into silence. She took her rosary from her apron pocket for comfort. It was a plain wooden affair, nothing like the elegant creations in silver, gold, and precious stones that her aunt Martine carried to Mass. Rose rubbed the smooth beads with her thumb and forefinger, focusing on the texture to calm her breathing.

"So, you wish to join our order." Mother Marie's voice was strong for a woman approaching seventy years of age. Her face was lined with experiences, sorrowful and joyful, but there seemed a peace about her that Rose envied.

"Yes, Reverend Mother," Rose said, looking down at her folded hands as she spoke.

"Sister Mathilde spoke very highly of you." With her smallest finger, Mother Marie traced a pattern, unseen to Rose, on the small wooden desk that separated the women. "She says you read Latin?"

"Yes, Reverend Mother," Rose said. "And Greek. And French, of course."

"Most unusual." Mother Marie assessed the young woman before her. "She says you have been quite successful with the education of one of the young native girls as well. Already learning their language. You would be an asset to us, but you were sent here to marry. We need wives in this colony even more than we need teachers to spread the word of God."

"Yes, Reverend Mother," Rose said. "But I cannot marry."

"I am sure you could find a young man in this colony to tempt you," said Mother Marie, echoing Sister Mathilde's words. "There are plenty to be had."

"Let me speak plainer, Reverend Mother," Rose said. "I will not marry."

"Marriage is a duty placed upon you by the King himself, a duty you accepted voluntarily, I would remind you." Mother Marie's eyes fixed on Rose, perhaps noticing a troublesome speck of defiance in the young woman's character. "This order has no need of those who are derelict in their duty."

"By no means, Reverend Mother," Rose said. "But I see that my duty has changed. I wish to serve my country and my king by teaching the new wives and girls rather than taking a husband of my own. I take those responsibilities to heart, I assure you, Reverend Mother."

Rose kept the calm in her voice, but did not avert her eyes as she longed to do.

"That's better," said Mother Marie. "And something I can well understand. The postulate period is one year. During that time you will live with the Sisters, pray, and study. After that, Sister Mathilde will report to me if she feels you are ready to enter the novitiate."

"Very well, Reverend Mother," Rose said.

"Sister Mathilde also says you wish to teach the native girls, and have been working with Sister Hortense as a sort of assistant. I agree this is an excellent use of your talents, and I wish you to continue learning their language. I want it to be the main concentration of your studies, even beyond Church doctrine," Mother Marie said. "It will serve you even better in your teaching, for we will rarely venture beyond the basic catechism with these young ladies. I trust you know your catechism well enough."

Rose nodded; she couldn't have spent three years in the Salpêtrière without knowing it as well as her own name.

"Excellent. I am pleased to have your skills at our disposal, my dear. You may go now and get to work."

"Yes, Reverend Mother." Rose offered a small curtsy as she stood. "And thank you."

"A pleasure, my daughter," Mother Marie said. "May God bless you on your path."

The first thing Rose learned as a teacher with an entire class of her own was that despite the bite in the October air, the Huron girls had far more success sitting and listening while outdoors for their lesson. The walls of the convent confined them, made them restless. Rose kept things very simple for their first session. She taught them two prayers, and explained their meaning in halting Wendat. Manon supplied her with a missing word, causing one girl with a long face and rather pointy nose to hurl an insult for which Rose needed no translation.

"Young lady, you will not speak in that way to a member of this class. Nor should you speak to anyone in such a manner." Rose's Wendat, though imperfect, was able to convey her message without any confusion. The offending child turned stone-faced for the remainder of the lesson, refusing to participate or respond for the entire hour.

Wonderful. Another Huron child who'll have no love for the French. Exactly what the Sisters asked me to do.

Rose didn't display her frustration to the children, but dismissed them with a forced smile and a genuine wish to see them back the next week. She did not anticipate Manon's detractor would be among them.

"Very well done, my dear," Sister Mathilde said, joining Rose in the courtyard as she collected her texts.

"Oh, I don't think it was any great success, Sister," Rose said.

"On the contrary, the girls seemed very attentive." Sister Mathilde opened the door for Rose, and pointed the way to the small room that served as her office.

"I fear the one girl—the one with the pointy nose—won't be back," Rose said, taking a seat opposite the Sister's plain pine desk.

"Don't you worry," Sister Mathilde said. "Our young Sarah, as we call her, will be back. Her mother is happy for the reprieve."

Rose didn't quite succeed in stifling her laugh. "I can imagine so. I didn't know we had given them French names."

"They would have been only too happy to tell you, if you had asked," Sister Mathilde said, leaning against the back of her rigid chair. "Allow me to offer you a piece of advice: Never hesitate to ask a question of your pupils. They will think more of you for taking an interest in them."

Rose felt herself shrink into the chair. Such a careless mistake.

"Don't fret on it. I imagine the girls could easily see your eagerness to begin the lesson. That has its virtues as well. But perhaps next week, spend a quarter of an hour getting to learn a bit more about the girls. Every scrap of information they share is a key to their minds and their hearts."

"Of course, Sister. They seem like sweet girls."

"They are," Sister Mathilde agreed. "Some of them remarkably so, especially our little Manon. She reminds me so much of my own daughter."

Rose stared openly at her superior, her mouth agape.

"I see I've stunned you." There was a glimmer of mischief in the old woman's eyes as she delighted in Rose's flabbergasted silence. "Remember, though we sisters are forbidden from marrying or having children once we've taken orders, there is nothing to prevent a widow from taking the veil."

"So your husband died?" Rose wished to retract the obvious question as soon as it left her lips.

"Yes. Our parents arranged our marriage when we were just eighteen. His father was a merchant, my father an even more successful one. I was a wife for two years before a fever claimed him. Just long enough for him to give me my little Rachel."

"And where is she now?" Rose imagined the girl must be grown by now. The thought of Sister Mathilde as a grandmother seemed somehow aberrant.

"For four years she was the light of my life, but she was never a healthy child. A simple cold claimed her from me, despite my efforts to keep her well. For many years I had a very hard time accepting that it was God's will. I confess it's still a point of contention between us." Though Sister Mathilde addressed Rose, her eyes glossed over as though looking back on her own past.

"So you entered the convent to escape your grief?" Rose asked.

"You think kindly of me. No. I entered to escape another arranged marriage. I also confess I was not fond of the first attempt. I pleaded with my father to let me take orders, and in the end, I had enough sisters for him to marry off that I was of little consequence."

Rose laced her fingers, not knowing how to respond to the information.

"But I must tell you, I have found great happiness in my order. Great satisfaction in teaching, prayer, and most of all bringing a measure of comfort to the women of this colony."

"I'm sure of that, Sister," Rose said. "There isn't a woman in our settlement who isn't grateful for your presence."

"Make no mistake, my girl. For as much as I have come to love my order, I would trade it all for one more day with my own daughter." Sister Mathilde's voice wavered almost imperceptibly. "Now hurry along and prepare your lesson for next week. And remember what I've told you."

Rose climbed the stairs, her thoughts churning. Sister Mathilde as a wife and mother did not register with the stately woman of God that she knew. The image of a young Mathilde with a baby at her breast seemed an unholy juxtaposition to the life she led now. But she'd survived marriage. She'd survived childbirth. She had carved a new life for herself out of the wreckage of the first, and seemed content with her choices.

Perhaps I could be as strong as the good Sister and accept the life I agreed to. But perhaps I'll be better off on this new path. . . .

Rose pushed the doubt from the pit of her stomach and settled into her task. Right or wrong, she knew that every path led to the same ultimate destination.

Chapter 15

Elisabeth

October 1668

Since Adèle had been born, the hardest part of the day was the lull between the lunch and dinner rush. Months ago, it was a welcome respite, now it was an abyss of awkward silence. Elisabeth avoided it by escaping to the convent or scrubbing every surface in the bakery or the home above stairs until they were inhospitably clean. She'd opted for the latter that day, and was pleased when she realized the hour demanded that she attend to her customers. Elisabeth hurried down to the shop to help Gilbert. He acknowledged her arrival with a nod and they busied themselves with customers for several hours. Welcoming smiles were offered, pleasantries exchanged. Elisabeth wondered if the customers noticed her insincerity, and Gilbert's, too. For the sake of the business, she hoped not.

"Supper?" Elisabeth asked when the last customer exited the shop.

"Please," Gilbert said. "Call me when it's ready. I'll be seeing to things down here."

"That's fine," Elisabeth said.

It's not fine! Elisabeth wanted to shout. *But I suppose it will have to be for now.*

She thanked the heavens that at least one good loaf of bread remained from the dinner rush so she didn't have to bake another. She loved baking, but it was the last thing she wanted to do when the shop closed these days. She made a good soup with freshly harvested vegetables and hearty chunks of salted pork. The odor in the kitchen was more than pleasant, the room scrubbed clean, and she even took a few minutes to straighten her hair and clothes.

An hour later, Gilbert ascended the stairs and took his place at the table.

"Thank you," he said as she placed his supper before him.

"Of course," Elisabeth said, patting his shoulder.

It was the only exchange of words during the meal.

Normally, Gilbert drank half a glass of wine with his evening meal, but lately he had taken to drinking two or more.

I'm so sorry I failed you, Elisabeth longed to tell him. *I'm so sorry you're stuck with a wife who can't give you a family.*

She managed to keep her tears at bay through dinner, but retreated to the bedroom once the dishes were cleared and cleaned. She muttered an excuse and disappeared into the room her husband had not slept in since Adèle's birth.

Elisabeth sat against the pillows and felt the tears roll down her cheeks. She ached for her lost baby. She cursed her battered body for taking too long to heal.

Worst of all, it seemed she was losing her husband as well, a little more each day.

Below, she heard Gilbert's footsteps on the wooden stairs and the crack of the front door as it shut. Perhaps he was going to use the outhouse. Perhaps he was going to the tavern. She didn't leave her bed to look.

Gilbert would not leave her. He had too much honor for that, was too devout in his faith, but Elisabeth wondered how long it would be before he sought comfort elsewhere.

She found solace only in her tears until she drifted to sleep and awoke to repeat the same scenes in the morning. Elisabeth stood in silence next to her husband, shaping the loaves of bread for baking before the breakfast rush. The sun had yet to rise, and Elisabeth felt fatigue to the marrow of her bones. Still, she pressed on.

"I can finish up here if you like," Gilbert offered. "You could get a little rest before we open."

"I'm fine," Elisabeth said, her voice barely audible.

"You look exhausted. I don't mind," Gilbert said.

"I'm fine," Elisabeth repeated, with more vigor than she intended. She reprised in a softer tone, "I'm fine."

"As you say," Gilbert said. "I'm going to the stockroom."

"All right. I'll be here if you need me." The stock had been inventoried two days before, but she was not going to argue with him.

The bread needed to sit for three-quarters of an hour before it baked, but Elisabeth could not bring herself to follow her husband's advice and rest. Idle hands led to an idle mind, and dark thoughts were not far behind.

Elisabeth scrubbed the counters and tidied up every surface in the shop. She was becoming used to moving without the added bulk of a baby, or to her breasts that had only just ceased to ache with untouched milk. The fatigue, however, still gripped her like a cruel iron vise. The discomfort when she disturbed the muscles pulled and torn in her thirty hours of labor lessened, but that was almost as unendurable as the ache. As the pain subsided, it felt as though little Adèle slipped farther and farther from this world. For two brief days, baby Adèle was the most beloved child in the colony. Her delicate features were perfect, and she spent her entire existence in the loving embrace of her mother.

Two months' time had not been enough to ease the pain of the mother who still replayed her daughter's final breaths in her mind every time she closed her eyes.

The dough risen, the fire mellowed and ready for baking, Elisabeth placed two dozen loaves in the vast brick oven. For an hour she coaxed the fire to a constant heat and rotated the loaves every fifteen minutes. The work was just engaging enough to occupy her hands and mind and offer her a small measure of peace.

A few moments before six o'clock in the morning, Gilbert emerged from the stockroom and took his place at the counter. Elisabeth unlatched the door and welcomed the first customers with a shallow smile. For three hours they sold bread and pastries at a steady pace. The reputation of Monsieur and Madame Beaumont's bakery had spread throughout the settlement. The business was an unqualified success.

"You ought to rest," Gilbert said when the breakfast rush had slowed to a trickle.

Elisabeth knew he was right, though she refused to indulge in the decadence of a midday nap.

"Would you mind if I went to the convent to see Nicole?" Elisabeth asked. She offered a small smile. "I promise I'll put my feet up."

"Go," Gilbert said, not returning the smile. "Don't worry about the dinner rush. I'll manage."

He turned and went back to the storeroom, Elisabeth presumed, to fetch flour for the afternoon stock.

I miss you, Elisabeth thought. *Come back to me soon.*

She placed a few leftover pastries in her basket and shoved down her guilt at leaving Gilbert to prepare for the evening rush by himself.

But it seemed clear that he preferred her to leave.

The walk to the convent was just long enough without becoming taxing. As a former resident, Elisabeth did not need to announce herself but found her way to the common room where Nicole sat knitting and Manon played by the fire.

"Eat." Elisabeth placed a pastry on a plate and handed it to Nicole with a look of mock severity.

"If you join me," Nicole said, returning the glare and placing an empty plate in front of her. Manon scuttled over to claim her pastry to enjoy in front of the crackling fire before the ladies could claim them all.

"Very well," Elisabeth said, remembering to prop up her feet as promised. "How are you getting along?"

"I'm managing," Nicole said. "And you?"

"About the same," Elisabeth said. "Bone weary most of the time. It's maddening."

"I understand how you feel," Nicole said. "This little one learned how to kick and has been keeping me up."

Elisabeth smiled for Nicole, but it did not reach her eyes.

"Oh, Elisabeth, I'm sorry," Nicole said. "That was stupid of me."

"Don't be silly," Elisabeth said. "I can be glad for you and sad for me at the same time. You're clinging to the good things right now, as you ought to."

"Thank you," Nicole said, relieved. "How is Gilbert?"

"He's quiet," Elisabeth answered after a moment's hesitation. She didn't feel right burdening Nicole with the truth.

"He'll come around," Nicole said. "He's grieving, too. He just needs time."

"I hope so, Nicole," Elisabeth said. "I really do. It's been two months and nothing has changed. If anything he's quieter and more distant than before."

The pair sat in silence for several minutes, watching Manon play with her growing collection of dolls. Clearly, the Sisters did not object to the novelty of a child in residence.

Rose appeared in the common room door, winded and looking as if she'd had a hectic morning.

"Pastry and milk?" Nicole offered.

"Please," Rose said, taking a seat. "Sister Hortense and I went to speak to the Huron people about Manon again."

"And?" Nicole sat upright, stealing a glance at the dark-haired waif on the floor.

"It's as we thought. Her grandmother was indeed very ill and passed away several days ago," Rose said. "The grandmother wasn't able to speak coherently for a long while, it seems. The tribe simply lost track of Manon. One family thought she was with another and so on. It happens. The chief seemed embarrassed."

"That explains why Manon was alone so much," Nicole said. "The old woman simply couldn't look after her."

"Right," Rose said. "And the grandmother was the last of Manon's family. The tribe didn't realize the girl was wandering so much. Apparently, she loved to spy on you, Nicole. She thought you were an angel."

"It's a miracle nothing happened to her," Elisabeth said, imagining Adèle at eight years old, alone in the woods. "Poor girl."

"She's clever," Rose said. "And a quick study. I've asked the tribe to let us keep her, at least for a while, to give her some schooling with the other girls."

"And what did they say?" Nicole asked.

"No, at first," Rose said. "They don't like the idea of adopting out one of their own. And most of the girls we teach are a few years older than Manon and not quite as impressionable. But since Manon is alone in the tribe, we convinced them it was in her best interest. If she were a boy, there would have been no persuading them. As it was, they worried that she wouldn't be happy without a family, though."

"She'll be with me," Nicole vowed. "After what she did for me, I can do that much for her. Luc would have died alone if not for her."

"I told them that," Rose said. "Sending her back to the tribe would be cruel to both of you. I think they're more apt to let her stay because of what happened to Luc."

"Thank you," Nicole said with brimming eyes.

Rose called Manon over and explained that she was welcome to stay with them if she wished. The child flung herself into Nicole's lap, sobbing and smiling all at once.

"There, there, sweet baby," Nicole said. "You're going to be fine."

Elisabeth looked at her friend and the lovely raven-haired girl in her arms and smiled, pleased that she was almost successful in stifling her pang of jealousy.

"Thank you very much, Nicole," Manon said distinctly. Though her vocabulary was growing at an impressive rate, she still concentrated on every syllable she uttered; hunting for the right words as a hunter stalks his prey.

Rose and the Sisters saw to most of Manon's education during her stay thus far, but Nicole directed the girl's French conversation. Elisabeth sensed the classes served as a diversion for Nicole, just as the bakery was a diversion for her.

"Don't thank me, dear heart. I'm glad to know I can keep you for a while longer."

"I want to stay always," Manon said, smiling at her foster mother.

"That makes me so happy, sweet girl." Nicole embraced Manon again. "Why don't you go supervise dinner? Sister Éléonore will miss you if you don't."

"What a good student," Elisabeth remarked as the Huron girl left the room.

"She is," Nicole agreed, with pride in her voice. "I think the Sisters intend her for the Church."

"And what do you want for her?" Elisabeth asked.

"Whatever will make her happy," Nicole said. "I have a hard time imagining her enjoying a cloistered life, but she is still a child."

"You're a born mother," Elisabeth said. "And a good one."

"Thank you," Nicole said. "It's easy to love her, though."

"That it is." A rare, genuine smile crossed Elisabeth's lips.

"Your turn will come," Nicole said, fumbling with the words. No one knew what to say to her. Condolences were maudlin and encouragement was patronizing. Elisabeth could not fault those who remained silent in her presence.

Elisabeth turned her attention to her teacup. "I'm not sure it will," she said, the china shaking in her hands. She'd avoided speaking in any depth on the subject, and saying the words aloud made it seem too real. "It's hard to make a baby when there isn't a husband around."

"What do you mean?" Nicole asked. "I saw Gilbert yesterday."

"In body," Elisabeth said. "We hardly speak. He finds any excuse to leave the room when we're alone."

"Oh, Elisabeth," Nicole said. "I'm so sorry."

"He's been gone every night for the past three weeks," Elisabeth said, the confession pouring from her. "I have no idea where he goes, but he's been drinking. I can smell it, and he looks like death in the mornings. I have to wake him now. He used to be up half an hour before we had to start baking, eager to start the day. But now . . ."

Nicole took Elisabeth in her arms and gave her silent permission to cry.

"I can't bear to lose him, too," Elisabeth said. "I know I've failed, but I don't want to be without him."

"How I wish I'd known," Nicole said. "I wish I could have been at your side. You didn't fail him, or anyone else. Adèle didn't live. She wasn't healthy, and for reasons we aren't meant to understand, she was taken from us. It wasn't your fault."

Elisabeth loved that Nicole used Adèle's name. To others she had just been "the baby." Use of the name acknowledged that Adèle had been a real person.

"But why is he so cold to me?" Elisabeth asked, pulling her shawl tighter, as though fending off her husband's frosty demeanor.

"If he feels cold toward you, he's a fool," Nicole said. "And I don't think he does, or is. You didn't fail him any more than Luc failed me. You want to blame someone, Elisabeth, because you think that will make this easier, but it won't. Sometimes tragedy is blameless. You have to accept it."

"I just wish I knew what to do," Elisabeth said.

"I can't choose your path," Nicole said, "but I'm sure you'll figure it out. You're a good wife, and Gilbert loves you. You will figure things out together."

"Would you like anything else?" Elisabeth asked toward the end of supper.

Gilbert's eyes snapped up from his plate, surprised by her attempt at communication. "No, I'm fine. Thank you."

"Gilbert, do you want to talk?" Elisabeth felt as blunt as a meat-ax but forged on anyway. "You've been so quiet. I know I have been, too."

Gilbert stood and placed his dish in the washbasin. "It's fine. I'll be downstairs." He bounded down to the shop. A few moments later she heard the door close as Gilbert exited onto the street below.

Rather than slink back into the bedroom for her evening cry, Elisabeth went to the window and tried to see where her husband was going. He turned right and continued on toward the main streets before Elisabeth lost him from her sight.

There were taverns in that direction and all manner of trouble. Whether he simply lost his sorrow in drink, or indulged in other vices, she knew not, but tonight would be the last night he ventured out without consequence.

I'm not letting you go so easily, Gilbert Beaumont, Elisabeth said to herself. *Tomorrow you will talk whether you like it or not.*

Elisabeth prepared to stand vigil on the lounge chair where Gilbert had taken to sleeping, but around midnight, she gave way to her fatigue. Sometime later, a persistent thudding at the door below roused her from her shallow sleep.

Bailiff Duval stood at the door, stern faced and annoyed at the call to duty at such a late hour. Gilbert stood beside him, unable to stand without aid.

"I believe this man is yours, Madame Beaumont," Duval said in a humorless tone.

"Indeed." Elisabeth took Gilbert's arm, no more amused than the disgruntled bailiff.

"I would suggest paying closer attention to your husband's comings and goings, madame," Duval said. "He's been drinking himself into a stupor at Simonet's every night for almost a month. Old Gustave Simonet had enough of him and called for me."

Elisabeth was not shocked that he, or anyone else, blamed her for Gilbert's misdeeds.

"Trust me," Elisabeth said. "I'll be having words with him very soon. Quite a few, in fact."

Duval looked satisfied, seeing what amounted to wrath in Elisabeth's blue eyes. He left the inebriated man in his wife's care. His smile told Elisabeth that he did not envy the morning in store for Gilbert Beaumont.

Elisabeth took no special care to keep quiet as she prepared breakfast. Although it was only four in the morning, Gilbert Beaumont was going to be on his feet and making bread whether he was ill from overindulgence or not.

She stifled a laugh as Gilbert stumbled into the kitchen, eyes bleary.

"Morning," he mumbled, as much to himself as to his wife.

"Good morning," Elisabeth replied with exaggerated good humor—and volume to match. "Have some breakfast."

The sight and smell of eggs, bacon, bread, jam, and frothy, cold milk was usually the highlight of Gilbert's morning. Today it turned him green.

"I can't," he said, pushing the plate away.

"You can, and you will," Elisabeth said, her voice brimming with rage. "And then you're going to get your arse downstairs and bake. And when the morning rush is over, you're going to come up here and we're going to talk about your behavior last night and every night for the past three weeks."

Gilbert stared at Elisabeth. His placid, sweet-natured wife was gone. He ate in silence, and Elisabeth imagined it took all he had to keep the food from resurfacing.

In the bakery they worked in tandem, no motion wasted, compensating for the late start and their fatigue. By the time customers arrived, both Beaumonts were shining with a layer of sweat, but prepared for the morning onslaught. Elisabeth sagged with relief when the last customer took her bread and left the shop quiet.

"Upstairs," she said, the angry wife replacing the respectable Madame Beaumont.

The couple ascended the stairs. Gilbert took his favorite chair and awaited a raking-down they both knew he deserved. Elisabeth remained standing, hands on hips like a schoolmistress calling out a wayward student for his shenanigans.

"Get on with it," he said, with no animosity in his voice.

"We're not up here for me to scream at you," Elisabeth said. "As tempting as that might be, it would solve nothing."

"Then why are we here?" asked Gilbert.

"I want to know what in Christendom is wrong with you," Elisabeth said, taking a seat across from her husband. "You won't speak more than two words to me. You leave the room at every opportunity. Now you're running out to the tavern every night, doing God knows what with God knows whom. I'm sorry that Adèle died. You have no idea how sorry. I'd give my life to change it, but you have to forgive me and move on."

"Forgive you?" Gilbert asked.

"The way you've been acting?" Elisabeth's voice wavered. "I know you blame me for what happened, but there was nothing I could do to prevent it."

Gilbert shook his head. "You've been thinking that I blame *you* for our daughter's death?"

"You don't?" Elisabeth's eyes searched her husband's for some insight into what he was thinking.

"My God, I'm sorry," he whispered. "I blame myself. You worked so hard while you were expecting. I let you do it. If I'd worked harder, made you rest, everything . . . would have been different."

Elisabeth took Gilbert's hands in hers. "No, my love," Elisabeth said. "I doubt there is a single thing we could have done to change things. Don't blame yourself. This was no more your fault than mine. Neither of us is to blame."

Gilbert took her in his arms.

"Why have you been running away from me?" Elisabeth asked. "We must have the most accurate inventory for any stockroom in the whole settlement."

Gilbert gave a weak chuckle, pulled her to his chest, and buried his face in her neck.

"I just sit in there," he said, eyes brimming over with tears. "I didn't want you to see me cry. You had enough to shoulder."

"We can help each other," Elisabeth said. "We don't have to do this alone."

"I was worried I was going to lose you," Gilbert said, giving into his tears. "For weeks you seemed so pale and weak, heartbroken. I thought you were slipping away. It scared me so much."

"I'm here," Elisabeth said. "And I am feeling better. Not myself yet, but better—and much better now."

"Promise me you'll rest?" Gilbert asked. "You must."

"Of course," Elisabeth said. "If it will ease your mind."

Gilbert stroked her hair. "I love you."

"I love you, too," she murmured, kissing his cheek. "So very much. And you're done with the tavern? I don't want to know what else . . ."

"Just drinking. It was just trying to forget, if only for a few hours," Gilbert said. "Never again. I'm sorry I made you worry."

Elisabeth continued pelting his cheeks and brow with downy-soft kisses, making up for weeks of missed affection. Gilbert stood, took Elisabeth in his arms, and carried her back to their bedroom. For an hour they lay together, talking, caressing, and mourning for their loss.

When duty beckoned in the shop below, Elisabeth dried his tears and her own with her sleeve and kissed his salty cheek before they left the room.

"I'm so glad to have you back," she said. The weight lifted from her shoulders and she mustered a real smile for her husband. She did not mar their happiness with her worry that the little wooden cradle in the corner would remain forever empty.

Chapter 16

Nicole

April 1669

Please sleep, angel. Nicole walked the dark corridor with baby Hélène, hoping the overtired infant would soon succumb to sleep. Nicole longed to stretch her legs in the weak spring sunshine and do her marketing, but until Hélène was asleep and entrusted to Sister Anne, she was captive. Afternoons were the most challenging time, but based on the stories she heard from other mothers, Hélène was a dream of a baby. Though Nicole thought to herself that if half the stories were true, half of the mothers in the settlement would have never borne a second child. Nicole kissed the satin skin of the baby's brow and smiled down at the lids that were losing their hard-fought battle to remain open. Hélène looked so much like her father that Nicole very often felt a pang of loss when seeing Luc's sweet blue eyes and mop of golden-brown curls on their daughter.

It was Thursday afternoon and the gentlemen had already come to call on the newest group of eligible brides. Girlish giggles escaped from the common room, recalling to Nicole's mind the youthful exuberance her own contingent had shared. *Can it only be two years since I arrived?* Nicole thought as she paced. *It seems like just a few weeks, but I feel as though I've aged three lifetimes.* The dark circles under her eyes testified to the truth of her musing.

Hélène was at last deep enough in sleep to be placed in her cradle with the doting Sister Anne. Knowing her free time was limited, Nicole grabbed her shawl and marketing basket and raced to the front door, not glancing into the common room where the ladies entertained the eager young men of the settlement.

Most days, Nicole was happy looking after Hélène and Manon and helping in various ways at the convent. Other days, she wished to run into the lush forests and never see civilization again. "You're just tired," Rose would say. "All new mothers feel this way." Though Nicole sometimes longed to throw it back in Rose's face that she had done nothing to earn her superior tone, she refrained. It seemed everyone, experienced with babies or not, had advice to offer, ranging from the sage and logical to the inane, stupid—even cruel and dangerous.

Pork, eggs, butter, cheese . . . Nicole did not trust her foggy brain to retain something even as simple as a shopping list. She repeated it to herself over and over, or else preparing dinner might be more challenging than it already was if Hélène was out of sorts.

The salty tang of blood and freshly butchered flesh was a permanent fixture of the Rousseau butcher shop. Nicole refrained from wrinkling her nose against the pervasive stink, as Madame Rousseau, a wiry woman with erratic wisps of hair the color of dishwater that refused to be tamed into a respectable chignon, was quick to take offense. All the same, Nicole hoped she would not need to wait a quarter of an hour in the airless room as the humorless woman tracked down from the back rooms the cuts of meat that Sister Mathilde required.

"You're looking well, Madame Jarvais," Madame Rousseau observed after Nicole gave her order. "No little one today?"

"I've left her with Sister Anne." Nicole rubbed her nose for a moment as if preparing to sneeze, in reality shielding her nose from the stench for a brief moment. *Stop gabbing so I can leave!* "It makes running errands so much faster."

"I can imagine." Madame Rousseau's deft fingers wrapped the thick chunks of pork, fit only for stewing, in brown paper. She handed off the parcel to Nicole, who placed the coins in the slight woman's outstretched hand. "It must be so nice to have the Sisters' help. Some of us had to watch our children ourselves."

Nicole blinked at the veiled insult, willing her tongue to remain civil. Sister Mathilde had warned about the importance of making—and keeping—friends. She took her parcel, stowed it in her basket, and turned from the store. Even plastered on an insincere smile for the hateful woman.

My God, it's unfair. I pay for my room. I work for the Sisters. I have the money from the homestead to pay my way—for now. Nicole knew the money wouldn't last long. Their homestead was not large and their home on it was a glorified shack, so the price she fetched was not exemplary. She had calculated she could live in comfort for eighteen more months if the Sisters would keep her. It wasn't an eternity, but it was enough time to make some sort of plan. She thought about her future in the moments before lying down and drifting to sleep. It cost her more sleep than it solved problems most nights.

Though most days she took the time to enjoy her stroll away from the convent and the demands of parenting, she now found no joy in the weekly excursion that was her only reprieve. At every shop she imagined judging glances and disapprobation from everyone she encountered, though no one repeated Madame Rousseau's odious jibes. She offered cold greetings and forced smiles for the shopkeepers, but avoided conversation. As was her usual custom, she saved her trek to Elisabeth's bakery for her last stop.

"Good afternoon," Gilbert greeted her. "The usual order for the good Sisters?"

"And spruce beer and pastry for us?" Elisabeth chimed in, entering the front room from the kitchen.

"Yes and no," Nicole replied, endeavoring to keep her expression neutral. "Just the things for the convent, please. I need to be getting back to Hélène."

"Is she well?" Elisabeth asked, her voice constricting in concern.

"Perfectly fine," Nicole said. "I just can't expect the Sisters to do my work for me."

Gilbert said nothing, but went off to the back kitchens as though looking for something of vital importance. *Perceptive,* thought Nicole.

"What's wrong?" Elisabeth pressed as she loaded two loaves into Nicole's basket. "You know the Sisters dote on that child."

"Nothing . . . just . . . nothing."

Elisabeth opened her mouth, but closed it once more. She took Nicole's hand from across the counter. "When you're ready to talk, come see me."

Nicole squeezed her friend's hand in turn, appreciating her lack of tenacity. She accepted her purchases and left for the convent. Despite what she'd told Elisabeth, she walked slowly back to the convent, Madame Rousseau's words tumbling over and over in her head. She entered the convent to find Hélène still curled in her cradle under Sister Anne's loving gaze and Manon sitting with Rose in the common room working on her lessons. *Such a burden on the Sisters, aren't they?*

Rather than pass the basket of food to Sister Éléonore, who ran the kitchen, Nicole waved her away and began preparations herself. The nun squinted her eyes at Nicole and left in a spin of movement that made her look like a cyclone—a very squat cyclone—who left order and repair in her wake instead of chaos. *Someone else I've offended,* Nicole scolded herself as she laid out the ingredients for that night's meal. *At least that time I deserved it.*

The mindless repetition of peeling and cutting the vegetables for the stew helped ease the tension from her shoulders. She focused on breathing in time with each deft motion of the knife and nothing else.

"Anxious to help in the kitchen this evening?" Nicole looked up to see Sister Mathilde at the kitchen door, but did not stop the methodic chopping.

"I always attempt to be useful, Sister."

"Of course you do, but you needn't dismiss Sister Éléonore from her own kitchen."

"I'm sorry," Nicole said, wiping her brow with the back of her hand and taking a pause from her attack on the produce.

"Then you must tell me what is bothering you. Though you are not of my order or my charge, I do feel responsible for your well-being all the same."

"It's ridiculous, Sister. A woman in town just implied that I was perhaps taking advantage of your generosity. It hurt my feelings, but they'll mend as feelings often do."

"Rubbish. Who said such a thing?"

"Madame Rousseau," Nicole admitted, taking the knife back in hand to the mound of potatoes before her as she divulged the full contents of the insult.

Sister Mathilde threw her head back in a full-throated laugh, uncharacteristic of the decorous woman. "How absolutely typical. She abuses you, but pawned her son off on the neighbor woman whenever she could. Not that I blame her. I've never known a baby who cried as long and loud as he did. Thank God little Jérôme grew out of it and into a strong young boy. Pay her no attention."

"But it does raise a valid question, Sister."

"How novel for the Rousseau woman to be of use. What question is that?"

"What shall I do with myself?" Nicole rubbed her eyes against the omnipresent fatigue. "I cannot stay here forever."

"No you can't," Sister Mathilde agreed, pulling a stool closer to Nicole and sitting at the scarred wooden table where Nicole worked. "As much as we love having you here. You need to find your place in the colony."

"I've thought about what I could do, Sister," Nicole said, exhaling deeply and rubbing her eyes. "I don't know if the Beaumonts need my help, but if they don't I'm sure there is someone in town who needs help. I'm capable."

"I know that, my dear, but our good King Louis did not send you here to bake."

Nicole allowed her meaning to sink in and had to swallow against the bile in her throat. "Luc has only been gone six months. . . ."

"I know, my dear. But think of this . . . women are few and precious here. You're a healthy woman, a hard worker, and a good mother. Many will see you here and think you are wasting your gifts and your childbearing years with us."

"Heavens above, I just had a baby three months ago. . . ."

"Maryse Rousseau is a bitter woman. Her comments came several months earlier than I expected . . . but I did expect them. If you were to accept suitors again, you'd have dozens of men coming to pay you court."

"Sister, I can't—"

"It seems impossible, I expect, but if you come down to the common room of a Thursday afternoon from time to time and make conversation, I think you'd find it easier than you think. It's unfair, I know, but life here seldom leaves us the luxury of working through our grief before moving on."

The tray, laden with beverages and cakes, shook as she placed it on the common room table. A few eyebrows arched as Nicole took a seat and joined the ladies as they welcomed the throng of suitors without the protective shield of Hélène, who was swaddled and sleeping with Sister Anne. *Please let me endure this without ridicule.* It was the highest aspiration she had for the afternoon.

For the first twenty minutes, Nicole thought she might be safe. Only six young men came to visit, each already paired off with a lady he had visited before. All the couples were engaged or days away from it. They would soon be gone, and the second new group of young ladies since Nicole's own arrival would be hard on their heels. Though Nicole's presence signaled her availability and the men would be sure to spread the word that there was an eligible woman to be had, perhaps there might be a week of solitude. Nicole's shoulders relaxed and she busied her hands with the skirt she was hemming for Manon. *A more productive afternoon than I bargained for.*

Footsteps entering the room broke Nicole's concentration and she looked up from the brown linen in her lap. Alexandre Lefebvre stood in the doorway looking as awkward as a nervous schoolboy. None of the ire from their previous encounter was present in his eyes. Nicole made an unnecessary survey of the room, knowing that each of her companions was occupied with a suitor.

"Some cider, monsieur? Perhaps some cake?" Nicole stood, folding the skirt in haste and placing it back in her sewing basket.

"Just cider, please." He took the seat nearest hers and accepted the cool beverage with a nod and slight smile.

Nicole helped herself to a mug of cider as well, deciding it best to keep her hands occupied with something, else her fidgeting would betray the state of her nerves. There was not a sentence in her mind that she felt was worth uttering aloud, so she stilled her tongue, allowing him to break the silence this time.

"I'm glad to see you are well," he said. "I had come to inquire after you when the child was born, but of course you were not feeling well enough for visitors."

"I . . ." Nicole stammered, wondering why he had taken the trouble to do such a thing when he had spent less than a quarter of an hour in her presence. At a loss for anything more intelligent to say, she could only offer a stunned, "How very kind of you, monsieur."

"What have you called the child?" he asked after a few seconds of silence.

"Hélène. It was my grandmother's name. I never knew her, but Maman always spoke so lovingly of her. I couldn't think of anything that suited her better."

"May I see her?" Alexandre asked. Nicole stared for a moment before she was able to remember her manners. Never before had she seen a man wanting to hold a child that was not his own. She scooped the baby up from Sister Anne in the adjacent room and returned, handing him the baby, making every effort to keep her from waking. He peered down at Hélène, and a genuine smile crossed his lips, transforming his face to that of a much younger man.

"She is a lovely baby," he said, his movements those of a man who knew how to handle an infant.

"She looks so much like her father," Nicole said, proud that her voice did not crack at every mention of Luc like it used to.

"Oh, I see plenty of her mother in her face as well," Lefebvre said. "You look like you have recovered your strength remarkably well."

"Yes," Nicole said. "I think I had an easier time than many."

"Perhaps repayment for everything else you had been through," Lefebvre said. "Occasionally, though rarely, the world can be kind."

"That seems more optimistic than I would expect of you, monsieur," Nicole said.

"I'm not so sure how optimistic I am," Lefebvre said. "But I'm not such a pessimist that I can't appreciate the good things when they do happen."

"Sensible," Nicole said, smiling at the dry humor.

"Congratulations," Lefebvre said, handing the child back to Nicole with care. "I am very happy for you."

"Thank you, monsieur," Nicole said, swaying in her seat to keep Hélène asleep.

"I was hoping you would permit me to come visit you on occasion. May I?" Lefebvre asked. His voice was very quiet, but there was a twinge of some emotion in it that Nicole could not quite identify.

"Of course, monsieur," said Nicole. "Company is always welcome."

"I'm glad for it," said Lefebvre, standing. "I cannot stay long today, I'm afraid, but I will see you next week."

"I'll look forward to it," Nicole said. Lefebvre bowed and found his way back into the weak April sunlight.

The rest of the room made the polite attempt not to gawk at Alexandre Lefebvre as he left, but Nicole made no such effort. She stared at the vacant door frame for five solid minutes before she returned to herself. Shaking her head, she left the room, knowing no one else would come to visit before Sister Mathilde ever so sweetly nudged the gentlemen out the door. Nicole returned Hélène to Sister Anne, then sought occupation in the convent kitchen. The since-appeased Sister Éléonore welcomed Nicole's help as she prepared the meal.

Rose entered the kitchen a half hour later as Nicole removed freshly baked buns from the oven to accompany the roasted chicken and carrots.

"Smells wonderful," Rose said, placing a basket of supplies on the worktable. It registered that Nicole's Thursday marketing duties had fallen to Rose. There was nothing in Rose's face that let Nicole think the added duty was irksome, so she let the matter pass.

"Thank you," Nicole said. "I think they've turned out well, thanks to an excellent tutor we all know."

"I had to tell you, there is a rumor going around town," said Rose, sneaking a roll before Nicole's swatting hand could make contact.

"Of course there is," Nicole said, carving the chickens to serve. "When is there not?"

"But you are not always a subject of them, now, are you?"

"Thank heaven, no I'm not. What have I done now?" Nicole did not bother to look up from her work, knowing full well Rose's reply before she spoke it.

"The rumor is that Alexandre Lefebvre came to visit you."

"And the settlement has us married by now, I expect."

"So it's true, then? And yes, you've got it just about right."

Nicole's laugh had only the slightest trace of resentment as it rang through the kitchen. There was precious little entertainment in the colony, and she could hardly begrudge them a juicy morsel of fresh gossip.

"A ten-minute visit," Nicole said, her shoulders still shaking. "If he'd been here a full hour, imagine what they'd say."

"Much the same, with more certainty," Rose said. "But I do have a piece of advice for you. Alexandre Lefebvre is a well-respected man in this colony. Do not encourage his attentions unless you know you can return them."

Humor did not shine from Rose's violet-blue eyes and Nicole knew she spoke the truth. There were few in the colony with the social standing to cross Alexandre Lefebvre without consequence. Nicole wasn't one of them.

I cannot marry Alexandre Lefebvre. The reality hit Nicole with the force of the Canadian winter wind as she awoke Thursday morning two weeks later. She would have to refuse him . . . and gently for the sake of her future in the settlement. He showed her civility, perhaps kindness during his visit, but there was nothing of Luc's warmth in him. She spent her morning searching for words, but found none that didn't seem ridiculous or cruel.

Nicole begged Sister Mathilde for an errand to win her a week's reprieve from Alexandre's attentions. Two hours later, basket piled with bread, meat, and cheese for the following week, Nicole decided it was safe to return. Dread filled her stomach as she saw Alexandre approaching. *Why can I not have a week in peace?*

"Madame Jarvais, allow me to see you home," said Alexandre, taking her basket.

"As you wish," said Nicole, not making eye contact and walking as swiftly as she could with Hélène in her arms.

"I hope you're well," Alexandre said, fumbling for a way to start the conversation. "I was disappointed not to see you at the convent."

Nicole offered a slight nod of the head and said nothing.

"Have I said anything to offend you?" Alexandre asked, puzzled by her cold demeanor. Nicole shook her head. "I have long wanted to apologize for my behavior when we first met. It wasn't gentlemanlike at all. I am sorry."

"It doesn't matter, Monsieur Lefebvre," said Nicole. "It was long ago."

"Yes it was," said Alexandre. "Is everything else quite all right?"

"Fine, monsieur," said Nicole.

"Oh, the blasted 'fine' of a female when she is anything but!" Alexandre's temper at last simmered to the surface. "Speak, for the love of Christendom, rather than ignoring me as you are. Tell me what I've done so I can make it right."

"Apparently, the whole settlement thinks you're courting me," said Nicole, no small amount of venom in her voice.

"They're right," said Alexandre. "So the very idea is repugnant to you?"

Nicole stopped and looked at Alexandre. There was something akin to hurt in his expression. "No," she said, her tone gentler. "But I can't court anyone, Monsieur Lefebvre. I just lost my husband six months ago. I'm just getting used to the idea of being a new mother. I just can't even conceive of anything more right now."

Alexandre let out a breath he hadn't known he was holding, and his expression softened as well. "I know how hard it is," he said with a caress of her arm so fleeting she thought she might have imagined it. "Forgive me. I was thinking only of myself."

"It's fine," said Nicole. "You couldn't possibly know. I'm sorry I was rude."

Alexandre shook his head, dismissing her apology.

"Please let me come see you, still," said Alexandre. "Even if you're not ready. I would still appreciate your friendship."

"You said you didn't mean to court me or anyone. That afternoon at the convent over a year ago." Nicole spoke the words like an accusation.

"You have a good memory, madame." Alexandre kept his eyes forward as he spoke.

"So you changed your mind?" Nicole probed.

"Not exactly," said Alexandre. "I saw you on the shore the day you arrived. I wanted to know you better then. My rudeness simply got in the way."

"Come visit if you like," said Nicole, adjusting the baby on her hip and taking back her basket as they had reached the convent doors. "But as my friend, please."

"As a friend," agreed Alexandre. "I know there have been plenty of times in my past I have been in need of one myself." He nodded a curt farewell and exited back to the dusty street.

CHAPTER 17

Rose

July 1669

"And what was the moral of that story?" Rose asked her pupils.

They sat in the fields not far from the convent, enjoying lessons in the summer sun. The children loved stories, and Rose spent hours digging for compelling material that featured strong moral lessons.

"Don't give your house to your son until you're dead, otherwise his wife might throw you out!" Sarah exclaimed.

The class erupted in giggles.

"That's not entirely wrong, Sarah. But what else can we learn?" Rose asked. "Yes, Manon?"

"To be kind to our elders and set a good example for our children to do the same." Manon spoke with confidence but not smugness. Still, Rose noticed the other Huron girls no longer treated Manon as one of their own.

"Very good!" Rose said, beaming at the child she considered a treasured niece. "That's all for today; you may go!"

Most of the girls bounded out of sight almost before the words were out of her mouth.

Manon stayed behind with Rose, returning to the convent rather than the tribe.

"You handle them well," a quiet voice said as Rose gathered her books and straightened her skirt. She looked up to see Henri Lefebvre not three feet from where she stood.

"Henri . . . Monsieur Lefebvre," Rose stammered. "What are you . . . I thought you were in the Antilles. . . ."

Henri laughed his throaty guffaw at Rose's sputtered greeting. "Indeed I was, but life on Martinique was not for me. I decided to return to France. My uncle persuaded me to pay him a visit before I return."

"Manon, why don't you head back? I'll be right behind you," Rose said as the young girl trotted off. "And how long will you be staying?"

"At least a month. The voyage here took almost two. I need time to get over the first trek before I start on another," Henri said.

"I don't blame you," Rose said, still shocked to see the man she thought was gone forever. Since he had left for Martinique all number of scenarios played out in her head. Henri hurt on some far-flung tropical plantation with no one to care for him. Henri back in France and playfully courting some brainless socialite. Henri moving on with his life and forgetting about her altogether. But here he stood, seemingly well, and with no bride in tow. *Surely he wouldn't come to see me just to flaunt a marriage in my face? Why should I care if he did? I* ought *to wish him well if he did.*

"So you're still serious about entering the Church?" Henri asked. "It seems your pupils adore you."

"And I them." Rose smiled at Manon's black braids bobbing away as she jogged along. "They're sweet girls. And yes, I hope to take the vows in a few more months."

"Did you miss me at all?" Henri asked.

"Of course," Rose said. She did her best to block out the dark weeks after his departure when she spent her days in silent study and prayer and her nights weeping for him. "I enjoyed our visits."

"May I call on you, while I am here?" Henri asked. "Like old times."

"That wouldn't be appropriate, monsieur," Rose said. "As a postulant, it wouldn't be right for me to have gentlemen visitors."

"I see. What if I were to accompany my uncle when he comes to visit your friend, Madame Jarvais? Would you sit with us?" Henri seemed eager, but not pleading.

He's being a friend.

Rose chastised herself. *He's forgotten marriage, but wants to see you before he goes back to France.*

"Perhaps," Rose said. "It depends on where I am needed."

"Rose . . ." Henri began. "I . . ."

"I'm sorry, monsieur. I have to accompany Manon before she gets too far ahead. I'll see you another time."

Rose started after Manon, who was now quite far ahead.

Henri, to Rose's relief, did not follow.

Back at the convent, Manon greeted Nicole with a kiss and ran off to the kitchen to persuade kindhearted Sister Anne that she was in great need of a small bite before supper.

Rose greeted her friend with barely contained fury.

"How dare you!" she hissed.

"How dare I what?" Nicole asked, baffled.

"You know what I'm talking about." Rose stormed up to their bedroom and slammed the door. Nicole followed, passing Hélène to one of the other girls before chasing Rose up the stairs.

"If you're determined to be mad at me, at least explain what I've done to make you angry," Nicole told her.

"Your precious Monsieur Lefebvre. He 'persuaded' his nephew to come for a visit." Rose paced, hands raking her black curls. "I'm sure you had nothing to do with that. You and your 'friend.' "

"Indeed, I didn't," Nicole said, astonished. "Weeks ago—months—Monsieur Lefebvre mentioned Henri had written. I asked if he was planning a visit, and Alexandre said no. I said it was a shame, but left it at that."

"And your dear Monsieur Lefebvre decided to persuade his nephew to visit anyway?" Rose asked, a mocking expression on her face. "Likely."

"Rose, stop," Nicole said. "What is wrong with you? I never met Henri. Why would I want to persuade him to visit? You told me you were friends, and I believed you. If Monsieur Lefebvre interpreted my words differently, I am sorry."

"Why else would Henri have come?" Rose buried her face in her hands. "Everything was fine. I've built a life. I don't need him."

"Why are you so upset? What aren't you telling me?" Nicole reached for Rose's hand, but Rose swatted her away.

"I should never have come here," Rose said. "I was better off in that death trap in Paris."

"Don't say that, Rose. Forget he's here, if his presence upsets you so much. Go about your days." Nicole's voice took on the tenor of a parent irritated with a petulant child.

"Right. Just . . . in the future, don't meddle in my business, please," Rose said, covering her eyes with her hands in exasperation.

"Fine," Nicole said, her voice dismissive. "It wasn't my intent."

Rose thundered down the stairs. At a loss for what to do, she went to the convent kitchen. She found the old scrub bucket and brush and started to scrub the kitchen floor.

"Sister Thérèse scrubbed that floor this morning, child," Sister Mathilde said, entering the doorway.

"It looks like it needs it again, Sister." Rose did not move her eyes from the floor beneath her.

"I think it's fine," Sister Mathilde said. "Stand up, girl."

Rose obeyed at once, though she resented the Sister's caustic tone.

"I hear Henri Lefebvre is back in the settlement for a time," Sister Mathilde said. "Am I right?"

"Yes, Sister," answered Rose.

"You know that, as a postulant, you are not to be in the company of men without a chaperone. I understand he walked with you this afternoon?" Sister Mathilde asked.

"I am aware of the regulations, Sister. I told him it was unseemly and that I could not see him." Rose controlled her tone as best she could.

"Very well," Sister Mathilde said. "Is this why you are upset, my child?"

"No. His return is disruptive, that's all." Rose dropped the brush in the wash bucket in defeat. She would find no solace in scrubbing.

"May I remind you, my dear, that these walls are not a refuge for the brokenhearted," Sister Mathilde said.

"You doubt my devotion?" Rose asked, standing to her full height and looking Sister Mathilde in the eye. "I work with the children hours on end. . . ."

"I do not doubt your dedication or your eagerness to work, my daughter," interrupted Sister Mathilde. "Only your motivation. Search your heart."

"And how are you getting along with your young pupils, Mademoiselle Barré?" Alexandre asked. "Henri says the group seemed quite captivated on Tuesday."

"Very well, monsieur," Rose said.

Why could I not come up with an excuse to be elsewhere? "They are dear girls. Most of them eager to learn as well."

"Wonderful," Alexandre said. "I cannot think of any more effective way of establishing good relations with the indigenous people than through their youth."

"Indeed, monsieur," Rose said, not eager to drag on the conversation. She directed her attention to the mending in her lap.

"Henri, have you plans after you return to France?" Nicole asked.

"Not as such," Henri said. "Father will have plenty for me to do near home. I think he's none too upset that I didn't care for Martinique. He gifted me his holdings there, but I plan to manage them from France as best I can. It's a gorgeous plantation, really. Fields of sugar cane that go on forever, the sea as blue as sapphires off in the distance. But while you have your incessant snows here, the sun never ceases to shine there. It grows so monotonous, it could never feel like home."

"I imagine you're a great help to your father," Nicole said, ill at ease with the tension.

Without a word, Rose gathered up her sewing and went to her bedroom. It was no use. She could not sit in the same room as Henri Lefebvre and listen to his idle chatter about running his family's affairs.

He's a good man, but he's not for me, Rose told herself. *My life is here; my work is here. I've made a life for myself and it doesn't include him.*

Rose decided to vent her frustrations out in the summer sun. The fresh air was refreshing and the muscles in her legs delighted in the exercise.

Too long indoors, Rose thought. *No wonder I feel so stodgy.*

She allowed herself to ramble for the better part of an hour before returning to the convent. Rose seldom ventured this far anymore, and had not asked for permission to leave, but she would accept a lecture from one of the Sisters in exchange for an afternoon out-of-doors. She wandered past the burgeoning shops and new homes. Past the church. Past the stables. Like everything else in the settlement she gravitated toward the river. The banks of the river where she could sit, undisturbed, and listen as the sounds of the coursing water drowned out her unsettled thoughts.

She sat down on the edge of the river on a clean spot of grass and looked out at the rushing water, trying to cleanse her mind of doubts. Her brow dripped with beads of sweat in the summer sun, but she didn't bother to wipe them away.

"If you wanted to hide from me, your old favorite haunt was probably not a good choice," Henri said, approaching from behind and taking a seat beside her.

Rose debated returning to the convent, as the Sisters would have her do, but did not want to be chased away from her moments of freedom.

"This isn't right, Henri," Rose said, still gazing out at the water. "We aren't supposed to be alone together."

"Yes, you're supposed to be locked in a darkened room, praying or poring over some Latin text, but here you sit," he countered.

"True," she admitted, picking at a blade of grass.

"Why does seeing me upset you so?" Henri asked, his gaze defiant, daring her to look away.

"I don't know," she answered, smoothing her skirt and preparing to stand. *Sister Mathilde will have your head for this. She forgave you walking with him once. She won't be so lenient a second time.*

"I think you do," he said. Something in his tone prevented her from standing. "You didn't want me to go in the first place, so you went into hiding. Now that I'm back, you have to face your feelings for me and it terrifies you."

Rose did not break her eye contact. She would not divulge her doubts to him, but could not find her voice to contradict him.

"I'm right, aren't I?" he asked.

Rose pulled her knees to her chest and rested her chin on them for a few moments.

"Yes," she said. "I missed you. I went to your uncle's after you left, hoping you were still there. . . ."

A tear rolled down Rose's cheek.

Henri brushed it away with his thumb.

"He told me you went to see him," he said. "In his letter. That's why I'm here. Nicole noticed how you had been and mentioned it to Uncle. He suggested I make the detour here in the chance that you might still care. It wasn't Nicole's fault. It was my meddling uncle and my optimistic heart."

Rose laughed as a few tears followed the first. "I owe her an apology."

"She'll forgive you," he said. "My uncle cares for her despite her hesitation. I can see why you get along so well. The most reluctant pair of brides our dear Louis ever endowed."

Rose laughed once more. "Perhaps."

"What about me?" Henri asked. "Should I forgive you?"

"For what, exactly?" Rose asked.

"You spent so much time convincing yourself that you don't care for me," he said. "We could have spent that time together. I should be furious with you. But instead . . ."

Henri leaned in, tentative at first, and placed his lips upon hers. She curled her arms around him and accepted his embrace.

"You aren't," she said, when he reluctantly pulled away.

"No I'm not," he said with a laugh. "Not even a little. Marry me? Please?"

Rose looked into his deep hazel-brown eyes and kissed his lips once more. A look of horror crossed her face.

"I can't," Rose said, starting to climb to her feet.

Henri grabbed her arm and pulled her into his lap, irrespective of passersby.

"You can," he said. "It's what you want."

"I do," Rose admitted. "But I love teaching the Huron children, and learning about them, too. I don't want to go back to France. I don't want to give it up and spend my days keeping house."

"I can't promise that you'll have all the time you want to teach," Henri said. "I want children, and that will demand a good deal of time from you. Still, I want you in my life. We can stay here if you wish, and you can keep teaching if you wish. I don't want you for scrubbing dishes and mending clothes." He kissed her callused fingers gently. "I want you for my wife. Please say yes."

At the mention of childbirth, Gislène Laurier's anguished face appeared in Rose's mind. *That could be me in less than a year.* She forced herself not to shudder at the thought. But as Henri held her in his lap, his face imploring, she could not deny him.

"Yes," Rose whispered.

Henri stood, pulled Rose to her feet, took her in his arms, and spun around like a gleeful child.

"Thank God," he said, kissing her before setting her down.

"To the convent," he said, taking her hand in his. "We have arrangements to make."

That night, after the children were settled, apologies offered, and tears shed, Rose related the tale of her proposal to Nicole.

"It just doesn't seem real," Rose said.

"I know what you mean," Nicole said. "For weeks after I married Luc, when people called me Madame Jarvais, I didn't realize they were talking to me and wouldn't answer! I am so happy for you."

"Thank you, Nicole," Rose said. "He is a good man."

"I'm sure the two of you will be very happy," Nicole said. "Was Sister Mathilde disappointed?"

"Not even surprised," Rose said. "She had us matched up long ago."

"Wise woman," Nicole said, not forgetting Sister Mathilde's intentions for the elder Lefebvre.

"And what about you?" Rose asked, broaching the subject once again. "You need to come up with a plan. And soon, if you're wise."

"I know," Nicole said. "I've thought about taking a place of my own, perhaps working for Elisabeth and Gilbert if they'll have me."

"Is that what you really want?" Rose asked.

"Not really, but it's a start."

"I suppose," Rose said. "But Alexandre is a good man. Don't break his heart."

"His heart isn't mine to break," Nicole said, shooting a weary glance in Rose's direction.

"Henri says that his uncle cares for you a great deal, in fact."

"Let's just be happy for you tonight, please?" Nicole asked.

Too buoyant to argue, Rose hopped out of bed and kissed Nicole on the cheek. "Thank you. I *am* truly happy."

"I know of no one who deserves it more," Nicole said, embracing Rose. "Though I confess, I'm curious to know what the dashing rogue did to change your steadfast heart."

Rose laughed as she climbed back under the warmth of her covers. "I'm not sure if it's something he did, really. It's as though I didn't have a choice. Not an obligation, mind you. It's just that I feel like I couldn't live without him. Not a full life, anyway."

"I remember feeling that way about Luc," Nicole said, some of the joy in her voice replaced by melancholy. "In the early days."

"I'm sure you'll have those feelings again," Rose said.

"No," Nicole said. "I don't need the flutter of young love again. But I do need a future for Hélène."

"You're wise," Rose said. The thought of Nicole's less-than idyllic future alone with a child tempered her own lightheartedness. Remembering the starry-eyed girl who asked Elisabeth about true love caused something to ache in Rose's chest.

"I haven't much choice. Hélène needs me to be," Nicole said, her voice fading with fatigue.

The conversation soon dwindled and Rose was left alone with her thoughts. She would marry Henri and fulfill her duty to the Crown. But it did not ease the fear that gripped at her bowels and caused her to shake at night. Try as she might, the visions of Gislène Laurier and Elisabeth Beaumont's children crept into her mind and refused to leave.

There must be a way to conquer this, or I will fail him. I will fail everyone.

Chapter 18

Nicole

July 1669

Rose and Henri were married one week later, with only Nicole and Alexandre in attendance. Henri beamed as the priest pronounced them husband and wife, and Rose smiled more than Nicole had ever seen. Henri had secured a fine stone house just three doors down from his uncle's home, and the couple retreated there as soon as the marriage was blessed. Rose wanted no lavish meal or throng of guests, but contented herself with the luxury of a very handsome deep-red gown that Henri procured for her as a wedding gift. It must have cost the earth with the fine fabric and three seamstresses hard at work for the entire week, but the bride was so radiant, Nicole thought it well worth the cost.

"Allow me to see you home," Alexandre said to Nicole as the happy couple disappeared from view.

"Please," Nicole said quietly.

"A successful wedding, don't you think?" Alexandre asked.

"Since the couple ended up married, I would say so," Nicole replied, mirth shining in her eyes. "They did seem happy though."

"I've never seen Henri so pleased," Alexandre said. "Not since he was a small boy."

"Rose, too," Nicole said. "She deserves happiness. The last few years in France were not kind to her."

"I envy their happiness," Alexandre confessed. "I was married once before. Has anyone told you?"

"No," Nicole said.

"I'm amazed. In a place like this, one's life is hardly his own. I was married two years before you arrived. Her name was Laurence. She was sweet and gentle, with lovely chestnut hair like yours." Alexandre's voice was low, almost reverent as he spoke of his late wife. "We had a son, Philippe. That winter was terrible. The consumption claimed them both in two days."

"I'm so sorry." Nicole's mind retraced its steps back to her first month in the colony and her first disastrous encounter with Alexandre and the conversation with Sister Mathilde that followed. She'd called him "poor man," and Nicole hadn't plucked up the courage to ask why he deserved her pity. But why had Sister Mathilde kept the secret from her? It would have served to soften her resentment of the proud man. Knowing she would never ask, she pushed the question from her mind.

"That's why I was so short with you when I saw you out in the snow that night," Alexandre said. "It was Laurence all over again. It was rude of me, and I'm sorry."

"There is nothing to forgive, monsieur." The past months had chipped away at the resentment she harbored toward him, but as he spoke of his past, the final shards melted like the last heaps of dirty snow in late spring.

"I know something of your pain," he said. "I've tried not to press, but I still want you for my wife. If you won't have me, at least let me send you and the baby back to France. I can't bear to see you alone. A woman needs protection in a place like this."

Return to France? To Papa and Maman and all the others? The prospect was delicious. For weeks, Maman would dote on her and the baby, feed them, coddle them . . . but then what would follow? The time would come for her to marry and she had nothing more to bring to a marriage than when she had left France. Alexandre's offer wouldn't include a dowry to marry another man. Nor could she bring herself to ask. And what could she muster for a dowry for

Hélène when the time came? And there was Manon. What future could a native girl hope to have in the old country? In the settlement, people looked askance at her. In France, people would stare, treating her like an exotic attraction from a menagerie.

The alternative was to stay and marry the somber man who stood before her. Nicole touched the pearl brooch her mother had given her and thought of a second wedding her mother would not see. It flashed before her—a quiet affair—just she and Alexandre, perhaps Elisabeth or Rose or one of their husbands standing as witness. He would have her outfitted before the wedding in clothing befitting a woman of means. Fashionable, but sturdy. He'd see her settled in the Lefebvre house within an hour of the wedding, and her life would never again resemble her modest beginnings.

Would the change be welcome? Nicole shook the thought from her head and looked into Alexandre's gray eyes. She had no choice.

"I envy their happiness as well, Alexandre," Nicole said, astonished with herself for using his given name. "But I must also think of Manon."

And of myself. Do I want to marry again? Alexandre won't leave me to freeze in a shack, but will he be kind? Do I have a choice?

"The Huron child? I know you're very attached to her." Alexandre's eyebrow arched at the odd bent in the conversation.

"I consider her my daughter." Nicole met Alexandre's eyes without wavering. "She risked her life trying to save my husband. I will not forsake her."

"I understand. I would not ask you to," Alexandre said, taking Nicole's hand. "Please, I must know your answer."

"If you don't object to two daughters in addition to a wife, I accept." Nicole exhaled as the words escaped her lips. She had made her vow.

"Nothing could make me happier," Alexandre said, his smile subtracting years from his face. "I'll take care of you all for as long as I take breath. You'll never want for anything again."

Alexandre kissed Nicole's cheek and her color rose to crimson. The whole settlement would know the news before she reached the convent door.

Nicole looked into the face of her future husband. He had none of the youthful mirth of Luc Jarvais, or even the almost-forgotten

Jean Galet. Alexandre Lefebvre was a man who had lived and knew the world. Still, Nicole realized her pain made her a poor companion for a green young man. Alexandre's experience was what she needed, and the same was true for him. But could she endure his cold manner? Would she ever be welcome in his circles? She had to trust that he would help her find a place in his world, but faith in a husband had been a virtue poorly paid in the past.

At least I can bring him a measure of solace, even if that is all I can bring to the marriage.

PART 2

Chapter 19

Elisabeth

June 1670

Elisabeth tried and failed to fasten her skirt around her thickening waist. Although it was hard to dress in the dark, concealing her growing abdomen that grew more and more conspicuous each day was impossible. With a defeated sigh, Elisabeth dug for the larger clothes she had worn during her pregnancy with Adèle.

It's just as well, thought Elisabeth. *Perhaps some of the whispering will stop. Concealing pregnancy is both illegal and dangerous here, anyway.*

Elisabeth, willing or not, heard most of the rumors and idle chatter in town. She knew nothing in the colony created more suspicion than a married couple that failed to produce a child almost every year. To be married for more than two years, and without a child, was all but unheard of. People whispered about the husband's masculinity, the wife's fidelity, or the couple's dubious attempts to thwart pregnancy altogether. Her swollen abdomen would do nothing but improve her standing with her fellow settlers.

Elisabeth had suffered two miscarriages since Adèle, and was not eager to sing the joyous news of her pregnancy just yet. With each miscarriage, Gilbert's suffering matched her own, and she was certain his worry even exceeded hers. For several weeks now, when she felt nauseated, she hid her illness with improvised excuses to leave the shop. When she could not bear to eat, she sneaked her soup back into the pot when Gilbert wasn't looking or forced a small serving down despite her protesting stomach.

However, she calculated she had just five months until the baby arrived, so the time for secrecy was over.

"There you are," Gilbert said with a smile. "I was wondering what was keeping you."

"Sorry, love," Elisabeth said, kissing his cheek. "I'll get right to work."

"Not to worry. Is that dress new?" Gilbert looked at his wife with an assessing eye.

"No. I haven't worn it for a while, though." She busied her hands measuring out flour, trying to keep her voice even.

A look of comprehension came over Gilbert's face. He looked both thrilled and petrified. Elisabeth had bled so much, and been so ill, after the last miscarriage that the priest had been called to offer her last rites. Father Cloutier had spoken to Gilbert about the fragility of women, and how he must not despair if God chose to call Elisabeth home. Her husband's scathing reply reached Elisabeth's ears, even in her sickbed. She wasn't surprised that the dour-faced priest had yet to return.

"How far along?" Gilbert asked.

"Four months. Maybe five. Almost halfway." She had not looked up from her mixing bowl, but was proud that her hands did not shake.

"Good," Gilbert said, embracing his wife. He pointed to the stool at Elisabeth's worktable. "Now sit."

She took her place with a smile and began her work.

"The more sitting you do, the less grief you'll get from me. Do we have an understanding?" Gilbert softened his orders with a soft kiss on her floured cheek.

"Yes, monsieur," Elisabeth purred.

"A blessing on obedient wives," Gilbert said with a chuckle. "I'll try not to be too much of a tyrant, though."

"Thank you," she said, knowing that her husband would gladly tie her to the chair to preserve her health.

* * *

After the afternoon rush, Elisabeth started for the stairs, excited at the prospect of a nap before supper.

The shop bell announced an arrival, so with a regretful look toward her bed, she turned back to the shop so Gilbert wouldn't need to leave the ovens.

The customer was a young boy, perhaps eleven or twelve years of age. His eyes appeared to take up the majority of his smudged face, and he offered no smile or greeting.

"What can I get for you, young man?" Elisabeth asked, hoping a gentle prod would get the child to speak. Rather than respond, he grabbed a loaf of bread from the nearest basket and ran for the door. Had he not stumbled over the threshold, he would have escaped, but Gilbert emerged from the kitchen and caught the boy before he made off with his loot.

"What is the meaning of this?" Gilbert demanded as he detained the boy by one struggling arm.

The boy stared at Gilbert, expression mutinous, but did not speak.

"Are you hungry?" Elisabeth asked, guessing the root of the petty theft.

The boy looked at her, looked down, and still said nothing.

"Come with me," Elisabeth motioned. Gilbert followed her to the bakery kitchen, dragging the boy behind him.

Elisabeth placed a plate with a large roll and a generous cup of milk before the boy. "Eat, then speak." She moved to ruffle his hair, but he dodged like a wary pup evading a kick.

A pang reached Elisabeth's heart as the boy devoured every morsel of food.

"Who are your parents?" Gilbert asked, softening as he realized the extent of the boy's hunger.

The boy opened his mouth to speak, but clapped it shut once more.

"You aren't in trouble," Elisabeth said. "We want to help you."

"My name is Pascal Giroux," he answered.

Elisabeth put another roll in front of him. It disappeared as quickly as the first.

"Your father is Raymond Giroux?" Gilbert asked.

The boy nodded. "You won't tell him, will you?"

Gilbert shook his head. "Your farm is a half day's walk from here. Is your father in town?"

"No, monsieur, I walked." Pascal looked at his grubby hands. "We hadn't nothing for breakfast. Wasn't much chance of anything the rest of the day, either, so I . . . came here."

"Things are that bad?" Gilbert asked.

Pascal nodded. "Maman's sick. Papa's not had good luck in the fields for two years. I thought you might not miss one loaf."

"Young man," Gilbert said. "You can't think that way. What if everyone took 'just one loaf'? Bakers everywhere would close their doors."

"I didn't think of it that way, monsieur," Pascal said, looking ashamed. "I just thought of my stomach. I was going to share it, though."

"I'm sure you were," Elisabeth said. "And you're young. I think the occasional error in judgment is forgivable—as long as it's not repeated."

Gilbert nodded. "It would have been far better to ask for help."

"Yes, monsieur," he said. "But isn't that begging?"

"Better an honest beggar than a thief," Gilbert said.

"I can't wait till I'm grown." The boy grew animated. "I'll earn my wages and won't ever starve."

"A noble ideal, son," Gilbert said. "And what is it you wish to do?"

"Anything but farming." Pascal spit the words out as though they tasted bitter. "It's too unsteady. One bad season and . . . Well . . ."

"It affects us all," Elisabeth said. "Bad crops mean flour prices rise, we must charge more, and fewer people can buy our bread. We're all at the mercy of the weather and other things we can't control."

"Well, I hate it," Pascal said. "How's a man to be certain of anything in this world?"

"He isn't," Elisabeth said, with a pat to her midsection. "We have to hope for the best and accept what happens."

"That isn't to say you can't give fate a push," Gilbert said. "God helps those who help themselves."

He turned to his wife. "You stay here. I'll see Pascal home. Hold some supper for me."

"You mean I don't have to walk?" Pascal asked, with tears welling in his eyes at the show of kindness.

"Of course," Gilbert said. "It would be full dark by the time you reached the farm. You don't want to get lost."

"Take this for his family." Elisabeth handed Gilbert a basket heaping with three or four loaves of bread and an assortment of rolls. Pascal's eyes widened. He embraced Elisabeth with the enthusiasm of a five-year-old.

"You're an angel, madame," he said.

Gilbert placed his hand on the boy's shoulder and led him off to the stables.

Two hours later, Gilbert returned, with Pascal in tow.

"An addition to our table tonight, if you don't mind, madame," Gilbert said in his teasing tone.

"Of course," Elisabeth said, this time successful in her attempt to ruffle the boy's hair. "I didn't expect to see you so soon again, though."

"I had a notion on the way to the Giroux place," Gilbert said. "If Pascal is as serious as he claims to be about wanting to earn his way in the world, I thought he might be of use to us here in the shop. He could be an assistant, for now, and if that works out, I might make him my apprentice one day. If you agree, of course."

"Please say yes, madame." The pleading look in the boy's eyes would have melted a sterner heart than Elisabeth's.

"I think it's a wonderful idea," Elisabeth said.

Once more, Pascal wrapped his arms around Elisabeth. She kissed the top of his dirty head.

A bath, she thought, *and before bed, too.*

"You won't be sorry," Pascal said. "I'll work myself to the bone, you wait and see."

"Trust to that," Gilbert said. "Madame Beaumont needs her rest and I intend to see that she has it. You are here, in part, to ease her load."

"Supper, gentlemen," Elisabeth said, placing a kettle of water on the stove to boil in preparation for the after-dinner scrubbing that Pascal did not yet know was in store for him.

Despite the two large rolls he had eaten only hours before, Pascal ate with the voracious appetite common to growing boys. With Elisabeth's appetite increasing as well, she anticipated a few longer spells before the stove in coming months.

Pascal took to his bath with the grace of a feral cat, but submitted to Elisabeth's orders in the end. She shuddered to think of the state of her guest room sheets if the boy had had his way. Once he was bathed and tucked away in his new lodgings, she soon heard the rasping of his sleeping breath.

"I hope you don't mind, Elisabeth," Gilbert said as they settled into bed a few minutes later. "It was a big decision to make without consulting you."

"With a little bit of training he'll be a lovely young man," Elisabeth said, grateful to be off her feet. "It's fine by me. Manon has been a great comfort to Nicole, and I'm sure Pascal will work hard for us. His parents didn't object?"

"When given the chance for their boy to have an apprenticeship at no cost? Giroux isn't such a fool as to turn that down. He rushed us out the door in case I changed my mind."

"I hope he won't pine too much for his family," Elisabeth said. "He is very young to live away from them."

"I doubt he will miss them much," Gilbert said. "If you'd seen their place you would know I had no choice but to take him on. God's truth, Raymond Giroux must be the laziest man in all of New France. His wife looks like she's working herself to death, and the children are half starved. The bread you sent was more food than they'd seen in a month."

"Poor Pascal," Elisabeth said. "No wonder he was so emphatic about making his own living."

"That's why I decided to hire him," Gilbert said. "He's seen the cost of laziness firsthand. He'd defend his father to his last breath, but I'd bet this very shop he's sick of depending on that man and being disappointed by him. He'll be the hardest worker in the settlement when he's grown."

"You're a good man, Gilbert," Elisabeth said, snuggling closer to her husband.

"I hope I'm right about Pascal," Gilbert said. "And I hope he's a quick learner so that you can get to resting."

"I can teach from a chair, my love," Elisabeth said. "And he needs us."

"I can't disagree with that," Gilbert said, wrapping his arms around her. "He'll need some schooling also. If he's under my roof I want him able to face the world when he leaves our service. My father made me go to school, dragged me there more than once, and though I had no taste for it at the time, I'm grateful now."

"That seems like a sound plan to me," Elisabeth agreed. Considering Pascal's brief tirade before his bath, she added, "Some of his vocabulary could use a little refinement."

"That it could," Gilbert agreed with a laugh. "I don't think his father guards his tongue very well."

"I'm sure you'll do better," Elisabeth said.

"I hope so, sweetheart," he agreed, his hand finding her abdomen and rubbing gently. He kissed her brow and pulled her close. "God strike me dead for saying this, but as much as I want you to have my child, I don't want to go through this again."

"I can't say I'm looking forward to it either, love," Elisabeth said. "But we'll weather the storm."

Gilbert said nothing, but squeezed his wife even tighter. *That's right, my love. Keep me close. Don't let me leave you, for I've no great desire to go.*

Elisabeth knew the fear would only subside with the birth of the child. She clung to her husband and hoped that they would somehow find solace in the next few months.

"Very good!" Elisabeth praised her young pupil. "Now gently form the dough into a ball like so and cover the bowl with a warm, damp rag. Then we let it sit for an hour before we bake it."

"Why can't we just put it in now?" Pascal asked. "It would be faster."

"Yes, but if you don't let the yeast rest, the bread won't rise. It will just stay in a tough lump. Not very nice to eat," Elisabeth explained.

"That must be how Mother makes her bread then," Pascal said. "Hard as a rock. I'll give her lessons when I visit home."

"She might appreciate that," Elisabeth said, uncertain whether Brigitte Giroux was the type to appreciate tutelage from her young son.

As promised, Elisabeth sat as much as she could and taught Pascal the trade, making him "do" rather than "watch." She soon realized that the boy would not have tolerated passive instruction well. After three days, Elisabeth trusted him with mixing and baking most of the bread, while she devoted herself to pastries and cakes. The inventory was finally keeping pace with the demands of the hungry settlement.

Each Sunday, as was the tradition of apprentices in the colony, Pascal returned home for a visit. He left with a heavy basket of bread and Elisabeth suspected he returned with a heavier heart. The longer he lived away from his family, the more he understood their dire situation and how little he could do to help them change it. Elisabeth sensed a growing tension between Pascal and his father, though the boy never breathed a word about the problem.

"You know you're welcome to stay with us on Sundays," Elisabeth said. "We'd be happy to have you."

"I know, but I want to see the rest of the family, especially Gabrielle." Pascal had a soft spot for his sister, who was a few years younger than he.

Elisabeth sensed that the little girl and the basket of bread were the only things that kept Pascal going out to the farm each week. The basket comprised the majority of their pantry. Even one missed visit would mean hardship for the Giroux children, so Pascal made the journey without complaint. He even refused to let Gilbert drive him home and back. He was learning something of his master's pride. While it would serve him well in time, she hoped he wouldn't allow his dignity to compromise his health.

"It will be fine," Pascal said. "The walk is good for me, and it lets me think."

"It can be a comfort," Elisabeth agreed. "My father lived for his daily constitutional. He said it energized him between bouts at the oven and teaching me his business."

"He sounds like a good man," Pascal said, with no small trace of envy in his voice. "A good teacher. If I ever have a son, I'll teach him a trade."

"A wise notion," Elisabeth said. She had no doubt that he meant what he said. Hunger had been a cruel education.

I will train you, young man. I will see to it that you have a good start in life. If your parents cannot do that for you, I must.

In such a short time, Elisabeth had come to think of Pascal as her own. Perhaps because she had not had children of her own yet, and because she could never consider her pregnancy as any sort of guarantee that she ever would. She was grateful for his presence as an assistant, for certain. The baby was becoming demanding of her energy, and there was no denying that Pascal lightened her burdens. Even without much training, he could fetch and carry, which proved an enormous help. But beyond that, he was a smart and affectionate boy. Elisabeth hated the harsh life he'd endured and hoped her child—or children, God willing—would never know such hardship.

"I think you've earned a break, son," Elisabeth said with a smile. "Take a pastry or two and enjoy some sunshine."

Never one to deny himself food or time out-of-doors, Pascal nodded enthusiastically and thundered from the kitchen through the shop to the freedom that lay beyond the bakery doors.

Elisabeth walked out of the kitchen to her seat behind the shop counter to see Pascal outside conversing with some of the other boys his age while they shared some of his pastry. Baked goods seemed a key to social success among his new social circle. *Enjoy some childhood, sweet boy. You've earned it.*

CHAPTER 20

Rose

June 1670

Rose wasn't quite sure how long she'd been staring into the void rather than hemming the trousers in her hands, but it was long enough for Nicole to clear her throat and call her friend back to the present moment.

"Rose, are you quite all right?"

"Fine," Rose answered, looking up from her mending. "A bit tired perhaps." *The ever-acceptable excuse for a young married woman. Never angry, sad, or lonely. Always tired.* Rose looked down at the frayed edges of Henri's trousers and tried to focus. Weekly, they met in Nicole's parlor to attend to these chores with the benefit of company to pass the time, but Rose wearied of the questions, no matter how much she cared for her friends.

"Do you think . . ." Elisabeth asked, patting her protruding midsection.

"No," Rose said. Her courses had just ended and she would have had no cause to think she could be expecting anyway.

However, people were already talking.

Almost a year. No sign of a baby.

"Your time will come," Nicole said with a gentle smile. Her own swollen belly betrayed her secret also.

Easy for the two of you to say, Rose fumed. *Both of you are well advanced in your pregnancies.* Rose took a breath and scolded herself. *They are good friends; I shouldn't think that way. I should be happy for them even if I can't be for myself. I have no desire to give birth, God knows, but it would be nice to be free of suspicious glances.*

"I'm sure," Rose said, aiming for a tone of nonchalance, and not quite hitting her mark. Changing the subject, she added, "The bakery seems to be doing a roaring trade, Elisabeth."

"So it would seem," Elisabeth agreed. "Gilbert has hardly had a moment's rest these past two weeks. I must say I'm grateful he's ordered me off my feet. He and Pascal are doing beautifully, so long as I oversee the morning pastries."

Nicole and Alexandre would be constructing a grand house in town that spring and renting out plots to farmers soon after. Alexandre had his fortune made.

"How about some cider?" Nicole offered, tiring of her knitting.

"I had best be going home, actually," Rose said. "Several matters need me."

If they thought her departure abrupt, Nicole and Elisabeth said nothing. Rose was grateful. She had no desire to answer their questions.

At home, Rose was not greeted, as she had hoped, by the aroma of dinner wafting from the kitchen. Not having the means that his uncle did, Henri's staff consisted of two: Agathe and Jacques Thiberge, an elderly couple who served the young Lefebvres. At least, they served to the best of their ability, but their stamina was not at its peak.

"Good afternoon, Agathe," Rose said. "Have you begun supper?"

"No, madame, I was just about to." Some ingredients had been gathered on the worktable, but no further progress made.

"Agathe, we're not in the custom of eating in the middle of the night. You need to remember to start meals earlier." Rose kept the frustration from her voice at some cost.

"My apologies, madame," Agathe said, not sounding contrite.

Discussing the matter with Henri would do no good. There wasn't an abundance of help to hire in the settlement, especially with limited funds.

"I'm afraid supper may be a bit late," Rose said, knocking on Henri's study door.

"Fine, fine," he said. He glanced up from his correspondence. "Anything else you need?"

"No, I'll leave you to your work. I'll call you for dinner."

"Thank you," he answered, already reimmersed in the papers before him.

Not knowing what else to do, Rose mounted the staircase and stretched out on a settee in her sitting room. Not feeling equal to a book, she closed her eyes and tried to relax.

Henri had withdrawn from the marriage, and Rose had, too. As much as she wanted to please her husband, Rose found his embraces impossible to endure. Every time he approached her, the specter of her uncle's caresses entered her mind and sickened her. The men were no more alike than a fine silk gown and a feed sack, yet she could not divorce herself from her past.

She pled for Henri's patience, but after a time his advances stopped. This relieved Rose . . . though the fact embarrassed her. After years of the finest training, she knew that a wife's first duty was to submit to her husband. She had come to this settlement to populate it, but she lacked the strength to allow it.

Rose half expected Henri to present her with an annulment notice, but he was too proud a man to let his marital unhappiness become a source of public gossip—any more than it already was.

The smells of Agathe's stew drifted up the stairs and beckoned Rose's appetite. Despite her deficiencies, Agathe was an impeccable cook, at least when it came to plain fare, which suited Rose just fine. A hearty mutton stew and crusty bread would be restorative on a brisk June night.

As was their custom, Henri and Rose chatted throughout the meal. The conversation never varied from the minutiae of the day. As always, they avoided the real issues. The tone remained cheerful.

The less the servants heard, the better.

"I must go to see my uncle later this evening," Henri announced toward the end of the meal. "I may be gone quite some time."

Rose wondered if this was a pretense to go elsewhere, but she dismissed the idea just as soon as it entered her mind. If Henri were going astray, he would not choose an alibi that she could so easily verify.

I wouldn't blame you if you did stray, Rose thought. *My poor Henri, you deserve better.*

"Of course. Would you like me to accompany you?"

"I have business to discuss," he said, pushing his plate forward. "I'd prefer you didn't."

"As you wish," she replied. Her tone was sweet. If she could not be a good wife, at least she was dutiful where she could be.

Henri had not returned by midnight. Although Rose kept her own room, his absence bothered her. Unable to sleep, she walked the corridors of the house she loved. It was not as grand as her childhood home, or her uncle's, but it was warm and inviting. The day Henri had brought her here she felt at ease within its walls.

The door to Henri's study was open. Rose decided to straighten his desk, as she sometimes did, as a small signal of her attention to his needs.

A letter, written in a bold hand, caught her attention:

> *M. Henri Lefebvre:*
>
> *Be advised that upon learning of your unsanctioned marriage to Mademoiselle Rose Barré, your father has, effective immediately, transferred the inheritance of his entire estate to your brother, M. Lionel Lefebvre. Your father believes the accounts that the women sent by the King to his colonies are common orphans at best, and remains adamant that you have made a "horrendous error in judgment" (his words).*
>
> *You retain your holdings on Martinique, as they were gifted to you, but you stand to inherit nothing at the decease of your father. He wishes to express his disappointment in your choice not to return to France and take your place as his son and heir.*
>
> *I do regret to be the bearer of these tidings, friend,*

but your father is obdurate on the matter, and I find no means to change his opinion.

Sincerely,

P. Leroux

Rose stared at the paper, disbelieving. Her father-in-law, a man she had never met, nor was she likely to meet, disapproved of her so much that he was willing to disinherit his eldest son. From all prior discussions, it seemed that Henri had always enjoyed a convivial relationship with his father.

Why has he not mentioned this to me? No wonder he fled tonight. Not only do I bring him no happiness in marriage, I have cost him almost everything.

Rose laid her head down on the desk and wept. She felt ashamed to indulge her emotions, but she was as unable to restrain the tide of tears as she would have been to dam the Saint Lawrence with her bare hands.

My poor Henri. If only I could love you as you deserve. I ought to go back to the Sisters and rejoin them. You could surely get an annulment.

The thought was so painful she had to push it from her mind.

She did not know how long she allowed the tears to flow, but when she was able to compose herself she went back to the task she had begun. Henri's office was tidy and efficient as it had ever been when she finished.

He already has a maid, such as she is, Rose chided herself. *It's not enough. You know what you must do.*

Rose ascended the staircase and entered her husband's bedroom, the one area in the house in which she spent very little time. It was not lavishly decorated, but his heavy silk bed linens and dark wooden furniture spoke of his good taste and breeding.

I was once a part of this world, too, she thought. *If they knew me, knew of my family, they wouldn't object to me . . . at least not if I were in France.*

She stood before his long mirror and, with great determination, removed her clothes. He had never seen her fully unclothed, and she wished to give this to him. She imagined few husbands in the colony saw their wives undressed with much frequency. It went against Church teachings, which urged modesty in all things—including the marital act—but Rose was beyond caring about trivial matters of doctrine.

Rose climbed into the bed and waited for Henri, drifting in and out of sleep as the time passed. She heard the door below open and close as quietly as Henri could manage. She smoothed her hair and positioned herself so she was lying atop the covers. Her heart beat a frantic pace as the knob to the bedroom door turned.

"Good evening, husband," she greeted him, her tone whisper-soft.

"Good evening, my wife," Henri said, his voice cracking as he looked away from her nude figure. "Wh-what are you doing in my bed?"

"I'd hoped it was clear," she said, daring a soft laugh. "I must be worse at this than I thought."

Henri approached her, bent over the bed, giving her a deep kiss on the lips. There was the sweet taste of his uncle's fine whiskey on his breath, but he was not intoxicated. He pulled away and rummaged through his bureau.

"Please put this on," he said, handing her one of his shirts. "I can't do this tonight. I can't take another failed attempt. . . ."

"I know," Rose said, pushing the shirt away. "I've been a horrible wife to you. I am so sorry. That all stops now."

She grabbed his wrist and pulled him into an embrace. She repeated in her mind, *This is what you must do for him.*

He was atop her, helping her to remove his clothes, all the while covering her with gentle kisses.

"Can you stay like that, just for a short while?" she asked, looking into his hazel-brown eyes. "Just let me get used to being this close to you."

"Whatever you need," he said. "My sweet darling." He brushed the hair from her forehead and kissed the bared skin. Her breathing evened as she adjusted to the intimacy. She wrapped her arms around his torso and nodded her permission.

Rose felt the muscles in her shoulders and neck relax as she found herself able to submit to Henri's kisses and caresses without revulsion. His hands were gentle, his lips not too demanding. She still trembled with nerves, but found, mercifully, that she welcomed his nearness. It would not happen overnight, but she knew as she lay with him that the time would come that she would be able to take pleasure in his arms. She could finally allow herself to love him as she longed to.

"What do you mean 'horrible wife'?" Henri asked in the hour before dawn as he cradled Rose in his arms.

"I wasn't able to perform even the most basic duty," she said, tucking her face into his chest. "I am so sorry I made you wait."

"I just wish I understood why," he said, stroking her hair with his free hand. "I've longed to make you mine for so long. I don't care that you weren't a virgin. I could tell, and it doesn't matter."

"No, I wasn't," Rose said, exhaling a breath she didn't know she had been holding.

"I know that matters to most men, but I don't care about your past. I don't care if some dashing young rogue stole your virtue and broke your heart. I care about your present and your future," he said, squeezing her tight to him as he had longed to do for months.

Rose felt the tears begin to stream once more, and she made no attempt to hide them.

"It wasn't 'some dashing young rogue,' as you put it. When my parents died, I went to live with my aunt and uncle. . . . He . . . forced me to lie with him."

Henri's grasp on her softened from lustful to tender. "To treat his own niece in such a fashion. I can't even imagine. A bout of drunkenness followed by a confession to your aunt, I expect?"

"It wasn't just one indiscretion. It went on for six months." Rose felt the blood drain from her cheeks and she curled her face into his chest. "When my aunt found out, she had me shipped off to the charity hospital like a common orphan the very next morning."

"My God, why didn't you tell me before?" Henri said. "I would have behaved so differently. It's no wonder you weren't able . . ."

"The past is the past, Henri. I should have been able to let it go. For your sake."

"Don't be daft," Henri said. "That monster scarred you as surely as if he'd carved your face with a knife. You can't just will that away."

"I tried for months," she said at length. "I wanted to."

"I know that now. It hurt, seeing you recoil from me. It still hurts, knowing how my touch must have made you feel. Forgive me for my impatience."

"There is nothing to forgive," she said. "Just continue to be patient. . . . It may be a while before I'm completely comfortable."

"Just tell me what you need," Henri said. "In this and all things, and I will be a happy man."

Rose took a deep breath and decided to broach a topic almost as painful. "I saw the letter on your desk. I was cleaning. I didn't mean to pry. I thought about running back to the convent and freeing you to return, but I couldn't . . ." She buried her face in his chest, wanting to hide from the truth that she'd cost him so much.

"Damn right," Henri said, tucking his finger under her chin so she was forced to look into the depths of his flashing hazel eyes. "If you'd pulled such a trick, I'd have dragged you back over my shoulder kicking and screaming."

"I didn't do it," she said. "It may not have seemed like it, but I love being with you."

"I'm so glad you're fully mine at last," he said, caressing the soft flesh of her bare upper arm. "I love you."

"As I love you," she said, snuggling her face into the soft hairs on his chest, slowing her breath and adjusting to the closeness of her husband.

Henri looked none too alert at breakfast the following morning, and Rose was sure she'd looked more resplendent in mornings past, but she felt a lightening of the mood that had to have been obvious to all. Servants or no, Henri kissed the back of her hand at the table, where they now sat side by side rather than across from each other.

CHAPTER 21

Elisabeth

July 1670

Get the pillow off my face! Elisabeth fought to scream, but she hadn't the breath for it. Someone shook her arm violently and she slapped at the intruder, only to feel her wrists seized by powerful hands. *I'm going to be murdered in my own bed.* She wanted to struggle further, but her muscles would no longer obey her orders. She tried to open her eyes, but pain gripped her as they fluttered open and she could not help but clamp them shut once again. *What has he done to me?* The intruder, a huge man, from what Elisabeth could tell, swung her over his shoulder and carried her from the bedroom.

She was jostled about as they descended the steps, and she heard the clacking and wheeze of the front door as they exited into the warm night air. As soon as they were outside, the man setting her on the stoop of a house across the street, fresh air impaled her nose and mouth like a lance. She was racked with coughing and heaves, unable to care that she lay prostrate in the street in her nightgown for all the neighbors to see. Tears streamed from her eyes, washing the poison away.

She did not know how long it was before she regained her bearings, but the first thing she noticed was that Pascal now sat beside her, his long, thin arm wrapped around her.

The second thing she noticed was that flames flickered in the windows, lapping at the wood, overdry from the unusually hot summer. Hungry like a wolf in winter, the fire ate away at the structure—the life that she and Gilbert had worked so hard to build.

Elisabeth stood in the street for a moment, watching her home engulfed in flames. She wrapped an arm around Pascal, and for just a moment she let grief consume her just as the fire consumed the parched timbers of their small home. Their shop. Their livelihood.

It's just a house. Just things, she scolded herself.

But the platitudes didn't comfort her. She'd left too many things behind before to do so lightly now. Trinkets that would mean nothing to anyone else, but they were her precious memories from home as well as her new life. All gone. She didn't bother to wipe the tears from her face.

The churning in her gut eased when she saw Gilbert's frame, laden with water buckets, marching toward them with several equally burdened neighbor men. Despite the creases of fear and worry on his brow, he was safe.

"Get to the Lefebvres. Now." Gilbert shouted the order in Elisabeth and Pascal's direction. She had no intention of disobeying Gilbert's command—if for no reason other than the baby's well-being—but her feet were not so compliant.

She stood and watched, helpless, as Gilbert and the other men formed a bucket brigade. Before long it looked like they might succeed in keeping the flames from spreading too far. She itched to join in, to help where she might, but her sore lungs and bulging stomach kept her from being useful. She breathed in a whiff of charred air and her shoulders sagged in defeat. Taking a final glance at her beloved home, she at last followed Gilbert's directive and dragged the bleary-eyed Pascal to the Lefebvre house, leaving her own behind.

A disgruntled-looking servant, named Paul, if Elisabeth's memory served, answered the door. He had been awake before she knocked, but disliked having his morning solitude disrupted before the house stirred.

"May I help you?" he asked, recognizing Elisabeth but not the boy. He looked her over, noting her disheveled hair and nightgown. Had he not known her, Elisabeth was sure he would have taken pleasure in turning her away.

"I am sorry to intrude, monsieur," Elisabeth said, understanding his annoyance. "Our home is burning. My husband sent me here while they fight the blaze."

"Please come in, madame," the servant said. "I pray the fire doesn't travel this far. It has been a very dry summer."

"Yes it has," Elisabeth agreed, glancing back over her shoulder. *Spare the neighbors, please,* she prayed silently, ignoring the pang of guilt at the realization that this was the first thought she'd had for them.

Nicole, having obviously heard the noises downstairs, descended in her nightgown and robe. She ushered Elisabeth into the dining room and ordered Paul to see to breakfast. Despite her state of undress, she ordered the servants about as though she were dressed as fine as Queen Maria Theresa herself.

"Where is Gilbert?" Nicole asked. The look in her eyes was that of a woman who had known loss.

"Fighting the blaze with the neighbors," Elisabeth said, refusing to indulge in her fears until she had reason to.

"It will all be fine," Nicole said. "You're safe, that's the main thing."

"From what I can tell from the upstairs window, the neighbors came to his aid. I wouldn't be surprised if the fire is out very soon," Alexandre said as he entered the room, his expression grim. "They've organized as well as they can. God knows we need a proper fire brigade in this settlement."

"Very true, Monsieur Lefebvre," Elisabeth agreed, trying to focus on his words as she pretended to eat.

"It may be the first fire of the season, but it won't be the last. You and Gilbert, and young Master Giroux, will stay with us while repairs are made, of course," Alexandre said.

"That is kind of you," Elisabeth said. "Thank you so much."

"Think nothing of it," Alexandre said with a dismissive wave.

Pascal sat in silence next to Elisabeth, pretending to pick at his breakfast. She placed her hand on his shoulder, as was her custom. The gesture, meant to be comforting, seemed to make him retreat more into himself. She had never seen the boy not clear his plate, but did not chide him. Despite the incessant hunger brought on by her baby, Elisabeth did not eat her usual helping, either.

"Monsieur Beaumont," Paul announced, showing Gilbert into the dining room.

Elisabeth leaped to her feet to embrace her husband, who looked bone weary.

"It's all gone," Gilbert said. "A total loss. The Audet house was badly scorched as well, but thank God no one else lost their homes."

"And you are unhurt?" Nicole asked, voicing the question that Elisabeth could not.

"Yes, though aged ten years in the course of a morning," Gilbert said without humor, taking a deep draft from a mug of milk.

"I would think so," Alexandre said.

"Well," Elisabeth said, at last able to speak. "At least the three of us are all well. The building can be rebuilt and things replaced."

Though she spoke the words, it was not easy to believe them. Some items could never be replaced: her father's recipe book, the two gowns Adèle had worn in her brief life. She even spared a thought for her mother's absurd handkerchief, embroidered to the point where it served no purpose. She had grabbed it on her flight from Paris on a whim, and she could never justify to herself why she had bothered. Those keepsakes could not be replaced any more than her father or Adèle themselves. Not to mention the house, which she had come to as a bride. The first home she had ever called her own.

Gilbert kissed his wife's cheek. The bakery had taken every coin he owned to build and had just begun to turn a real profit. It was harder for him to put things into perspective.

"Build in stone this time," Alexandre said. "I wouldn't be surprised if they don't make it a law soon anyway, as many fires as we have."

"It's a sound idea," Gilbert said. "But mercy knows where I'll find the money for stone."

"I'll lend it to you," Alexandre said.

"I can't accept that," Gilbert said.

Elisabeth could guess that stone would cost a fantastic sum of money. Debt was the curse of the colonist, and Gilbert had been proud to avoid it before now. It took no convincing for Elisabeth to see they wouldn't be able to escape it any longer if they wished to remain in business.

"You're the best bakers in the settlement," Alexandre said. "It's a sound investment. With a solid building and good equipment, your business will double, if not more."

Elisabeth knew this was an offer that a sensible man like Gilbert could not turn down.

"You have an agreement, Lefebvre," Gilbert said.

"I—I should be getting home," Pascal said with a stammer, placing his napkin on the table.

"What do you mean?" Elisabeth asked.

"It's my fault the shop burned," he said. "I wanted to light the fire in the oven so the two of you could get more sleep."

"You sweet boy," said Elisabeth, wrapping her arms around Pascal. More than once, Gilbert groused about having to waken to get the oven lit and mellowed to the right temperature a full hour before they could begin baking.

"Son, it was an accident," Gilbert said. "It could have happened to me, or to Elisabeth. That house was as dry as a pile of November leaves. I'm sorry it happened, and I don't want it to scare you. I'll train you up on oven duty as soon as I have one to light again."

Pascal nodded at his master. Elisabeth kissed the boy's cheek and embraced him.

"We couldn't do without you," she said with a teasing smile. "I've grown too accustomed to the help."

"I've never been happier to hear a thing in my life," Gilbert said. "And stay used to it, too. Pascal is going to be a full apprentice next year, and he'll need all the practice in the kitchen he can get."

"Once your new shop is built, there will be no want for work," Alexandre said.

"From your mouth to God's ears, my friend," Gilbert said, raising his mug. "For there is never too much of that to be had."

* * *

For the first time, in what seemed like an eon, Elisabeth slept past dawn. She made her way down the stairs the following morning, still unaccustomed to the fine surroundings. Her head split in two and her stomach was as unsteady as in the early days of her pregnancy. Though everyone was gathered in the dining room for their breakfast, Elisabeth persuaded a passing maid to fetch her a cup of tea to the vacant parlor. *Just a few moments of tranquility before I face company.*

Elisabeth chose a plush chair, close to the window that afforded a good view of the river. The parlor was impeccably furnished and gracious like those of Anne Martin's elegant friends. Nicole, however, had the talent for making wealth and opulence seem welcoming and approachable. Elisabeth felt comfortable sitting on the velvet chairs and placing her cup on the marble side table. Perhaps it was Nicole's presence. Perhaps it was Alexandre's lack of pretension, despite his position. Whatever it was, Elisabeth was glad for their hospitality.

The maid emerged with the tea and departed, calling no attention to herself. The dainty china cup, painted with pink-and-white lilies, was eerily like the pattern her mother used to embroider on every cloth surface she laid her hands on. The flower of the French royalty. Anne had grander visions than life had fit her for, and Elisabeth spared a rare charitable thought for her mother. *You would have been an excellent noblewoman. Your father made a bad match for you based on the interests of his own pocket. Papa deserved better than you, but you deserved different from what you were given, too.*

The greenish mixture in the cup was no proper tea, but an herbal approximation that was the best anyone could do in the colony. Elisabeth closed her eyes and dreamed that the fragile cup contained a rich brew of real Arabian coffee. Many mornings, she and Anne had enjoyed their cup of coffee in silence. One of the few things they shared was a love of the brew, and they chose not to spoil their enjoyment of it with conversation.

One sip of the bitter tea reminded Elisabeth that Arabian coffee was no more attainable in the settlement than the moon itself. One of the little sacrifices she never knew she would have to make when she left. Compared to the other sacrifices thrust upon her in recent days, it was insignificant, but Elisabeth found it easier to focus on the annoyance of inferior beverages than the real losses she was faced with.

Enough sulking. Gilbert and Pascal don't need to waste their strength comforting me.

Elisabeth stood, handing the cup off to yet another maid, and entered the dining room. She did not plaster a false smile on her face, but banished the grief from her countenance as best she could.

Just then, the babe inside her offered a reassuring nudge. *There's plenty to be going on for.*

CHAPTER 22

Nicole

August 1670

The Lefebvre house bustled with activity after the temporary addition of the Beaumonts and Pascal. Nicole was pleased to have her friend in residence, and was in no rush to see the new shop complete. There was seldom a day when Rose did not make an appearance as well, eager to spend as much time as she could with her friends, while they both had ample leisure time to socialize.

"How pretty you look in blue," Nicole said, draping a length of lovely linen over Elisabeth's shoulder. "Fitting the three of you for new clothes is the most fun I've had in ages."

"The color does suit you," Rose said. "We should make a little gown for the baby from the scraps."

"You and Alexandre have been too generous to us." Elisabeth sighed, not for the first time.

"You needed new clothes," Nicole said. "Alexandre wanted me to hire a tailor, but I wanted the fun of making your wardrobe ourselves. Aside from looking after Hélène and Manon, I don't have a lot to do. Alexandre isn't used to a wife who works."

"I'm sure you'll adapt," Rose said with a smile.

"That worries me, too," Nicole said, more sober. "I don't want everything to change."

"But it does," Elisabeth said, "and we're better off embracing it."

Nicole smiled. "You're the best-suited of us for life here. You grew accustomed to this place long before Rose and I did."

"I left behind far less than either of you," Elisabeth said. "You had a family who loved you. Rose had her duties at the Salpêtrière. I wouldn't have had the shop for much longer. All I had to cling to were the memories of my father, and a mother who didn't care."

Nicole didn't answer. Letters from home arrived less and less often, which came as no surprise. Her family had moved on with their lives—lives that no longer included her. She wouldn't want them to pine for her, anyway.

"Well, you're certainly easier to fit than Pascal," Rose said. "That rascal could hardly stand still."

"He can't bear to sit idle," Elisabeth said. "So much like Gilbert."

"At least Gilbert could stand long enough for us to take a proper measurement, for pity's sake," Nicole said. "I'm worried none of Pascal's things will fit at all."

Elisabeth laughed, taking her seat now that her own measurements were complete. She took up a pair of trousers she was fashioning for Gilbert. These would be much finer clothes than the Beaumont family had worn before the fire. Nicole hoped that their generosity wouldn't grate too much on Gilbert's pride.

Alexandre had told Nicole to see to the replacement of the Beaumonts' household goods, and had allocated a generous budget. For his own part, Alexandre helped Gilbert contract for the construction of the new shop, with an apartment above, on a plot near the center of town.

Nicole understood that although the cost was minimal to Alexandre, it was an enormous sum to Gilbert. Nicole tried to give her gifts with sensitivity and discretion. She knew Gilbert and Elisabeth felt beholden enough already.

"It seems a shame to make so many dresses when I won't be able to wear them once the baby is here," Elisabeth said. "That is, I hope I'm back to my old size soon enough once he or she is here."

"This little one won't be the last," Rose said.

"No," Nicole said, thinking of her own precious bundle that was not yet noticeable under her skirts and stays.

She frowned as the memories of her pregnancy and labor played through her head. She was not looking forward to reliving the last month of pregnancy, or the childbed. Alexandre was thrilled, and longed for a son, though he would not say so directly.

Three hours later, Gilbert had sturdy trousers, and Pascal had a starched new shirt for church and Sunday school well under way.

"The three finest seamstresses in all of New France," Alexandre said, entering the salon as they tidied up their bits of cloth and thread. "It looks like you put your afternoon to good use."

"Yes, indeed," Rose said, smiling at her uncle-in-law. "Your wife has quite the eye for fabric."

"I'm pleased to hear it." Alexandre placed an affectionate hand on Nicole's shoulder. "You'll forgive me if I claim her from you now."

Nicole followed her husband to his office. According to their semi-weekly tradition, Nicole sat in the stiff chair opposite Alexandre's desk as they went over the household accounts together.

"Well done," Alexandre said as he looked at the ledger. "There isn't a better house manager in all of France, I'd wager. The household expenses have gone down by a wide margin since you and the girls moved in."

"Thank you." Nicole refrained from saying that the only thing she had to do was eliminate the waste the servants caused when Alexandre wasn't looking. In the beginning, the staff was not overly happy to have an attentive mistress, but seemed to be accepting her supervision. Managing a staff, Nicole learned, was not much different from managing a family, and Nicole had seen her mother do that with skill for many years.

"The governor is having a ball two weeks from today," Alexandre said. "You need a new gown. Take money from the household funds and have one of the local seamstresses concoct something fashionable for you. Don't fret about the cost."

"Alexandre, that isn't necessary. Surely I have something that would do."

"This is an important function," Alexandre said. "I need you dressed accordingly."

"Very well." There was no use arguing when Alexandre gave an order.

"Most women enjoy spending money on such things." Alexandre looked at Nicole as though trying to solve a complex mathematical problem.

"I must not be like most women," Nicole said. "I'd rather see the money spent elsewhere, or, better still, saved."

"You're a wise woman," Alexandre said, sitting back in his chair and rubbing his tired eyes. "But this is a case of money well spent. You're not accustomed to a world where appearances mean as much, if not more, than substance."

"No I'm not. And I fear I don't like it."

"Neither do I," Alexandre said. "But it is the world I was born into. And there are worse things in the world for a man than seeing his wife well dressed, so please accommodate me. I'll be up to see the children shortly."

Nicole recognized her dismissal, and ascended the stairs to the nursery where Hélène played with her nurse and Manon sat immersed in her studies.

"Mamah!" the child cried.

Nicole smiled and took her from Eloise.

"Was she a good girl this afternoon?" Nicole asked.

"As always," Eloise said. The girls loved the nursemaid, and while Nicole had no qualms about the kindly old woman's care, she felt an occasional stab of jealousy. Running the household did necessitate the help, however, and Eloise was wonderful with the children.

"And how goes the studying, mademoiselle?" Nicole asked.

The candlelight reflected off the top of Manon's black head as she pored over her Latin grammar.

"Very well." Manon looked up from the text with a smile. "How was your day, Maman?"

"Just fine," Nicole said.

It was hard to believe that the child did not speak a word of French only two years before. Manon had shown a scholastic aptitude far beyond her peers, and now took private lessons from the Sisters after the classes with the rest of the Huron girls concluded for the day.

"Tell me, what has Homer to say today?" Alexandre asked as he entered the nursery.

Manon, as always, gave a perfect account of her lessons and expertly answered all of Alexandre's grammar queries. He nodded his head in satisfaction. Manon understood herself to be dismissed. She took her text and retreated to her bedroom.

The nurse followed suit, taking leave to her own small chamber.

"And how is Papa's little angel?" Alexandre asked, bouncing the joyful toddler on his knee.

Hélène's response was a drool-soaked grin and squeal.

"Manon is coming along so well in school," Nicole said. "Rose says the Sisters have rarely seen the likes of her."

"Very good," Alexandre said, kissing the child on her plump cheek. "Do you think they intend her for the Church?"

"Likely," Nicole said.

"You don't want her to become a nun?" Alexandre asked. "It would be an excellent choice for her, studious thing that she is."

"If it's what she wants, I'll accept it," Nicole said. "But I worry that life will be too confining for her."

"Time will be the best judge of that," Alexandre said, dismissing the subject. "And what future for you, little cherub? A handsome duke? Nay, only a prince in shining armor for my girl."

Nicole smiled at her husband's exuberance, but his obvious preference for Hélène over Manon troubled her. Outwardly, Alexandre was kind, never raising his voice or a hand in Manon's direction. He ensured the Huron girl was well dressed, well fed, and had the best of everything. However, Nicole understood far better than her husband that material goods and physical comfort were not the same as genuine affection.

The adults dined together each night precisely at seven o'clock. Manon, Hélène, and Pascal ate together in the kitchen an hour before.

"Three more weeks until the shop will be complete," Gilbert

said one night, after yet another day of overseeing the construction. "Were it not for your influence, Lefebvre, it would take three times as long."

"Glad to be of use," Alexandre said. "Heaven knows there is plenty of building to do in this colony. The builders need to keep focused and finish a job before they take on the next. I'm not sure the governor was wise to bar the formation of guilds within the settlement. It seems to me the organization would help."

"You may be right," Gilbert said. "But the guilds are harmful in some respects as well. They insist that the workers and even apprentices earn wages in addition to their meals. It may discourage some from taking them on, which may deplete the supply of skilled laborers in time. And there's precious few of them already." Nicole nodded. Many who came from France did so in exchange for three years of free labor. Most masters worked hard to ensure their workers were well taken care of, but had little in the way of liquid money to repay their help. Alexandre was aware that people like Gilbert traded in kind rather than in cash for most things, but it was a reality, Nicole expected, he couldn't fully understand.

"That could be amended within the system," Alexandre said. "But the main thing is, you'll be installed in a month or two more, and open for business soon after, I trust."

"As soon as I can manage it," Gilbert said. "Best to open doors and get established before winter."

Nicole ate in silence as the men conversed. Gilbert was now indebted to another man in order to establish himself, as were most men in the colony. It would take four years, at least, to clear the debt, and Nicole had seen more than a few of the colonists struggle or fail to pay their debts. The consequences were sometimes dire. Nicole hoped Alexandre would prove a gracious creditor. She tried to temper the nagging worry that her husband might be steering Gilbert into too large an enterprise. She pushed the worry away.

It was not her place to doubt her husband.

The evenings passed pleasantly in the company of the Beaumonts. Conversation never lacked, and they often retired to bed much later than anticipated. Elisabeth and Gilbert, along with Pascal, occupied the guest rooms on the west side of the house, while

Alexandre and Nicole each had a room down the hall from the nursery on the opposite side.

The arrangement was not what Nicole was used to. She and Luc had shared a bed for the duration of their marriage, as did her parents and all of the other couples in her acquaintance. After her marriage to Alexandre, Nicole learned that separate rooms were traditional for the upper classes. *So cold. So formal. I can't see why anyone would want this.* For all the comforts of Alexandre's home, Nicole questioned whether she'd been wise to marry above her station. She felt sure she'd never be a part of Alexandre's sphere and even more certain that she didn't want to be.

There was no knock at the door that night, nor did she expect one for at least six months. Not until the baby was born and she had time to heal. On nights when Alexandre did not make an appearance, Nicole would have, in the space of a single heartbeat, exchanged her husband's position for that of an honest blacksmith who chose to share a bed with his wife.

"Excellent, madame," said Yvette Babineaux, Nicole's seamstress. "This color suits you well. I haven't seen satin as fine as this in three years or more. You will be ravishing."

The dress *did* fit well, and did not bring undue attention to the thickening of her midsection. The soft pink silk felt decadent. It was the finest garment Nicole had ever owned, and she felt a twinge of vanity when she saw her reflection in the mirror. She looked like a fine lady, even if she was not one by birth.

What wouldn't I give for Maman to see me dressed this way, Nicole thought. *She would know that she would never need to worry about me going without ever again.*

"Thank you, Madame Babineaux," Nicole said. "You've done splendid work."

"It was a pleasure, madame," Yvette said. "There isn't much call for finery here, so jobs like these are particular fun."

Nicole paid the sum, plus a handsome bonus, and dismissed the woman from her chamber. The ball was an hour away, the dress finished just in time for their departure.

Margaux, the servant who acted as Nicole's personal maid when the occasion warranted, saw to her hair and a dusting of cosmetics. Just as the maid was about to take her leave, Alexandre's knock at the door startled Nicole from a reverie she didn't know she had fallen into.

"Come in," she said.

"You look beautiful," Alexandre said. "This dress will be the making of young Madame Babineaux. Once the ladies see this, she'll be the most sought-after seamstress in New France."

"I hope so," Nicole said. "That's why I hired her. I hoped to give her business a boost. The way she dresses and carries herself, I thought she would be capable."

"That's my bride," Alexandre said. "An eye for talent. The dress is as perfect as the lady in it. It only wants one thing."

Alexandre removed a small leather case from his breast pocket and opened it to reveal a strand of creamy white pearls. He removed them and clasped them around Nicole's neck, then turned her toward the mirror to admire the effect.

"Lovely," he said.

"Thank you," Nicole said, her hand rising to her throat. The simple strand of pearls had to be worth the price of a small farm.

"I thought they would accentuate the brooch you're so fond of," Alexandre said, playing with a tendril of chestnut hair that draped on the creamy skin of her neck.

"My good luck charm," she said, fumbling with the gem at her bosom. "It was my mother's. She asked me to sell it for money to buy land, but the jeweler said they were just imitation pearls. Since it was worth so little, it wasn't worth selling. I do like having it, though."

"You did well to keep it, my dear," Alexandre said. "Because those aren't glass pearls at all. Perhaps not the finest specimens in Paris, but they are genuine, I assure you."

Nicole choked on her emotions as Alexandre's words registered. She had been swindled . . . and her family had been deprived of a much-needed source of income.

"Do you think I could sell the brooch here?" Nicole asked.

"Why would you want to be parted from your keepsake, dearest?" Alexandre's brow furrowed as his wife's expression grew more absent.

"The money would help my family," Nicole said. "I would never have kept it if I knew it would fetch a price."

"Don't worry about it, dear," Alexandre said, handing Nicole her shawl. "I will make it right."

Of course he would, Nicole thought to herself. *So many problems are so easily solved when you have money.*

"Just do me one small favor," Alexandre said.

"Of course."

"At least *pretend* to have fun this evening," he said, his smile teasing.

"If I must," Nicole said, returning his smile with less vivacity. "But only for you. May I have just one moment?"

Alexandre nodded and left Nicole before the mirror. She hardly recognized the woman who stood before her in the reflection. She was not born into a life of silk and pearls, but here she stood. Perfectly dressed. Perfectly coiffed. Though she did not feel the part of a society maven, she knew she looked it. *I don't want to be a part of this world, but I will try for you, Alexandre.*

The governor's mansion sparkled as though made of diamonds. Gemstones shone on the ladies' necks, and the chandeliers glittered with crystals. . . . The beauty dazzled Nicole into silence. She had never seen such opulence, which rivaled her grandest visions of the finest salons in Paris. The majority of the colony's functions occurred during the social season, just after Christmastide, but the arrival of the King's advisor and a top civil authority from France required an exception. Thankfully, the late August evening was cool. The satin gown would have been stifling a month before.

"Breathe," Alexandre reminded her, seeing his wife's discomfort.

"What am I doing here?" Nicole asked in a whisper. "I'm a farmer's daughter. I don't belong here. I feel as if, any second, someone is going to shout 'Imposter!' and throw me into the street."

"Half the people here aren't nearly as highborn as they would have you think. The other half have plenty to hide, I assure you. The trick is to think you fit in with this despicable crew, and you will."

"If you dislike them so much, then why are we here?" Nicole asked.

"The governor has the ear of the Intendant and the Intendant has the ear of the King," Alexandre answered, his expression matter-of-fact. "It's all about influence."

Nicole nodded. Alexandre's business was complex, and she had little interest in it, aside from assisting him as best she could, but it didn't take business sense to know that nothing but good could come from knowing the right people.

Nicole plastered a smile on her face and followed Alexandre's lead.

". . . and do you think the King's ministers understand what that law will mean for the colonists?" Alexandre was deep in conversation with one of the governor's underlings, a small, sniveling man whose name had escaped Nicole.

"You look positively radiant," said the deputy's wife, Ursule.

She scrutinized Nicole's figure, with a lingering glance at her midsection. There was a trace of either disappointment or jealousy in her face. "I've always been partial to pink. . . ."

Nicole listened as Ursule prattled on. She responded politely as needed and kept one ear on Alexandre's conversation. Any information Nicole could glean might be of use to Alexandre later.

Nicole felt a wave of relief as the butler announced dinner and the party dispersed to the massive dining hall.

Outside in, Nicole thought, remembering the rules for flatware.

Shortly after they were married, Alexandre had started coaching her in the etiquette of the aristocracy.

"Remember," he had said. "The upper class knows itself through mannerisms. Eating a certain way, speaking a certain way, and acting a certain way are ways to let the elite know you are one of them."

Nicole's mother had been adamant about good manners at the supper table, but her directives were nothing compared to the list of rules to which Nicole now found herself subject. Fear loomed in her brain that someone would see her use a fish fork for the appetizer and have her flung out for her deception.

The food was elaborate, the presentation exquisite. Quail, *foie gras,* creamy sauces, delicate pastries, and more, all served in abundance. The best wines from France flowed freely. Nicole tried to choose her flatware by sneaking a glance at her husband's hands before she ate. Despite her nerves, she had to admit the food was beyond any meal she'd ever eaten before. However, she understood that ladies did not eat overmuch at these occasions, so she was careful to sample the dishes but little more.

"Dancing next," Alexandre whispered in his wife's ear.

Nicole groaned to herself and longed for the warmth of her bed.

As couples made their way to the ballroom, Nicole took Alexandre's arm and followed. The strains of a minuet sounded from the small orchestra. Couples took their places on the dance floor. Nicole had practiced the steps for two weeks and hoped against hope she would not fall on her face. Alexandre was more than adept at dancing, however, and she found it easy to follow his lead.

"It's not that bad, is it?" Alexandre asked after several minutes.

"Not as long as you lead. I can manage the steps, or at least pretend."

"You're catching on to the whole charade marvelously," Alexandre said with a laugh. "You're one of us now."

"I'm not sure how I feel about that."

"Nor am I," Alexandre said. "But I'm happy you're trying."

"My pleasure." Nicole was mostly telling the truth. The evening had not been quite as torturous as she imagined it might be.

"Ah, Lefebvre," said a buoyant voice, approaching.

Alexandre broke from dancing to shake the governor's hand.

"Let me congratulate you on such a lovely bride," the governor said, "as I haven't yet had the chance."

"Thank you, monsieur gouverneur," Alexandre said with a subtle inclination of the head.

"The King has not failed to send the finest flowers from his kingdom for our poor settlement, has he?" the governor asked in a grandiose voice.

Nicole could not hide her blush, but did not avert her eyes.

"Better than that," Alexandre said. "I ought to send him a letter of thanks, for I'm certain he has sent me the finest jewel from his treasury."

Nicole wasn't sure whether to grimace or laugh. She despised these courtly manners.

"In that case, Lefebvre, you must allow me the pleasure of a dance with your breathtaking bride," the governor said. "You could not deny an old man such a rare pleasure."

"Indeed, I could not. Please enjoy yourselves."

Alexandre bowed and handed Nicole to the governor's hands. He led her to the center of the dance floor. Despite his considerable size, the governor was not without grace. He was as accomplished in dancing as her husband, no doubt the product of a social education that had started in the earliest days of childhood.

"And how long have you been in New France, my dear?" the governor asked, looking down at Nicole with interest as he led her about the dance floor.

"Not yet three years, monsieur," she answered.

"That long?" he asked. "What a pity we have just now met."

"A shame indeed, monsieur," Nicole said, trying to emulate the manners and expression she had seen in the other ladies. She did not hint at the truth that until she had married Alexandre, she was well beneath his notice.

"Your husband has quite the mind for business, madame. You must be proud."

"Immensely so," Nicole said, with a genuine smile. "I've never met his equal."

"It's good for a wife to be so generous with praise for her husband's accomplishments," the governor said.

"As all wives should be. But then, I am fortunate to be married to such a praiseworthy man, monsieur," Nicole said. "It makes the task much easier."

The dance was coming to its end, and Nicole gave what she hoped was a graceful curtsy to her partner. From the corner of her eye, she saw Alexandre bowing to a gray-haired, elegant woman not far away. She hoped to make her way back to him but was tapped gently on the shoulder.

"Might I have the pleasure?" asked a balding man in his forties or fifties. Nicole nodded her assent and was not left without a partner for the next two hours.

"Will you allow an old man to dance with his wife?" Lefebvre said as another of the governor's deputies led Nicole to the dance floor.

"In one night you've become the *grande dame* of New France society," Alexandre whispered, with mirth in his shining gray eyes. "I've never seen the like of it."

"Very funny," Nicole said. "I've never been so relieved to see anyone in my life. My feet are killing me."

"Then we'll escape back home once this dance is over," Alexandre promised. "But you must tell me what you said to the governor."

"He commented on your business skill, and I agreed with him, as any good wife would do," she said. "I hope I haven't said anything I oughtn't."

"Quite the contrary, dearest," Alexandre said. "I believe you said all the right things. He wishes to see us in his offices on Monday."

"Us?" she asked. "Both of us?"

"Yes," he said. "I believe you have bewitched him. And I don't blame him for wanting to see more of you. You are the most beautiful woman here."

"Then keep your promise and take me home," Nicole said, smiling as the song ended.

"A distinct pleasure, madame," said Alexandre, offering his arm.

Though Alexandre claimed the meeting was likely a social formality, Nicole had never seen her husband so anxious. The governor, however, had grander plans for Lefebvre, as Nicole suspected. When they returned home, Nicole saw to it that the dinner was a meal of special magnificence. The finest hens, well seasoned and roasted with a careful eye, graced the Lefebvre table along with creamed potatoes, Elisabeth's good cakes, and a bottle of champagne that Alexandre himself had brought over from France. It was becoming popular with the elite in Paris, though Nicole had yet to adjust to the shock of bubbles bursting in her mouth, releasing a tidal wave of flavor.

"To Seigneur Lefebvre," Gilbert toasted.

"Seigneur Lefebvre," the others chorused.

Alexandre beamed a radiant smile and raised his glass to his guests and family. Nicole knew this was the day he had hoped for since setting sail for the New World six years before. He was now a lord in his own right, with land to rent, tax, and govern like any of the landed gentry in France.

Nicole beamed back, knowing her husband would be the kind, fair landowner he had always longed to be.

Chapter 23

Rose

September 1670

"How shall we spend the day, my beautiful Madame Lefebvre?" Henri asked, his tone buoyant at the breakfast table. "I cannot bear to face a day of work on one of the last fine days of the year."

Rose offered him a smile, pleased to see the furrow of worry absent from his brow. Their reserves were dwindling and they needed income. She knew it pressed on him, but she didn't want to add to his burden by bringing up the subject overmuch. "As long as I spend the day with you, I'm happy to set aside my needlework for a spell."

"I honestly don't know how you ladies manage that awful stuff," confessed Henri. "It looks so boring."

"It's knitting I loathe," Rose said. "But I've always been partial to embroidery. It's refreshing, in a way."

"I suppose I can see that," he said. "I feel the same way about riding. I'd sooner go without my arm than my horse."

"Will we be able to keep him?" Rose asked. "I imagine it's expensive. . . ."

"Never fear, darling, Abraxas is safe. Uncle Alexandre will keep him in hay for us if the need arises." Rose nodded her approval.

The palomino gelding was a source of pride and pleasure for Henri and she hated the idea of seeing them separated.

"He's a good man," Rose said.

"That he is," Henri said, a grin appearing on his lips. "And, what's more, he hates my father, so my disinheritance infuriates him."

"Why does he hate your father so?"

"It began as nothing more than the second son's resentment of his older brother," Henri said. "But Grandfather was so determined to keep his estate in one piece that he left Alexandre with nothing other than his God-given wit. Thankfully, he has plenty of that."

"That he does," Rose said. "How unfeeling of your grandfather not to leave *something* for his son."

"To make matters worse, Alexandre is thirteen years my father's junior. He was still at university when Grandfather died," Henri said. "Had Grandmother not insisted, I'm sure Father would have pulled his funding."

"You honestly think so?" Rose asked. "How terrible."

"I would not put such a thing beyond my father's capabilities," Henri said. "He is more concerned about money than any man I ever met. My brother, Lionel, is just like him. I think, ultimately, Father would rather leave the estate to Lionel. I have always been too independent, too adventurous with my money, for Father's liking."

"I'm so sorry, Henri," Rose said. "There is no way he would change his mind?"

"I doubt it," Henri said. "And in my heart of hearts, I'm glad. We would have had to return to France when he died, and I much prefer the freedom here. France stifles me."

"I'm sorry it was all because of me," Rose said. "I don't want our marriage to be the cause of discord."

"It makes no difference," Henri said. "You are worth a dozen fortunes."

"You flatterer." She gave him a playfully scornful look. "The sad part is that if they knew who my family was, they probably would have approved of me."

"Which lends credence to my idea that he was looking for reasons to disinherit me," Henri said. "I am out from under my father's thumb, and it doesn't suit him, but it suits me well. Don't think any more on it."

"I agree, not today. Not while the autumn sun shines."

"Indeed, Madame Lefebvre," Henri said. "We should spend the day out-of-doors. A picnic. I know just the spot."

"That sounds wonderful." Rose shared her husband's love of the mountains and woods of Quebec. After three years of clean air in New France, the thought of returning to Paris, even without the confinement of the Salpêtrière, sent Rose into a cold sweat.

Agathe was given orders to prepare a basket with the finest lunch she could procure, and the couple took off, both mounted on Abraxas rather than bothering to hitch the horse to their small open carriage. Abraxas was a massive horse, with a thick golden coat well suited to the climate. He bore the extra passenger with ease and seemed elated with the chance to exercise his legs in the fine weather.

"Here we are," Henri said.

"I can see why you love to ride," Rose said, rubbing the horse's nose and offering him an apple from the picnic basket. "Abraxas is such a sweet animal."

"Best horse I've ever ridden," Henri said, patting the gelding's golden shoulder. Turning to his wife, he asked, "What do you think of the view?"

They stood in a large clearing that allowed a view of the Saint Lawrence to the south. Mountains loomed to the north and east. The odor of the evergreens wafted heavy in her nose. "It's stunning," Rose said, setting out a blanket on the grassy field. "How did you find this place?"

"It's ours. Or will be. This is part of Uncle's estate. He will rent this to us and he's agreed to make some vast improvements to the existing farmhouse, just there." He pointed to a small, but sturdy-looking stone building off in the distance. "It will be infinitely cheaper than our place in town. It won't be a luxurious life, but it will be a comfortable one. If you consent, of course."

"I'm not sure I understand," Rose said, looking up as she set out Agathe's inviting dishes. "Do you think you could be happy as a farmer?"

"I wasn't made for manual labor, I admit," Henri said, as he took a seat on the blanket. "I will help manage Uncle's lands on-site and make sure that the tenant farmers do their part for us and us for them. Like most of the *seigneurs,* Uncle prefers to live in town, but knows the absence of the *seigneur* does not inspire the farmers to hard work. Between Uncle and me, we'll have the most successful estate in all of New France."

"And you hope they'll make you a *seigneur* as well," Rose speculated.

"Well done," he answered. "It will probably be several years before the governor thinks of me, but my uncle's influence can't hurt."

"I imagine not," Rose said. "Is this what you want?"

"Without question. To make my own way without my father trying to control every aspect of my life? It's what I've always dreamed of."

"Then how could I object?" Rose asked, looking over the landscape. "I would love nothing more."

Rose looked out at the vast expanse of land and admired the stately mountains and proud pines. They would make for lovely scenery in the coming years. Whether they could provide equally good companionship was a thing far less certain.

The plans for their removal to the estate took time. They would need a crew to renovate the old farmhouse and to make their plot of land welcoming. Their plot of land was small, with the majority reserved for the tenant farmers. The terrain was too precious to be wasted for anything other than cultivation. Henri decided it would be the following spring before they took residence—perhaps summer, if luck was not on their side. Rose feigned indifference to the delays, but was happy with anything that prolonged their removal to the country.

"You aren't too unhappy to leave town, are you?" Henri asked one night as they snuggled in each other's arms in the moments before sleep. Tonight was one of the nights where his closeness was comforting rather than stifling.

"No," Rose answered, idly tracing patterns on his chest with her fingertips. "Though I will be sad to be so far from Nicole and Elisabeth. I'll miss them terribly."

Henri kissed his wife's forehead. "The distance isn't all that great."

"With household duties and winter weather, our visits won't be frequent," Rose said. "But one cannot have sweetness in life without sacrifice. I'll manage, darling. Don't fret for me."

"Fretting about you is one of my fondest pastimes," Henri said with a teasing grin. "You wouldn't deny me the pleasure."

"No," Rose said. "I've denied you all the pleasure I ever plan to."

"That's what a man likes to hear," he said.

A few weeks later, Rose sat in her favorite chair by the window, embroidering frills on a small dress.

"And what has my lady so engrossed?" Henri asked, startling his wife, who shrieked at the unexpected sound of his voice.

"Heavens, you scared me," Rose said. "Just my sewing."

"Remind me to wear a bell 'round my neck like a cow for the next time you sit transfixed with your fancy work," Henri said. "I was in the room for a full three minutes at least."

"I get absorbed, that's all," Rose said.

"Well, wake yourself from your reverie for a few moments," Henri said. "We're going for a walk."

"It's rather chilly for a stroll." She looked out to see the limbs of the evergreens swaying in the bitter September breeze that had settled in overnight.

"We won't be out long," Henri said. "Come, I've something to show you."

Seeing the excitement, near giddiness, on her husband's face, Rose could not bring herself to object, no matter how comfortable her seat nor how warm the fire.

They walked to the stables, not far from the house, where Henri lodged Abraxas. A sturdy-looking mare, not advanced in years but old enough to have mellowed, stood in the stall beside Henri's beloved horse. She had Abraxas's shining golden coat, but stood two or three hands shorter.

"This is Amethea," Henri said. "Abraxas's sister. I thought she would be perfect for you."

"She's gorgeous," Rose said, nuzzling the horse's soft nose with her own. "But can we afford her with all that is going on?"

"It's a necessary expense," Henri said. "You'll need a sound horse of your own when we move out of town. Getting her now allows you time to learn to ride."

"Thank you so much," Rose said, sliding into her husband's embrace. "She's wonderful."

"You have to promise to ride her faithfully," Henri said. "Horses need exercise."

"I'm not sure it's the best idea in my current condition," Rose said, moving his hand to her belly. "We wouldn't want to risk the health of your future heir."

It took a few moments for Henri to comprehend her meaning, but then he lifted her into his arms.

"No, we most certainly don't. We"—He twirled Rose once gently and placed her back on firm ground. "We'll find a stable boy. Borrow Pascal Giroux when he needs a break from the bakery.

"How far along?" He cleared his throat against the threatening tears and kissed her cheeks softly.

"Not more than two months. Early days yet." Rose smiled up at her husband, biting her lip at the sight of his feeble attempts to keep his tears at bay.

"Promise me you'll rest, my sweet one. Promise me you'll have the servants attend to whatever it is you need. I'll hire you a maid if we need to." His embrace was gentler than usual, already protective of the new life they were responsible for. Rose knew Henri was eager for a family, but he'd refrained from discussing it since the early days of their marriage. At first, her reluctance to join him in his bed made the topic unnecessary and painful. Later, her revelations about her uncle must have made him nervous to press her about any aspect of intimate life. Rose tightened her arms around him, grateful that he'd tempered his enthusiasm and happy she could finally give that measure of happiness back to him.

"I think I'll be able to manage as we are, darling." The cost of a personal maid couldn't be borne for years yet, as much as Henri wanted to give her that luxury. "But I promise I'll take care of this little one as best I can."

"Thank you, my love." Henri finally gave in to the tears and let them spill down his cheeks as he held Rose against him.

"I'm just sorry it was such a long road to get here." Rose reached up and kissed his cheek, oblivious to the passersby who might see the display.

"But we got here, my dearest wife, and that's all that matters to me."

The following afternoon, Rose took her usual seat in Nicole's parlor, armed with her sewing. Though only a few stitches from complete, she brought the small gown she'd been working on the previous day.

"I've never seen you take such pains for a baby gown," Elisabeth said, taking her eyes from the star-patterned quilt she had fashioned from odd scraps.

"I thought I'd make a special effort this time around," Rose said, not looking up from her work.

"I've heard the Laurier woman is expecting again," Nicole said, her knitting needles not missing a beat. "I know you were there for her last time. Has she asked you to come again?"

"No," Rose said. "My days of midwifery are over. Unless either of you need me, of course."

"Rose—are you?" Elisabeth's voice betrayed her reluctance to broach the subject. *God knows they probably think Henri and I can't have children by now.*

"Yes," Rose said, looking up at her friends with a soft smile. *They'll never know what our troubles were. Let them think it was just a problem of nature and not my reluctance to be a proper wife.*

The trio stood and embraced, not without a few tears.

"Oh, I am so happy for you!" Nicole exclaimed. "Our babies will be such dear friends."

"Let's hope so," Rose said. "I don't know what I'd do without either of you. What I *will* do without you when I am out on the estate, for that matter."

"It's not that far," Nicole said. "We'll be together all the time."

"You sound like your nephew-in-law," Rose chided. "You're a mother and a wife. You know that can't be."

"Well, niece-in-law, I promise we'll make an effort," Nicole said, taking Rose in her arms. "And you will stay here when the baby is born. If you need a doctor it will make things far less complicated."

Rose exhaled. The realities of the birth hadn't even registered with her. The baby would arrive in spring at least, so she wouldn't have to contend with winter storms preventing her from getting to town. Henri would agree to stay with his uncle for a month or so. He would not prevent her from doing so, in any case.

"Thank you, dearest aunt-in-law," Rose said, kissing Nicole on the cheek.

"Merciful heavens, that makes me sound old," Nicole said with an uncharacteristic giggle.

"Baby clothes," Elisabeth declared, reclaiming her seat. "You'll have baby Lefebvre outfitted before the afternoon is out."

For the next hour, Nicole spoke of her early days mothering Hélène in the convent. Elisabeth spoke of her baby's impending arrival. Rose chimed in on occasion, smiled, kept up with her sewing. All the while it sank in that she was wholly unprepared for the enormous task that lay before her.

Childbirth still terrified her, but less so. On a daily basis, she saw women walking about the settlement, babes in arms, no worse for their toils. But in seven months, an innocent life would look to her for love, comfort, and protection. She was confident in her ability to provide the first two. The latter caused her worry. Her uncle had also sworn to protect her when she was twelve years old.

She found herself gripping her needle and gown too tightly, causing a cramp in her forefinger and wrinkles in the fabric. She set the handiwork down on her lap, and focused on the prattle of her two dearest friends. Focused on their words of love. Nicole mothered two lovely girls. Elisabeth fostered the young Giroux boy and would soon welcome her own child. Despite Elisabeth's losses, she seemed calm. Nicole didn't seem wrought with worry as her needles clack-clack-clacked together, a soft wool blanket forming beneath them. Inch by inch, Rose willed her muscles to unwind, her breath to deepen.

She would be a mother. The choice was no longer hers. The best gift she could give her child was a mother with the courage to face the cruel world he or she would inherit. *Would that I could have your courage, ladies, but I suppose I must find my own.*

Rose designated the small bedroom next to their own as "baby's room." Rose knew it was ridiculous, as they would be long removed from the cozy town house before the baby's arrival. *Every bird needs her nest,* she told herself. For weeks she tidied the space, filled it with the dozen baby gowns she and her companions had crafted in the space of an afternoon, and prepared it for the little bundle she found herself longing to hold.

Henri smiled at his wife's antics, but said nothing. Rose suspected he thought her over-eager to welcome their child into the world—something he could not fault in his beloved wife.

But he didn't see the scrubbing.

She took pains to keep her hands from cracking and bleeding. She made sure Agathe never noticed her labors. In fact, she forbade either servant from disturbing the space unless their duties demanded it. She spent more time in the nursery that would never house her child than in any other room in the house.

The more time passed, the more she dreaded leaving their home for the far-flung estate. She would miss her friends, miss the comfort and society of the town, and she would lose this haven she had created for their child. The small corner of the world where she felt certain she could keep her sweet child safe from all the perils that lay beyond its doors.

CHAPTER 24

Elisabeth

November 1670

The crowd inside the Beaumonts' new bakery was the largest Elisabeth had ever seen. Pascal, who had turned thirteen and become a full apprentice, manned the ovens with Gilbert. The new bakery assistant, Pascal's younger sister Gabrielle, served customers and took payments. At age nine, she was Pascal's closest sister both in age and affection, both now thrilled to be reunited under the same roof. Pascal had spoken so often of her and seemed so downtrodden after his visits home that Elisabeth persuaded Gilbert to approach the Giroux man about letting her come on as her assistant. It wasn't the formal apprenticeship they had for Pascal. As she was a girl, this sort of arrangement was rarely bound by contracts, but it was a good opportunity for Gabrielle to make a place for herself in society. And going to bed with a full stomach was a more immediate advantage that the reedy child seemed painfully grateful for.

The bakery kept up with local demand, but only just. Though exhausted, Gilbert was proud of the thriving business.

On Gilbert's orders, Elisabeth spent the day upstairs, resting. In the past week, she had not even ventured out to see Nicole or Rose, but relied on them to visit her for company. She still insisted on making dinner, but was grateful that Gilbert always set aside two loaves of bread for their meal.

"How are you feeling, sweetheart?" Gilbert asked as he came upstairs, Gabrielle trailing behind. "You look tired. Did you stay off your feet?"

"Except for making dinner, yes," Elisabeth said. "I haven't the stamina for anything else."

"Gabrielle will see to dinner until the baby is born and you've recovered," Gilbert said. Turning to Gabrielle, he added, "You can leave the shop an hour early to see to supper. Pascal will take over your duties, and I'll manage the ovens during that time."

"I would love to," Gabrielle said. "I love to cook when there is good food to be made."

"I won't argue," Elisabeth said, smiling at Gabrielle's exuberance. "I've neither the energy nor the desire."

"Sensible," Gilbert said.

Elisabeth stuck her tongue out, teasing her husband for his bossy demeanor. His worry grew worse as her time grew nearer, so she rarely protested his commands. The more she helped him keep his calm, the calmer she felt herself, which in turn made the coming ordeal less strenuous.

Gilbert stroked his wife's hair, causing young Gabrielle to smile. Elisabeth imagined seeing a couple that cared for each other was a novelty for the girl.

"I never want to leave," Gabrielle said. "Your home is so clean and cheerful."

"I'm glad you're happy here." Elisabeth had grown fond of the child in the past three weeks. "But the time will come when you want to start a family of your own."

"Maybe when I'm much older, like you," the child said, her expression serious, "but not before."

Gilbert smiled at the unintended insult, but neither he nor Elisabeth took offense. Gabrielle was a hard worker, cut from the same cloth as her brother, and had even better natural skill in the kitchen than Pascal. Elisabeth hoped to train the girl in the pastry making soon, but for now Gabrielle was needed with the customers.

The entire Beaumont house went to bed shortly after dinner, because the work demanded early mornings. Elisabeth had not toiled as hard as the others, but found herself just as anxious to find her bed.

Almost the moment she lay down, however, she felt a strange pop in her abdomen and a surge of waters. A wave of pain followed, as her muscles contracted. A second contraction came hard upon its heels.

"Elisabeth," Gilbert said. "What's wrong?"

Unable to speak because of the pain, she pointed to her swollen belly.

Without another word, he threw on his coat and went to fetch the midwife. Elisabeth heard him shout for Gabrielle to attend to Madame, and that he would be back shortly.

The labor pains came closer and closer until Elisabeth felt no reprieve between them. The pains stole her breath and caused her to scream into her sheet, but it was not the wrenching agony when Adèle was born. It wasn't the unbearable cramping when she lost the others so early on. This was different, as though her body were working with her instead of against her. She was able to keep her wits about her well enough to keep from scaring poor Gabrielle out of hers.

It's going to be fine. This baby will live. He's had long enough to grow. He's strong. Stronger than the others. She forced herself to repeat the words, but there was still the gray specter of doubt as she recited them. An uncomplicated birth didn't guarantee a healthy child.

Gilbert ushered in the midwife, Sylvie, a kindly woman of fifty-odd years, along with Rose and Nicole, who promised faithfully to let Sylvie perform her duty without their interference. Gilbert motioned for Gabrielle to follow him into the parlor where he would hold vigil until one of the ladies brought him news—whatever it was.

"I'll leave you ladies to your work." Gilbert's face was the color of Elisabeth's bedsheet and as torn as she'd ever seen him. He didn't want to leave his wife in her hour of need, but he didn't want to see her in pain or impede the midwife as she worked.

"Kiss me," Elisabeth rasped before he escaped the bedroom. "Please."

She had her eyes closed against another surge from her midsection, but felt the brush of his lips against her wet brow. *I'll do my best not to fail you again, my love, for there is no chance that I'll allow our hearts to be broken again.*

The implication of that made her heart ache. She would have to force Gilbert to sleep in another bed, night after night, until her courses stopped. After a time, any man would be forced to find comfort elsewhere. Gilbert would be more discreet than most. He would always love her, but there was nothing stopping him from falling in love with another. She wiped away a tear and focused on Sylvie's instructions. *There are other things to worry about at the present moment.*

Nicole stood to Elisabeth's right and Rose to her left, anticipating her need for a cold compress to her forehead or a hand to grasp to help her through one of her surges.

"You can push when you feel ready, my dear." Sylvie spoke in tones just above a whisper to Elisabeth and all the expectant mothers in her care. For this reason among others, she was one of the most sought-after midwives in the settlement.

With every push, Elisabeth hoped she was bringing a child to his first breath and not his last. The pain kept her thoughts in a maelstrom that flung them from hope to despair when they were coherent at all. Above all the image of Gilbert's face, manfully hiding his tears, alternated with his face resplendent with joy. One of the two would be before her soon enough.

"Such a fine young lad I've never seen," proclaimed Sylvie as she handed the swaddled babe to his father. "Your wife did well, Monsieur Beaumont."

"As I knew she would," Gilbert said, beaming at his son. "Little Pierre, you are a handsome thing, aren't you?"

"I think you're a might biased, my darling," Elisabeth chided with a smile.

"As well he should be," Sylvie said. "I declare I've never seen a child so alert this soon after birth. He's going to be extraordinary, mark my words."

"May we see him?" Gabrielle asked from the doorway.

"Of course," Elisabeth said. "Little Pierre will be happy to meet you both."

"Should he be so purple and wrinkled?" Pascal asked.

Gabrielle jabbed him in the ribs with her elbow. "That isn't nice, Pascal! He's lovely," she added, peeking into the blanket-cocoon.

Sylvie chuckled. "He'll look better in a few days, don't you worry."

"I hope so," Pascal said. "Else, I don't think he'd get on well with the other boys."

Gilbert jostled the boy's shoulder, freer from worry than he had been in months.

"To bed with both of you," he ordered, pointing to the door. "We have a bakery to run in just four hours."

"Rest now, madame," said Sylvie, as she prepared to take her leave. "I'll come back in the late morning to check on you."

"Thank you, Sylvie," Elisabeth said, grateful to have had her gentle influence in the room.

"My pleasure," she said, as she left the couple to admire their son.

"Thank *you* so much," Gilbert said, returning Pierre to his mother. "I can't believe I have a son at last."

"I know," Elisabeth said. "I was worried it would never happen."

"Me too," Gilbert confessed. "Should I sleep in the other room?"

"You stay right here. I'm doing as well as can be expected," Elisabeth said, inviting him to bed. "Much better than the last time."

"Thank God for that," Gilbert said. "Rest while you can. I'm sure he'll be hungry soon."

"Too true," Elisabeth said. "Thank you for letting me name him after my father."

"It seemed only right," he said. "Though I'd like the naming of the next Baby Beaumont, if you don't mind."

"Provided I get to hear the choices in advance," she said, so euphoric after giving birth that she would have promised him anything.

"I was thinking Fabien for a boy, in honor of my father," he said.

"And Elisabeth for a girl. . . . We could call her Lisette. I want our daughter named for the best woman I know."

"The next after that will have to be little Gilbert, for his papa," Elisabeth said, taking Pierre from his father's arms and cradling him to her breast.

"He's a little Canadian, isn't he?" Gilbert asked, peering over Elisabeth's shoulder at the baby. "He'll probably never see the country where we were born, just as Pascal and Gabrielle will not."

"That's sad, in a way," Elisabeth said. "I loved Paris so much."

"But wonderful in another," Gilbert said. "We have given him a country all his own. A nation to conquer, if he is strong enough."

Three days later, on a bright Saturday morning, Elisabeth and Gilbert took Pierre to church for his baptism. It was the first time since the re-opening that the shop had been closed, except on Sundays.

Rose and Henri, the godparents, stood at the altar holding the sleeping babe as the priest offered the blessing. Pierre stirred in Rose's arms when the holy water was sprinkled on his forehead, but didn't display his capable lungs, much to his parents' relief.

The child could not have two godmothers, but Nicole had wanted to contribute to the festive occasion, so she had organized a reception at her home after the ceremony. Hélène's baptism had been a quiet proceeding, so soon after Luc's death, so Nicole made Elisabeth allow her full rein to create a lavish affair. The dining table fairly sagged under the weight of the scrumptious dishes.

"Sit, Elisabeth," Nicole said, ushering her to a plush chair placed toward the center of the parlor. "Enjoy the attention the wee man is getting. I'll fetch you a plate."

"Thank you," Elisabeth said, keeping an eye on whoever held Pierre and watching for signs of illness in the guests. Sharing her newborn, even with their nearest friends, was not easy.

The Giroux family attended the fête, due to their children's connection with the Beaumonts. The poor farmers looked ill at ease in Alexandre Lefebvre's spacious residence.

"Please have a plate of something," Elisabeth said to Pascal's parents, indicating the dining area.

"Very kind of you, madame," Raymond Giroux said, "but I think we're going to take our leave."

"What a shame," Elisabeth said. "You traveled quite a distance. You ought to stay and enjoy yourselves a bit longer."

"Thank you, madame," Brigitte said. "We'll collect Pascal and Gabrielle and be off."

"I was going to bring them home in the carriage this evening," Gilbert said as he entered from the dining room. "I'd be happy to take you all, to spare you the walk. The evening air is getting brisk."

"We don't need charity, Beaumont," Raymond said, his tone disdainful. "We'll take our children and go."

"We want to stay, Papa," Pascal said, approaching his father. "We'll be home tonight."

"You don't tell me what's what, boy," Raymond said. "I'm still your father. I see now where you're getting your big ideas. I won't have you looking down on me. This job of yours is ending now."

"Monsieur, this is neither the time nor the place for this discussion," Alexandre interjected. "Monsieur Beaumont will see your children home this evening. If you are not inclined to eat and celebrate the birth of this child, you are free to leave."

"Think we own the world, do we, Seigneur?" said Raymond, though his tone was much less menacing. "These are my children. I won't have anyone tell me what I can or can't do with them."

"Papa, please, can't we stay a bit longer?" Gabrielle asked.

Raymond slapped her smartly across her face.

"Did you hear me, girl?" he asked. "We're going home."

Pascal, noticing that Gabrielle's nose was bleeding, grabbed his father's collar. Giroux's eyes widened with sudden fear.

"Damn you to the deepest fires of hell, old man!" Pascal hissed. "If you ever lay a hand on her again, I'll see you hanged. I'm a full apprentice. I have a contract you can't do a thing about. And Gabrielle isn't going anywhere, either.

"The Beaumonts are good people and raising us better than you ever thought of doing. Get your own damned coat, and see yourself out. We won't be home this Sunday, or any other."

Pascal released his father's shirt and stared at him with fury.

"Fine, you ungrateful little shit," Giroux spat. "May I never see either of you ever again."

"Easily arranged," Alexandre said, stepping between the boy and his father. "I trust you can find the door."

Nicole ushered the weeping Gabrielle from the room while Elisabeth wrapped her arms around Pascal. The boy was shaking, with anger or regret, she knew not.

"Don't worry," Elisabeth said. "He's gone; it's over."

"That no-good piece of gutter sludge," Pascal said, still shaking in Elisabeth's arms.

"Young man, you ought not speak of your father in such a way," said Father Cloutier. Elisabeth had begged for any other priest to baptize her child, since he'd refused to baptize the first, but the Church had not given them a choice.

"The boy speaks the truth," Elisabeth said.

More than one head turned at the woman who dared to contradict the priest.

"The Bible commands us to 'honor thy mother and thy father,'" the priest began, in a tone brimming with authority.

"And so Pascal does," Elisabeth said. "By staying to honor the baptism of his brother. Pascal and Gabrielle live in my house, and are as much my children as Pierre. If you'll excuse me, I need to see to my daughter's injuries."

The priest stared at Elisabeth, his mouth agape.

Madame Beaumont had dismissed him as she might an ill-behaved child.

"How are you, sweetheart?" Elisabeth asked, stooping to Gabrielle's height to inspect her injuries.

Nicole had washed the blood from Gabrielle's face, but spots still marked the front of her best dress. She fought bravely to stem the flow of tears.

Elisabeth noticed, with satisfaction, that Rose had retreated to the kitchen with Pierre when the confrontation began.

"Her nose isn't broken," Nicole said, answering for the child. "She may have a black eye tomorrow, but I think she'll be all right."

"I'm s-so s-sorry for ruining the party," Gabrielle stammered.

"Don't you think on that for a moment," Elisabeth said, embracing Gabrielle as she had her brother. "All I care about is keeping you safe. And Pierre is far too little to care about what happens at his party."

"He is lucky to have such a sweet *maman,*" Gabrielle said.

"And such a sweet big sister and brother," Elisabeth said. "You'll stay with us as long as you wish to."

At this, Gabrielle began her tears afresh and tightened her grip around Elisabeth's waist.

"Perhaps we ought to cut things short and get this lot home early," Gilbert said, entering the room with Alexandre.

"Yes." A devilish grin played at Alexandre's lips. "You'll want to be rested for tomorrow's sermon. Father Cloutier's lecture on filial duty will be most enlightening."

Alexandre was wealthy. He could dare to mock the clergy if he chose. It could make him unpopular in the colony, so most times he kept his remarks to himself, but Elisabeth had heard him speak with disdain about the priests and even some of the Church directives. Nicole, Elisabeth was sure, held her tongue on the matter for the sake of matrimonial accord.

"Yes, I think I've had more than enough excitement for an afternoon," Elisabeth said. "Please take us home."

As promised, the Sunday sermon focused on obedience to parental, and clerical, authority. Elisabeth was not the only one to notice the priest's too-frequent glares at the Beaumonts' pew. Pascal sighed at one point, and Elisabeth saw Alexandre's shoulders shaking with stifled laughter three rows up.

So long as this doesn't damage business, I can endure it, Elisabeth thought to herself. At least little Pierre slept through the Mass, not attracting any more attention to the family than was already directed their way.

Father Cloutier nodded stiffly to the Beaumonts as they left, and didn't offer his usual pious farewell.

The Beaumonts joined both sets of Lefebvres in the courtyard in front of the church as they did most Sundays. In the midst of their conversation, Gabrielle clutched Elisabeth's hand. Raymond and Brigitte Giroux appeared, haphazardly washed and in their best clothing, with a troupe of dirty children following them. The family looked hungry and overtired from the long walk into town.

Raymond and Brigitte stopped to talk with the priest, and cast indelicate glances at the Beaumonts.

"Home," Gilbert said, when he noticed the Girouxes at the door of the church. His voice betrayed the seriousness of the situation.

They left the courtyard at a faster pace than they would usually take on a Sunday morning, with the Lefebvre families hard on their heels.

"Pascal and Gabrielle, will you please play in the parlor with Manon and Hélène? We'll call you in when it's time for luncheon," Elisabeth said.

The children all complied, as the eldest three were great playmates and accepted the presence of toddling Hélène with cheer.

"This is not good," Gilbert said, once the children were out of earshot.

Elisabeth had already begun setting the table and setting out pastries to occupy her hands.

"There is not a thing Giroux can do about Pascal," Henri said. "He's a legal apprentice and all but your property for the length of his contract. Unless they can show you've mistreated him, the contract can't be broken without your consent.

"Gabrielle is another matter."

"I know," Gilbert said. "I wish we'd formalized her agreement, too."

"It would have been wise to draw up a contract making her your servant," Alexandre said. "She's young for it, but no one would have looked askance."

"Is there nothing we can do?" Nicole asked her husband. "Speak to the governor?"

"He wouldn't want to intervene," Alexandre said. "It's precisely these sorts of domestic squabbles with which he wants nothing to do."

"We can't let her go back," Elisabeth said, setting down a plate of rolls with too much fervor. Half of them spilled onto the table. "I know they beat her."

"It isn't a crime to discipline a child," Alexandre said.

"We aren't talking about spanking an errant child," Gilbert said. "You saw how he hit her."

"Within his legal rights, even so," Alexandre said. "I'm not agreeing with it, merely pointing out what a judge would say. The man is a beast, but he is her father. He has rights, whether he deserves them or not."

"I don't understand why he wants her back," Elisabeth said. "He was more than glad to send her to us, just as he was with Pascal. Why has he changed his mind? What have we done wrong?"

"That's just it," Nicole said. "You've done everything right. If you whipped Pascal, or kept Gabrielle in rags, he wouldn't care. But as it stands, he's jealous."

"It seems so unfair," Elisabeth said, tracing the designs on the embroidered tablecloth with her finger.

"To a man like Giroux it's incredibly unfair . . . to *him,*" Henri said. "To see his children in comfort when he has none is a great injustice to his mind."

"Again, his motives and character matter little," Alexandre said.

"What are we to do, Lefebvre?" Gilbert asked.

"I wish I knew," Alexandre said. "But I would prepare for the worst."

The bailiff, accompanied by Father Cloutier, collected Gabrielle the following week.

"Please don't make me go," Gabrielle implored. "This is my home."

"No it isn't, child," the priest replied. "Your home is with your rightful parents, whom you must honor and obey."

Gabrielle had never gone to Mass before her stay with the Beaumonts, but respected the Church with a child's faith. Yet for all her natural obedience, the girl glared at the priest, her expression lined with fury.

"Your father never beat you, did he?" Gabrielle asked, as if daring him to answer.

"I accepted my punishments and learned from my mistakes."

The priest's condescending tone made Elisabeth feel ill. This was not a toddler, or a simpleton, but a bright young girl being sent back into misery.

"And when I'm being beaten for no transgression, Father, what is my lesson there?"

Neither Gilbert nor Elisabeth checked the girl's defiance.

"Patience," Father Cloutier said, grabbing her arm. "Go pack your bag, girl, and be quick."

"Let me go," Gabrielle said. She twisted from the priest's grip and ran to her room. She emerged a few minutes later in the tattered dress she'd arrived in.

"Where are your things?" A look of annoyance colored the priest's round face. "I'm anxious to have this settled."

"This is all I came with, sir," Gabrielle answered. "I won't take the things the Beaumonts gave me to see them sold for drink."

"Do not insult your father, child," the priest said.

"Are we going or not?" Gabrielle snapped.

The bailiff started to take Gabrielle by the elbow, but she resisted. Head held high, she walked to the carriage and entered on her own.

She looked back at the Beaumonts and gave a quick wave before sitting back in her seat. Elisabeth guessed that was as long as she could stand to look without breaking down in tears.

Pascal, wordless through the ordeal, retreated to his room. Though Gilbert had tried to talk to the boy, he would not speak of his sister's removal, other than to curse his parents.

"Poor boy," Elisabeth said. "I feel almost as badly for him as for her."

"He feels guilty that he can stay and she was taken away," Gilbert said, embracing his wife.

"I should speak to him," Elisabeth said.

"That would make it worse," Gilbert said. "Let him have time."

"I suppose you're right," Elisabeth said, breaking away with a kiss as she heard Pierre's cries.

"Back to work, for all of us," Gilbert said. "I'm going to rouse Pascal as well. He'll have time to brood as he kneads the bread. The work will do him good."

"Make sure he doesn't take out his anger too extravagantly on the dough or the bread will be tougher than old chicken." The couple exchanged a hollow laugh and returned to their duties.

Elisabeth scooped up her tiny son to give him his morning meal. She smiled into his face and felt the glow of love pass through her.

"My dear little man," she cooed, as he took her breast with enthusiasm. "Maman loves you so."

Despite her maternal contentment, Elisabeth's heart also traveled along the rocky dirt road with Gabrielle, who she loved as a daughter. She murmured a prayer that they would not be separated long. For the first time, Elisabeth did not have much faith in an answer.

Chapter 25

Nicole

December 1670

Nicole's feet ached worse after each ball. Each time, she swore this ball would be her last until the baby came, but somehow Alexandre could always persuade her to go to just one more.

"Are you unwell?" Alexandre asked, as his wife collapsed into her favorite chair.

"No more than usual," Nicole said. "Tired, but nothing unexpected."

"Thank you for going," he said. "I don't care for this dancing nonsense any more than you, but it's important to be seen at these functions."

"I know," Nicole answered, resting her feet on the little velvet tuffet. "I'll be glad when the season is over, though."

"Too true," Alexandre said. "Before we retire, I'd like to show you plans for the new house—to know if it suits you."

"I'm sure it will," she said. "Though I don't understand why we need to move at all."

"The city is growing, dearest," he said. "Building a fine house at the city center is a smart investment. We'll need the room for entertaining, not to mention the children."

Nicole couldn't find any argument there. Their dining and sitting rooms were becoming inadequate for the large dinners they hosted as part of their social circle. The constant kicks to her midsection said that an ample nursery was wanted as well. For all the work that accompanied babies, Nicole preferred their company to that of Quebec's elite.

"Very well, show me," Nicole agreed, following him to the study.

Alexandre spread a large scroll of paper over the top of the broad mahogany desk, and she looked on as he explained the plans.

"Must we . . ." she began, but she closed her mouth before the thought escaped.

"What?" Alexandre asked, looking up from the plans to his wife. "Go ahead."

"Separate bedrooms," Nicole said, blushing. "Why are they necessary?"

"Convention, I suppose," Alexandre said. "It's what I'm used to. Isn't that your preference also?"

"I see nothing conventional about it," Nicole said. "I've never known a married couple who kept separate quarters."

"It's very common among the families of my acquaintance," he said. "If we sell the house, anyone who could afford it would expect the rooms arranged that way. I forgot . . ."

"That I started my life as a poor farm girl?" Nicole asked, arching her brow.

"With the operative words being 'started life,' " said Alexandre. "Though I intended to say you 'were not born in the same circles I was.' No one could tell where you started, Nicole. You've blended into society marvelously well."

"Glad I'm not an embarrassment," she said, not entirely teasing.

"Enough of that," he said. "Regardless of birth, your education fit you for better things. You ought to be proud."

"I am," she said. "It's simply a lot to take in. Our current house is twenty times grander than the one I grew up in, yet we're building one finer yet. It baffles me that there's a need."

"You think of home often, don't you?" he asked.

"All the time," Nicole confessed. "It was the same when I was expecting Hélène. I pine for my mother, wanting advice. I wish you could meet her. My sisters and little Georges would not even know me now."

"I'm sure their memories are better than you give them credit for," he said. "As for the house, is everything to your liking?"

"It's lovely," she said. "Just see to it that there is plenty of light and ample space in the nursery, and it will be wonderful."

"I'm glad you approve," he said. "I hope to finish construction within a year. Then we won't have to bother moving until after the baby is born."

"All the better," Nicole said.

"You've been pale lately," Alexandre said. "Do you feel well?"

"As well as one might hope," Nicole said. "Too many hours indoors, particularly in ballrooms."

"The weather has been remarkably fine for December," Alexandre said. "Tomorrow we'll bundle up the children and go see our property, if you like."

"That sounds wonderful," she said, glad for any excursion that didn't involve a ball gown or politics. "Speaking of the children, I should check on them before I retire."

"Good night, dearest," he said, offering a polite peck on the cheek.

"Good night," she responded. Of course he would not be joining her.

In the nursery Manon and Hélène slept the untroubled sleep of beloved children. Nicole watched their even breathing and serene faces. In the moonlight, Manon's brown skin and black tresses contrasted so beautifully against the white pillowcase. Hélène's golden-brown curls fell in a halo over her pale forehead.

My sweet girls, Nicole thought. *Sleep well. I envy your peace.*

Nicole made her way to her own room. Sleep would be fitful, just like it was this far along in her pregnancy with Hélène. She sank into the plush mattress and felt her aches and pains subsiding by inches.

You finally drew up the courage to talk to him about bedrooms, Nicole thought, *but it got you nowhere. He dismissed you, as he always does when you disagree. He's a good man. You should be happy. You're provided for and your children will want for nothing. Luc Jarvais would never have been able to do for them what Alexandre is doing. . . .*

It was rare that Nicole thought of Luc anymore. When she *did* think of him, she thought of his decision to go trapping, and could no longer dismiss it as the action of a man who wanted to provide for his family. He was selfish and reckless to leave her alone. He was selfish to have married her at all before he had a house that could withstand the winter. She felt an occasional pang of regret that Luc hadn't lived to meet his daughter, but the loss of Luc Jarvais no longer stung.

She was Nicole Lefebvre now.

Remember that, Nicole scolded herself. *Being lonely in marriage is better than being alone . . . especially here.* But while Luc had left her alone in body, Alexandre left her feeling just as lonely when he was in the same house. For all the comfort, was she any better off than she had been? Seeing her daughters well cared for answered the question as soon as she formed it in her mind, but the knowledge did little to warm her bed at night.

Alexandre's magnificent horses carried the sleigh past the outskirts of the settlement and on to the Lefebvre holdings. When they arrived, Manon descended to frolic in the sparse blanket of snow. Hélène longed to join her sister, but Alexandre kept the wiggling toddler in his arms to keep her dry.

"It's beautiful," Nicole said as she took in the immensity of their holdings. Ice-covered trees glistened in the weak sun.

"I can't believe all this is yours."

"Ours," he said. "Were it not for your charms, the governor might not have noticed me. You've every bit as much a right to this land as I."

Nicole squeezed his hand. The law thought otherwise, but his words were kind.

"If you could do anything with this property, what would you do?" he asked.

Hélène gave up her struggle and laid her head on his chest as they strolled across the land.

"I would give it to my father," Nicole said without hesitation. "He dreamed of a farm this grand. He longed to buy more land in France, but was never able."

"The plague of the Old World farmer." Alexandre looked at the mountains in the distance. "The best of years, they eat like kings, but even then, they remain cash poor. In bad years, it's disaster."

"I know," Nicole said. "I lived it."

"It's a little better here," Alexandre said. "Fewer taxes, fewer laws. The peasant farmer has a fighting chance."

"So it seems." The subject of her family bruised Nicole's feelings, so she walked along in silence.

"Nicole," said Alexandre. "I know you aren't happy."

"It's of no matter," Nicole said. "My condition makes me sensitive, that's all."

"I should tell you," Alexandre said. "I've sent for your parents and younger siblings to join us. I hope I haven't overstepped my boundaries."

Did I hear him right? She stared dumbly at her husband.

"Wh-what?" she stammered.

"They should arrive by summer," he said. "Not in time for your mother to help when this baby comes, but perhaps the next one. The sailing periods are so short—I couldn't get them here sooner."

Nicole felt warm tears on her cheeks and hastened to wipe them away.

"Please say something," Alexandre said. "Have I upset you?"

"Quite the opposite," Nicole said. "I've missed them so much."

"I know." Alexandre wrapped his arm around her. "I promised I would make it right, remember?"

"I never dreamed you would send for them. I thought you meant to give them a bit of money for the brooch."

"Why would I do so little when I could truly help them, and make you happy in the process?" Alexandre asked. "I confess you're so unlike the women of my acquaintance, dearest. The women I knew before were content with jewels and frocks. You're made of sterner stuff, and thank God for it. I just wanted to do something to show you . . ."

"I don't deserve you," she said as she dried her tears. *He will not see them again.*

"So you're pleased?" he asked.

"Of course," she said, taking his hand. "I only hope they will be happy here."

"As do I. A friend of mine in Rouen visited your parents and arranged the matter. He seemed to think the farm wasn't much more productive than when you left. Your father will do far better with healthy new lands here." Alexandre gestured to the panorama in front of him. "Half of this will be his to farm and make a living. When he dies, it will pass to our children."

"Can you afford such a gift?" Nicole asked. Acres upon acres stretched before them.

"In truth, the *seigneurs* make little money off the land compared to other enterprises," Alexandre said. "It's more important that we manage the property well and keep troubles to a minimum so that the governor and the Crown have less to worry about. With Henri overseeing things on-site, we hope to operate the best-run estate in New France."

"I'm sure we will," Nicole said with pride.

"We'll have some sturdy young lads clear the land for him," Alexandre said. "It's awful work, I gather. I've told Henri to have a solid home built for them as well. They won't be able to plant this year, but everything will be ready the following spring."

"Thank you," Nicole said, embracing her husband while trying not to disturb the sleeping Hélène. "I don't know what I could ever do to make this up to you."

Alexandre rubbed her swollen belly. "You do enough as it is."

"Up you get," Nicole murmured as she nudged Manon awake from her nap on the sofa. The girl offered a brief but mutinous look before standing up and smoothing her dress.

It was just before eleven at night on Christmas Eve. They would be late for midnight Mass unless they left at least forty-five minutes early. Traveling in the snow was always a challenge, but the added gloom of midnight made the trip a serious undertaking.

Bundled in their warmest clothes, the Lefebvres climbed aboard Alexandre's sleigh.

Any other night of the year, the town would be asleep, but few in the settlement—even those of middling faith—missed the celebration of the Nativity. The lavishly decorated church glowed with candlelight for not only the traditional Mass, but choral singing and Nativity pageants as well.

"They put on a good show," Alexandre whispered after a performance of *Panis Angelicus*. "But I envy the little one."

Hélène nestled against her mother's bosom, sound asleep. She was far too young to be interested in Latin, no matter how beautifully sung. Manon's attention never wavered from the altar.

Nicole noticed Elisabeth nudge Pascal awake more than once during the service. Though almost three years Manon's senior, the Beaumonts' apprentice took little interest in church.

Monsieur Rosseau, the butcher, cast a disapproving glare at Manon. His opinion that she didn't belong in the church was not a rare one. People always glanced at Manon in public, and not always with kindness in their eyes. Nicole shot a murderous look at the old man. He must have understood her meaning full well as his bewildered eyes reverted forward where they belonged. *Listen to the sermon, you clout. It will do you more good than thinking poorly of a small girl.*

Nicole fought to restrain her tears. As much as she considered Manon to be her flesh and blood, the rest of the colony would never see it that way. No matter how high Nicole climbed on the social ladder, Manon would not be allowed to follow.

Sweet, serious girl, Nicole thought. *I hope we've done right to take you from your people. I hope you are happy.*

Just after one o'clock in the morning, the Lefebvres and their nearest friends returned home from Christmas Mass. They were welcomed by a warm fire and the smell of roast goose wafting from the kitchen.

"Nothing better than returning home from a drafty church to a good meal," Alexandre said. "To the table, everyone."

"Manon, why don't you put the baby Jesus in the crèche before supper?" prompted Nicole. "It's Christmas now."

Manon reveled in the chance to have a role in the festivities. With the crèche complete, family and friends sat down for the meal. The staff had prepared a feast fit for the holiday: roast goose, creamed potatoes, carrots, chestnuts, cider, and a few bottles of the better wines from Alexandre's collection.

"Everything looks perfect, Sophie," Nicole said as the cook placed the last dish on the polished wooden table. "I'm only sad I can eat so little these days."

The maid smiled at the compliment. "Never mind, madame. Most of this can be reheated, as good as new, for you later. Enjoy what you can."

"Thank you, Sophie," Alexandre said, by way of dismissal. "We'll let you know if you're needed."

The squat woman bowed to the master of the house and took her exit.

Too familiar with the servants. In front of company, too. How absurd, but I suppose it's what he's used to.

"I've never tasted goose like this before," Pascal said, proud to be eating with the adults. "When I had it before it was greasy and stringy."

"A risk with goose, to be sure," Alexandre said. "But Sophie is among the best cooks in the settlement. Tell me, young man, have you heard from your sister?"

"No, monsieur," Pascal said, a dark cloud passing over his face. "It's been almost a month, but I expect Papa won't allow her into town."

Elisabeth patted the boy's shoulder.

Nicole suspected Pascal felt his sister's absence keenly, especially at Christmas.

"You three must be glad for the holiday," Nicole said to change the subject. "I doubt you've slept much the last few nights."

"You speak the truth," Gilbert said, the bags under his eyes affirming his lack of rest. "We couldn't run the ovens long enough."

"To a prosperous New Year," Alexandre said, raising his glass. "I think you've re-established yourself beyond expectations, Beaumont."

"Thanks to your help." Gilbert raised his glass in return.

"It seems my uncle has been quite the benefactor to us all," Henri said. "We'll be installed on your estate this spring if all goes well."

"The sooner the better," Alexandre said. "Although we'll miss having you and Rose in town."

"We'll miss it, too," Rose said, her tone low, "but we'll visit as often as we can manage. You must promise to come see us as well."

"I doubt I'll be able to keep my wife away," said Alexandre. "She'll have her own horse and carriage to do as she pleases."

"Really?" Nicole asked, her expression shocked.

"Yes, really," Alexandre said with a laugh. "I was going to tell you on New Year's Day. Merry Christmas, dear."

"Thank you," Nicole said. With the exception of bringing her family to the settlement, the gift was the most extravagant she had ever received.

"You'll be the envy of all the fashionable ladies in town," Alexandre said. "Just promise to make good use of it and take Didier or Guillaume to drive you."

"Of course," Nicole said. She had never driven a carriage and had no desire to learn.

The jacket she'd bought Alexandre for the new year now seemed trifling by comparison, but with the baby's delivery approaching, she had no wish to venture out to the shops before the holiday.

The rest of the meal continued with the same good cheer with which it had begun, but Nicole retreated into herself.

Fashionable—*that word again. Always so important how we show ourselves to others.*

By the time the meal ended, at half-past three in the morning, Nicole was more than happy to see the others leave so she could find her bed.

"You've been quiet," Alexandre said as they shut the door. "Do you dislike your gift?"

"How could I not love it?" Nicole asked. "It's just so generous. I could never return the gesture."

"Nor would I expect you to," he said. "Come to my study. I have another gift for you."

"There's more?" she asked, eyes wide.

"Yes, and you're to accept it without complaint," he said, with mock severity.

"If you insist, good sir," she replied.

When they reached the study, Alexandre unrolled the house plans on his desk.

"Have you changed the plans?" Nicole asked. She saw no difference in the design.

"Only the purpose of the rooms," he said. "If we ever need to sell, the next owners of the house will expect separate bedrooms."

"Of course," Nicole said.

"However, this room does not need to be a bedroom while we live there." He pointed to the area designated as her bedroom. "You may use it as a private sitting room, or an office—as you choose."

"Then you want me to . . ." Nicole fell silent, too embarrassed to speak the words.

"Share my bed," Alexandre said, voice low. "I realized that your previous comments were intended to express how important that was to you. I dismissed your opinion at first. I'm sorry."

"Don't apologize, but yes, I would prefer it," she admitted.

"Thank you for telling me," he said, wrapping his arms around her in an uncharacteristic display of affection. "You're a very patient woman, putting up with a man who does not always listen."

Nicole sank into the embrace. "You've been so generous of late. I know it's your nature, but has something happened?"

"Other than giving me a child?" Alexandre asked. "I love Hélène as my own, but this is different."

"I understand," she said. "But what about Manon? She is my daughter every bit as much as Hélène."

"The Huron girl means a great deal to you, I know," Alexandre said. "But, I confess I can't think of her as our own."

"Because she's a native?" Nicole asked.

"No, though I suppose it doesn't help," he said. "Don't mistake my meaning. I'm fond of her, and glad to have her here. She's as smart and dutiful a child as I've ever seen. It's just that my affection doesn't run as deep as a father's ought to."

"I didn't know you felt that way." Nicole pulled away from his embrace.

"I am sorry," he said. "If I could change my feelings, please know that I would. Manon will always be welcome in our home. I will give her everything she wants or needs, as I would my own daughter. Please don't doubt that."

"No, of course not," Nicole said, feeling an ache grow in the pit of her stomach. "I just worry she'll notice the difference and feel resentful."

"She has a far more comfortable life than she has ever known before," Alexandre said. "I hope that she'll realize how well off she is."

"As do I," Nicole said, brow furrowed.

"Enough of that for now," Alexandre said. "It's very late, or, rather, early, and we both need sleep."

"Agreed," Nicole said, knowing sleep would elude her.

As they ascended the staircase to Alexandre's room, Nicole noticed the door to the nursery was a few inches ajar. Nicole closed the door, careful to make no noise, and prayed the darling raven-haired girl hadn't heard a word of their discourse.

CHAPTER 26

Rose

Early March 1671

Rose tossed a heavy log onto the crackling fire and pulled her chair as close as she dared. Their small stone home was well built, but did little to ward off the wicked spring cold. Rose lay back in her chair and willed the fire to heat the room as quickly as it could. While she waited, she rested and felt the movements of the baby who grew inside her. The helpless little being that would depend upon her for everything. When he appeared in two months, her life would transform, and Rose both longed for and dreaded his arrival.

Observing the birth of Nicole's son, Frédéric, had calmed Rose on one front. Not every birth was traumatic. Not all tears were tears of grief. But would she be able to protect the innocent child? Shelter the baby from all the evils in the world? Even her own papa had not been able to protect her from her uncle. When she voiced her fears to Henri, his response was always the same: "No, you can't protect him from everything, nor should you, so don't fret about it."

He didn't understand . . . there was no stopping the worry.

Henri and Rose had moved into the house only three weeks before. Though the winter cold held fast, the majority of the crew's work was inside, so the winter weather wasn't a terrible hindrance to their task. Ultimately, Rose was glad that the move had not taken place any later. With a small staff, setting up housekeeping had taken all of her energy. Rose missed the activity of town, of having Nicole and Elisabeth close, but seeing Henri so happy made the sacrifice worthwhile.

Rose had almost drifted off to sleep when a series of thumps at the door startled her to her feet.

The door swung open with a gust of brisk spring breeze.

"Get clean wet rags!" Henri shouted as he entered.

Rose assumed he intended the order for Mylène, one of the two servants they'd hired to replace the elderly staff when they moved from town.

Henri entered the sitting room with a battered Gabrielle Giroux in his arms. She was unconscious, but the rise and fall of her chest showed that she breathed.

"Set her here," Rose said, indicating a lounging chair.

When the servant entered with a basin of warm water and rags, Rose took them from Mylène's hands and washed the dirt and blood from the young girl's face. All her visible skin was bruised, scraped, or caked with dirt and blood. Rose only assumed the damage was the same under much of her ripped, muddy dress.

Rose assessed the girl's injuries and found no sign of broken bones, though the bruising was severe.

"Let's take her upstairs to a bed," Rose said. "Mylène, a clean nightgown, please."

When they reached the bedroom, Rose changed Gabrielle from her ragged clothes and handed the rags to the servant with orders to burn them. Gabrielle didn't wake, which made Rose worry that the beating might have caused permanent damage. A lump rose in her throat at the thought of the sweet, curious girl reduced to a simpleton. She thought of the childlike women shackled to the walls of the putrid cells in the Salpêtrière and could not stem the flow of tears, though she did not let them impede her work.

Henri waited outside the room, pacing in the hallway.

"She hasn't stirred," Rose reported as she emerged and shut the door behind her. "Even though Mylène and I dressed and cleaned her. Do you know what happened?"

"I was out surveying the land with a prospective farmer when I saw her running toward me," Henri said. "She collapsed before I reached her.

"Her father's place isn't far from here. She must have recognized me. . . . She didn't start running until she drew close enough to see my face."

"Poor child," Rose said, wiping away her tears. "I'll stay with her. I'm not sure what else to do."

"Don't tire yourself out, or you won't be of any use when she does wake," Henri said. "I'll fetch the doctor to see if he knows what else can be done to help her."

Rose took up her vigil by Gabrielle's side, holding the girl's small hand in her own, now soft, long since healed from the cracks and calluses of her past.

"Please wake, Gabrielle," Rose murmured, not knowing if the child could hear. "You're safe now, darling."

A few minutes later she tried again. "Wake up, Gabrielle, I'll get you some broth and bread. You must be hungry."

And later still, "You can go to the Beaumonts' as soon as you're well. I promise."

She kept up the encouraging offers until Henri returned with Dr. Germain. Father Cloutier and the bailiff came, too, unwelcome additions to the party.

"I'm sorry," Henri murmured to Rose as they drew aside to make room for the doctor. "They saw me leaving the doctor's in a hurry and asked what happened. Father Cloutier offered to pray over her. I couldn't stop them from following along."

"I'm not worried about them now," Rose said. "Let's just attend to Gabrielle."

Henri nodded assent and they returned to the bedroom.

"Her breathing is sound," the doctor said. "But I cannot tell how bad a blow she's taken to the head."

"If the child is stable, she ought to be taken home," said Father Cloutier.

"I wouldn't risk moving her," the doctor said.

"She's not going anywhere," Rose said. "Not until she's awake and well."

"Young woman . . ." the priest began.

"Out in the hallway. Now," Henri ordered.

The men obeyed. Rose followed, leaving the doctor to continue his examination.

"You heard my wife and you heard the doctor," Henri told the priest. "Gabrielle is not well enough to be moved. Moreover, I won't have her sent back home until I learn how she received those injuries, and why she ran away in the first place."

"She is a disobedient child fleeing from her parents' authority," Father Cloutier said. "It's not your place to harbor her."

"You sorry excuse for a man," Rose said, her temper breaking. "Are you blind to the child's bruises and cuts?"

"Her father has the right to punish her as he sees fit," the priest declared.

"This is not punishment, you monster!" shouted Rose, the memory of her own abuse surfacing. "This child has been beaten almost to death. She may die yet. Are you willing to send her back for more of the same?"

"How dare you speak to me in such a tone?" the priest demanded.

"I will dare to speak as I please in my own home—get out of my house. You are not welcome here."

"And you can go with him, Bailiff," Henri added. "You may return when you have an order from a judge, and not before."

"You may trust to that, Lefebvre." Cloutier turned his back to Henri and Rose and found his way downstairs with the bailiff on his heels.

"Off to inform her good-for-nothing father, no doubt," Rose muttered. "Worthless scum, the pair of them."

"Not so loud," Henri said. "Insulting a priest won't earn you friends in this settlement."

"I don't need friends who take up with such an evil man," she said.

When she returned to Gabrielle's side, Rose asked, "Any change, Doctor?"

"None, I'm sorry to say," he replied. "I've done what I can. Keep her still and hope she wakes."

Rose did her best to keep her composure. Gabrielle needed her to be strong. "Thank you, Doctor."

"Don't thank me," Dr. Germain said. "I wish I could do more. With cases like these, either she'll recover or she won't. God's will, I suppose."

"As you say," Rose said. "If you think of anything that might help her, please let us know."

"Of course," he said. "But be prepared for the worst."

"Let me see you home, Doctor," Henri said. "You must be tired."

"Indeed," he said. "Thank you. And good luck to you all."

Rose squeezed Henri's hand as he left the room. She returned to her seat by Gabrielle. Though the child slept soundly, Rose took some comfort from her even breathing.

It was more than an hour before Henri returned.

"You ought to get some sleep, darling," Henri said as he entered the room.

"Not until she's awake," Rose said. "I don't want her to find herself alone in a strange place."

"I'll stay with her awhile," Henri said. "And I'll wake Mylène or Yves to take a turn before I sleep. If her situation changes, someone will come for you."

"Very well," Rose said. "I'm about ready to fall asleep as it is."

"I sent word to Elisabeth and Gilbert," Henri said. "No doubt they'll visit in the morning."

"Thank you," Rose said. "I imagine Pascal will be in a state."

"Justifiably so."

The tears Rose endeavored to control burst through her determination. Henri took her in his arms.

"I know," he murmured. "Come, let me put you to bed."

Exhausted and disconsolate, Rose submitted without argument. Once tucked into bed, she heard Henri leave with a quiet click of the bedroom door.

He'll take good care of Gabrielle, Rose thought, just before the fatigue took her away.

"I've asked Yves to look over Gabrielle," Henri said as he climbed into bed sometime later. "Go back to sleep, darling."

"She doesn't know him," Rose said, stifling her yawn with the back of her hand.

"He can assure her she's safe and he'll come get us. I promise."

"Poor child," she said into his chest.

"Yes," Henri said. "Get some rest so you can be of use to her."

The Beaumonts and the elder Lefebvres arrived together the following morning.

"Merciful Lord," Elisabeth stammered when she saw Gabrielle's still-sleeping body. Aside from the bruises and cuts, she was also thinner than when she had left the Beaumonts' care.

Gilbert held his wife's hand, his expression grim, when the child did not respond to their voices.

To Rose's surprise, Pascal did not rage, but held Elisabeth's hand and stared at his sister.

"Demon," Elisabeth breathed. "Only a devil would do this to a child."

"Too true," Rose said. She held baby Pierre, who cooed and patted Rose's chest with his fat hands, unaware of the situation. "I'll leave you with her for a while."

"Thank you," Elisabeth said, taking a seat in the chair Rose had occupied since dawn.

Gilbert and Pascal accompanied Rose to the sitting room where Henri, Alexandre, Nicole, and their children waited.

"Is there anything that can be done, Uncle?" Henri asked.

"Normally, these matters aren't for the courts," Alexandre said. "The judges don't like to meddle in domestic affairs. This is an extreme case, however, and we may be able to see Giroux prosecuted, if we can find enough evidence that he did this. If the child doesn't survive, it would be a murder case."

"She's going to make it," Pascal said, trying to control his voice.

Gilbert embraced the boy, but made no promises.

"I took the liberty of speaking to the judge," Alexandre said. "Asked him to send a bailiff to question Giroux. We have a public account of him hitting her, which creates the necessary suspicion to support a questioning, at least."

"Thank you," Gilbert said, his face ashen, an arm still around the shaking Pascal.

Rose sent Manon to occupy Hélène and the babies, leaving the adults to wait. Henri paced, while Nicole produced some knitting that she hadn't touched in over a year. Alexandre borrowed paper and a plume from his nephew and wrote out an account to send to the judge. As a *seigneur,* his testimony would be valuable to the court.

Two hours later, the bailiff approached the house, along with Brigitte Giroux and three small, dirty children. Henri opened the door, though his face was anything but welcoming.

"Madame Giroux was hoping to see her daughter," the bailiff said, far more polite than the previous night.

"I know I haven't the right to ask for anything from you," the woman said. "But I'd like to see her."

"Come with me," Rose said, from behind Henri. She could not bring herself to deny the woman entry.

Rose escorted Brigitte up the stairs while the three smaller children flung themselves at their brother. The bailiff stood just inside the door, as if prepared to leave as precipitously as the night before.

"Elisabeth, Madame Giroux would like a few moments with Gabrielle," Rose whispered as she knocked on the open door frame.

Without releasing Gabrielle's hand, Elisabeth wiped the tears from her face and stared at Brigitte. Rose saw a mixture of loathing and pity in Elisabeth's face. After a long moment, Elisabeth kissed Gabrielle's hand and left the room without a word for the shabby woman.

"I'm sorry," Rose said to Elisabeth. "She came with the bailiff."

"Gabrielle is her child," Elisabeth said.

Rose could see in Elisabeth's face how much it cost her not to tear the Giroux woman in half in front of the bailiff and the whole passel of Giroux children. Not for the first time, Rose admired her friend's tremendous restraint.

Rose could see in Elisabeth's face that Gabrielle's condition had not changed. Gilbert briefly caressed her shoulder, almost absentmindedly. Rose suspected anything more demonstrative would cause him to betray his own calm façade.

"We miss you, Pascal!" the youngest Giroux child said. He was a boy of about five years, named Jean.

"I miss you, too," Pascal said, hugging his brother close.

The other children, a girl of seven and a boy of eight, did not dare to speak in front of the strangers.

Rose examined the Giroux children, trying to remain undetected. They were underfed and filthy, but none had visible bruises or scars.

"Children, come with me," Rose said, motioning to the young Girouxes.

They looked at her with distrust, but followed when their brother prodded them forward.

"Mylène, please find the children something to eat," Rose said at the door to the kitchen. "And anyone else, if they're hungry."

The maid welcomed the children and fed them their fill. When Rose emerged from the kitchen, Brigitte had returned to the parlor, her visit with her sleeping daughter concluded.

"Welcome to our home, though I wish it were under pleasanter circumstances," Rose said. Her words were kind, though given with an icy countenance.

"Thank you, madame," Brigitte said to Rose as she descended the stairs. "I had to see her. . . ."

"We understand," Rose said. "What happened to the child?"

"It was Raymond," Brigitte said. "When she came home without her fine clothes, he was in a rage for weeks. I suppose he's been taking it out on her ever since."

"She refused to take them with her," Elisabeth said.

"She told me," Brigitte said. "Yesterday evening, Raymond complained there wasn't food. Gabrielle suggested he get a job and earn some. Raymond flew into a fury. . . .

"After she ran away, he took off, and he hasn't returned. I expect he knew he'd be in trouble, the way she looked when she ran out."

"Have you any idea where he might go?" Alexandre asked.

"No, monsieur," Brigitte said.

"Why didn't you stop him?" Rose asked. "Or stop Gabrielle and get her to a doctor?"

"I had no idea she was hurt so bad," the woman answered. "Honest, I didn't. Just thought it was a few bruises, like before. As to why I didn't stop her . . . I hoped she'd run to you good folks. We should have never taken her from you. Raymond is a terrible stubborn man. Hated to see his children well off when he wasn't."

"As we thought," Henri said. "He should have been happy that others were willing to do for his children what he would not."

"I know, monsieur," Brigitte said. "But arguing with Raymond is as much a waste of time as yelling at a tree."

"Will you wait at home for him to return? Or help the bailiff look for him?" Alexandre asked.

"No, monsieur," Brigitte answered, not daring to look at him directly. "After this, I'm through with Raymond. I have a brother in Trois-Rivières. I'm hoping he'll take me and the little ones in."

"We know where the brother lives," the bailiff said. "If we need Madame Giroux in future, we'll be able to find her."

"Good," Alexandre said. The bailiff had anticipated his question.

"Will you keep my girl safe?" Brigitte asked Rose. "Take care of her for me?"

Better than you ever took care of her, you miserable woman.

"Of course," Rose said, managing a weak smile.

"God bless you," Brigitte said. "I am sorry. Will you please tell her that much?"

"We will," Elisabeth said, intervening. "Because I believe you are."

"Thank you," Brigitte said. "I'll not bother you again."

The children flocked to their mother, with extra bread in hand, and exited the house.

"We're on the lookout for Giroux," the bailiff said with a bow as he left. "We'll let you know if there's news."

Henri shut the door behind them, and the entire room seemed to breathe a collective sigh.

"They have to find him," Pascal said. "Punish him for what he's done."

"They'll try," Gilbert said. "But he has lots of space to hide."

"He's not that clever," Pascal said. "He won't hide well."

"We can hope not," Alexandre said. "I'll put my resources into finding him, I assure you."

"Thank you, monsieur." Pascal looked at Alexandre as though the *seigneur* were King Louis himself.

"I'm going to sit with Gabrielle," Rose said, handing over little Pierre, who insisted on his mother's arms when he saw her descend the stairs.

Gabrielle lay as still as before. Rose knew that she could not live long without waking to eat and drink. Her slight frame had almost no reserves to sustain her.

"Wake up, darling girl," Rose said, exhaustion coming over her like a wave. "You're safe. We love you, and want you back with us."

It took some persuading, and a tantrum from little Pierre, to convince Elisabeth to return home when evening came.

"Someone will stay with Gabrielle all night," Henri promised. "We'll send for you if she wakes."

"Let's go, sweetheart," Gilbert said. "Pierre needs his bed and his *maman*."

"Very well," Elisabeth conceded, embracing Rose. "Take care of her for me."

"As if she were my own," Rose said. "Get some rest so you can help her when she wakes."

"That sounded familiar," Henri said, with a rare smile, as he closed the door.

"Always prudent to remember sage advice," Rose said, returning the smile. "No matter how unreliable the source."

"Unreliable," Henri said, feigning disbelief. "Madame, you wound me."

Her smile faded. "What a day."

"Indeed," Henri said. "I hope to heaven they find the bastard and see justice served."

"I don't have the energy for anger," Rose said. "I'm going to sit with Gabrielle awhile."

For more than an hour, Rose sat, stroking the back of Gabrielle's hand and the soft skin of her cheek. *This is no world for a child.* Rose's free hand rested on her stomach. *I'm so sorry I'm bringing you into such a miserable place.*

Mercifully, Gabrielle's chest continued to rise and fall. Rose couldn't be sure if it was the truth or wishful thinking, but Gabrielle's breathing seemed to grow stronger. *It's a blessing you're strong, my dear girl. You've been called on to use that strength far more often than a child should.*

* * *

The following morning, Rose rushed to dress in the predawn hours. Yves gratefully surrendered the chair beside Gabrielle's bed when Rose arrived and left to seek a few hours' rest before his workday began at sunrise.

"Good morning, Gabrielle," Rose murmured. "You're warm and safe, my darling."

She noticed a twitch of movement in Gabrielle's face in response to the words. At first, Rose thought she had imagined it. But then she saw the tiniest movement in Gabrielle's hand. It was all she could do not to scream her excitement.

"Henri!" she called, keeping her voice even. "Come here, please!"

"What is it?" Henri asked from the doorway, not yet coherent.

"She moved. Her face and her hands," Rose said.

He looked at the girl as Gabrielle's right hand twitched again.

Henri ushered Rose from the room and spoke in whispers. "It's not a bad sign, but let's give the Beaumonts a few more hours of sleep before we send for them." Although he wouldn't say it aloud, Rose could tell her husband didn't want to encourage her hope too soon.

"You're sure we shouldn't fetch them?" Rose asked.

"No need," Henri said. "If I know Elisabeth Beaumont, and I do, she'll be here in less than an hour."

As he predicted, the Beaumonts arrived just a quarter of an hour later, bringing a massive basket full of breads and pastries.

"I'm hoping to persuade you all to eat today," Gilbert said. "And, also, the baking kept Elisabeth busy."

Rose left her friend alone with Gabrielle and occupied herself with Pierre while the men ventured out-of-doors to find a useful occupation for Pascal. The boy had little patience for idle waiting.

"Such a big wee man," Rose said to Pierre as he drooled from the corner of his smiling mouth. "And soon, I'll have my own to care for. Will you like to play with him when you get bigger?"

Pierre had Gilbert's rich brown hair, his mother's expressive brown eyes, and a smile all his own. Though Rose feared the horror the world could deal to these sweet children, she understood why people accepted the risk. To see the joy in the baby's face filled Rose's heart with unmitigated delight. She smoothed the locks from his forehead and kissed the soft skin. *Perhaps I will enjoy this after all.*

"She's awake!" Elisabeth called from the bedroom.

With the infant in her arms, Rose ran upstairs to see Gabrielle for herself. The girl was pale and listless, but breathing soundly and awake.

"Thank heavens. I'll go fetch the men. They'll want to see her," Rose said, passing Pierre to Mylène, who also sought the reassuring sight of Gabrielle's curious green eyes alert and taking in her surroundings.

Rose ran for the door and hoped the men had not ventured far. After four or five minutes of a solid jog, she saw them off in the distance.

"She's awake!" cried Rose. Whether they heard her, or inferred the reason for her arrival, Gilbert and Pascal came running toward the house while Henri made for the barn and his horse to fetch the doctor.

Rose called for Mylène to prepare warm broth, bread, and water for Gabrielle. Rose ascended the staircase, passing Pierre to Yves as she went.

Her heart sang to see Gabrielle was still alert when Rose entered the room once more.

"I'm so glad you came back to us," Rose said, holding Gabrielle's free hand. Elisabeth already held the other. "You gave us quite a scare."

"Thank you for helping me," Gabrielle said. "I'll try not to scare you again."

CHAPTER 27

Elisabeth

April 1671

"Stay in bed, Gabrielle," Elisabeth said. "I'll get supper."

Though she kept her tone light, Elisabeth's expression betrayed her concern. Gabrielle seemed cheerful, but in the weeks since her awakening and her return to the Beaumonts' home, the young girl's color had not returned and she tired far too easily. Her lack of recovery frightened her new mother.

Gilbert had set up a "daytime bed" for Gabrielle in the family's main living area, so the girl could feel part of the goings-on without straining herself.

Elisabeth tried to focus on the venison and vegetables she chopped for a stew, but found her eyes wandering to the frail figure beneath the quilt.

I've lost three babies. I'll not lose my Gabrielle as well.

An hour later, the smell of the stew wafted down the stairs and lured Gilbert and Pascal from the shop.

"My word, you're a good cook, woman," Gilbert said by way of greeting as he placed the bread on the table and kissed his wife on the cheek.

"Pleased to hear it," Elisabeth said, glancing from her husband to Gabrielle.

He followed her gaze, and a frown flickered across his face.

"I'm going to eat at the table tonight," Gabrielle said, not waiting for acknowledgment before she stood.

"Sweetheart, I can bring you your food on a tray," Elisabeth said, rushing to the girl's side. "You need to rest."

"I'll never get stronger if I don't move around," Gabrielle said.

Elisabeth looked to her husband for support, but he offered none.

"She can try, for a little while," Gilbert said, pulling out the chair for Gabrielle and taking her arm to help her into place. He turned to Gabrielle. "If you get light-headed, it's back to bed, though."

"Of course," Gabrielle agreed.

"Good girl," Elisabeth said, still not convinced of the wisdom of letting the girl sit upright, even for a meal. "Eat as much as you can, but don't strain yourself."

"You're putting us on," Pascal said with an impish grin. "We know you're just trying to shirk your share of the work."

His levity was superficial. As much as Elisabeth worried, she knew Pascal worried more. The boy had said that Gabrielle was the only blood relative he still claimed.

Just as everyone was seated and served, there was a knock on the door below.

Gilbert rolled his eyes. "Monsieur Lucas has probably forgotten his supper loaf again. I'll help him out, to avoid the wrath of Madame."

The Beaumonts laughed. Madame Lucas's temper had a reputation throughout the settlement. When he returned, however, Father Cloutier and Bailiff Duval trailed him.

At the sight of the men, Elisabeth hesitated a brief moment and gestured to the two free seats at the table. "Would you join us for supper?"

I'd sooner dine with the Girouxes, but I will not have people speaking against my hospitality. Thank goodness I made extra, though I'll have to improvise for tomorrow's midday meal.

"Thank you, Madame Beaumont," the priest said as he took a seat.

Elisabeth forced a smile and served the two men generous helpings of stew.

"Your reputation as a cook isn't exaggerated," the bailiff said, eating with zeal.

The priest looked at his companion's table manners with disdain. He ate with careful movements that seemed all but choreographed.

"We come with news," Father Cloutier said. "Regretfully, Raymond Giroux's body was found this afternoon. It appears he had an unfortunate encounter with a wild animal, God rest his soul."

"Better than he deserved," Pascal mumbled.

"Young man, this is your father we discuss," Father Cloutier scolded.

"I know, and I meant what I said." To his credit, Pascal's tone was not defiant but resolute.

"You must honor your father, even in death," the priest replied. "The Bible commands it."

"As you say." Pascal didn't look up from his plate.

"Are you feeling all right, Gabrielle?" Elisabeth asked, noticing the girl had paled.

"Not as well as before," she said. "I should rest. Father, was that all your news?"

"Yes, child, though I would ask you to remain at the table a little longer."

Elisabeth noticed a flash of annoyance on Gilbert's face, but her husband hid his irritation admirably.

"I do have some additional concerns to discuss with you," the priest continued.

"Very well, Father," Gilbert said.

"The Ursulines are willing to give Gabrielle a home. Given her circumstances, they are willing to waive the usual endowment that accompanies a candidate for the novitiate. She could ask for no better opportunity."

"The Sisters are kind," Elisabeth said, remembering her own happy weeks in the convent. "But Gabrielle is welcome here."

"I worry, madame, that this may not be the best environment for her," said the priest.

"How could you think so?" Elisabeth asked. "We care for her like a daughter. She's fed, clothed, and taught a trade, as well as instructed on how to run a home. She's better off than many girls her age."

"And when it comes time for her to marry, what then?" asked the bailiff, finding his voice after his third helping of stew.

"She'll have the best dowry we can muster," Elisabeth said, snatching plates from the table and placing them on the washboard.

"You would be willing to do so much for a child that is not your own?" The priest's eyes widened.

"You see us in our pew each Sunday, yet you seem surprised to find the principles you preach lived out here?" Gilbert sat back in his chair and crossed his arms over his chest. "You offend us, sir."

"Not my intention, I assure you," Father Cloutier said. "Though I have concerns about your wife as a guardian for a young, impressionable girl."

"And what, pray tell, makes my wife's conduct questionable?" Gilbert's hold on his temper was tenuous at best. The telltale vein in his forehead throbbed.

Elisabeth did not trust herself with words. Instead, she served dessert and cider.

"The talk in town is not favorable." Father Cloutier took a dainty bite of Elisabeth's prized *millefeuille* pastry. "People say you run the bakery as equals, though the Lord requires a woman to submit to her husband's authority."

"My wife is the better baker, Father," Gilbert said, pushing his plate forward. "I seek her opinion in all things because God has blessed her with superior skill. A humble man can—and should—admit this."

Father Cloutier harped on humility from the pulpit without end. He appeared none too pleased to have his arguments brought against him.

"I hear you are also teaching her to read and write," the priest said.

"Necessary for the business," Gilbert replied. "I'm teaching Gabrielle as well. I would mention, the Ursulines would educate her, also."

"Only so she could be of service to God," the priest began.

"Learning to read in service to one's husband and family is also a Godly virtue," Gilbert said. "Father, my wife spends every waking moment taking care of her family with at least the same love and devotion you have for your church. Say what you will about me, but her conduct is irreproachable."

Elisabeth bit back a smile as she recalled her behavior the morning Duval brought her intoxicated husband back from the tavern. *Perhaps not irreproachable, love.* As much as Elisabeth wished to defend herself, she held her tongue. Her husband's defense would be far more persuasive.

"Monsieur Beaumont—" the priest began.

"No more, Father," Gilbert said, standing and walking to the stairs. "I have worked since before dawn, and I'm bone tired. Please see yourselves out."

The priest left in a huff. The bailiff trailed after him like a scolded dog following his master.

"I don't want to leave," Gabrielle said. "I don't want to become a nun."

"Nor will you have to," Elisabeth said.

"How can you be so sure?" Pascal asked, voice brimming with venom. "He seems bent on getting his way, as usual."

"The Sisters know me," Elisabeth said. "They won't take Gabrielle from my care without reason."

"True," Gilbert said, reclaiming his discarded dessert. "And like it or not, the priests can't contradict the nuns as much as they like to think."

"Back to bed, sweetheart," Elisabeth said, offering her arm to Gabrielle. The girl was noticeably shakier on her walk back to bed. "Please don't worry."

"I'll try not to," Gabrielle said. "Is it strange that I feel sad about Papa?"

In all the upset over Gabrielle's future, Raymond Giroux had been almost forgotten.

"Not at all, dear," Elisabeth said, smoothing a brown lock from Gabrielle's forehead. "My *maman* and I didn't get along, but part of me still misses her."

"How could anyone not get along with you?" Gabrielle asked.

The earnest wonder in her face made Elisabeth smile.

"I have that effect on more people than you might realize," Elisabeth confessed. "But I've learned a lesson along the way."

"What's that, Maman?"

It was the first time Gabrielle had used the term. Elisabeth had to clear the emotion from her throat before she answered. "The longer I live, I find the people I struggle to get along with were never worth getting along with in the first place."

"The man is as stubborn as a constipated jackass," Sister Mathilde declared the following afternoon, when she heard about the encounter with the priest.

It took all of Elisabeth's restraint not to sputter cider on the convent floor.

"Laugh if you will, young madame, but it's the truth," the nun said as she placed her cup on the table with vigor beyond her years.

The common room remained the same as it had when Elisabeth lived there. Only the young inhabitants had changed. They seemed to Elisabeth quite a bit younger than she had been when she arrived, but she realized that was just the result of passing time.

"I don't deny it," Elisabeth said. "I just don't understand why he's so fixated on our family."

"I'm sure he has his reasons," Sister Mathilde said, smoothing the wrinkles from her habit. "He rarely acts without them. It boils down to the fact that women scare him, and educated, independent women scare him most of all."

"What nonsense," Elisabeth said, taking one of Pierre's nightgowns from her bag for hemming. "What man is scared of women?"

"Most of them." The Sister arched her eyebrow. "Why do you think they spend so much energy putting us in our places?"

"I never thought of it that way, Sister."

"Of course not," Sister Mathilde said. "Your father raised you like a son, and your husband treats you like an equal. You haven't seen it as many times as I have."

"I suppose you're right," Elisabeth said, but she wondered how much the men were to blame. Her mother had wanted her under a man's boot, too. Men may have created the cage, but mothers clipped their daughters' wings and shoved them inside.

"And there he is now. Great shock, I'm sure," Sister Mathilde said, shaking her head as a black-clad figure passed the window on the way to the front door.

Moments later, a younger nun escorted Father Cloutier to the common room. He frowned with annoyance at the sight of Elisabeth.

"Madame Beaumont, I had not expected to see you here."

He took the seat nearest Sister Mathilde without awaiting an invitation.

"Perhaps not," Elisabeth said. "I seldom have time to visit the Sisters as I'd like, but Monsieur Beaumont thought a walk and an hour of conversation would do me good."

Elisabeth patted her increasing midsection. With all her ministrations to Gabrielle, she had not noticed her missing courses until they were more than a month overdue.

The gesture was not lost on Father Cloutier, but he did not acknowledge it.

"Just as well that you're here, I suppose," he said. "I've come to speak to Sister Mathilde concerning the Giroux girl. I think she should move to the Sisters' care immediately."

"She's not well enough to move," Elisabeth said, stowing the baby's garment in her bag. "Last night's supper was her first out of bed."

"The Sisters will provide her with medical care."

"Father," Sister Mathilde said, "although we would gladly take the child in if she wished it, or if she had no other options, I cannot take on the burden of nursing and feeding an extra person if the faithful of our community have offered to do it for us."

Sister Mathilde sat as tall as her curved spine would allow. Her blue eyes did not waver.

"I understand your reluctance, Sister," Father Cloutier said, "but you did agree."

"I agreed that she would be welcome here if no other option existed," the nun replied. "The request surprised me, given how useful Gabrielle has been to the Beaumont family, and they to her. Now that I know she is wanted in their home, I see no reason to move her here."

"You would go back on your word, Sister?" the priest asked.

"I will not," Sister Mathilde said. "If Gabrielle Giroux desires to join our order, or if the Beaumonts cease to offer her care, I will welcome her under my roof. She is a hard worker, and would be an asset here. However, my duty in this settlement is finding wives for the settlers. New France needs mothers more than Sisters. Gabrielle is better off with the Beaumonts unless God calls her otherwise."

"Sister, I have prayed extensively on the matter." The tenor of Father Cloutier's voice attracted the attention of several young ladies in the room, who until then had at least pretended to be engrossed in their knitting.

"Mademoiselle Giroux has not." Sister Mathilde's tone was no gentler than his. "No person should assume a religious vocation lightly, as you ought to know, nor should a child ever be forced into one. The Reverend Mother and I will not accept a candidate who does not wholeheartedly wish to devote her life to the Church. The decision is Gabrielle's and hers alone. Until she recovers, and unless she wishes to join the Church, she will remain with the Beaumonts."

"Sister, if they were the faithful Christian couple you claim, they would have several children by now, not just the one. Their lack casts doubt upon their faith and character."

Elisabeth's jaw dropped.

Sister Mathilde silenced her with a look before responding. "Madame Beaumont is not as young as some of our other brides, Father, and her pregnancies have not been easy. Surely you do not blame her for the loss of her first child, or for the two she has lost since then?"

"I . . . was unaware . . ." the priest began.

"It is not for want of duty that Madame Beaumont lacks a houseful of children," the nun continued. "Perhaps the Lord has sent the Giroux children to fill it, since her womb cannot."

"Sister, I doubt—"

"Father Cloutier, this matter is one for the convent to decide," Sister Mathilde said. "I will visit Gabrielle when I can, to ensure she is mending properly and receiving proper care."

"I am disappointed in your change of heart." The priest stood.

"And I in your willful misinterpretation of my offer. Good day, Father." Sister Mathilde did not rise to see him out, but gestured to the exit.

All eyes in the room were fixed on the priest as he left, slamming the door in his wake. A few nervous giggles escaped from the knitting corner, but Sister Mathilde's sideways glance silenced them at once.

"Thank you, Sister," Elisabeth said, once she found her voice.

"Please, child." Sister Mathilde took a sip from her cider. "Crossing that man is always a pleasure. Thank you. But tend to that girl of yours," Sister Mathilde said. "Give him no reason to complain."

For a month, life continued normally at the Beaumont household. Once a week, Sister Mathilde, assisted by Sister Anne, visited and checked on Gabrielle. The child grew stronger every day and delved into the books that Sister Mathilde furnished. Gabrielle's intellect would never equal Manon Lefebvre's, but she seemed just as eager to learn.

One Thursday afternoon, an hour or so after Sister Mathilde left and Elisabeth installed Gabrielle in a chair by the window to enjoy the warm June sunshine, Elisabeth heard raised voices in the bakery below. She exchanged a glance with Gabrielle and descended to the shop.

"Duval, you know how I run my business." Gilbert stood nose to nose with the bailiff, face flushed an angry red.

"Rules is rules, Beaumont," the bailiff said. "If you can't abide by 'em, you can't do business."

"Let me see your mandate."

"Here." The bailiff produced the document.

Elisabeth wondered how much of the bailiff's annoyance was due to the fact that a "little man" like Gilbert Beaumont could read.

Gilbert scanned the paper and thrust it back. "This law was passed over a year ago. Why has no one complained before now?"

"That's not my business, Beaumont. Someone has complained. Comply with the law, or we'll take away your license to bake. Is that clear?"

"Fine; get out of my shop." Gilbert pointed to the door.

Duval exited, shoulders back and nose aloft. His job was done.

"Of all the pompous imbeciles . . ." Gilbert sputtered.

"What was that about?" Elisabeth asked.

Gilbert raked his fingers through his hair and paced. "Apparently, when we raised prices two months ago, we exceeded the amount decreed by law."

Elisabeth stopped. "But the price of wheat almost doubled. We all raised our prices. We less than all the others."

"Don't I know it," Gilbert said, pinching the bridge of his nose as he did when a headache was coming on. "People would have paid another two *sous* a loaf at least, but I didn't want to raise it any higher than I had to."

"Did Duval speak to the other bakers?" Elisabeth asked. She busied her hands wiping the counters with a cloth.

"I don't know," Gilbert said. "I should have kept my head and gotten more information, but I was angry."

"I don't blame you," Elisabeth said, discarding the cloth. "We've a right to be angry. This isn't a Paris bake shop, after all. We only have so many suppliers for flour."

"Too true." Gilbert's voice sounded hollow. The voice of a man with no answers.

"We'll manage, Gilbert." She looked up at his broad, sturdy face and planted a kiss on his cheek, ignoring the possibility of a passerby seeing her from the street.

The crowd outside the shop hurled angry insults as Gilbert closed the doors. Bailiff Duval smiled and dispersed the disappointed customers.

"They seem so angry," Gabrielle said from her seat in the corner.

"Without bread for supper? They've a right to be." Elisabeth took a bucket of soapy water and attacked the countertops with a brush. With the forced decrease in cost, they couldn't afford to buy the ingredients to keep their customers supplied.

"Duval is set to put us out of business, plain as plain." Gilbert swept the floor in time with Elisabeth's scrubbing.

"Don't give that vile man the credit." Elisabeth flung her brush in the bucket, causing the water to slosh on her skirts and the counter.

"He hasn't the brains or the desire. It's Father Cloutier. He wants the shop shut down because of me."

"What do you mean?" Pascal paused from scouring the oven.

"Don't worry," Elisabeth said. "I have an idea to fix this. Gabrielle, can you manage the supper?"

Gilbert opened his mouth, but swallowed his question. A moment later, he changed his mind. "What do you plan to do? Nothing foolish, mind."

"Of course not." Elisabeth's frosty expression quashing her protective husband's protests. "For the moment, I intend to pay a call on the Escoffiers."

Quentin Escoffier's bakery sat a ten-minute walk from the Beaumonts'. Though Elisabeth was not well acquainted with Quentin Escoffier or his wife, Thérèse, their exchanges had always been pleasant. She hoped they would give her the information she required.

"Madame Beaumont!" the jovial Quentin exclaimed when he recognized her figure at the door. He emerged from behind the counter and shook her hand. "I would not expect to see you here in the middle of the afternoon."

Elisabeth took a quick inventory of the shop. She saw plenty of loaves of every description, therefore plenty of profits to cover the cost of flour. The cakes and pastries were few and unimaginative, though she approved of the cleanliness and order.

"I take it Bailiff Duval has not been here?" Elisabeth asked.

"Should I expect him?" Quentin asked, releasing her hand.

"I doubt it." Elisabeth told him about the bailiff's threats, the closing of the Beaumonts' shop, and her theories concerning Father Cloutier. Gabrielle's case was well known in the settlement. No one grieved for the loss of Raymond Giroux.

"Thank you for the warning, madame," Escoffier said. "Is there anything we can do for you?"

"I can't think of anything that will help, Monsieur Escoffier. If we aren't allowed to charge a fair price, we may well be forced to close our doors for good."

"I will pray for you, madame," Quentin said, his expression grave.

"I appreciate it. Thank you." Elisabeth, as a token of respect for her fellow baker, purchased a small cake for her family before returning to the closed shop.

Gabrielle, with help from Gilbert and Pascal, had produced a respectable mutton stew in Elisabeth's absence. Even so, they ate in silence. The impending closure of the bakery hung heavy over their table.

The following afternoon, the supply of salable bread ran out two hours before closing. As expected, Bailiff Duval had stopped by twice to inventory the shop and disperse the angry crowd in the afternoon.

"If you cannot keep the people supplied, we can give your license to one who can," Duval threatened.

Gilbert retired to douse the ovens for the day. Elisabeth ignored the bailiff and locked the door.

"Not so fast!" Escoffier called from the street. His wife, Thérèse, and four apprentices from the other bakeries in town accompanied the baker. They carried baskets brimming with fresh-baked bread. "I believe you need these loaves, madame."

Elisabeth, eyes wide, ushered the group into the shop. They emptied the baskets into the cases, fully restocking the store in a matter of moments.

"Prayers are good," Escoffier said, "but I realized you could use loaves even more."

Elisabeth felt the tears spill over onto her cheeks as she embraced the small, round man.

"You're a guardian angel, Monsieur Escoffier."

"Nonsense. I am a man with a sense of justice. Do you hear that, Duval?" Escoffier rounded on the bailiff, who had entered the shop with a flood of eager patrons. "You cannot bully these good people. Who will bake bread for our citizens if the bakeries close? Will you?"

"Leave the Beaumonts alone, and find something better to do with your time!" a patron shouted. The others grumbled agreement.

Duval exited the shop without a word.

"What happened?" Gilbert asked, entering to see his shop bustling once again.

"Your brother bakers stood up for you and your wife, Beaumont," Escoffier said. "We won't see your business ruined."

Gilbert nodded, unable to speak. From behind the counter, Elisabeth smiled at her husband. She remembered the kindnesses of her father's patrons and colleagues in Paris. She was not so surprised as he. She only hoped the gesture would be enough to keep the law at bay long enough to save the business from ruin.

CHAPTER 28

Nicole

July 1671

The ship came into view just before noon.

Nicole gripped baby Frédéric to her chest, racing heart lulling the infant into a slumber.

Hélène squirmed as she held Alexandre's hand. She was anxious to meet the mysterious "Mamie" and "Papi" that everyone spoke of.

Manon stood still, a picture of decorum. Her face showed mild curiosity, but no stronger emotion, at the arrival of her adoptive mother's family.

"Can we take them to see Papa's land this afternoon?" Manon asked, looking up at her mother.

"No, *chèrie,* they'll be exhausted from the journey." Nicole adjusted Frédéric as she spoke. Her sturdy son was a bigger burden to carry than his delicate sister had been. More energetic, too.

Exhausted, at best. The voyage is hard enough on the young, let alone those who are past their best days. Nicole gripped her son, not giving her fears credence by voicing them.

It seemed like hours before the passengers disembarked, but Nicole soon saw her family on the gangplank. She rushed to them and grasped her mother, as though convincing herself that Maman was a real person and not a shadow from her dreams.

Words failed as tears choked Nicole.

"My darling girl," Bernadette said, admiring her well-dressed daughter. She wiped her own tears. "You've grown into a beauty. I knew you would."

"Don't keep her all to yourself!" Thomas chided with a smile. "I never thought I'd see my girl again." He enveloped Nicole and the baby in his arms.

"This is your grandson, Frédéric," Nicole said, passing the baby to her mother. "And these are my daughters, Hélène and Manon, and my husband, Monsieur Alexandre Lefebvre."

Thomas took his son-in-law's hand and shook it. "God bless you, son. Thank you for looking after my daughter."

"She is a treasure, monsieur," Alexandre said, with no trace of his usual courtly flattery. "I'm glad that you can be reunited. Shall we continue our conversation at home?"

The Lefebvres had yet to move to the new house, in the heart of the settlement, but their current residence was enough to awe the Deschamps family. It lacked the refinement of a Paris apartment or the grandeur of a country estate, but it was among the finest in New France. Nicole had rooms prepared for her family to rest in comfort and reacquaint themselves with their eldest daughter and her family before they made the move to their lodgings at the farm.

That afternoon, Thomas asked his son-in-law for a carriage tour of the settlement. Nicole was surprised and pleased to see her father so energetic after his journey.

Claudine, Emmanuelle, Manon, and Georges eagerly joined them, leaving Nicole and Bernadette behind to put the younger children down for naps.

"Maman, you and Papa will stay here," Nicole said, showing her mother the second bedroom. "But the maid will see you settled. Let's have some refreshment in my sitting room."

"Your sitting room, my my." Bernadette smiled and gave her daughter a roguish wink as they entered the plush little parlor. It was clearly the domain of the lady of the house as evidenced by the pink and green fabrics and the glints of light that bounced off the walnut furniture. Bernadette looked at her daughter, wide-eyed. This room alone was at least half the size of the farmhouse they'd left behind. The only piece of furniture that would have looked at home in their old farmhouse was the sturdy chair Luc Jarvais had purchased for his bride.

"You'll get used to it, Maman. It wasn't easy for me, either." Nicole poured the cider into cups and offered her mother a biscuit from the platter.

"I'm going to look like a beggar among your friends," Bernadette said, admiring her daughter's fine dress.

"Nonsense, Maman. You'll be welcome everywhere. Besides, I have winter cloaks for you and Papa already, and dresses made for you and the girls. I used Manon as a model, though it was hard to think of the girls having grown so big."

"They are almost ladies, aren't they?" Bernadette sighed as she folded a nightdress. "How did the little native girl come to you?"

"She found my first husband after he had been shot by one of the men in her tribe." For the first time in years, Nicole shed tears for Luc Jarvais as she told her mother the story.

"The girl seems very quiet and ladylike," Bernadette said when her daughter had finished. "You've done an excellent job of raising her."

"I'm not sure how much I had to do with it." Nicole smiled as her mother took a second biscuit. "She was born a lady. The Sisters and I just helped her along. She's so bright, Maman."

"I have no doubt. She's a lucky girl to have you."

"She saved me, Maman. If she hadn't stayed, I don't know that I would have had the strength to move on. Those first few months . . ."

"You would have managed," Bernadette said. "You don't give up on anything. All the same, I'm grateful the child gave you some measure of comfort."

"It doesn't seem real that you're actually here, in my very room," Nicole said, embracing her mother.

"There were times I didn't think I would make it," Bernadette admitted.

Nicole remembered Elisabeth's ministrations when she was so ill on her own voyage. She nodded.

"Still," Bernadette said, "I can see why the King is so set on keeping this land. It's beautiful. I can't believe how well you've done for yourself."

"Alexandre is a good man," Nicole replied, averting her eyes.

"Your father and I could never have settled you half so well." Bernadette's tone was as wistful as it was truthful. "We went 'round and 'round when you asked for our blessing to leave. I thought I was right then, and I know it now. I couldn't be prouder."

Nicole bit her tongue. She was comfortably settled, to be sure. But she felt that Elisabeth and Rose deserved far more credit for their successes than she did for her own. Nicole knew she was of use to Alexandre, but each day she despised her role in society more. She lived for the days when she stayed at home, tending to Hélène and Frédéric and helping Manon with her lessons. Those were the days she felt useful.

For over an hour, mother and daughter caught up on the goings-on of the past four years. The dozen letters they had exchanged, while prized and reread until the paper grew too thin to handle, could not convey all the details of life on either side of the ocean. Bernadette listened, enraptured, to tales of Rose's change of heart and marriage to Henri, and Elisabeth's bakery, and the incidents with the Giroux family. Nicole smiled at her mother's gossip about their former neighbors and the news of her older brothers, Christophe and Baptiste, now fathers themselves, with thriving farms in France.

"This will be the prettiest dress I've ever had!" Claudine breathed, holding up the basted-together garment and admiring herself in the mirror.

"It was nice of Monsieur Lefebvre to buy us the fabric," Emmanuelle said, fondling the length of blue-and-gray silk brocade she had selected on their afternoon tour of town.

"You must have something nice to wear when you come visiting from the farm," Nicole said, knowing how a gift so lavish would have turned her own head at the age of twelve.

Nicole insisted on making her sisters' dresses at home instead of allowing Alexandre to hire a seamstress. She had missed sewing with her sisters and was anxious to reclaim at least a portion of that experience. Besides, the girls would have to sew for themselves on the new farm, as they had on the old one.

"I wish we could stay and live in town." Claudine pouted at herself in the mirror, though the sight of her soft pink dress-to-be seemed to cheer her.

"Papa could never handle a life in town. Not even one as small as Quebec," Nicole said as she cut the pieces for Emmanuelle's dress. "You'll love your beautiful new house. You won't miss town at all."

"Not likely," Claudine said.

Seeing Claudine's even stitches, Nicole had to admit that her mother's teaching skills had not faltered in the years since she had left.

"Nothing ever happens on a farm," Claudine complained. "Town is where the excitement is."

"How can you say that, Claudine?" Emmanuelle, less enthusiastic about sewing, buried herself in a book she had borrowed from Alexandre. "Farms are full of life. We'd starve without them."

"Listen to your sister," Nicole said, arching her brow. "I've only met one other eleven-year-old who speaks such sense. And speaking of the sun, there it shines."

Manon stood at the entry to the sitting room with a shy smile on her face and a thick book clutched to her chest. "I'm twelve, Maman."

"Of course you are, but you spoke almost as much sense last year as you do now." Nicole winked at her daughter. "Where is your fabric, sweetheart? We can baste all the dresses together by supper if we don't dawdle."

"I didn't get any fabric, Maman," Manon said. "I'm off to study. Latin examination tomorrow."

"Your papa didn't offer you a length of fabric along with your aunts?" Nicole asked.

Claudine and Emmanuelle snickered at being called aunts to a girl practically their own age.

"He did, Maman, but I have enough clothes. Too many, in fact. I didn't need another dress."

"As you wish, darling," Nicole said. "We would have enjoyed your company, though."

Something in Manon's expression made Nicole's maternal hackles raise in alarm.

"Is everything all right, sweetheart?"

"Fine, Maman. I need to study this passage before supper."

"Give Horace my regards." Nicole smiled at her daughter as she padded from the room.

"Imagine wanting to study that stuff instead of making dresses and having fun." Claudine shook her head as she stitched.

"She's a smart girl," Nicole said. "She enjoys her studies. Speaking of which, Maman said a few more hours with a book wouldn't do you any harm."

Emmanuelle nodded agreement.

"Maybe, but not Latin," Claudine said, setting the garment down. "If I'm going to read something, it better be in French. One language is enough for me."

Emmanuelle rolled her eyes. Manon didn't need to worry about Claudine ever staking a claim to the title of family scholar.

"May I speak with you?" Manon stood at the nursery door and spoke softly, so as not to disturb the younger children.

Hélène was already tucked into bed and Frédéric settled with his nurse.

"Of course, darling. Let's go to your room." Nicole extinguished the candle and blew a kiss to the sleeping Hélène.

Manon's room was cheerful, and close to the nursery, but private, as appropriate for a girl on the cusp of womanhood. A large mahogany desk that had once been Alexandre's dominated the space. It was covered with books and stacks of paper, each one organized in a system that only Manon understood completely. The girl sat on the edge of her bed and motioned for Nicole to do the same.

"What do you want to talk about? It has been a big week, hasn't it?" Nicole tucked a wayward strand of hair out of Manon's face and stroked her cheek.

"You're happy now that your family is here, aren't you?" Manon looked at the pattern on the wall beyond Nicole's shoulder rather than making direct eye contact.

"Having us all together makes things complete." Nicole patted Manon's hand as she spoke. "Do you enjoy having them here?"

"They're nice." Manon's voice rang with sincerity. "I can see why you missed them so."

"What aren't you telling me, Manon?" Nicole asked.

"I miss my people, Maman." Manon managed to look at Nicole. "The Huron girls don't consider me one of them anymore. It doesn't feel right."

"I'm so sorry. I could speak with Sister Hortense, arrange some visits to the Huron village. Would that help?"

"I don't think it's enough, Maman." Manon's voice was resolute, bolder now that the issue was out in the open. "I've turned my back on who I am. My mother—my birth mother—my grandmother, my tribe—they all deserve better from me."

"I can't imagine they would be anything other than proud of you. You're accomplished in Latin and Greek, the smartest girl in your class," Nicole said.

"And there are days when I can barely remember my native tongue." Manon looked out her window at the starlit night. "I love living here. I don't want to leave you, but now that you have your family, you don't need me anymore. I should return to my own people while I still can."

"Manon, I couldn't bear to part with you." Nicole rose and placed her hands on Manon's shoulders. "You're my daughter. You belong with me."

"You have treated me as your own," Manon said, "but you have a daughter, and a son, and sisters. Other people here don't welcome me the way you do. I know that makes you sad, and you would change it if you could, but it won't change. I see it every time we go to church, every time we're in town. People look at me like I don't belong."

"I don't care about what they think." Nicole turned Manon around. "Do you think they're more important to me than you are?"

"No, but it matters to me," Manon said, her voice unwavering. "These are your people. They're right, I don't belong, and if I stay here much longer I won't belong with my own people anymore, either."

"Manon, darling—"

"Maman, that isn't even my name. Not truly."

Nicole sought words, but found none. The candlelight danced off her cheeks as her shoulders trembled.

"Don't make this harder than it has to be, Maman." Manon embraced Nicole. "I'll always love you, but this is something I have to do."

Nicole was helpless to hold back her tears as she shut her sitting room door behind her and found her place in the plain wooden chair Luc had gifted her at their wedding. The rustic piece of furniture looked as out of place in the feminine parlor as a fur trapper at a royal ball, but she had insisted on keeping it, nonetheless.

"Nicole, what's the matter?" Alexandre bounded across the room before she could speak. He walked her to their bed and held her as the sobs racked her body.

"Dearest, you must tell me what's wrong." Alexandre stroked Nicole's tear-softened face.

"Manon wants to leave us." The words were bitter on her tongue.

"For the Church?" Alexandre asked. "It was never your first choice for her, but it seems a good fit. She's young to enter the convent still, though, isn't she?"

"She doesn't want to take the orders." Nicole steadied her breath as she wiped her tears. "She wants to go back to her people."

"Why on earth would she want that?" Alexandre's expression looked as though Manon had announced a plan to swim the Atlantic.

"She doesn't feel welcome here." Nicole stood, freeing herself from Alexandre's arms. She looked in vain for something to tidy or clean. "She feels like an outsider here. She said she always would."

"Absurd." Alexandre began to disrobe. "Don't fret over that ridiculous notion. She'll be more sensible in the morning. She just feels a bit put out with your family here. Once they've settled in the country all will return to the way it was."

"I don't think so. She spoke so forcefully." Nicole sat on the bench in front of her mirror and brushed out her long chestnut hair to give her hands an occupation. "You know how she is. She wouldn't say it if she didn't mean it."

"I'll speak with her tomorrow, dearest." Alexandre approached his wife and stooped to kiss her shoulder. "Regardless of how she feels, she is better off with us than anywhere else. She's a reasonable child. I will persuade her that her place is here."

"Please do speak with her, dear heart," Nicole said. She had seen Alexandre's persuasive tactics, and they were formidable.

She placed the brush on the vanity and looked into her own weary brown eyes, for once wishing she could feel more confidence in her husband's success.

Despite Nicole's pleas and Alexandre's reasoning, Manon stayed steadfast in her decision to return to the Huron. Nicole tried, and failed, to keep the tears at bay as she helped the sweet girl, her eldest daughter, prepare for her departure.

"You must take the cape, Manon, I insist." Nicole placed the folded garment of navy-blue wool back in Manon's small bag. "You know what winter is like. I know you want to dress like your people, but I don't want you to freeze. This may come in handy someday. I want you to keep it."

"Very well." Manon snapped the leather bag closed and took a last look around her bedroom.

"Please—are you sure . . ." Nicole said.

"You promised," Manon said, gripping her bag.

"Please," Nicole said, gripping Manon's shoulders, "at least promise to visit?"

"I don't think that's wise." Manon fidgeted with a strap on her case.

Nicole took Manon in her arms. She refused to entertain the thought that it might be for the last time. She wanted to scream at her. To wail. To plead with her to stay where she belonged. More than anything she ached to have the devoted eight-year-old child who had led her through the forest to Luc's body back in her arms. The child who would never have dreamed of leaving her. That child was gone, however, and Nicole knew more than a little about homesickness and the yearning for family. Nicole lingered in the embrace, knowing how empty she would feel when it was over.

"You will always be my girl."

Nicole stared at her plate and managed a couple of mouthfuls of the roasted chicken and creamed potatoes, but no more.

Around her, Claudine and Emmanuelle chirped about their afternoon in town, while Alexandre and Thomas discussed spring planting strategies. No one mentioned Manon's absence, or seemed to mind it at all.

Only little Hélène had shed tears for her missing sister.

"Darling, eat your supper," Bernadette chided.

Nicole placed her fork beside her plate and shot a reproachful look at her mother. "I'm not hungry."

"You're not upset about the native girl, are you?" Claudine asked.

"My daughter? As a matter of fact, I am. She left a few hours ago. Am I to forget her already?"

"No one said that, dear." Bernadette continued with her meal.

Nicole stood, throwing her napkin on her plate. She took no leave of the table, but didn't care about the breach of etiquette.

What good is being the lady of the house if I am not above the rules on occasion?

Nicole retired to her room and changed into her nightgown before she realized it was hours too early for bed. She busied herself with long-neglected yarn and knitting needles, making a massive rectangle that might evolve into a scarf or blanket that wasn't needed, but finding a measure of solace in the occupation.

An hour later, Alexandre knocked softly at the bedroom door, a custom that made Nicole smile under other circumstances.

"Ready for bed already?" he asked. "I looked the house over for you after dinner."

"I was in no mood for company." Nicole cast the needles aside. The lump of knitted fabric was now twice the size of a scarf, but less than needed for a blanket of any practical size.

"I imagine not," Alexandre said, removing his coat and placing it over his chair. He sat on the edge of the bed to remove his boots.

"She made her decision, dearest. We must respect it. There's nothing more to be done."

"We should have tried harder, Alexandre." Nicole looked out the glass, hoping Manon was safe. "We should have done more to make sure she knew she was wanted."

"What more could we have done, Nicole? You raised the girl as your own, clothed her and fed her when you could ill afford it. I did what I could, as well, and she repaid us all by leaving. If I have any feelings on the subject, it's anger and betrayal on your behalf. This was a spectacular demonstration of ingratitude."

"It doesn't matter now, does it?" Nicole mused, tracing the outlines of the pattern on the brocade chair. "She's gone. I've lost a part of my heart."

"You know I cared for the girl, and I am sorry for your sake, but don't dwell on it overlong. She's with her people, and you with yours. We have two children and will have more." Alexandre bent down by his wife. "Not to mention two boisterous sisters, a strapping young brother, and doting parents that I imported for you."

Nicole smiled at his concern and warmth. He was not a demonstrative man, not in his day-to-day actions, but that only made his grander gestures more meaningful when they occurred.

"I will try," Nicole said, reaching forward to kiss him. "But it will take time."

"If it didn't, you would not be the woman I love." He brushed a lock of hair from her face. "But you will heal. I'm sure of it."

Nicole looked into the deep gray eyes of the man she loved. He was good and kind, but he would never understand her love for Manon or the debt she felt for the girl who had dragged her into the snow in hopes of saving Luc Jarvais.

CHAPTER 29

Rose

August 1671

Little Benoît nuzzled his mother's breast, contented with a stomach full of milk, and drifted into the blissful slumber of a well-loved infant. Rose smiled down at his peaceful face, wanting to laugh at the cooing noises he made in his sleep.

She placed Benoît in his cradle and left the little nursery with all the stealth she could muster. She lifted her eyes heavenward and wished for a solid two-hour nap. If he did not sleep, he would be unbearable for Mylène. Leaving him with her, even for an afternoon, was still torture. It had been impossible at first, but she bowed to her husband's pleas to trust the capable servant with the baby's care for a few hours.

Rose sat in her favorite chair, pulled close to the window to take advantage of the cooling draft. She rummaged through her mending basket looking for a pair of Henri's breeches.

Such thrilling work. Rose stretched the muscles of her neck that rebelled against her stooped posture. She knew that moving from the settlement out to the homestead would isolate her somewhat, but the extent to which she missed the town and the company of Nicole and Elisabeth had surprised her. The first months on the homestead had been so busy that Rose had no time left to notice loneliness. Setting up house and preparing for the baby had taken all of her time and precious energy. Now that Benoît was growing stronger and sleeping through the night, her mind grew restless, though her body remained occupied.

The hem stitches were lazy, but they would hold.

Rose tried to invest herself in household tasks, but they did nothing to stimulate her brain the way her teaching and studying had. She had mentioned her discontent to Henri several times, but he urged her to be patient. When he became a *seigneur,* with land of his own, they would return to town and she could take a more active role in society. Until then, she had to be content with the life of a country wife.

Rose changed from her housedress and prepared a finer garment, left behind from her months in town. The green satin overcoat, pale pink stomacher and underskirt, and stiff petticoats felt foreign and uncomfortable now.

As a girl, she had worn such clothes for play, but with passing years she had traded satin and silk for wool and linen, just as Latin and Greek had given way to mending and dusting.

At times, Rose cursed the education that made housekeeping so monotonous, but she could never bring herself to wish it away completely. It had saved her from the drudgery in the Salpêtrière and made her a suitable wife for Henri. A simple woman would have bored him.

Rose scolded herself for not taking more interest in running her home. Hundreds of women lived less comfortably than she, without complaint. She refused to blame Henri for her *ennui,* though she did spare the occasional unkind thought for her father-in-law for disowning Henri because of his marriage. She would never see the man, so she could see no harm in it, and she found some secret delight in wishing him ill.

More and more, though, she thought about Vérité's—Pauline's—predictions for her future in New France. The dilapidated house, removed from society, a husband half-gone savage, bearing child after child until her body wore out, and complete and utter boredom through it all. Pauline had missed many key details—Rose's husband was genteel and her home was comfortable, at least by colonial standards, but the loneliness and boredom . . . In that, at least, Pauline had been correct.

Henri entered the room, sweating from the exertion of a day on horseback under the August sun. He removed his soaked chemise and washed his torso with Rose's dampened cloth.

"How are your holdings, Seigneur?" Rose asked with a teasing grin.

He approached her from behind, pressing his bare chest against her linen shift and kissing her neck, left exposed by her upswept hair.

"Perfectly well, Dame Lefebvre. Though not mine . . . Neither are we Seigneur and his lady—yet."

"Soon, I hope," Rose said, tilting her head, inviting more.

"You're so beautiful," he said, his breath soft on her neck as he kissed it again.

"Thank you, sweet husband of mine," Rose said. "You ought to dress so we aren't late."

"What if I don't care that we're late?" He turned her around to face him and pulled her body close to his. He bent down and kissed her—slow, passionate, probing on her waiting mouth.

She welcomed his embraces now, and since Henri knew the source of her occasional apprehension, he knew when and how to give her space on the rare instances where she needed it.

Henri deepened the kiss as she wrapped her arms around his neck as a signal that she was willing. Too eager for the bed, he freed himself from his breeches, lifted her against the wall, and raised her shift, entering her when his probing fingers felt the least amount of wetness. A dozen thrusts and he climaxed. Breathing labored, he picked her up and carried her the five strides to the chair in the corner of the room that he used to pull on his boots in the mornings. He cradled her in his lap and stroked her mussed black curls.

"Sorry, my darling. I'll give you your chance later."

"No need to apologize, beloved," Rose said, nuzzling the sweet, musky-scented curve of his neck. "I missed you today, too."

"You're unhappy, aren't you?" he asked.

"I miss town," Rose said. She knew that telling the truth would hurt him less than withholding it. "I miss the girls. I miss the people."

"I wish I could promise that we could move back soon, but you know I can't."

"Don't fret," she said. "I just have to find happiness here. You've done nothing wrong."

"I can't help but think you would have been better off with someone who could provide you with more than this." He gestured to their small, plainly furnished room.

In many ways the move to the country had been even harder for Henri than for Rose. She had learned to live in meager conditions before. He had not.

"If you had never come along, I'd be Sister Marie-Rose by now." She cast a violet-blue gaze into his hazel one. "Teaching Latin to native girls and scrubbing the floors when Sister Mathilde wasn't looking. Don't ever apologize for saving me."

Rose settled into the plush chair in Nicole's parlor, allowing her muscles to relax in the absence of a screaming baby demanding her attentions. Three stitches into her embroidery, she stiffened, expecting Benoît's cries to summon her away from her work. *He's with Mylène. He's well and safe. Relax and enjoy your time away.*

While Rose embroidered and Nicole knitted, Elisabeth stared at the Lefebvres' parlor wall. Rose peered over her shoulder to the spot that had her friend so transfixed. It was as handsome a wall as Rose had ever seen, but there was nothing particular that ought to have captivated Elisabeth.

"I thought at least a spider might be crawling up the wall, the way you stare," Rose remarked.

"Just ignore me," Elisabeth said, reaching for her cup of cider. "Try though we might, we can't supply the people with the bread they want at the prices Duval claims we must."

"You can't keep this up," Nicole said. "You'll make yourselves ill."

"I don't see what choice we have," Elisabeth said. "We owe your husband the earth and Gilbert is too proud to give up on the shop and try something else. Not to mention, the very idea breaks my own heart."

"You won't have to, I'm sure," Nicole said. "And don't worry about the money. As Alexandre always says, 'It's never wise to be shortsighted with a long-term investment.' "

"More important, have there been any developments with Gabrielle?" Rose asked. The memory of the girl clinging to life, her pale skin indistinguishable from the bleached sheets, haunted her still.

"Would that God had sent Father Cloutier into oblivion instead of into our lives. And the wretched bailiff along with him." Elisabeth's blue eyes flashed.

Rose reached over and took her hand. "You of all people don't deserve the foul man's attentions," Rose said.

"I'd wager my favorite knitting needles he's been sent here to the very edge of civilization because no one wanted him back home," Nicole said.

Elisabeth nodded a weak chuckle, but Rose's hand clapped to her mouth.

"You're a genius, Nicole," Rose said, rubbing her temples in thought.

"Naturally," Nicole chortled, "but what have I done to demonstrate my mental prowess this time?"

"We need to get Father Cloutier transferred—and far away, too," Rose said. "Heaven knows a personal vendetta against a good family like the Beaumonts does the settlement no good. The bailiff doesn't matter; he's just the priest's henchman. If we cut off the head, the hand won't be of much use."

"How on earth can we manage such a thing?" Elisabeth asked. "The bishop would be unlikely to have an audience with us, let alone act on our request. Chances are, the bishop would just support old Cloutier and leave us to our own devices."

"You're not wrong," Rose said. "We can't be so direct. We must go through the governor. He's the only one with any influence at all over the bishop."

"Alexandre has said time and time again that the governor wants nothing to do with these sorts of domestic matters," Nicole said, setting aside her knitting. "Though the issue of a priest involving himself in commerce might not please him."

"I'm not sure he needs to know the details," Rose said. "All he needs to know is that it would please the lovely Madame Lefebvre, wife of Seigneur Lefebvre, and things may fall into place."

"Do you really think he would listen to me?" Nicole asked. "And how would I contrive a reason to meet with him?"

"Oh, I think he'll listen to you," Rose said. "Especially if his mood is softened by good food and music. You must host a ball."

"Alexandre has been harping that we ought to have one, though I was thinking of waiting until autumn," Nicole said, sitting back in her chair, the guest list, menu, and linen inventories all but printed on her forehead. *Not quite the shy farm girl from Rouen anymore, are you?* Rose smiled at the confidence.

"Give me three weeks," Nicole said. "We'll have him gone, or we'll have thrown a magnificent party for no purpose. We'll be no worse off than before in either event."

For the last half of September, Rose and little Benoît all but took up residence in town. They stayed with Nicole and Alexandre to help Nicole prepare for the ball.

Elisabeth and Gabrielle helped, too, as often as the bakery could spare them, which usually meant when Gilbert and Pascal were tending the ovens mid-morning. Henri came, too, when the demands of running the estate permitted.

Days of linen pressing, menu planning, wardrobe gathering, and planning each minute detail had left Nicole crazed, but Rose's calming influence kept her in check. One afternoon, four days before the ball, Rose stood to stretch her back, stiff as starched cotton from too many hours hemming napkins following too many other days penning invitations in her finest script. Rose feared the blue ink would never fade from her fingers.

Parisian society ladies had linens, china, silver, and crystal stocked neatly in armoires, ready for shining, ironing, and polishing by their massive household staffs. Nicole had settings to entertain twenty to thirty guests, but a ball for a hundred or more was beyond her stores. They had to purchase, borrow, and make the rest in the short time they had allotted themselves.

Rose was about to force herself back to her hemming when a commotion from the entry drew her attention. She and Nicole left the parlor to find Henri, Alexandre, and Thomas Deschamps engaged in a frantic conversation.

"No idea which direction they went?" Alexandre asked.

"None," Thomas said. "I followed the tracks as far as I could, but I know they headed west for a little while."

"I'd wager they headed into town," Henri said. "I'm surprised we didn't see them on the way."

Alexandre nodded. "Seems most likely."

"Will someone explain what's going on?" Nicole asked.

"Your fool sisters have taken the horse and wagon and taken off," Thomas said, temper rising in his cheeks. "I'll take a whip to them when we find them."

"As Henri says, they're probably coming here," Rose offered. "Claudine hasn't stopped talking about the town since she arrived on the farm."

Rose had come to know Nicole's family well, since they were her closest neighbors. She agreed that Claudine was too impetuous, but the girl's independent spark had also endeared her to everyone. However, bookish Emmanuelle was Rose's favorite.

"We must organize and search our way back toward the homestead," Alexandre said. "I hope they haven't broken a wheel or lamed a horse."

"Or run into the natives. Bernadette is ill at the thought," Thomas said, his face grim.

Rose wished to contradict him, remembering her sweet-faced pupils and wonderful Manon, but she held her tongue. Abductions did happen, and two unescorted girls could run into trouble on their own.

They split into three search parties, two people each: Nicole with her father, Rose with Henri, and Alexandre with a servant, each equipped with horses, wagons, and routes to search.

"We'll meet back here in four hours, whether we find the girls or not," Alexandre said. "If you find them, bring them here and send riders to find the other teams. The servants have instructions to do the same, should the girls show up here in the meantime."

Rose nodded. Her uncle-in-law had a plan for everything. That afternoon, however, no one begrudged his abilities to manage a situation.

For the first hour, as they drove the northern route, Rose scanned the roadside and kept her thoughts as positive as she could. However, she grew tense as the minutes passed with no success. She willed herself not to fidget, lest she might drive Henri to distraction.

Dusk fell. Rose cursed herself for not bringing at least a light cloak.

The girls are worse off than you.

As she prepared to light the lantern, she heard a scream.

"Over here!" It was Claudine. "Please help!"

Henri pulled the horse to the side of the road and leaped from the wagon. Rose jumped down with only a hint more decorum, owing to her petticoats.

Claudine was covered in mud from head to foot. When she realized who had stopped for her, she flung herself, mud and all, into Rose's arms, babbling through her sobs.

"Emmanuelle is hurt," Henri shouted from the girls' upturned carriage. "She may have a broken leg—the horse most assuredly did. I've put him out of his misery."

Rose shook her head. "Load Emmanuelle in the wagon and I'll sit with her," she called to Henri. "Claudine, you must calm yourself and sit with Henri. Can you manage that?"

Claudine offered a feeble nod and climbed up to the seat Rose had vacated.

Henri carried Emmanuelle with ease, as though she weighed no more than a bag of flour, but he held her as though she were made of porcelain. Her face was far too pale and she shook from pain and shock.

"Shall we take them back to our house?" Rose suggested as they settled Emmanuelle in the back of the wagon. "It's closer. We could send Yves to tell the others."

"No, she needs a doctor," Henri said. "Moving her will get her medical care much faster."

Rose kept Emmanuelle as still as possible on the ride. Henri tried to keep the ride smooth, but the rutted roads made the effort moot. He urged the horses along, seeking a balance between caution and speed.

Nicole and Thomas stood in the entry, removing their cloaks, when Henri and Rose arrived. Claudine gripped Rose's hand and Emmanuelle lay limp in Henri's arms.

The Lefebvre house flew into action. Servants were dispatched to the doctor, Claudine was bathed and dressed in a clean nightdress, and messengers were sent to inform Madame Deschamps of her daughters' whereabouts.

The doctor pronounced that Emmanuelle had fared much better than the horse. The girl had a badly sprained ankle and a twisted knee, but it would mend in time if she rested.

"What have you to say for yourself?" Thomas asked Claudine when the doctor had left. His tone calm, in the manner of the weather before a storm.

"It's my fault, Papa," Claudine said, tears welling up in her large brown eyes.

"I've no doubt of that," Thomas said. "Your sister would never consider such a fool thing on her own." He glared at his daughter. "You cost me a horse, as well as a wagon, and could have killed your sister. Give me a reason not to lock you in the cellar for the rest of your days."

Claudine wiped the tears from her cheeks with the sleeve of Nicole's dressing gown. "I can't, Papa."

"That's the first responsible thing I've ever heard come out of your mouth, girl." Thomas sat back in the chair and rubbed his tired eyes.

"Where were you going?" Nicole asked. "What was so important that you had to sneak away from Maman and Papa?"

"I was coming here," Claudine admitted. "I wanted to help you prepare for the ball. I thought it was terribly mean of you not to let us help. I convinced Emmanuelle that once we were here you'd be glad to see us."

"You never stopped to think that Maman might need your help at the farm more than we do here?" Nicole asked. "She has enough to do, keeping Georges in line and running the household, without you scaring her half to death."

"I didn't think of that," Claudine said.

"Clearly," Nicole said. "You never once thought about anyone but yourself."

"You're right." Claudine stared down at her feet. "It's just so boring out on the farm, with nothing to do but housework and chores."

"I should have invited you to come help," Nicole said in hushed tones, stroking the back of her sister's head as she still clung to Rose. "I didn't think pressing linens would be any more exciting here than at home."

Claudine emitted a weak chuckle. "At least I'd be around more people."

"Schooling," Rose said after a few moments' reflection. "You need schooling."

Claudine looked up at Rose, her face uncertain.

"You could come to my house, you and Emmanuelle both, and take lessons. I'm sure we can work things out with your mother. It would be a good diversion for you." *And me as well.*

"Latin and Greek and all that boring stuff?" asked Claudine, her voice small.

"And poetry and needlework and history . . ." added Rose.

"That might not be so bad," admitted Claudine.

"Not to mention a good smattering of etiquette and household management," added Alexandre. "Our young Madame Lefebvre comes from solid Parisian stock, Mademoiselle Claudine, and has much to teach you and your sister once she's recovered."

"I'd like that," said Claudine. "Though I'm not as smart as Emmanuelle."

"Then you must work twice as hard," Alexandre said. "I don't want people to say my sister-in-law's education is lacking when you come to stay with us."

"I—I can come stay with you?" asked Claudine.

"Provided you work hard, I think it would be wise once you're of age to make a match." Alexandre cast a brief glance at his wife. Rose guessed that this was not the first time the matter had come up between them.

Nicole nodded her assent. "But I warn you, we'll accept none of your nonsense here, and you must prove yourself in the meantime."

"I will," said Claudine, her face sincere. "I will work very hard, I promise."

"Trust to that. And if you had acted like a young lady tonight, you might have stayed and helped your sister prepare for the ball, but now no such invitation will be extended," said Alexandre.

"Oh please, let me come. I'm so terribly sorry," Claudine begged, her eyes alight.

"No, I don't think we'll go so far as to reward your behavior so well," Nicole answered. "But there will be others if you earn the privilege. You need the skills Maman can teach you more than you need to know about throwing parties. Dream all you want of living in a grand house in town, but whether you live on a farm or in a palace, there is no one better than our mother to teach you how to run it."

"And it's better than you deserve," said Papa, breaking his silence. "If you ever give me such a fright again you'll be dancing on my grave."

"I'm so sorry, Papa," said Claudine, crossing the room and embracing her father. "It won't happen again."

"I should hope not, girl," Thomas said, his words gruffer than his voice. "I expect you to toe the line around here and help your mother, 'boring' or not. You've a life of work ahead of you—not just balls and fancy dresses. If you can't learn to be a proper farmer's daughter and learn the value of a day's work, I won't send you off to your sister, invitation or not."

Thomas wrapped his arms around his daughter, visibly relieved that she was unharmed. Though Édouard Barré had been gone for quite some time, the sight reminded Rose of how much she still grieved for his loss. Other than during the brief period before her uncle's true nature was revealed, she had not had the luxury of mourning for her beloved father. Since that time, life had not allowed for her to indulge her emotions. As she saw the exhausted girl enfolded in her father's loving arms, she felt a slight twinge of envy for that same embrace and protection she'd longed for so often over the past nine years.

CHAPTER 30

Nicole

September 1671

Needing a break from the preparations for the ball, Nicole took her carriage out to see her family's new farm. Thomas Deschamps looked out over virgin fields gifted to him by his son-in-law with a glint of excitement in his eyes. In the years before she left France, Nicole had seen those warm eyes filled with defeat and exhaustion far too often. Now, she delighted in the potential and possibility he saw.

The growing season was short and he couldn't grow the same variety of crops that he could in France, but her father would learn and adapt.

Thomas draped his arm over his daughter's shoulders and squeezed her close.

"You've given me so much, my girl." Emotion was thick in his throat. "I didn't think I had it in me to start over, but I feel like a boy again in this new world. Thank you, my sweet girl."

"Papa, for all you've given me, I wish I could do more."

Nicole looked over the rolling fields, so unlike her native Normandy, but now just as familiar and beloved. She had gained so much from New France—a husband and children she adored—

and now, she had the gift of her past as well, in the form of her family.

She had lost much, too. She thought of Luc and Manon.

But with her father's arm wrapped around her shoulder, the knowledge that her mother and sisters were ensconced in their new house, thirty minutes away by carriage, warmed her heart as it hadn't been for months. Years, if Nicole were truthful to herself.

Though I have a husband, children, dear friends . . . nothing seemed like home until my family was here. Perhaps Manon has someone who will make her feel at home again.

Nicole offered up a silent prayer that this could be true. There was no part of her heart or soul that didn't wish Manon every happiness, but she still ached. She ached for the months when only Manon's selfless love gave her comfort in the gloom of the days after Luc's death. The sweet child who stole into her bed on the coldest winter nights and stuck her frigid toes against Nicole's leg.

But the future bore down upon them all, like a runaway horse, prepared or not. Nicole considered the tiny secret in her womb. One she had not announced, wishing to keep the delight to herself for just a little longer. This baby would never replace the darling girl who had rescued Nicole in so many ways, but the child would be cherished and welcomed all the same. Still, the fact that Nicole could not give the same love and acceptance to Manon dealt a blow to her heart she feared would never mend.

Nicole entered the foyer of the Lefebvre house in a velvet gown the color of an evergreen resplendent with health, like the boughs that festooned every bare surface, owing to the want of flowers in autumn. Alexandre escorted her, standing tall, almost regal in a black-and-gold *justaucorps* that coordinated with, but did not match, his wife's ensemble. The detail was no mistake. The candles, the china, each ingredient in the myriad dishes the impeccably clothed staff would serve . . . not an element was left to chance. Nicole oversaw it all, and surveyed the room with satisfaction

Whatever happens now, you must act as though it was the plan all along. Do not fuss with the greenery. Do not shift a candle placed an inch too close to the other. Don't fuss with the odd wrinkle on a

tablecloth. You are above the minutiae now and must enchant your guests.

"You're a miracle worker," Alexandre whispered as the first guests entered the hall.

"I did as the situation required," Nicole purred with a wink after she'd curtsied to a lesser deputy of the governor. "If I must conjure up a miracle, what else am I to do?"

"I cannot tell you, but will say I'm the luckiest man alive," Alexandre said as the deputy's stodgy wife departed for the drawing room.

"I'm sure it's convenient having a capable hostess for a wife," Nicole said, her tone absentminded. *Who would have ever expected me to be a society wife?* Her mother's face, aghast at the mountain of linens and the stacks of china, would stay with her for the rest of her days.

"Don't ever think that's why I married you," Alexandre whispered.

"Not once," Nicole said, her voice brimming with solemnity. "Since you had no reason to suppose I'd have any skill at it when you asked me for my hand."

Alexandre threw back his head in a full-throated laugh. He seldom laughed, but when he did, Nicole could not help but share in his mirth.

The last guests arrived, and Alexandre escorted his wife to the dining room that gleamed with polished glass and clean china. They sat down to a meal befitting the finest houses in Paris. The staff, instructed as to how every portion of the meal must be served, missed not a step. From the crisp linens to the rich soup, presented with a flourish, Nicole could not find fault.

Henri tasted the creamy soup, thick with the earthy flavor of squash and seasoned with precision. "You've hosted the event of the season and it's only a half hour in. She's a triumph," he whispered, but the truth of his words was evident.

Henri sat to the left of his uncle. The governor sat at the head of the table, his rank sufficient to dispossess even the host.

Nicole, rather than engage in the conversation, listened and noted. What sort of liquor did the governor prefer? To which seamstresses did his wife offer her custom? Noting. Filing away for later use. No detail was worth overlooking.

Without her interference, Rose and Alexandre managed the conversation with grace. The governor and Rose discussed a comedy of Corneille's that he had seen in Paris during a visit the year before. Alexandre mentioned Henri's efforts on the estate, but not in detail. No one would ever conduct business at a social event. From the expression on the governor's face, he was entertained by Rose's wit and pleased with Alexandre's and Henri's labors. And not at all disappointed in the meal.

"So much wonderful food, Madame Lefebvre," said the governor, as one of Elisabeth's delicate cakes was set before him, the capstone to the repast. "I can't imagine where I'll stuff another mouthful, I'm afraid."

"Many thanks, Monsieur le Gouverneur," Nicole said. "But it would be such a shame if you did not at least sample the dessert."

"I could not bear to disappoint you, my dear Madame Lefebvre." The cake was a perfect tribute to autumn, apples and toasted almonds encased in Elisabeth's signature pastry—an elegant marriage of buttery and flaky textures that did not impede the flavor of the fillings, but withstood their robust consistencies. The governor took his fork, anticipation plain upon his face. He savored the first small morsel for several moments. The six people closest to him sat silent in suspense.

"A masterpiece," he declared. "An absolute masterpiece."

"I am so glad you think so, Monsieur le Gouverneur. The artist who created it, Madame Beaumont, sits not three places from you." Nicole gestured in Elisabeth's direction.

The governor looked surprised that Elisabeth, refined as any lady, attired in a rich cornsilk-blue damask, could have created such a pastry. The Beaumonts looked like established members of society, not humble bakers.

"Beaumont . . ." said the governor. "Yes, I remember your name. My staff buys my bread and cakes from your bakery. You're an asset to the settlement, madame and monsieur."

"I thank you, Monsieur le Gouverneur." Elisabeth's voice was strong, but she said no more.

Alexandre had coached her to leave things here. The governor had witnessed both her skill and her gentility. Their problems would be presented later, and in the proper fashion.

"Seigneur Lefebvre, might I claim the privilege of opening the ball with your lovely wife?" The governor's expression in Alexandre's direction was of a man who did not expect to be disappointed.

"Of course, Monsieur le Gouverneur. Such is your right," Alexandre said. *And so we intended for you to do from the instant this ball was conceived.*

Nicole consented for the governor to lead her to the dance floor, and followed his steps with more poise than he showed, but not so much flourish as to make him look too far inferior.

"I'm impressed with my own ability to walk, let alone dance, after so fine a meal, madame," the governor said, laughing at his own joke. The smell of the meal, paired with what had to be a rotting tooth on his breath as he guffawed, turned Nicole's stomach, but she retained control of her countenance.

"I'm so pleased you enjoyed our little feast," Nicole said, the smile plastered on her face. "I thought the dessert was especially nice, myself."

"Indeed," the governor agreed. "Your friend is rather talented. Am I right in thinking that she has something to do with the Giroux family? I remember the good Father prattling on about them. Can't say I followed all the details. He does tend to go on, you know."

"You're correct as usual, Monsieur le Gouverneur," Nicole said, pleased for the direction of the conversation with so little need for manipulation. "The Beaumonts have apprenticed the eldest Giroux boy and have taken the eldest daughter in as a sort of assistant since their father passed on."

"A kind gesture, to be sure," the governor said, his hand on her back wandering an inch too low for comfort. "Though I seem to remember Father Cloutier thinking the arrangement wasn't all that suitable. He wanted the girl for the Church, if memory serves."

"I fear Father Cloutier is an unhappy man. I think he pines for the bustle of the city," Nicole said, doing her best to feign concern for the loathsome man. "Not all men are robust enough to appreciate the rugged beauty of our settlement, are they?" She allowed her fingers to trace the ridge of his shoulder. A bold gesture, but from the expression on the governor's face, a welcome one.

"No indeed, my dear." The governor's hand inched lower. Nicole averted her gaze for a split second to see Alexandre watching from the sidelines, attentive but subtle. *Just keep your calm, I don't like it any more than you do.*

"Indeed, in a settlement such as this, I feel our spiritual leaders must understand and support the needs of our political leaders, don't you agree?" Nicole returned her gaze to the governor's watery-blue eyes.

"Of course," he said, though Nicole suspected he barely registered her words.

"It surprises me that an astute man like Father Cloutier would advocate for a young, healthy girl like Mademoiselle Giroux to be taken in by the Church when there is a family willing to bear the expense of bringing her up," Nicole continued. "Doesn't the settlement have a greater need for wives than for clergy?"

"You're completely right, my dear," the governor said.

"I'm so glad you agree," Nicole said, offering him a wide smile. "Would it be too bold of me to suggest that you bring this to the bishop? I'm sure he'd be glad of a young priest who is more willing to learn our ways and support our fine leaders. And poor Father Cloutier would be much happier to retire in his homeland. I do so worry about him."

"Your kindness does you credit, my dear," the governor breathed. Nicole hoped her grimace was none too evident. "Of course I'll speak to him." The old man's hand slipped just a hint lower as the strains of the quintet came to a stop.

"All my thanks, Monsieur le Gouverneur," she said, stepping out of his grasp with a deep curtsy. "And I'm so sorry our dance is over. I could not bear to deprive the rest of the assembly of the pleasure of your company."

Nicole made her way back to Alexandre, but spared a wink for Elisabeth on the way.

Social event of the season, indeed.

CHAPTER 31

Elisabeth

September 1671

Gilbert raised his glass, brimming with fine French champagne worth more than he would earn in three weeks of baking.

"To the Lefebvres and the finest social event of the season," Gilbert said, wrapping his arm around Elisabeth, who clinked her glass against his. *How fine you look in your elegant suit of clothes, my love, but your plain wool jacket and breeches covered in flour become you even more.* She smiled up at her sturdy husband, appearing well rested and happy for the first time since Gabrielle's injury. *Please God that the governor makes good on his promises to Nicole and I can keep my sweet-natured husband for good.*

"An unqualified success, my dear," Alexandre said, nodding to his wife. "You'll find yourself flooded with social calls for months. Any woman in attendance is going to want all your secrets for throwing such a party."

"How thrilling," Nicole said, her tone dry. "But if tonight's efforts improve things for the Beaumonts, I won't complain about a string of wasted mornings."

"Amen to that," Elisabeth said. "If that odious man gets shipped back to France, I can't imagine that our problems won't ease."

"With regard to the Giroux girl, certainly," Alexandre said. "No one but Cloutier has any interest in seeing her removed from your care. But the bakery is another matter. If another official takes a notion to enforce the royal edict, you'll find yourselves in the same predicament."

"I've thought of that," Gilbert said. "But I can't think that there's anything we can do. The edict makes perfect sense for a baker in Paris, but if we can't set the prices to allow for the cost of flour, we can't do business."

"And I'll continue to speak on the matter to the governor, even the Intendant, if I'm ever in his earshot. In the meantime, there is a way around the regulations. Have the patrons deliver their flour to you and order what they want to be made from it at whatever price you agree to. If you conduct things like this, the law can't touch you. Even the King can't dictate what you make under commission."

"It will complicate some things," Gilbert said. "And it may be an inconvenience to the customers."

"They'll adapt," Elisabeth assured him, making mental calculations she would share with her husband when they were alone. "And we could expand the business to more of the outlying farms. Pascal can be sent to collect flour one day a week and deliver the finished products the next."

"I believe your wife is as talented a businesswoman as she is a baker," Henri said, accepting a refill of the sparkling wine from his uncle. "You may count us among your first customers in your new delivery service. Mylène has some skill in the kitchen, but her bread is nothing to yours."

"Done!" Elisabeth said, shaking Henri's free hand. "And count on a platter of pastries every week for being the first to offer us your custom."

"My waistline won't thank you for that," Rose said, laughing as she traced the lip of her glass with her pinky. "But I'm sure I'll suffer through it."

"It will be a sacrifice, but I'm sure we all will," said Henri, patting his flat stomach.

Warmth enveloped Elisabeth as she looked at the faces of her husband and dearest friends. *What would have become of me if I'd ended up in Trois-Rivières or Ville-Marie? Or worse, if Maman had found a way to keep me prisoner in Paris? Sometimes fate can be kinder than our fondest wishes.* Elisabeth squeezed her husband's hand and laced her fingers through his. He took the signal, and it was less than a quarter of an hour before they found themselves entering the bakery in as much silence as they could so as not to disturb Pascal, Gabrielle, or baby Pierre.

Rather than going above stairs, Gilbert lit a candle, sat on Elisabeth's stool, and pulled her into his arms.

"Just twelve hours ago, I knew with every fiber of my being that we were going to lose this place," Gilbert said, resting his chin on her head. "And now I feel, I honestly feel in the pit of my gut, that we might have a chance to keep going."

"And keep Gabrielle," Elisabeth said. Over the past week she saw the shadow that crossed Nicole's face whenever someone mentioned Manon. She would be every bit as haunted as Nicole if Gabrielle were taken from her.

Gilbert's embrace tightened around her. "I couldn't even bear to think of that."

"You're a good man, Gilbert," Elisabeth said. "And a good father to our children. All of them."

"Well, nature hasn't been too helpful giving us a family in the usual way, so it just made sense to collect a couple more, didn't it?"

"Indeed, my love," Elisabeth said, thinking of the growing babe in her womb who caused her worry each day. She would not be convinced there would be a child until he or she was screaming lustily in her arms. "Though I wish more than anything that we'd have more luck in that area. We ought to have our own tribe by now."

Gilbert cupped his wife's face in his hands, forcing her to look in his eyes. "Sweetheart, don't you waste a moment fretting on all that. If we're meant to have more children, we will. If not, I have the most loving family in all the settlement, and don't need a dozen babies to prove that to the likes of Father Cloutier."

Elisabeth leaned her face in to reach Gilbert's, her mouth finding his. She parted her soft lips and yielded to his hungry kiss.

Three weeks later, the Beaumont bakery was a place transformed. Word of their delivery service spread to the homesteads, and farmers arrived every hour with their sacks of flour in tow, grateful to be free of the task of baking their bread each week. While Elisabeth knew how to stock a traditional bakery, the organization of the delivery business was foreign to her. Pascal took on this task, showing a remarkable capacity for management. He devised systems for organizing the flour deliveries, the orders, picking up flour from farther afield on Thursdays, and delivering the baked bread no later than Friday morning. Gilbert saw to the majority of the bread baking, Gabrielle kept the shop, and Elisabeth saw to the cakes and fine pastries that the authorities had yet to regulate.

Gilbert saw this in Pascal when he took him in. An eye for talent, just like Papa. Her heart swelled each night when he boasted that there had been no miscalculations in the orders, nor any wasted flour. More than one farmer had come in from the far reaches of the settlement to praise Pascal to Elisabeth and Gilbert. The answer was always the same: "We would expect nothing less from a Beaumont."

Elisabeth set a platter of her favorite *millefeuilles* in the case and reached for the broom to tidy before the dinner rush when the bell at the door sounded. Father Cloutier stood in the entry, looking as friendly as a wolf snarling over a hunk of discarded meat.

"You meddlesome whore of Babylon, how did you manage it?" he demanded by way of greeting.

"Gabrielle, go on upstairs and start supper, sweetheart," Elisabeth asked, squeezing the girl's shoulder. She leaned in to whisper, "I'll be up before too much longer, don't worry."

The girl obeyed without hesitation, and Elisabeth waited until she heard the door latch at the top of the stairs before she looked back to the priest.

"Now, how may I help you, Father?" Elisabeth asked, treating him with the same sugary condescension she had used with the roughhewn sailors on the crossing.

"Don't play innocent with me, you witch," Cloutier said, his face purple with rage. *Please God don't let the despicable man have an apoplexy here. I don't want his wretched ghost spoiling my pastry cream.*

"I'm afraid you'll have to tell me what you mean, Father," Elisabeth said, not abandoning her pretense. She swept the floor as though he were no more than a farm boy, unworthy of her full attention.

"I'm being sent back to France. To some backwater in the south," he spat. "And don't act like you aren't responsible for it."

"Father, I am but the wife of a humble baker," Elisabeth said, careful not to claim the title for herself, though at some personal cost. "How do you imagine I have the influence to make such a thing happen?"

"I don't pretend to know your conniving ways," he said, still standing only a few paces inside the door, speaking loud enough for the passersby to hear. "All I know is that you are to blame for this. You're an independent, evil woman and you will pay for your sins."

"I have no doubt of that," Elisabeth said. "We all will on the day of judgment, as you remind us each week. But I assure you that I had no knowledge of your transfer before now. Though I cannot say that I am sorry to see you go."

"You will still refer to me as 'Father,' you impertinent hussy," he thundered. "Do you not know I am a man of God? You dare speak to me in such a way? Have you no shame?"

"Indeed I do. But though you are a man of God, I believe you are also a man. And a flawed one at that. You have taken it upon yourself to attempt to ruin my family, though we intended no insult on you. At the end of the day, *Father,* I would rather be held accountable for my sins than yours. I pray you will think on that before you treat anyone in your new parish as callously as you have treated all of us."

"Do not believe that you will get away with this, you harlot," the priest said, his tone now low and threatening. "You have no idea who you are meddling with."

"Oh, I think I do," Elisabeth said, gripping the broom until her knuckles glistened white. "I think you're a small-minded man with more ambition than good sense who has been shunted from post to post for the past three decades because no one can stand to have you at the pulpit for long. Have I got the measure of it, *Father?*"

"I pray that the man who replaces me will continue to watch over you and work to purge this good settlement of your evil influence," he pronounced. "I pray that he will be a true man of God."

"As do I, *Father,* though I think you and I have very different ideas of what that looks like. Now I will bid you good day." Elisabeth pointed to the door with her broom, using every ounce of her restraint not to fling it at his head. *And when the new man comes, and I know he is a true man of God, I will take him—by his hair if necessary—to consecrate the land where my Adèle is buried. She will not be denied her eternal rest because of you.*

As the priest spun with a flourish he smacked into Gilbert's broad chest. The priest offered no greeting or apology, but slithered past him onto the street, making his angry path back to the church.

"What was that all about?" Gilbert asked, his brow arched.

"What else could it be?" Elisabeth answered, grasping his face and bringing him in for a kiss. "We've won."

Elisabeth tucked little Pierre into his cradle, and escaped for a few moments of solitude into her empty kitchen. Pascal and Gabrielle slept, secure in the knowledge that both were in their rightful home. Gilbert spent his hour below stairs preparing what he could for the following morning. Rather than retire to the bliss of her soft mattress, she put the kettle to the fire and prepared a cup of herbal tea.

She sipped the bitter brew and willed herself to put aside the venom that rose so quickly to the surface when she recalled the memories of her mother. She pulled from the vault of her memories the few pleasant thoughts she'd kept hidden, shadowed darker and darker since her father's death.

The first doll she remembered. A cloth doll with a sweet face that Anne was always happy to provide with new frocks that matched Elisabeth's. The time that Anne took Elisabeth to the opera when she was twelve years old, allowing her daughter her first dress that was cut for a young woman and not a girl—Elisabeth long considered that the day she'd become a woman. And the coffee. A silly thing, but something they loved.

For several days, Elisabeth toyed with the notion, but she brought herself to take out a sheaf of paper, quill, and ink from Gilbert's small desk, where he kept the bakery's books. Though

Elisabeth was still slow in forming her letters, the calm of the night allowed her the full concentration she needed for the task.

Dear Maman,

I take pen in hand to wish you well, from the depths of my heart. We did not part well. We have not always been friends. I want to tell you, while we have time on this earth, that I forgive you for your moments of callousness. I know you wanted me for greater things, even though they were so very far from the things that I myself wanted, or indeed will ever want, from life. You didn't understand me, you probably still don't, but you are not the first mother to do so. You will not be the last.

You have a grandchild. A beautiful boy, named Pierre for Papa. It is my dearest wish that he will grow to be a fine young man like his namesake. I know you didn't appreciate Papa as well as he deserved, but I am now able to see that he did not give you your due, either. Neither have I. You are resourceful. You are ambitious. While those qualities drove you and I apart, they are part of who you are, and I should have tried harder to find the virtue in them.

You had great plans for me. I see that now. You wanted a grand life for me, and I have found it, Maman. It might not be the life you pictured, but it is as grand a life as I could have dared to hope for. I have a good, hardworking husband, a healthy son, and friends dearer to me than the sisters I never had.

In your last letter, you said you no longer had a daughter. I hope, truly, that you reconsider, for there is never a day when a daughter does not need her mother. I will welcome your letter with a glad heart as I would welcome your person with open arms.

Your loving daughter,

Elisabeth Beaumont

It wasn't for Anne's sake that Elisabeth wrote the letter, but for her own. She needed a release from her mother's specter, but disowning her mother with the same disregard as Anne had shown her would not free her. Her loving father had told her on more than one occasion that forgiveness was a mighty weapon when wielded with love and compassion. It was only now that Elisabeth had the strength to welcome her mother back into her life. If Anne ignored the invitation, that was her own affair, but Elisabeth had done what she could to mend the rift.

Still hearing Gilbert below, Elisabeth did not see any point in seeking out her bed. She found her sewing kit and her crisp white handkerchief. She had some lovely pink thread and began to watch as the delicate flowers took shape on the white background. The more she stitched, the more it seemed there was a bare space for another bloom.

CHAPTER 32

Rose

February 1672

"I really, really, really hate Latin," Claudine announced, laying her head on the wooden desk in defeat. "I'll never wrap my head around the stuff. I told you I wouldn't." True to her word, Rose welcomed them for four hours every afternoon for their studies. Henri had converted a small room into a classroom, allowing the girls to escape from their home for a few hours and Rose to stay within earshot of the baby.

"That simply isn't true, my dear," Rose said, patting the girl's back. "You've already made progress. A month ago you couldn't read a syllable of Latin, and now you're able to conjugate verbs and make out simple poems. You *are* making progress."

Their curriculum was an evolving thing as Rose endeavored to follow in the Ursulines' footsteps and played to her pupils' strengths and weaknesses. Since the sisters opposed each other in their talents, Rose found that every lesson pleased one Deschamps girl as much as it dismayed the other.

Claudine raised her head and gave a baleful look Emmanuelleward. "Not as fast as she is."

"Emmanuelle, what do you love above all things?" Rose asked, turning to the studious child, who just then looked up from her text. Her leg, still sore months after the accident, was propped up on a cushion while she studied.

"Study," Emmanuelle said. "Reading. Languages. All of it."

"And what do you do in your spare time?" Rose asked, standing to her full height and smoothing her dress.

"I read," Emmanuelle said, placing her book aside and making eye contact with Rose as though she were answering questions for an examination. "Latin and Greek from our text sometimes. Mostly French because it's what Monsieur Lefebvre has in his library to lend me."

"And, Claudine, what do you do in your spare time?" Rose asked, turning to the older sister.

"I sew and embroider," Claudine answered, sitting up straight. "I enjoy doing fancy work."

"As do I," Rose said with a smile. "So, Claudine, is it so surprising that your sister should excel in Latin and you in needlework when you devote so many extra hours to those pursuits?"

"I suppose not," Claudine admitted. "But Latin is so terribly dull. I'll never use it in my life, I know."

"Wouldn't you like to understand the prayers in church?" Rose asked, sitting down at her own desk so she could sit at the girls' level.

"I don't see why," Claudine said. "God understands them, so what difference does it make if I do?"

"You sound more like your brother-in-law every day," Rose said.

"Good. I hope to be just like him," Claudine said. Rose wasn't quite sure if she should smile or shake her head. Alexandre's irreverence and bitter jibes were tolerated because of his status and his ability to know when to hold his tongue—neither virtue had Claudine yet attained. Goodness knew Nicole's sweet temper was needed to balance out his acerbic tongue. No matter how unsuited she had felt for life in the upper crusts of society, he needed her unique blend of gentleness and social cunning to maintain his standing. Rose could tell her friend derived as much satisfaction from her role as Elisabeth did from running her bakery. She had envied them their place, many times, but now she had her teaching and her family to which she could devote herself.

"Darling, what is it you *want* from life?" Rose asked, taking Claudine's hands in her own.

"A husband, a comfortable home in town," Claudine answered without pause.

"Things most girls wish for, to be sure," Rose said. "But do you think those things alone will bring you happiness? What of friendship?"

"Oh, I want lots of friends," Claudine responded, her eyes wide and earnest. "A nice group of girls to trade stories with and who will tell me how pretty I look."

Rose refrained from rolling her eyes, knowing Claudine would turn a deaf ear to everything she said if she did. "Remember, darling girl, admirers and friends are rarely the same thing."

"So how goes progress with your young scholars, my love?" Henri asked that evening as they climbed into bed.

"Not too bad. Emmanuelle is as smart as a whip and eager to please. She reminds me so much of Manon." A frown crossed Rose's face at the thought of the sweet girl who seemed so very far away. She had spent more than a few hours sharing tears with Nicole over the departed girl. She prayed every night for Manon's safety . . . and hoped that the child could find some measure of happiness among her people.

"And her rascal of a sister?"

"Just as you describe—a rascal," Rose said. "I worry for her. She's better suited for a Parisian ballroom than the wilderness."

"Just like her auntie Rose?" Henri asked, wrapping his arm around her and kissing her forehead.

"Hardly," Rose said. "These days it seems as though Paris might as well be as far away as the moon. To tell the truth, I would not wish it any closer."

"You don't long for the fine clothes? The elegant salons?" Henri asked, no trace of humor in his voice.

"No," Rose said, the certainty in her voice shocking even herself. "There are days I miss being in a town, I admit freely. But I have learned some lessons our young Claudine is not yet able to. I have a loving husband. I have a strong son. I have two dear friends who mean more to me than a legion of two-faced courtiers . . . and if I am very lucky, in seven months or so, I may be blessed with a daughter as well."

"You minx!" Henri said, sitting up in bed. "Is this how you tell me I'm going to be a father once more?"

"Ah, so it's you who longs for the life of a courtier," Rose said, sitting up nose to nose with Henri, her eyes flashing with glee. "Shall I make a formal declaration before our families so they might give us their blessing?"

"No need, my love," Henri said, pulling her onto his lap. "My God, I am the luckiest man alive." He pulled her face to his in a kiss that, less than two years prior, would have caused Rose to recoil in fear. Tonight, she was able to breathe, to embrace her husband, to love him as she had longed to do during all the months of cold and solitude of their early marriage.

"And I, the luckiest woman to ever draw breath, my darling," Rose said, returning his kisses, breathing in his masculine scent—honest sweat and pine—as though it were a fine perfume.

She looked into his hazel-brown eyes and was unafraid. Could not bring herself to remember ever being so. She motioned for him to wait, but this time not to brace herself or steady her nerves. She only wished to revel in the freedom from the ghosts of her past.

Epilogue

Rose

March 1672

"She's beautiful." Rose swaddled the rosy infant girl and placed her in Nicole's arms. *Another daughter for New France. Nicole has done her duty. We all have.*

"I think we'll call her Sabine for one of Alexandre's sisters that he was fond of. He's been dropping hints for weeks now."

Was fond of. Rose rubbed the back of her finger against the baby's downy cheek. Alexandre's sister was alive and well, but it seemed like everyone in the Old World was spoken of in the past tense. *And so the Old World is for most of us. Dead and buried. Some of us with happy memories, others all too happy to be rid of the past.*

"That's a lovely name," Elisabeth cooed. Rose could see the maternal lust tinged with heartbreak in her eyes. Despite another loss, Elisabeth would want to try for a baby again, and soon. Pierre wouldn't be a baby much longer and would need brothers and sisters to tussle with on the bakery floor. Rose admired her perseverance and wondered if her heart were strong enough to bear such pain over and over again.

"Shall we invite Alexandre in to meet his daughter?" Madame Deschamps asked, taking a brush to Nicole's sweaty mane. *How quickly we try to erase all the signs of our hard work. We ought to let our husbands see how brutish this business is. They might have more sympathy for us.*

"Just a few more moments. I'm not quite ready to share her yet."

"Take all the time you need, dear. I'll just go end his suffering. Do you mind if I tell him that he has a new daughter?" Nicole's mother whisked away the soiled linens from the bed and passed them off to one of the maids who stood waiting in the hall. She'd quietly managed the birth with the efficiency of a Parisian surgeon. Rose marveled at the woman, beginning to stoop with age, who moved with the grace and dignity of someone far above her station.

"Of course. Thank you, Maman."

"No thanks are needed. Ever." Madame Deschamps kissed her daughter's brow. *Another granddaughter. A daughter married as well as she could ever hope to be. Two young daughters who stand to make great matches themselves with her help. I can't imagine many women in New France could be much happier.* Rose smiled at her friend's mother as she left the room, wishing her own mother might have had the chance to attend her labors.

But it wasn't to be. Nor was there any sense brooding on the matter.

"I'm so glad you were both here for me." Nicole slid down in the bed, looking duly weary from her day's work.

"It was our honor, Madame la Seigneureuse, I assure you." Rose relieved Nicole of her precious bundle to allow her some rest. The baby slept contentedly already, looking quite as exhausted as her mother from the ordeal.

"Rest," Elisabeth ordered. "You've earned it."

In their years in the colony, the three of them had borne six children, fostered three, and there would be more in the years to come. When they boarded the ship, they knew this was the plan, but to see it realized so completely warmed Rose's heart. In her days with her father, she'd been taught to be respectful of the Crown. When she lived with her aunt and uncle, the monarchy was spoken of with absolute reverence . . . but after her tenure in the Salpêtrière the King had fallen in her estimation. Not for any particular action, but as a symbol of all that had kept her in prison those long years.

Privilege. Rank. Influence.

Things she never had, despite being born into that sphere. Despite being a gentleman's daughter, she had always been one letter away from spending the rest of her days in a dank death trap.

As she looked at the dear baby in her arms, Rose knew this child would never have to fear the wrath of her father or brothers landing her in a cell. There was no purgatory masking as a charity hospital here. This New France offered the freedom dear Sister Charité had promised, and Rose knew the precious child in her arms would know all the wonders that freedom would bring.

And the freedom it had finally granted her.

AUTHOR'S NOTE

In 1663, Louis XIV and his ministers devised a plan to strengthen their claim on the Canadian colony and stave off British advances. The French decided to send marriageable women to the male-dominated population of New France, and thereby fortify the population and its ties to the new land. Other countries tried similar measures, but none on the scale and with the governmental and clerical support as the French.

Many settlers lived a nomadic existence, creating wealth through fur trapping and trading. The hope was that French women would marry the settlers and provide a "civilizing" influence, increasing the men's interest in farming. The French counted on these men to defend their land if the British invaded, and thought they would do so more valiantly if their livelihood were tied to the land they fought for. The plan would also result in a generation of "little Canadians" who would grow up and take their parents' places as permanent—and loyal—citizens of the French colony.

These brides became known as the *filles du roi,* "King's Daughters," because Louis XIV offered the women passage, a trousseau, and sometimes a dowry in compensation for leaving France. These women were poor, orphaned, or, sometimes, too expensive to marry off in their native land. They came from every corner of France (a few were not even French), but largely from Paris and the northwestern part of the country. Many of the Parisian recruits were one-time residents of the Salpêtrière, a mammoth charitable institution called a "hospital," but which had little to do with healing. For many, it proved a death trap.

Because so many women came from this atrocious prison, the rumor began to circulate that the "King's Daughters" were prostitutes, and that Louis attempted to solve two problems: ridding Paris of social pariahs and populating his colony in one efficient move. The Baron de la Hontan, a traveler and "historian" of his time, supported this rumor (along with other fantastic claims) and, as a result, this mistaken but widely held belief was popular for centuries. The realities were these:

- Seventeenth-century French prostitutes often suffered venereal diseases, which would have made them infertile—a poor choice for building a population of French Canadians. Later, King Louis did send women of questionable morals to his holdings in the Antilles, but his aims were different.

- Each woman was required to have an affidavit of good comportment signed by her priest in order to depart. Clergymen would not risk their own reputations by supporting a woman of poor moral quality.

- The clergy had a huge influence on the running of the colony. Women acting inappropriately would have been (and sometimes were) deported back to France. Unlike Britain, which expelled troublemakers to overseas holdings, France did not allow lawbreakers in its devoutly Catholic colony.

- Prostitutes were not widely arrested and placed in the Salpêtrière until the 1690s, almost twenty years after the last of the King's Daughters departed for Canada. The women of questionable conduct were held in La Force, the hospital prison, and were not considered eligible for emigration.

- Very few children were born out of wedlock in New France; this would not have been the case if the women had proclivities toward prostitution.

With this information, we can deduce that if any of the King's Daughters were prostitutes in France, they were few in number and probably reformed before leaving for Canada. Today, though exonerated by historians, the King's Daughters remain little more than a footnote in history books. It is for this reason that this book exists.

My purpose is not to depict these women as angels. They were not. They were real women with struggles, aspirations, and fears, who had the remarkable opportunity to help found a nation. If they had a common virtue, it was bravery. They left a prosperous, flourishing France, sacrificing all they had, with little chance of return, in order to marry strangers and raise families on a foreign and often dangerous frontier.

The characters in this book are of my own invention. Through these fictitious women, I endeavor to relate the struggles and triumphs the King's Daughters experienced as they voyaged to and settled in the New World. I share their stories so you, the reader, can better understand the sacrifices of the women who helped found French Canada and who share a genetic link with two-thirds of the people who live there today.

With my humble thanks,

Aimie K. Runyan

A READING GROUP GUIDE

PROMISED TO THE CROWN

Aimie K. Runyan

ABOUT THIS GUIDE

The suggested questions are included to enhance your group's reading of Aimie K. Runyan's *Promised to the Crown.*

DISCUSSION QUESTIONS

1. Why do you think the author chose to write the story from three points of view rather than as a single narrative? Why do you believe she chose to create three fictional characters rather than selecting a historical figure to document?

2. France was in a period of relative prosperity during the era of the "King's Daughters" program, yet there were scores of women who wanted to participate. What do you feel were their motivations and aspirations?

3. What were the main difficulties French women, particularly those who lived in cities, most acutely suffered upon arrival in New France?

4. Rose's situation was terribly common; for slight offenses, women could be imprisoned by their families for the rest of their lives. We see that the "charity hospital" where Rose lives is an abysmal place, but when offered the chance to leave the Salpêtrière, Rose hesitates. In fact, many women who were offered their freedom chose to stay in the hospital. Why do you think a seventeenth-century woman would opt to remain imprisoned?

5. Elisabeth seems to have the easiest time adapting to life in New France. She claims she "had less to leave behind," though the truth of that statement is questionable. What about her personality enables her to make the transition more easily than her peers and to embrace the tumultuous changes in her life?

6. Many of the women who agreed to become "King's Daughters" spent a good amount of time in convents, boarding-houses, and with "sponsor families" before marriage. The

Sisters made sure their domestic skills were up to standard and gave them plenty of advice on selecting their husbands. What do you imagine the key pieces of advice were and do you think Nicole followed them?

7. Rose decides fairly soon after her arrival that she wants to enter the convent. This decision could have been socially ruinous for her, despite the revered status of the Church in the colony, especially after she rejects a promising suitor. Why do you think her choice was frowned upon, and why was Sister Mathilde so hesitant to let Rose take orders?

8. Aside from the emotional heartache of her miscarriages, Elisabeth and Gilbert also face some social stigma for their childless state. This is especially true because of their openly affectionate nature toward each other. What do you believe are the reasons for this social pressure and what does it say about the expectations for marriage in seventeenth-century Quebec?

9. We see Nicole's transition from the shy farm girl to the capable social maven during the course of the book. What enables this transformation and growth?

10. How does the fire symbolize Elisabeth's relationship with her mother, and what else could it symbolize about her future?

11. What are the reasons for Manon's departure, both stated and implied? Do you feel she was justified in her decision to leave?

12. In the end, Rose is able to overcome her trauma to enjoy her marriage, but she will always carry the scars. How do you think this will affect her relationship with Henri and her children moving forward?

13. The portrayal of the clergy throughout the book is varied. The nuns are depicted as industrious and motherly, while Father Cloutier, in particular, is shown as petty and scheming. What do you feel is the reason for this contrast?

14. Alexandre could have used his pull to influence the judicial system in the Beaumonts' favor when the bailiff decides to enforce the King's edict on the bakery. Why do you feel the women took this more subtle approach, and do you think the women's back-channel approach ultimately was effective?

Please turn the page for an exciting sneak peek of
Aimie K. Runyan's next historical novel

Duty to the Crown

coming in November 2016 from Kensington Publishing!

Chapter 1

Manon

May 1677, Outside the Quebec Settlement

Only for her little brother would she venture onto the white man's land—especially *this* white man's land. The air had not yet lost the cruel bite of winter, and Manon longed for the warmth of her longhouse. She had several miles left to trek and medicine to brew before she could rest. Young Tawendeh was ill with fever, along with half the village. Most were not grievously ill, but it was enough for concern. She had seen fever turn from mild to lethal in an hour, so she took no chances. Her remedies were the best chance for a quick recovery, though she feared few would accept her help until they were too far gone.

The path through the forest was far more arduous than if she skirted its perimeter, but the cover of the trees protected her from view. The scent of pine danced in her nose and perfumed her skin. Manon considered it the smell of her home and her people. She cursed the feeble light of the dusk hour when the towering evergreens blocked much of the weak spring sun. When true night fell, she would be able to track her path by the stars, but only if she could see them free from the overhanging limbs. She did not fear the night or the animals that lived by moonlight. A child of the forest, she knew the most dangerous creatures lived not in trees, but in the growing town to the southeast of her village.

"What have we here?"

Manon froze at the sound of the raspy male voice.

"A bit far from home, aren't you?" he continued.

She turned, very slowly, not wanting to give the man any reason to strike. Alone, in the forest, he would face no consequences if he attacked her.

"Stupid thing," he drawled. "You don't understand a word I'm saying, do you?"

"I am just passing through, monsieur," she spoke softly, but in perfect French. She did not allow the tremor in her heart to reach her voice. She would not let this dirty farmer know she feared him.

"This is my land." The man, hunched and weary from a day's labor, straightened to his full height. "You're trespassing here."

This is not your land, you foul creature. Nor any man's. Manon kept the thought to herself; it would only spark his temper.

"I mean no harm, monsieur." The courtesy tasted bitter on her tongue, but she sensed his considerable self-importance. "I am going home. This is merely the shortest route without cutting through your fields."

"I don't care for trespassers," the man insisted. "What's in your bag?"

"Nothing of interest, monsieur." Manon spoke the truth. White men had little use for plants they could not eat.

"Let me see in your bag, you little savage." The large man's stench nearly overpowered her as he stepped close and grabbed her wrist, snatching the deerskin pouch with his free hand. "Nothing but weeds. Are you trying to cast some kind of spell, witch?"

"No, monsieur." She fought harder to swallow back her fear. A whisper of the word *witchcraft* could see her dangling from the gallows. "I am merely gathering herbs to heal fever."

The man spat without releasing her wrist. "You were stealing those weeds off my land. I could see you hanged."

He wasn't lying. She paused for a brief moment to consider whether she could inflict enough damage on the brute of a man to enable her escape when he took a step closer.

"Don't be upset," he said, caressing her cheek with a dirty finger and moving closer still. Close enough that she could smell his rancid, whiskey-laced breath. "You're too pretty for the hangman's rope. We might be able to work something out."

Anger flashed in her eyes. This grimy man spoke as if she were the dirt beneath his feet, and he was going to force her to tell her full identity. Something she'd sworn never to do.

"I don't think so." Manon broke his grasp on her wrist and stepped backward. "This land is *not* yours. It belongs to Seigneur Lefebvre." She spat his name like a curse. The lord of these lands had once been her protector, but she hated using his name to earn her freedom all the same.

Before she could react, one of the farmer's massive hands slammed into her cheek, and stars dotted her vision.

"How dare you," Manon growled. "I know the *seigneur*. I was known as Manon Lefebvre to your people. The *seigneur* would not appreciate your behavior toward me. But please, continue, if you wish to lose every inch of your lands."

Manon saw a shimmer of fear in the farmer's eyes.

"Likely tale, you brown trollop," he said, voice wavering. "How do I know you aren't lying?"

"Madame Lefebvre's parents live less than a mile from here," Manon said. "They will vouch for me and my right to be here. I'm sure they'll welcome the intrusion over a bag of weeds that means nothing to any of you."

"You're lying," the man pressed. "Trying to trick me."

Her hunter's instincts forced her heart to slow and her breathing to steady. If he fought, she would defend herself, but killing—or even injuring—a white man would cost her her life.

He had to go with her to the Deschamps' house.

"Monsieur, I speak the truth," she said, returning to a respectful tone. "The Deschamps can assure you that the *seigneur* has no objection to my presence here."

The man hesitated at her mention of the *seigneur* and his parents-in-law. Anyone might know the landholder's name, but his wife's family was not of the first circles.

"Fine, then. Lead the way, if you know it so well."

She started west, toward the cultivated fields. Her moccasins made a slap-slap-slapping noise on the hardened earth. She moved quickly, but not fast enough to give the farmer cause to think she would run. He trudged along a few paces behind her, breathing labored from the exertion.

Hurry up, you great moose! I need to get home.

Less than ten minutes later, Manon knocked on the door of the small but inviting farmhouse. Though visitors here were scarce, the flickering of the fire and the smell of good food radiated the kind spirit of its mistress.

An old woman answered the door. She no longer stood as straight as she once had, but moved with efficiency. No spark of recognition lit the woman's eyes as she looked with a furrowed brow at the unknown girl.

"Manon!" The cry came from behind the woman. It was the first time anyone had called her by her French name in ages, and it fell hard on her ears.

Familiar chestnut hair and soft eyes came into view. It had been five years since Manon last saw Nicole Lefebvre, the woman she once considered her mother. The years had been kind to Nicole, leaving only a few lines of experience around her eyes and a bit more fullness to her hips. Nicole dressed in fine fabrics, perfectly cut and tailored, as one would expect from a woman of status, even in her small community.

"Hello," was all she could utter as Nicole took her in her arms. She felt a few decorous tears fall from Nicole's cheek onto her own as they embraced.

"Look at how you've grown, my sweet girl! You're practically a woman," Nicole said, then, seeing the red handprint on her cheek, she cradled Manon's face in her hands to inspect the injury. "What's happened to your cheek?"

"A misunderstanding," she answered. The red print would soon be a bruise, but would fade in time. Nothing to worry over, especially with Tawendeh's condition apt to deteriorate the longer she was away. Manon did not say that the Huron people had long considered her a woman. She had learned years before that the French had the luxury of long childhoods.

"Welcome, Manon," said a commanding voice from the dining area.

Alexandre Lefebvre, her one-time foster father, entered the living area and bowed, very slightly, in her direction. Manon offered him a barely perceptible nod, like a queen acknowledging a stable boy. The farmer shifted his weight from one foot to the other, his considerable size causing the floorboards to creak, calling attention back to himself.

"I am sorry to disturb you," Manon said, the French language still feeling odd on her tongue. "Your tenant found me gathering herbs in the forest, at the edge of your lands. I assured him that you would not object to my presence, but he preferred to hear it from you directly."

"The young lady speaks the truth, Rocher," Alexandre said to the farmer. "She is welcome anywhere on my lands and is not to be harassed, is that understood?"

"Yes, seigneur," the man said with a bow. "Forgive the intrusion. Can't be too careful, you know." The man cast a knowing look in Manon's direction. *Yes, because my people are the dangerous ones. You have that much to fear from a woman half your size alone in the woods?*

"Quite," Alexandre said. "You have other things to attend to, Rocher. Have a pleasant evening."

The farmer shook his head at the sight of Dame Lefebvre embracing a native girl, and bowed his way from the house.

"I'm sorry to have bothered you," Manon said, her tone still formal. "I must return home."

"Nonsense." Nicole took Manon's hand and led her to the table where the rest of the family sat. "You'll stay for supper."

"I cannot," Manon said, patting Nicole's hand. Now that Nicole was Madame Lefebvre, her hand was free of the calluses earned from a hard day's work. It pained her to refuse the hospitality of the woman who had been so kind to her, but she would not be able to sit still while Tawendeh was ill. "There is a fever in the Huron village. My brother is among the ill. It can become serious so quickly."

Nicole responded with the quizzical furrow of her brow at the mention of the word *brother*.

"Adoptive brother," Manon explained. She was an orphaned only child when she'd first met Nicole some nine years prior. Her aging grandmother had been less and less able to keep track of her young granddaughter, so Manon roamed unchecked. Her favorite thing to do was to wander into the woods and follow the brown-haired French angel who lived in the run-down cabin near the Huron village. She had never spoken to this lovely creature with her foreign clothes and creamy skin, but love-starved Manon could only imagine she was as lovely and sweet as she looked. When Manon happened upon Nicole's husband, grievously injured by a Huron arrow that was meant for a stag, Manon found the angel and dragged her to the dying man. In the end, they were too late. Nicole adopted Manon and they were inseparable for the three years that followed.

"You'll be in want of supplies if the fever spreads. We'll send you with all we have." Nicole transformed at once. She was no longer just a loving mother and dutiful wife, she was a commander. The women of the house set to work gathering anything that could be of use when treating the ill: blankets, clean rags, and more food than Manon could hope to carry in four treks to the village.

Manon forced herself to keep from fidgeting as she waited for Nicole and her mother to assemble the supplies. She could be of no use, nor could she refuse the food and supplies her people needed. She stood and observed the family as they bustled about on her behalf rather than sitting down to their own supper. Nicole's parents had only spent a few weeks in Manon's company. They seemed to have a vague recollection of her, and welcomed her into their home. The chatter of immaculately dressed children only served to make the small farmhouse seem all the more welcoming.

"Your family has grown," Manon said, to break the awkward silence.

"Without question," Nicole said with a laugh as she folded a thick woolen blanket. She indicated a beautiful girl of eight with golden-brown curls. "You remember Hélène, of course, and Frédéric. Sabine was born shortly after you left and Cécile and Roland arrived early last year."

Hélène was the child from Nicole's first husband, born only a few months after Manon had come into Nicole's care. She had stood by Nicole's side when the dark-haired, sturdy boy called Frédéric, the very image of his father with dark hair and flawless ivory skin, entered the world. He greeted Manon with wide eyes and a head cocked sideways with unspoken questions. *An imp, just like Tawendeh.* The toddling twins, blond and mischievous, were too absorbed in playing with their wooden horses on the dining room floor to notice the guest. Shy Sabine clung to her mother's skirts and looked at Manon with curiosity, weakly returning the native girl's gracious smile.

"What lovely children," Manon said in earnest. "You have been blessed."

"Amply," Alexandre agreed, taking his place by his father-in-law's side at the table as the women continued gathering. He reintroduced the Deschamps family without the slightest indication that her arrival caused him displeasure. *Not that he would ever voice it.*

Nicole's parents, two younger sisters, and little brother had come to the colony nearly six years before when Manon was still a ward of the Lefebvres. Not long after the Deschamps arrived, Manon realized Nicole's original family had usurped her place in Nicole's life. Claudine and Emmanuelle would take Manon's place in her heart. Alexandre, Manon was sure, thought to please his wife by moving her family to the New World, thereby easing her homesickness and worry for their well-being. In so doing, however, he cut out Manon's place in their family and replaced it with Nicole's own sisters. Perhaps it wasn't by happenstance, either. Manon's presence with the leading woman in their small society already caused stares from the rest of the settlement. The elder Deschamps had clearly endured hard labor. Their faces showed the signs of too many days in the sun. Still, both looked plump and hardy, thanks to the bounty of their new land. They wore plainer clothes than the Lefebvres, but still fit in better in the settlement than Manon in her deerskin robes and moccasins.

Claudine Deschamps surpassed her sisters in looks, though perhaps not in grace. She was seventeen—almost exactly Manon's age, with dark brown hair and eyes that shone. Emmanuelle was almost sixteen and stouter than her sisters, but her hazel eyes that contrasted with her mahogany hair merited a second look from the young men of her acquaintance.

"You've been well then, my dear?" Nicole asked as she placed a massive loaf of bread in a basket with a jug of soup.

"Yes." Manon paused to look at the perfectly roasted venison on the plate that Madame Deschamps placed at the table, praying none could hear the rumbling of her stomach. New World foods cooked in the French tradition; foreign and familiar, all at once. "I've been trying to learn the methods my people use for treating illness. That's why I came. I was gathering herbs, for a remedy, for my little brother. I wouldn't have ventured so close to your lands otherwise."

"You're welcome to gather all the herbs you need here, darling," Nicole said with a glance toward her husband.

"Of course," Alexandre acknowledged, "though I would avoid Rocher. He had an unfortunate encounter with an Indian man a year or two back and is a tad leery, as you surely noticed."

"I'll bear that in mind," Manon said, keeping her less charitable thoughts to herself. Nicole flitted about the kitchen gathering more things to place in the basket. *I'll be lucky to make it home before daybreak carrying such a burden. Please do hurry.* The images of Tawendeh growing weaker and more feverish plagued her, but she would not shame herself by appearing ungrateful.

"You're sure you can't stay?" Nicole's eyes looked pleading as she scanned the room for anything else she could send along in the overflowing basket.

Claudine took a seat across the table from her brother-in-law and cleared her throat too loudly for it to be anything but a hint to her sister to sit down to the family meal. Nicole could not see that her younger sister was staring intently at the back of her head, seething impatience. Manon's view was unobstructed.

"I wish I could, truly, but I must tend to my brother and the others. And I wouldn't wish to intrude on a family meal."

"Manon, your visit is not an intrusion. Please promise you'll come see me?" Nicole took Manon's hands in hers, gripping as though to prevent her from slipping away a second time.

The thought of walking through the settlement, dressed in her deerskins, and knocking on the door of one of the finest houses New France could boast caused her empty stomach to churn. "I cannot promise, but our paths may cross again."

"I hope so, sweet girl." Nicole's eyes shone as she took Manon in her arms for a long embrace. Manon accepted the overladen basket that Nicole thrust at her and thanked her and Madame Deschamps extravagantly. It was enough food to feed her family for at least two weeks and one fewer worry for her as she nursed Tawendeh back to health.

Darkness had set in, though the waxing moon cast plenty of light to see Manon home. A fine carriage could not pass the rough paths to the Huron settlement; only a rugged wagon could make the journey. Nor would Manon accept the loan of a horse, so she set off toward home on foot. The faces of Nicole's abundant family flashed in her memory one by one. Nicole's darling children, proud husband, loving parents, and lovely sisters. *You've filled my place admirably, Maman. Nicole. I hope, truly, that you've been happy.*

Mother Onatah looked up from her young son, who was still drenched in sweat and mumbling incoherently despite the cold cloths she applied to his forehead and face.

"No change." Manon's words were not a question.

Mother Onatah acknowledged them with a grim nod. Though the fever had yet to take a death grip on the boy, they both knew not to treat any fever with frivolity. *Yarrow tea, sooner rather than later.*

Manon added the herbs to her mortar to make a thick paste to boil into a pungent tisane. Too weak to protest, Tawendeh swallowed the potent, bitter brew and reclined back into his mother's embrace.

"What can we do now, Skenandoa?" Mother Onatah's black eyes glimmered with the unshed tears of her concern.

"We wait." The response was cruelly honest, but she would not give her adoptive mother false hope.

Mother Onatah had welcomed the frightened twelve-year-old girl as her own when Manon returned without warning from the French settlement. Onatah had stood before the council, claimed the girl as a daughter, and given her the name Skenandoa—*deer*—owing to her long limbs, graceful gait, and skittish nature. She was thus made an official member of Big Turtle clan, but Manon learned quickly that the Huron distrusted her French ways and her education as much as the French distrusted her brown skin and accented speech.

Still, Mother Onatah had given her a home, and it was better than no place at all. As the older woman ministered to her son, Manon scanned the house for an occupation. The small longhouse was in disarray. Manon had been gone for hours and Tawendeh commanded all his mother's attention. She began by organizing the pouches of dried herbs she'd strewn about that afternoon when she discovered her stores had run low. *I'll not make that mistake again. I'll gather herbs every week during the growing season for the rest of my days. My carelessness could have cost Tawendeh his life.* Chastising herself, she added more kindling to the fire and urged the flame higher in case more yarrow tea was needed.

"He's sleeping," Mother Onatah whispered to her. "You ought to do the same."

"I couldn't sleep, Mother. Not while things are unsettled."

"Then go for a walk and come back ready for rest. I'll have need of you in the morning."

"Very well." She didn't bother trying to persuade Mother Onatah to take a turn at sleeping herself. While Tawendeh was in danger, neither would sleep until her body forced her into repose.

Manon stood outside the longhouse, breathing in the midnight air—crisp, but mingled with the woodsy tang of chimney smoke. The light of the waxing moon bathed the village, preventing Heno, the chief's son, from taking her by surprise.

"There you are, my beauty," Heno said, emerging from the wood. His name meant *thunder* in their language, no doubt the Chief's attempt to inspire confidence in their allies and fear in their enemies. Thus far, the strategy had proven effective, for his son grew strong and tall—the perfect hunter-warrior.

"Good evening, my brave hunter," she said, offering the handsome young man a kiss as she took him in her arms.

"How is young Tawendeh?" he asked, pulling back slightly from the embrace and tucking a loose strand of her hair behind her ear.

"Improving," she said. "Mother Onatah ordered me to get some air while she tends him."

"I'm glad she did," he said, closing the gap between them and leaving a trail of soft kisses on her face, careful not to disturb the bruise.

"The white man?" he asked, tracing the edge of her puffy cheek with his finger.

She nodded. He growled softly in response. "How are the others?" Manon asked, resting her cheek against his broad chest to hide the injury and change the subject. She wouldn't let the stinking French farmer ruin her time with Heno.

"Fifteen more have fallen ill. No one has died yet, but a few of the elderly and one of the children look close." He spoke as though reporting back to the council about a scouting expedition or a hunt. *He has to detach himself, or else it would be too painful.*

"If only they would let me . . ." Manon began.

"I have spoken to anyone who will listen. They will come around. They'll have to." Heno ran his fingers down the thick braid of black hair that extended down past her lower back, and gripped her even closer.

I just hope they will accept my help before it's too late. There was nothing to be done, though. Any attempt to persuade them would only make them more wary.

"I need you," she breathed between kisses.

"With pleasure, my beauty." He pulled out of her embrace and led her to their favorite clearing, the place they had met for the past two years when the weather was fine. On colder nights they coupled in whatever warm corner they could find.

Though the night air bit and dew covered the grass, Heno's warm, muscled body drew her mind from the chill.

His mouth was ardent. His hands moved over her body with the confidence of an established lover. The man who taught her the art of love, despite all her misgivings in the early days. Adjusting to the ways of the Huron, where people viewed adolescent exploration as innocent and natural, took a while to accept after three years of Catholic indoctrination.

Manon lay in his arms for minutes—perhaps even hours—sated and impervious to the cold.

"I want to make a child with you," Heno said, breathing in her ear.

"Please don't start this again. I beg you. Not tonight," she said. "I can't bear to argue."

"If you have my child, Father will be forced to let us marry," Heno reasoned.

"He needn't do any such thing. And if he refuses, I'd be alone, with a child to raise." Her grip on his arm grew tighter and she had to keep herself from digging her nails into his flesh. Few raised ire in her as much as their chief.

Heno perched up on his elbows, taking her chin with his thumb and forefinger, forcing her to look into the depths of his serious black eyes. "I'd never let that happen, Skenandoa."

"You're the son of our chief. You'll do exactly as you're bid." She brushed his hand away. "You're the prince of your people, no freer to do as you please than a prince of France."

"I can't imagine the prince of a great country not being free to do precisely what he likes." Heno's jaw grew taut as it often did when she mentioned the French.

"Listen when your father speaks," she said. "His decisions have nothing to do with his happiness, but rather the welfare of his people." *And that means seeing you married to a sweet, obedient girl who cares for nothing more than the traditions of our people and securing your lineage.*

"That almost sounded like a compliment," Heno said.

"Whatever the issues I might take with your father, self-interest is not one of them," Manon said. "Though I will never care for the man who cast out his sister for taking me in."

"I wouldn't say Onatah is cast out," Heno said. "She still lives with her tribe."

"Marginalized, because she showed me kindness," Manon said.

Heno sighed deeply, whether frustrated by her logic or his father's irrational fear of outside influence, Manon knew not.

"I will have you for my wife, my beauty." He took her chin again, this time kissing her, claiming her mouth with his.

"Nothing would make me happier, my brave hunter," Manon said as he pulled away.

For a moment she indulged in her favorite fantasy: a life where the tribe accepted her as Heno's wife. A pillar of her community. A healer. A mother. She allowed herself to consider it only rarely; in her heart she knew it would never happen. But as she lay in Heno's arms, optimism flowed through her veins, nourishing her body like manna.

"I love you, Heno," she whispered, cupping his face and kissing his lips, savoring his taste like she would her last meal. "For now, just love me and let the future settle itself."

"Always, my beauty." He shifted to reclaim his position atop her, but Manon placed her hand on his chest. She gently pushed him to his back and straddled him, claiming her pleasure as the midnight wind stung her skin. For a few moments, she was neither Huron nor French. She was free of everything except her love for the beautiful man beneath her.

CHAPTER 2

Claudine

One of Alexandre's stipulations of Claudine and Emmanuelle's staying in town was that they would obey Nicole as readily as they would their own mother. Had it not been for her brother-in-law's decree, Claudine would never have agreed to wake moments after the cock's crow to take supplies to the Huron village with her two sisters and their longtime friend Gabrielle Giroux. She wanted to scoff at the idea of traipsing through the woods with blankets and food to people who had not requested and who would not welcome their interference. But she stilled her tongue. Even if it meant enduring a morning in the woods, it wasn't worth risking Nicole's—or worse, Alexandre's—ire.

"Will one of the servants be driving the carriage?" Emmanuelle asked Nicole, who had come to ensure the girls were up and preparing for the day. Emmanuelle wasn't overly fond of horses since an unfortunate accident when she first came to the colony resulted in a seriously injured leg and the loss of a much-needed horse.

"Pascal Giroux will drive us in the wagon he uses for deliveries. It can maneuver better on the narrow roads than anything we have. Since we're taking supplies, we'll need some room." The Giroux girl, Gabrielle, was the same age as Emmanuelle, and was included in many of their outings. She was the ward of one of Nicole's dearest friends, Elisabeth Beaumont, who along with her husband ran one of the most successful bakeries in the entire colony. Gabrielle and Emmanuelle were great friends, but Claudine had little interest in her aside from her considerable skills with needle and silk.

"We'll be down for breakfast shortly." Emmanuelle smiled at Nicole, who backed out of the room with a nod. *Always sister's pet.*

"Why in Christendom do we have to go out all that way to haul blankets and broth to people we don't even know? Didn't we send enough along last night? Can't Nicole send someone if she *must* send more?" Claudine asked to no one in particular.

"Because Manon meant a great deal to Nicole, and she wants to help if she can."

Claudine rolled her eyes and bit her tongue. Emmanuelle always had a response for everything, and it was usually what Nicole and Alexandre wanted to hear. Worse, Emmanuelle offered her explanations as though she were explaining a sum to a befuddled child. *Maddening.*

Breakfast was a harried affair, Alexandre eating leisurely while Nicole chided the girls to eat quickly so they could get underway. There was an unspoken censure in Alexandre's eyes, but he rarely contradicted his wife. She was so often the model of propriety and restraint that he must have felt obliged to overlook her few eccentricities. In particular, her affection for the Huron girl that Claudine sensed he never fully understood.

As they left the settlement, the houses and stone buildings gave way to trees and the wide, well-maintained roads gave way to narrow, rocky paths. Emmanuelle and Gabrielle chatted as they often did, but Nicole kept her eyes fixed to the path as though she and not Pascal were driving the wagon. Claudine looked at the endless evergreens and wondered why she had ever thought this would be some magical fairy kingdom where she would never be in want of diversion and handsome suitors. In her years in the settlement, she had yet to reconcile the shattered dreams of her twelve-year-old self, though she was now a woman approaching eighteen.

Claudine, having devoured the few letters Nicole had sent home, leaped at the chance to come to the New World, where her sister had married so far above her circle. When Alexandre's agent came to offer them passage to this New France, Claudine nearly screamed at her father's hesitance to leave their barren land. It hadn't taken much persuasion in the end. The voyage provided futures for the girls and their younger brother, Georges. What was more, their elder brothers would absorb the barren land into their own farms, giving them both sizable holdings. The land could rest fallow and it would bear crops again. It would still belong to a Deschamps, and that was as much as their father could have hoped for.

She'd pictured a shining metropolis, and was crestfallen when she learned she'd be living on a farm much like the one where she was born. The house was infinitely better. The land was fertile. But it was still a farm, and one that seemed to be a thousand miles from anywhere interesting. The fledgling town, while nothing to the lively bustle of Rouen, was immeasurably preferable to living out on her parents' homestead. She loved her sister for taking them in and vowed she'd make a good match since she had the gift of connections to some of the best society New France had to offer. If she had any luck, she'd find a man of good sense who wanted to return to France—maybe even the bustle of Paris—and would take her away from the monotony of country life forever. Somewhere there had to be a young man with dark hair and flashing eyes who would whisk her away to a life—if not of luxury and leisure—at least of adventure and varied society. She clutched her wool cloak tight about her shoulders against the damp spring air. *He has to exist somewhere.*

In the meantime, Claudine lost herself in poetry. Permanently placed next to her bed was a love-worn copy of ballads by the *trouvères*—the courtly poets of medieval times—that a bookseller had given her when he realized her arresting brown eyes could actually read. It was ragged then, and wouldn't have fetched more than a few *sous* from the small population interested in his wares. Claudine had read it to the point where the corners were indelibly smudged with her fingerprints. While Emmanuelle read widely, Claudine found solace in the one tome. The depictions of gallant knights and maidens took her away from the tedium of farm life and chores even after hundreds of readings.

The Huron village came into view; rows of longhouses dotted the small clearing. A few men stood at the edge of a large fire, scowling like bears awakened midwinter at the small envoy of French who had just descended upon them.

Nicole stepped down from the wagon first. Claudine waited, her breath caught in her throat, as her sister approached the men. Nicole shook visibly, but stood as proud as the Queen herself.

Please, God, don't let them be as unfriendly as they look.

Claudine had never seen such a living arrangement in her life. The building was high, even by French standards, and seemed to go on for a solid mile. There were pelts from deer, beaver, bear, and other animals covering nearly every surface of the immense building. It seemed Manon had managed to convince the council to separate the ill into a longhouse by themselves. The sick slept on beds built onto the wall like shelves—not unlike the bunks on the ship they had sailed on from France. The only noises in the longhouse were the wheezing and chattering teeth of the fever-riddled and the crackling of the fire in the pit where Claudine, Nicole, and the others watched Manon tending the contents of her thick cauldron. Nicole stood next to Manon, while the others gathered a step behind her, anxiously awaiting a command from one of them.

"You shouldn't be here." Manon barely looked away from the vapors slithering up from her pot as she stirred.

And a welcome to you, too. I guess you're too good for a wagonload full of supplies and five pair of helping hands. I won't be the one holding up the departure if Nicole bids us to leave.

"You need help, Manon," Nicole said, stepping forward. "Please tell us how we can be useful."

"By going home. I promise." Manon's eyes were framed by sagging dark circles of exhaustion.

"You heard her, Nicole. She doesn't need our help. I'm sure she's quite capable of managing things on her own." Claudine stepped forward and put her hand on Nicole's arm to lead her back to the safety of the wagon, but her sister would not move.

"Give us something to do," Nicole implored. Claudine crossed her arms over her chest and restrained a sigh. Nicole's coolness in public, her composure, was always something Claudine admired; yet in the presence of this common girl, all of that restraint was gone. Nicole was once again the awkward farm girl from Rouen.

"I need more fresh water and yarrow flowers," Manon said at length, as though speaking a dire confession.

"I'll fetch the water," Pascal said at once from the dark corner of the longhouse where he had been lingering in silence, exiting before anyone could call him back. *He's a smart young man, probably trying to keep away from the fever. It'll be a miracle if we don't all catch our deaths.*

"What does yarrow look like?" Emmanuelle asked. Manon produced a stem with clusters of dainty white flowers like a riot of miniature daisies.

"As much as you can find. It's the only thing that seems to be helping."

"Let's go," Gabrielle chimed in, gesturing to the door with the basket she held firmly in her right hand. "I think I saw a patch not more than a mile from here along the road when we came in." Claudine followed Emmanuelle and Gabrielle, both of whom walked briskly to the main road that connected the Huron village to the French settlement. *Anything to be out of there and away from those people. Who knows when they'll decide they've had enough of us and choose to send us on our way by force? Or worse. I doubt her concoction even works. It'll probably do no more than give them a bitter taste in their mouths and a sour stomach.*

As Gabrielle promised, the abundant yarrow patch was a ten-minute walk from Manon's longhouse. The gentle spring rains and nurturing sun had yielded wildflower patches thicker than Claudine had ever seen.

"Let's use knives and cut the stems higher up, rather than pulling," Emmanuelle suggested.

"That will take longer and I don't want to have to come back for more." Claudine knelt and began yanking the stems from the ground, roots and all, ignoring Gabrielle's glare.

"The plants won't grow back if you aren't gentle with them," Gabrielle warned.

"I'm not wasting more time gathering weeds than I absolutely have to." Claudine gripped another yarrow stem and yanked it from the earth.

"Claudine, the Huron depend on these herbs for their medicine. Treat them carefully." Emmanuelle sounded so very much like Nicole that Claudine raised her head to see if their older sister had followed the three of them to the clearing. Claudine gritted her teeth at the rebuke. *Don't forget I'm the older sister. Learn your place.* But her censure went unvoiced. The world seemed to side with Emmanuelle and there was no winning.

"Fine. You two can sit here rolling in the weeds. I'm going back."

Claudine thought about walking back to the settlement on her own. Perhaps she could entertain Alexandre with tales of how his wife was carrying on with a pack of savages with no regard for his respectability and position, but town was miles away on a path she didn't know.

She sat down on a boulder just out of view of Emmanuelle and Gabrielle and let the tears flow down her cheeks. Nicole had told her countless times that she was supposed to be a pillar of the community and the first to volunteer her services to those in need. It was supposed to feel noble and self-sacrificing, not tiresome and aggravating. *This isn't how things were meant to be. I am going to disappoint them both and they'll send me back to the farm for the rest of my days.*

It was another quarter of an hour before Emmanuelle and Gabrielle met Claudine at the boulder where she had been sitting, having gathered enough of the yarrow to satisfy the demand, or so they hoped. To Claudine the overflowing basket looked like a pile of weeds big enough to treat several fever-ridden villages, but she didn't presume to know what went into the brewing of a tisane to cure fever.

Knowing long walks in cold weather irritated Emmanuelle's lungs and worsened her limp, Claudine took the overfilled basket and strode ahead. She was almost a hundred yards ahead of her sister and Gabrielle when the longhouse came into view. *Thank the Lord we didn't get lost. I'll learn to knit blankets for the poor after this so perhaps I might at least be able to be of service to the less fortunate from the comfort of the settee.*

Manon sat beside an older woman who lay very ill with the fever. Manon held her hand and muttered words in her native tongue. The woman was petite to begin with, but the glow from sweat and the quaking of her shivering body made her look like a child. A weak child.

"I have your flowers for you," Claudine announced, trying to call Manon's attention back to her. Manon simply held up one hand to command silence. Claudine wanted to fling the weeds at Manon's head in exasperation, but stood frozen to the floor. Nicole stood a few yards away, as transfixed by the scene as she was. Though Nicole was always the center of activity . . . always the one to organize everything . . . she stood immobile and useless. At seeing her sister in such a state, Claudine felt an ache in her stomach as though she were witnessing something unnatural—something wrong—like the dust flying off her father's barren field when she was a girl.

The fragile woman took a rasping breath, exhaled, and did not take another. Grim faced, Manon closed the woman's eyes. She stood, took the basket from Claudine, and returned to her cauldron over the fire where she added new flowers to the mixture.

Emmanuelle and Gabrielle now stood next to Claudine, and their eyes followed Manon as well. Claudine found the nerve to look at Nicole and raise a questioning brow. Nicole looked up from the deceased woman and crossed to her and the other girls.

"That woman was Manon's adoptive mother," Nicole whispered in explanation. Claudine looked at Manon, kneeling transfixed in front of the simmering cauldron. *Poor girl. No one deserves to lose a mother so young.* There were no words or gestures that Claudine could conjure up that didn't sound ridiculous, so she stood in place and waited for someone to offer up an order. It was perhaps the first time in her life she would have been glad of a useful occupation, and consequently, the first time one wasn't eagerly waiting on the tip of her mother's or sister's tongue.

After a few agonizing minutes of standing idle, a few men, mostly older, entered the longhouse. The man at the front was tall and imposing with a face that bore more lines of experience and labor than Claudine had ever seen in her life. He was only a fraction as intimidating as the man to his right. Years younger, several inches taller, and clearly furious, he was not a man Claudine would ever dare to speak to, let alone provoke.

Claudine clutched her skirt to hide the trembling of her hands. Her breath stopped short in her chest, the lack of air causing the fire to take on an eerie halo. *We're all going to die here.*

Manon stood and approached the men, no fear discernable in her face. The oldest man spoke a few words in his language, and Manon nodded. The conversation continued a few moments longer, until a young boy, perhaps seven years old, ran to where she stood and flung his arms around Manon's waist. She spoke several words in return. Though Claudine could parse none of the words, she recognized authority and confidence when she heard it. Were it not for the crackling fear in the air, Claudine was certain she'd feel a prickling of envy at Manon's bravado.

The men exited the longhouse, the younger man lingering a few moments. He said a few words to Manon, kind ones, if Claudine interpreted correctly. She returned a terse, quiet reply and turned her back to him. The fierce-looking man's face seemed to soften for a brief moment, but almost as quickly, he resumed his mask of hostility and followed in the footsteps of the tribe's elders.

Manon knelt before the boy, who now wept openly in her arms. Her brother, Claudine presumed. He buried his face in Manon's shoulder and sobbed for his mother. Claudine swallowed back some tears, not entirely sure why they were there. This was not her grief.

"Darling, what can we do?" Nicole said at length.

"Help me gather our things and take me into town so I can find work, please." Manon's confidence was gone, her words a mere whisper.

"Why?" Claudine blurted out.

"That man was the Chief of this clan. He has ordered me to leave. He believes the fever to be my fault."

"How positively idiotic . . ." Claudine rolled her eyes in the direction of the door.

"Be that as it may, he is the Chief and I am no longer welcome here. I was only allowed to stay under his sister's protection as it was, and now that she is gone, I must leave."

"His own sister is dead and his first act is to banish the child she chose to raise as her own?" Nicole's jaw set, her teeth visibly clenched. This look never boded well for the person who caused it. This time, Claudine feared her sister's wrath might bring down the fury of the entire Iroquois nation on the five of them. *Calm yourself, sister.*

"So it would seem. Would you help me?" Manon's look was at once proud and pleading. What options did she have but to ask for help? A life foraging in the woods would be no life at all.

"Manon, you needn't even ask. You will stay with us as long as you wish. We'll leave at once."

"Tawendeh must come as well. I promised Mother Onatah . . ."

"My dearest girl, I could not ask you to abandon your brother. I daresay there is always room for one more in the Lefebvre nursery."

"Thank you," Manon whispered.

"Let's be on our way," Nicole urged.

Claudine nodded, her agreement as fervent as it had ever been. She, Emmanuelle, and Gabrielle gathered up Manon's and Tawendeh's sparse belongings. In all her life, Claudine was never so thrilled to find herself in the back of a rattling wagon on a bumpy road. She hoped for Nicole's sake her brother-in-law would be as happy with the new additions to his family.